RUINS ON STONE HILL

HEROES OF RAVENFORD
BOOK 1

F.P. SPIRIT

Copyright @ 2018 F. P. Spirit
Cover Art by Jackson Tjota
Cover Typography by Amalia Chitulescu
Interior Design by Designs by Shannon
Edited by Sandra Nguyen
ISBN 978-0-9984715-7-0

Thanks to Tim for creating the world of Thac, and to Eric, Jeff, John, Mark and Matt for their roles in bringing the Heroes to life. Also, thanks to the rest of my friends and family who gave their time and support into the creation of this book.

BOOKS BY F.P. SPIRIT

The Heroes of Ravenford

Ruins on Stone Hill

Serpent Cult

Dark Monolith

Princess of Lanfor

The Baron's Heart

Rise of the Thrall Lord

City of Tears

Arinthar Collections

Tales From Thac

TABLE OF CONTENTS

The Red Warrior..5

A Strange Alliance... 13

The Road to Ravenford.. 20

The Charging Minotaur.. 27

Maltar 38

Into the Dead Forest 49

Bugbears 58

Stone Hill... 70

Inside the Ruins.. 83

Through a Mirror Darkly.................................... 95

In the Dungeon 107

Necromancers.. 116

Unexpected Reunion 126

Stone Golem 134

The Ancient Scroll... 146

Wizards' Duel 157

Ravenford Keep 171

The Truth about Lloyd...................................... 181

Troubled Hearts 191

Back to the Bendenwoods 201

Orc Ambush 210

The Cave Guardian.. 217

The Elven Bard 224

Down the Well...238

Captive Audience 252

Lost in the Caves...260

Bringing Down the House.......................................272

Celebration 286

The Enchanted Hammer 297

Giant 305

Return to the Ruins...316

A Cry in the Night..325

Battle in the Dead Forest...................................337

The Serpent Cult..350

Eastern Thac as depicted at the Great Library of Palt on the Isle of Lanfor. Though there are still ancient copies on parchment, this visual representation of the map is magically maintained by the librarians there. This is evidenced by the addition of recent towns such as Ravenford and Vermoorden. However, it should be noted that landmarks such as Cairthrellon are still represented here, even though the great elven city "disappeared" over 500 years ago.

- Lady Lara Stealle, High Wizard of Penwick

1
THE RED WARRIOR

Speed and silence, deadly both

The aged ash trees reached toward the sky. Glimpses of deep blue peeked through the treetops, the light of the afternoon sun barely penetrating the dense forest foliage. The fresh scent of the surrounding trees and bushes, mixed in with the earthy aroma of grass, wafted on the cool crisp air. A trace of dust lingered, churned up by the wheels of the wagons that had traveled the well-worn dirt road, cutting a path through the looming forest.

Other odors also rose from the earth: the musky, warm smell of horses, the heady memory of wine, some pungent herbs, and dried hay. These scents were attached to a group of travelers. Horses pulled wagons filled with boxes, barrels of goods, and beverages that the caravan owners were carting to their destination. The wagon floors were lined with hay in a vain attempt to make passengers more comfortable.

The clip-clop of horse hooves, the squeaking of turning wheels, and the creaking of wagons announced the caravan's presence along the dirt road. Bright-voiced birds and rustling leaves accompanied its passage through the forest.

Glolindir sat in one of those wagons on a pile of hay—his back propped against a box of goods with his cloak thrown over it in an attempt to make the seat more comfortable. Being an elf, Glo did not look much different from a human. Standing at about six feet tall with flaxen hair, blue eyes, and fair skin, he was perhaps a bit thinner than most humans, but the only trait that gave away his heritage was his pointed ears.

Glolindir had been lulled into a half-trance by the rocking motion of the wagon, and the soft sounds of the forest. The young elf was quite content, until he realized that something was different. There was a subtle change in their surroundings, but he could not quite tell what it was. He opened his eyes and gazed around, straining his senses.

His friend, Aksel, was doing the same. A few minutes ago, the gnome had been lounging across from him on a second pile of hay. Now Aksel was standing up, his three-foot frame tensing as he listened with his own pointed ears.

They were both transfixed, trying to place what was amiss. Aksel gazed at him. Glo shook his head at the silent question that passed between them. They were missing something obvious, something that was just at the edge of their awareness. Both friends turned to gaze at Seth.

The halfling sat in the front of the wagon next to the driver. His small frame, just barely shorter than Aksel's, was dwarfed next to him. Seth's head was slightly cocked as if also listening.

Listening. That was it! There weren't any forest sounds. The birds had stopped chirping their songs, and even the rustling of leaves had died down. Glo continued to strain his ears, but the surrounding woods remained quiet. He opened his mouth to say something when a strange sensation washed over him. It hit him like a crashing wave, making every nerve taut. His heart raced, sweat gathered across his brow, and he felt a bit light-headed.

Aksel must have noticed his sudden change in condition. "Are you alright?"

Glo ignored the gnome, his eyes darting from side to side. He searched for any sign of danger, yet saw nothing to warrant such an intense reaction. *What is causing this sense of dread?* It suddenly dawned on him—it was his familiar, Raven. He was linked empathically to the tiny magical beast, and these feelings of fear were coming from her!

Glo stood up and poked his head out of the wagon, looking up into the trees. *Where is she?* He scanned all around, his heart still pounding. *There she is.* He spotted her up the road ahead of them, winging her way back in a state of utter panic.

Aksel's head suddenly appeared next to him. "What's going on?"

"It's Raven. Something has her really spooked—something on the trail ahead."

Aksel raised an eyebrow. Seth's eyes narrowed. Even the wiry old wagon driver knew something was wrong. He glanced over at Glo and said, "Son, you don't look so good."

Glo steadied himself. "I'll be fine."

They scanned the woods ahead, three pairs of keen eyes scrutinizing either side of the trail.

"Over there!" Seth pointed up ahead off the trail to the left.

Glo focused in on the spot, but at first saw nothing. Abruptly something moved. It looked like the top of a bow. Glo strained his eyes, trying to get a better look. *Is that an arm?* Yes, he saw an arm—a bare green arm. It was sticking out from behind a bush and holding a drawn bow with a nocked arrow. As he continued to watch, a gust of wind briefly blew the bush aside. For just an instant, he got a look at a face.

It was not quite human, but brutish, almost monkey-like with green skin and two short tusks protruding from the lower jaw. Glo was momentarily startled. He'd seen such a creature before, but only in books back home. *That's an orc!* A wave of nervousness passed through his body. Orcs were nasty creatures—carnivorous humanoids who did not mind feeding on the flesh of people. They were all in grave danger.

Aksel and Seth must have seen it as well. Aksel let out a soft gasp, and Seth's eyes went dark, a twisted smile crossing his face. Glo pushed down his rattled nerves, and took a deep breath.

"Orc!"

His voice startled the driver, and the man nearly fell out of his seat and off the wagon. He recovered and pulled hard on the reins, bringing the wagon to a complete halt. The driver then turned, dove into the wagon, and crawled back behind the barrels and boxes.

The reaction had caught Glo by surprise. He tore his eyes away and peered out ahead of them. The other wagons had also stopped.

Aksel distracted him yet again. "Where did Seth go?"

In all the commotion, Seth had disappeared. Glo scanned the area, his heart pounding in a frantic rhythm. He finally caught sight of Seth stealthily crawling under the stopped wagon in front of them. He was about to cry out to him, when a whizzing noise came out of the forest. Glo instinctively ducked down into the wagon, Aksel beside him. A split second later, two arrows embedded themselves into the seat above. Both elf and gnome flinched at the sight.

Glo swallowed hard. "I think he's headed toward the front of the caravan!"

Aksel merely shook his head. "Doesn't surprise me."

Glo silently hoped that Seth knew what he was doing.

Aksel mirrored his thoughts. "I just hope he knows what he's doing."

"He was well-hidden beneath the wagons." Though he tried to sound comforting, Glo was equally worried about their friend. In fact, he was concerned about all of them. Orcs were not creatures to be trifled with. This was a deadly situation—one they just might not survive.

Seth crawled under the two lead wagons. He stayed on his belly until he made it to the front of the caravan. Once there, he scanned the area. Up ahead he spotted the two sentries, who were supposed to protect the caravan, on the ground unmoving, with numerous arrows protruding from their backs. Seth did not blanch. He was used to death; he had experienced it up close more times than he cared to admit.

A brief image of his old master came unbidden to him. The

halfling momentarily shuddered as he relived the moment his tutor died—disappearing in a conflagration of fire before his eyes. He could feel the heat as it wafted over him and he smelled the sick odor of burning flesh. Seth woke up many a night in a cold sweat after witnessing that same scene over again in his dreams.

The halfling shook himself. This was neither the time nor the place. Swallowing hard, he forced down the memories, allowing his training to kick in. Seth scanned the rest of the area around him, but there were no more bodies to be seen. The others must have heard Glo's warning and ducked inside. Bowmen were now returning fire from the wagons, but it was not enough to keep their attackers at bay.

The orcs began to charge, green faces snarling, from the trees on either side of the road. A few of the vile creatures were felled by arrows, but two of them made it to the lead wagon and tried to climb aboard.

Seth stood up, a sharp dagger suddenly appearing in his hand. He barely slouched as he crossed under the wagon, till he stood face to kneecap with one of the orcs. The creature was so close that the fetid odor of unwashed flesh and filth filled his nostrils. Seth scrunched his nose in an effort to avoid the smell. *Gods, don't these things ever bathe?*

The wagon tilted as the orc lifted one leg off the ground and began to hoist itself up the side. The screams of the people inside spurred Seth into action.

Speed and silence, deadly both. His master's creed echoed in his thoughts as he rolled out from underneath the wagon and leapt up behind the vile, smelly brute. The bristly hair poked Seth's skin through his black leathers as he grasped the oversized left ear of the orc, his hand slipping slightly from the greasy filth on the rough skin. With practiced ease he brought his dagger to the creature's throat.

Once again, he heard his master's voice: *All things with heads, from animals to men, need blood to reach their brains. Open those channels and the life will pump out of any foe.* Seth's blade moved across the orc's throat, quick and clean, cutting a deep gash clear across. The brutish fiend tried to reach back and grasp its attacker, not realizing that it was already as good as dead. Seth let go and dropped softly back down to the ground.

He immediately launched himself into a forward roll beneath the wagon, the body of the slain orc hitting the ground behind him with a loud thud. Seth caught a glimpse of a second orc on the other side of the wagon. He continued rolling until he came out behind it—his dagger in hand as he leapt at the monster. Seth grabbed on tight, and with a quick slash of his dagger dispatched the second creature.

A sudden premonition, perhaps from his years of training, made Seth flip off the orc's back. A second later, a flurry of arrows buried themselves into the falling body. *No honor among these creatures,* Seth thought. He swiftly launched himself underneath the wagon again and gazed out from his hiding place. A group of orcs approached the wagon, bows nocked with arrows. The lead creature squinted with its glowing red eyes and pointed to the place where he had just disappeared.

Abruptly, the four lead orcs fell to the ground, their previously nocked arrows flying haphazardly in all directions. The three behind tripped over their companions and landed in a heap on top of them.

Seth darted out from under the wagon and chanced a quick look down the line of wagons. He saw Glolindir standing in their original wagon, his staff in his left hand and his right hand outstretched. Seth flashed the wizard a quick smile, and Glo winked back. *Handy having a wizard around who can put enemies to sleep!*

As the fallen orcs tried to get up, they were riddled with arrows from the wagons. Within seconds, all the vile creatures were lying on the ground in a heap of ugly flesh.

Seth ran out to the pile of enemies, making certain the top ones were dead. He then dispatched the remaining monsters before they woke up from their magically induced "nap." All the while, he kept eyes and ears open for attackers, but no more emerged from the surrounding woods.

It looked as if they would make it out of this after all, when the underbrush parted up the side of the trail. A brute of an orc stalked out of the woods. It was huge, with massive shoulders and long, wicked tusks dripping with saliva. In its right hand, it held a curved sword easily twice the size of the little halfling. Glowing hate-filled eyes surveyed the caravan and the fallen bodies of its brethren.

Right, Seth thought. This monster was beyond anything they could handle. Still, he was not the type to give up. His mind raced, searching for some tactic to use against the beast.

The monster stared at the wagons for a moment, then lifted its head to the sky, letting forth a savage scream. The ferocity of it shook Seth to the bone. The creature then lowered its head, lifted its huge sword, and charged toward the wagons with a vicious growl.

Glolindir spotted the monstrous orc at the same time as Seth. The wizard waited till it charged, then lifted his arm and pointed a finger at it. As he did so, mana, the energy that flows in and around all things, gathered within him. He drew the energy inward with concentrated will and focused it with a gesture. All that was needed now was a verbal command to trigger it.

The orc had closed half the gap to the lead wagon when Glo spoke the words that released the spell, *"Nullam Telum."* A projectile of arcane energy leapt from his finger and spiraled out toward the charging creature. The purple missile met the beast in midstride and connected with an audible *thud*.

The monster appeared neither shaken, nor hurt. Instead it merely glanced down at its chest, reached up with its free hand, and touched the smoldering spot.

Glo's eyes went wide. This huge orc was far tougher than he imagined—he had severely miscalculated. He watched in horror as the creature dropped its hand and turned its feral gaze toward him. An evil grin spread across the monster's maw, then it charged.

Glo froze in place, unable to move a muscle. He had been so sure of himself. He had studied his spells and creatures and practiced his art tirelessly. Yet none of that had prepared him for this. Here was a real live monster bearing down on him, fully intent on ripping him limb from limb. It swiftly closed the gap between them and would be on him in seconds.

My father was right. He was woefully unprepared to cope with this. At that moment, he wished that he had listened to his father's advice and stayed in the safety of their elven home.

Aksel climbed out of the wagon just in time to see the creature rushing toward them. "Well, that doesn't look good."

"Agreed," Glo said through barely moving lips.

When Seth saw the monstrous orc charge his friends, he threw aside all reason. There was no way the two of them could handle that monster alone. He wasn't sure if he would be much help, but he had to do something.

Seth took off at a dead run. The monster was moving quickly, but if he could intercept it he might be able to distract it away from his friends. Swiftly reaching the second wagon, he leapt up the side. Seth landed on the soft wagon top and raced across it, precariously balancing on the thin fabric. He stopped at the very edge, and was about to launch himself onto the beast's back, when shouts came from the front of the caravan. Seth paused, chancing a quick look toward the lead wagon.

Down the road and closing fast was a rider dressed in red armor, yelling something that sounded like *Pen-ick*. The warrior repeated the cry as he closed in on them, and Seth heard it clearly this time—Penwick. More orcs appeared at the head of the caravan, but they now turned toward the approaching rider with startled grunts and noisy growls.

Seth turned back toward the monstrous orc, but to his surprise, the beast had pulled up short. It had turned toward the approaching challenger, curiosity written on his hideous face. Luckily, Seth's reflexes kept him from falling. Otherwise, he would have ended up landing on the beast's face—not the most ideal place to be.

The crowd of orcs stared all around, as if unsure what to make of the lone rider. Finally, they mustered up their courage and charged to meet him—all except for the huge one. It seemed to have forgotten all about Glo and was now glaring at this brazen newcomer.

Seth glanced over at his elven friend. He was white as a sheet, still frozen in place. Seth's lips twisted sideways as he turned back toward the coming battle. The rider had nearly reached the caravan and now stood in his saddle. A second later, the figure launched himself off his horse, unsheathing two large swords as he arced through the air. The red-armored rider landed in the midst of the orcs that had charged to meet him. Before any of them could touch the man, his blades began to swing around.

This guy is huge! Seth thought. He was a head taller than the monsters, easily as large as the huge orc standing below him. Despite his great size, his moves were swift, weightless. He twisted and twirled, dancing through the attackers, blades darting in and out. One orc after another fell. The big man mowed down their enemies like a scythe cutting through weeds.

Seth glanced back at the wagon and saw Aksel standing next to Glo, trying to snap the wizard out of his fear-induced trance. Below him, the monstrous orc had not moved. It stared intently at the warrior, seemingly oblivious to everything else.

The fight continued on, orc after orc falling. Some of them pulled back from battle and drew their bows. Abruptly, four of them fell to the ground, motionless. The two remaining orcs jumped back in fright, glancing around to see what had felled their comrades.

The corner of Seth's mouth lifted slightly. Aksel must have finally gotten through to Glo and the wizard was back to work. Seth reached into a pouch on his belt and pulled out two thin black knives. In one swift motion, he flicked his wrists, letting the knives fly from his fingertips. The triangular projectiles covered the distance to the two orcs in less than a second and stuck with a soft *thwack*. Both creatures fell to the ground, a thin black dagger between their eyes.

Seth glanced over his shoulder, but the huge orc remained motionless, its attention on the large man mowing down its brethren. Seth turned back toward the fight just as the red-clad warrior felled his last opponent. The man stood alone now, orc bodies strewn all around him. His face was covered in sweat from exertion, but did not seem to be breathing heavily at all. The forest had gone quiet; the rest of the orcs were either dead or asleep. Some heads popped out of the other wagons, cautiously peering up and down the trail.

Abruptly, a bone-clattering scream shattered the silence. All of those heads quickly disappeared back into the wagons. The huge orc's head was reared toward the sky, its maw still hanging open from that unearthly cry. It slowly dropped its head and glared balefully at the warrior. The orc stood there for a few moments, then charged its new foe, its heavy footsteps causing the wagon to shake underneath Seth.

"Look out!" Seth did his best to hold on. The warrior glanced up and gave him a brief smile, then rushed forward to meet the charging orc. Large as he was, he somehow managed to move with incredible speed. He hurtled toward the monster, his two great swords spread out on either side.

Man and orc collided head on; two titans locked in combat. Their muscles heaved in testament to the ferocity of the struggle. Yet the warrior turned aside the fierce slashes from the monster's huge blade. The creature swung at him again and again, grunting and heaving as it tried to cleave the man in two. Instead of dancing around this opponent, the large man stood his ground. He deftly parried those tremendous blows with one sword then the other, all the while slicing away at the vicious beast's hide.

The monster had no real skill with its sword—most likely relying on its strength to overwhelm opponents. Soon the orc's thick skin was deeply gashed, its greasy, green body streaked with trails of blood.

Seth took advantage of the distraction and dropped down off the top of the wagon. He crept forward to the last remaining sleeping orcs and silently dispatched the rest of them. When he looked back up, the two titans were still locked in combat.

The beast suddenly changed its tactics. Instead of another huge overhand swing, it pulled back and slashed at its opponent's torso. If the blow had landed, it would have chopped the man's arm off and cleaved him halfway through. The warrior swiftly blocked with a downward parry that sent the monster's blade flying in an upward arc. As the wicked blade slid off the man's sword, it caught him in the upper left arm.

That's not good, Seth thought. Skilled as the warrior was, there was no way he could fend off the monster with one arm. It looked like they would have to jump in to help him after all. He glanced over his shoulder and saw that Glo and Aksel had climbed out of the wagon and were watching the battle.

Seth motioned to the wizard. "Can you put it to sleep?"

Glo stared back at him, his face haggard and drawn. "I can't! My concentration is... gone."

Double not good. Spell-casting was draining, every spell taking a toll on the caster's mental reserves. Glo, still a novice, was mentally exhausted and could not cast a spell without a long rest. Seth turned his attention back to the battle. To his surprise, both man and beast had stopped fighting. The warrior had stepped back and was examining his arm, one eye still on the orc.

At the same time, the monster glowered at the man, its barrel chest heaving from exertion. The beast abruptly laughed, a deep guttural sound that raked its entire body. The noise sent chills through the halfling. He recognized what that meant. The monster was gloating before its final kill.

The large man did not seem intimidated at all. In fact, a grin spread across his face. "Good one!"

Seth stared incredulously at the man. *Is he nuts?* Then it dawned on him—this was only a young human, in his late teens at best. Appearance wise, he looked the same age as Glo, Aksel and Seth, but that was still relatively young for a human. Perhaps he didn't realize the danger he was in.

The beast had stopped laughing. It watched the man carefully, its expression uncertain.

The young warrior's smile faded, replaced with a tranquil expression. He held his blades out to either side, fanned away from his body. A second later, those blades began to glow. The light from the swords flared, and then burst into flame.

Seth raised an eyebrow. He had seen many things in his short life, but he had never seen anything like that.

The flaming blades must have unsettled the huge orc. The creature took a step back and muttered something unintelligible in its guttural tongue.

Without warning, the young human leapt forward and began a blinding offense that sent the orc backpedaling. The flaming swords burned brightly, sparking as they met the monster's huge blade. Any blow that touched the creature's skin caused the flesh to smoke and sizzle.

As the warrior continued his relentless assault, the smell of burning orc filled the air. The monster was driven backwards, cursing and screaming until the warrior landed a blow that jarred the creature's huge sword loose. The wicked blade arced through the air, landing a few yards away, well out of the orc's reach.

The beast screamed in frustration, rearing back from the twin fiery blades, bellowing into the sky. With almost no warning, the creature lunged at the young man, trying to crush him under its great weight. Seth thought the man would be flattened, but instead the warrior braced himself, pointing his two swords forward.

The monster realized its peril too late. It could not stop itself and neatly skewered its body on the young man's burning blades. Time froze as the creature hung there for a moment, the back of the twin swords protruding from its massive body. The beast shuddered once, fell backward, and landed with a loud thud, a final grunt escaping its lips.

The warrior stood over the brute, dripping with sweat, his chest heaving as he took in long deep breaths. The orc lay there, its massive limbs still twitching in the dirt. Finally the spasms subsided, and the beast lay completely still.

2
A STRANGE ALLIANCE

Human, elf, gnome, and halfling—a very unlikely union

The red warrior stepped over the monster, the fiery blades now cold as they protruded from the orc's carcass. He reached down and yanked out each blade, blood covering them up to their hilts. The warrior stepped back, took a deep breath, and sat down on a nearby rock.

Seth heaved a sigh of relief, scratched his dark hair, and cast a look at the mass of dead surrounding them. He rose from his crouched position and strode over to the big man. Glo and Aksel were only a few steps behind him, each wearing expressions of amazement. As he approached the man, he noted as heads popped out of the other wagons once again, cautiously peering up and down the trail.

Seth returned his attention to the warrior. This man was definitely tall, probably over six feet, with broad shoulders and muscular all over, but not overly so. Brown tousled hair capped his youthful features, his deep blue eyes watching with interest as the halfling approached.

"Nice job with those throwing knives." The warrior wiped the blood from one of his blades.

Seth's lips twisted sideways.

"Not so bad yourself with those giant pig stickers."

The big man laughed. "Thanks! My name's Lloyd. What's yours?"

"Seth."

Lloyd extended his hand. "Well met, Seth."

Seth reached up and grasped the large hand, his own dwarfed by it. This Lloyd had a *very* strong grip.

"That was a neat trick with those flaming swords."

Lloyd shrugged. "Oh, that? That was nothing. Just a little something my father taught me."

Glo's voice rang out from behind him. "Well, I thought that was amazing."

Seth glanced over his shoulder as Glo and Aksel joined them. The wizard appeared quite impressed. "I've never seen anything like it. How did you do it?"

"I'm a *spiritblade*," Lloyd replied, as if that explained everything.

"A spirit—blade?" Glo looked slightly puzzled. "Is that some sort of martial art?"

"Sort of. A spiritblade is kind of a martial disciple of the sword. We learn to use our minds and spirits as well as our bodies to wield our weapons. The spiritual energy enhances what we do, and sometimes makes it look like, well, magic."

Seth whistled low. "That's very interesting. Where'd you study?"

"With my father. He's one of the best in the world."

Glo smiled. "He must be very proud of you." His smile suddenly faded, replaced with an embarrassed expression. "Oh, where are my manners? I'm Glolindir. And this is Aksel."

Lloyd stood up and extended a hand to Glo. As he shook the elf's hand, Seth noticed as Glo winced a bit. The big man then reached down and shook Aksel's hand. When he was done, the gnome drew his hand back and rubbed it gingerly.

"How's your arm feeling?" Aksel asked, still massaging his hand.

"It's fine." Lloyd moved his left arm around to support his claim. "As a spiritblade, you learn to ignore pain."

"Pain is one thing, but it won't do you any good if it gets infected."

A look of doubt crossed Lloyd's face. "That's a good point."

"I can take a look at it for you if you like." Aksel's concern was clear, but he was trying to be polite nevertheless.

"Are you a healer?"

Aksel nodded. "A cleric."

"Okay." Lloyd sat down on the boulder and sighed. Aksel sat down next to him.

Lloyd removed the twin sword sheaths that were strapped over his back and then peeled off what turned out to be an armored red leather shirt. His left arm had a gash along the upper part, but was also black and blue around the cut.

Aksel examined it closely. "Ah, we'll have that fixed in no time." He placed his hands on the arm, and a white glow began to emanate from them. The light moved its way along Lloyd's arm, and the wound itself began to glow; the cut closed before their eyes, and the skin took on its normal color.

Glolindir had seen healers at work before, but divine magic always amazed him. He knew that clerics manipulated mana much like wizards, but while arcane casters used intellect to concentrate their will, divine casters relied on faith. Almost any injury or ailment could be cured via this divine intervention. In fact, a cleric with enough experience could even resurrect the dead.

As Glo watched Aksel in action, he realized that his friend was particularly good at what he did. It was not just the healing power he displayed, but Aksel genuinely cared about the person he was healing. He showed concern for his patient's mental and emotional state as well as the physical, talking gently with Lloyd and assuring him as he applied his divine power. While Aksel continued to heal Lloyd, Glo's mind wandered back to the battle.

"Sorry I wasn't of much help back there. I only stepped out from behind my books a few weeks ago, and I guess I'm not quite as battle-ready as I thought." Glo was furious with himself for freezing up the way he did.

Seth snorted. "Heh, battle-ready. Is that even a thing for a wizard?"

Glo glared at the halfling. Seth folded his arms and glowered back at him.

Aksel interrupted the staring contest. "Don't sell yourself short. By my count, you put eight of those creatures to sleep."

Glo smiled wanly at the gnome. "Maybe, but I froze when it came to taking care of that huge one."

Lloyd's expression was one of understanding. "Ah, that can happen to anyone. You should have seen how green I was the first time I went hunting bandits. Good thing my dad was with me." An embarrassing smile spread across the young man's face. "Anyway, I agree with Aksel. I am good with swords, but not quite adept at dodging arrows. You and Seth took out those archers mighty handily, and I, for one, am grateful."

Glo began to feel a bit better about the whole thing. At that point, the rest of the wagoneers joined them. They gathered around and thanked all four of them for fending off the vicious assault. A tall, graying man addressed the foursome.

"Lucky you were all here, or we would have all been goners for sure." He introduced himself as the caravan leader, Reise. He asked Lloyd if he would travel with them on the rest of their journey to the seacoast town of Ravenford.

Lloyd gave a boyish grin. "Sure, but after that I am heading out to Tarrsmorr."

Aksel stared at him for a moment. "What are you headed there for?"

"I'm looking for work, of course. I want to use my skill with the sword to help others." Lloyd paused, searching for the right words. "Things have kind of quieted down in my hometown. I could have joined the navy, but I wanted to travel a bit and lend my blades where they would be most needed."

Seth snorted. "Well, you might want to rethink your decision about Tarrsmorr."

"Why's that?"

Glo explained further. "The three of us were just there looking for work. Unfortunately, the town is pretty quiet. Not much work to be had for adventurers. So we decided to try our luck on the east coast."

"Rumor has it there's some strange happenings out there," Seth added.

Lloyd swept his gaze over them. "So where exactly are you headed?"

Aksel answered this time. "We were actually thinking of traveling to Penwick…"

Lloyd's expression grew incredulous. "Penwick? Why, that's where I'm from! Trust me, there's no work in Penwick, either." He proceeded to tell them how he, his father, brother, and sister had assisted the army in chasing the last bandits out of the Penwick area. It seemed that the entire family was as skilled as the young man.

Aksel spoke tentatively as he finished healing Lloyd's arm. "You could travel with us. Like you, we want to lend our skills where they are most needed. You would be a welcome addition to our little group."

Lloyd stood up, waved it around a few times, and smiled down at Aksel. "Thanks. My sister's the healer at home. She's always patching us up, even though we give her a hard time. Guess I never realized just how lucky we were." Lloyd glanced at Seth and Glo. "And as for you two, you both covered my back pretty well in that fight. All in all, I'd say we make a pretty good team."

"Then, it's official." Aksel put his hand out. Lloyd stared at it for a moment then bent down and placed his hand over Aksel's. The trace of a smile crossed Glo's lips as he looked at the large human hand dwarfing the gnome's. The entire thing seemed a bit overdramatic, but Aksel and Lloyd both had serious expressions, so the wizard decided to follow suit. He bent down and placed his hand solemnly over the others.

All eyes turned to Seth. The halfling stood there for a moment, then rolled his eyes toward the heavens.

"Well, if it will make you happy." He stepped forward and put his hand on top of the others.

The four of them stood there for a moment at the edge of the forest, hands joined. Human, elf, gnome, and halfling—a very unlikely union of races.

Finally, Seth stepped back. "Okay, enough with the picture-perfect moment. Now what do we do?"

Aksel smiled. "For now, we continue with the caravan to Ravenford. After all, at least one of us is getting paid."

Seth's face took on an innocent expression. "Does this mean that Lloyd has to split his fee with us?"

Glo and Aksel exchanged glances. They both looked at Seth and then at Lloyd, not sure what to say.

Lloyd's expression was unreadable at first, but then he burst out laughing. "O…kay," he said when he could finally get the words out. "I can see who is going to be the treasurer of this little group!"

"Seth? Treasurer?" Glo shook his head in disbelief. "Isn't that like giving the wolf the key to the barn?"

Seth shot him a dirty look, but then saw the thin smile on Glo's lips. "Very funny."

The corners of Aksel mouth upturned. "If his money handling is as good as his cooking, then we better just bury our money in a hole and call it good."

Lloyd, Glo, and Aksel all burst into laughter. Seth just shook his head.

As the merriment died down, Reise rejoined them. "We've finished gathering our comrades' bodies and have stowed them in the wagons."

Aksel stood up, sobering at once. "Very good. I will go and perform last rites over them." The little cleric left to perform his somber duties.

Reise's face still looked disturbed. "Anyway, we can move out whenever Cleric Aksel is done. If we leave soon, we can be in Ravenford by nightfall."

Lloyd went to gather his things, while Seth and Glo headed back to their wagon. As they strode along, Glo dropped his voice to a whisper. "So, when were you going to tell us you were some kind of assassin?"

Seth stared up at him with a dark expression. "Seriously? The proper term is *ninja*. And the art of *Ninjutsu* is about surprise and deception. It is not a topic for idle conversation."

Glo was taken aback by Seth's vehement response. The combination of stealth, speed, dexterity, and knife handling made Glo think of an assassin. Add to the fact that Seth dressed mostly in black. Glo did not mean to offend his friend, but now realized that the label had some pretty negative connotations.

"My apologies, my friend. What I should have said is that I am greatly impressed by your prowess. Lloyd was right. You had all our backs covered in that fight. I am not certain we would have survived it without you."

Seth responded in a flat tone. "Thank you." His lips twisted to the side. "You weren't so bad yourself. Now we just need to get you over your stage fright."

Glo shook his head and smiled. A short while later, Aksel rejoined them. Seth climbed up onto the wagon and took his original seat. "Treasurer," he murmured, "I think I like the sound of that."

Aksel and Glo exchanged glances and grinned.

3
THE ROAD TO RAVENFORD

The entire western sky appeared on fire

The caravan continued east along the road and quickly exited the dense forest. It was late in the day, but the sun still shone bright in the sky behind them, hovering over the dark green trees of the Bendenwoods. The forest spread behind them as far north and south as the eye could fathom. The black heights of the Korlokesel Mountains rose up on the western horizon then curved to the north, winding around the woods like a gigantic dark serpent.

Grasslands stretched out before them, the road unraveling across those plains and fading into a thin ribbon before completely disappearing off in the distance. Sporadic groups of trees sprung up here and there, but none were the size of the woods they just left. A range of rolling, tree-covered hills appeared to the north. These were known as the Vogels and would parallel their path eastward all the way to the sea. The grasslands stretched to the southern horizon, although a glimpse of a wide flowing river was viewable at times. This river, the West Raven, also paralleled the east road but eventually combined with the Berribrun just west of Ravenford. From there, the Raven River flowed through the center of town and emptied into Merchant Bay, a huge body of water that opened out to the sea beyond.

The first signs of dusk appeared in the east as the small wagon train wound its way along the open road. Glo sat in the driver's seat of the third wagon, firmly holding onto the reins, silently wondering how he had ended up in this position. He distinctly remembered admiring Lloyd's horse, a white and brown spotted paint, and the two of them talking about horses in general. What followed afterwards was still vague in his mind. Their wagon driver had asked him about horses. He had said something about the lead driver dying, and before Glo knew it, the old man handed him the reins. Glo told them this was a big mistake, but between encouragement from Aksel and Seth and Lloyd's promise to ride beside them, he finally gave in. Secretly, he thought that Seth only agreed to it so he could watch Glo make an idiot out of himself.

As it turned out, there was very little to worry about; the road was surprisingly smooth, and the single set of reins managed the team of horses nicely. Glo settled comfortably into his new position with Aksel and Seth on the front seat next to him. As promised, Lloyd rode alongside. Glo glanced at the young warrior. He made an imposing figure, the sun gleaming off his red leather armor giving it a crimson sheen. Yet, despite his intimidating size, Lloyd was rather low-key outside of battle. He rode along quietly, listening to stories about their homelands and the lands to the west. At the moment, Glo was describing his home city.

"Cairthrellon lies many miles west of here, in the great forest of Ruanaiaith. But unlike other cities, Cairthrellon is a part of the forest—alive, beautiful, and ever changing."

Lloyd gave him a puzzled look. "How is that possible?"

Glo paused a moment, searching for the right words. When he began again, his voice was filled with passion.

"Imagine walking through the forest and finding cascading waterfalls, secret glades, green shaded arbors, and grottos as sad quiet music plays across the moonlit meadows. As you continue to wander, you come across unexpected beautiful statues, enchanted thickets, and sparkling fountains that seem to spring randomly from otherwise placid ponds. You can hardly see the houses as they meld into the landscape, and in the center of all of this you find a keep of translucent quartz that changes colors with the seasons..."

The elf's voice caught, a hint of moisture in his eyes.

Lloyd's face softened, stirred by the elf's description of his home. "It sounds beautiful, Glolindir. If I may ask, why did you leave?"

Glo wasn't sure how to answer. It was a complicated situation. His people were a stubborn lot, and they didn't care much for non-elves, but he did not want to tell his new friends that. They reached a curve in the road, and Glo used the excuse to delay his answer. Once they made it around the bend, he responded.

"Let's just say I had a difference of opinion with my father. Had I stayed at home, I would never be able to use magic like I do now."

"You mean freezing up at crucial moments?"

Glo glared at Seth. The halfling wore a wicked grin. Aksel, in-between the two, coughed violently into his hand.

"I think I understand," Lloyd said behind him.

Glo gave the halfling one last dark look, then swung back to face the young warrior. Lloyd's expression was one of sympathy.

"If I had stayed in Penwick, there wouldn't have been anything near the *fun* we just had."

Seth's mouth half twisted. "You've got a strange idea of fun there, Lloyd."

Lloyd broke out into a grin. "Yes, maybe I do, but you have to understand; I am a martial adept of the sword. We live for battle."

"I think the keyword there is live. That doesn't always go well with battle," Aksel noted.

Lloyd threw back his head and laughed. "Very true, master cleric; my sister would often say the same thing."

The foursome fell silent. Lloyd took a few minutes to scan the road ahead, but all remained still. Satisfied that nothing was amiss, he soon rejoined them. "So what about you, friend Aksel? What is your home like?"

Aksel seemed taken off-guard by the question. "Caprizon? Well it's certainly not alive like some folks' homes." He cast a sidelong glance at Glo.

Glo brushed off the front of his cloak with an impish grin. "We can't all live in style."

A brief smile crossed Aksel's lips. "Touché. Anyway, it is a bit different. There's a tall ravine where the Stilwyndle River empties into the Sea of Riazel. Caprizon is built into the cliff-sides of that canyon."

Lloyd appeared baffled. "So then how do you get around?"

"There are ladders—lots and lots of ladders. And there are cable cars, both up the sides of the cliffs, as well as across the canyon."

Lloyd appeared impressed. "That sounds like fun!" His horse seemed to agree, choosing that moment to whinny, tossing its head up and down.

Aksel's expression seemed distant, as if lost in thoughts of home. "It can be. I have to admit, living on flat land like all of you took some getting used to."

A short laugh escaped Seth's lips. "That's because the rest of us are normal."

Aksel narrowed an eye at their halfling companion. "Really? Then why don't you tell him about the great city of Ilos?"

Seth's face took on a dark expression, his body bristling. "Because there's not much to tell."

Lloyd interrupted the duo. "Ilos? Isn't that way up north?"

Seth cast Aksel a dirty look, then turned to face Lloyd. "Yeah, it's pretty much a run of the mill city. Not part of the forest and not hanging at all crazy angles on the sides of a cliff."

"Except that it's all made of stone," Glo added.

Lloyd looked impressed. "The whole city?"

Seth nodded. "Pretty much." He appeared quite uncomfortable talking about his hometown. It was something Glo had noticed since he first met Seth a month ago.

Lloyd's curiosity had been piqued. "Why would anyone do that?"

"Let's just say they got tired of rebuilding it every time it got burnt down."

"Invaders?" Lloyd's voice took on a slight edge.

"Parthians." Seth almost spat the word.

"Parthians." Lloyd's grip on his reins tightened. "They did the same thing to Penwick during the Second Parthian War."

"They burned the whole city?" Seth asked softly. There was an uncharacteristic trace of sympathy in his voice.

Lloyd's face turned red with anger. "More than half of it. Once the Parthians were defeated, the town was rebuilt; but then came the Golem Thrall Master and his stone armies. Penwick was overrun, and a large section of the city was burnt to the ground."

As if to emphasize his words, a strange reddish glow flared up behind them. It cast long crimson shadows on the road ahead. Glo and Lloyd both turned in their seats, and Aksel and Seth stood up to look over the top of the covered wagon.

The sun had almost set behind the Korlokesels, with only the top of the disc still visible, and that had turned a flaming red. The rays fanned out and lit up the clouds above—the entire western sky appeared on fire. The timing was eerie, as if the sun god Arenor himself acknowledged the tragedy that had befallen Penwick.

Glo tried to imagine what he would do if his home had been burnt down. It was a very real threat when one lived in the forest as the elves did. Thankfully, the trees were enchanted with spells to resist burning, but magic could only do so much. Not knowing what else to say, Glo spoke with as much sympathy as he could muster. "Your people must have been devastated."

Lloyd was still staring at the sunset, his face awed by the raw display of nature. When he turned back around, there was a grin across his brash young face. "We're a resilient people."

It was good to see him smile, but then, just as abruptly, his expression darkened. "The worst of it was when the Warlord Eboneye raided us. That was only twenty years ago."

The young man closed his eyes and took a deep breath; the muscles in his face relaxing. Glo glanced at Seth and Aksel, wondering if they knew anything about this Eboneye, but the two of them merely shrugged.

"Previous invaders occupied the city—but not Eboneye. His

men were bent on looting and pillaging with no concern for who they killed or what they destroyed. We had no choice but to fight back. The army had been routed, but a resistance was formed. They fought a slow, pitched battle against the pirate forces and eventually won back the city, but it took months."

Lloyd's face was now ashen. "Most of Penwick was leveled…but worse than that, nearly half the population died. When it was over, there were so many corpses that they could not all be buried. The bodies had to be burnt to avoid spreading disease."

Lloyd was so upset that his voice cracked. He turned his head away, his fists clenched tightly on the reins of his horse. Glo looked from Seth to Aksel and saw the horror mirrored in their expressions. He felt he should say something to Lloyd, some words of understanding, but the words would not come.

The sun had finally set behind them, darkness overtaking the countryside, creating pockets of shadows underneath the trees. Seth stood up and lit a lamp that hung off an iron hook welded onto the upper frame of the wagon. Once lit, the lantern illuminated the road in front of them with a warm glow.

Glo glanced at Lloyd. His face was hard to see, but he appeared to be lost in his thoughts. "So…what's Penwick like today?" he asked, attempting to lighten the mood.

Lloyd didn't answer at first. Finally he replied in a quiet voice. "Today? It has been mostly rebuilt."

Lloyd began describing the current condition of his home: the tall buildings, the great bridges, the public gardens, and the large temple dedicated to the god Arenor. As he spoke he became more and more animated. "…and there are sections of the city that rival the great capital of Lymeridia."

"It sounds beautiful," Aksel said wistfully.

The young man gave an enthusiastic nod. "It is. The Barony of Penwick stands strong and proud these days; its influence reaches as far north as the city of Lukescros and as far south as the town of Haggentree. And at sea, the Penwick navy is unmatched along the coast. Our ships patrol from Colossus Point to Southpoint and are avoided and feared by even the vessels of the 'great' city of Dunwynn."

Lloyd now sat straight in his saddle, all traces of grief gone. Glo was glad to see the young man back to normal. He was also quite impressed with the fighting spirit of the people of Penwick. Glo glanced at Aksel and Seth. The former bore a look of admiration, while the latter wore his usual smirk.

Seth was the first to comment. "That's quite a tale. So what exactly happened to this Eboneye?"

Lloyd's answer was quite zealous. "Don't worry—he got exactly what he deserved. The Lord Kratos Stealle saw to that. Of course, he wasn't a Lord back then, but he was a spiritblade—*First Blade* in the resistance. After the last big battle with the pirates, Eboneye tried to escape. Lord Stealle followed him to his ship, and defeated him in one on one combat. The ship went down in the harbor, and the pirate warlord was never seen again."

Aksel sounded impressed. "This Lord Stealle was quite the hero."

Lloyd cleared his throat, appearing quite uncomfortable. "Yes. He's actually Admiral of the Penwick Navy these days."

Glo pulled the reins as they came to another curve in the road. "With someone like that around, I doubt Penwick has much to fear from anyone."

"Amen to that!" Lloyd patted his horse.

The conversation turned to lighter topics. The night had turned pitch dark, the moon not quite up yet. Lloyd galloped to the front of the caravan and scouted the area ahead. As it turned out, the rest of their journey was uneventful. A couple of hours later, the wagon train finally reached its destination, the seaport town of Ravenford.

4

THE CHARGING MINOTAUR

May the leaves of your life tree never turn brown

By the time the caravan reached the town, it was late in the evening. The first signs of civilization were evidenced by the light of an occasional farmhouse along the roadway. As they continued eastward, the farms appeared more frequently, until they finally entered a tended orchard. When the caravan exited the grove, the travelers caught their first view of Ravenford. The foliage on both sides of them parted and the town lay sprawled before them, houses lit up and twinkling. On a hilltop to their left stood a castle, the keep's windows ablaze, lighting up the citadel. The castle walls were lined with torches, the shadows of the occasional patrol of guards visible along the parapets.

The town itself spread away from them, down to the river and across the other side. A pair of well-lit stone bridges spanned the river, and a few docks jutted out from the opposite shore. Various-sized vessels stood moored at those docks, their silhouettes casting dark shadows on the banks behind them. The rest of the town continued south from there. The lights stretched on for some distance, and farther back, a hill rose up, crowned with what appeared to be a temple. The eastern edge of the town stood upon the shores of Merchant Bay, those calm, clear waters almost mirror-like as they spread to the far horizon. The moon had just risen, its silver light splitting the waters of the bay like some giant knife that reached from the eastern skyline all the way to the shores of the sleepy little seaport town.

A small guardhouse stood alongside the road just outside of town. The guards briefly stopped the wagoneers, but on recognizing them, let the caravan through. Glo noticed strange looks from the guards as their wagon passed. Once out of earshot, Seth turned to his friends. "These people need to get out more. You think they'd never seen an elf, gnome, or halfling."

The caravan stopped in front of a group of buildings at the foot of the hill from the keep. There were a number of signs here: *Fine Food & Drink, Mason, Leather Goods,* and *Wine and Ale.* This late in the evening most of the shops were closed. The food store was still lit up, and as they pulled up, an older gentleman came out to greet them.

Glo did a double take. This balding, grey-haired gentleman had elven features, but with a fuller face like a human. *He's a half-elf.* It surprised him to find one where there were purportedly no elves. Elven/human marriages were rare enough since elves were quite long-lived—their lives measured not in decades, but in centuries. The difference in lifespan alone made such unions difficult. Not only would the elf outlive their spouse, but their children as well, making cross-race marriages nearly intolerable for elves. Glo could not imagine falling in love with someone only to watch them wither away in a few decades.

While all this went through Glo's mind, Reise disembarked. He greeted the half-elven store owner, explaining to him all that had happened. The store owner, Pheldan, was elated to see them. It seems that they were the first caravan to make it here from central Thac in months. As the conversation continued, another figure exited the store—a young woman, perhaps in her late teens. Long dark hair reached down past her shoulders, framing a diamond-shaped face.

Her complexion appeared quite pale. Her features were also elven, though not as pronounced as Pheldan's. She turned out to be the store owner's granddaughter, Xelda.

Glo, Seth, and Aksel disembarked, retrieving their belongings from the wagon while Lloyd dismounted and hitched his horse to a post in front of the store. Reise and the shop owners came up to greet them.

"These are the folks who saved the wagon train…" Reise began.

"An elf!" Pheldan cried. "And a gnome and a halfling. What an odd trio!"

"Grandfather!" Xelda's eyes widened. "Where are your manners?"

"Oh. Yes, you are quite right. My apologies, gentlemen. I am Pheldan and this is my granddaughter, Xelda."

Glo, Lloyd, Aksel and Seth introduced themselves in turn.

"Thank you for saving the caravan and our goods," Pheldan said when they were done.

Aksel responded with a deep bow. "We are glad to have been of service. I'm just sorry we couldn't save those poor guards and the driver."

Reise's voice was heavy with sadness. "They were good men and far too young to pass on; but again, thank you. Please accept these tokens of our appreciation." He took out his purse and paid Lloyd his promised fee. Furthermore, he refunded Glo, Seth, and Aksel their passage fare. Glo raised an eyebrow—that was quite generous of the caravan owner.

Aksel cleared his throat. "Thank you. That is more than kind of you, but now I think it best if we be off. We need to find accommodations for the night."

"Please, go down to the Charging Minotaur," Pheldan responded. "My good friend, Telpin, owns the place. Tell him that Pheldan sent you. He will set you up nice and comfortable."

Glolindir was touched by the gesture. "Thank you, my friend." He added in formal Elvish, "*Aa' lasser en lle coia orn n' omenta gurtha.*" It meant *May the leaves of your life tree never turn brown.*

The old half-elf's eyes welled up with tears. "Why, I haven't heard Elvish since mother left us." He turned to his granddaughter. "Xelda, did you hear that?"

The young woman nodded to her grandfather. "I did indeed." She turned toward Glo. "He's been trying to teach me Elvish ever since I was old enough to walk." She gazed from Glo to her grandfather, her eyes dancing with amusement.

"But she claimed she would never use it. If you had just listened to me, you could give this nice young fellow a proper reply." The old man folded his arms across his chest and fixed his granddaughter with a triumphant stare.

Xelda glared back at him. "Really, Grandfather?" She looked at Glo and said in nearly perfect Elvish, "*Aa' menle nauva calen ar' ta hwesta e' ale'quenle*". It was a well-known elven farewell. *May thy paths be green and the breeze on thy back.* She followed it with a perfect curtsey.

Pheldan stared at his granddaughter, flabbergasted. "Xelda, you've been holding out on me!"

It was her turn to fix him with a stare. "Not really. I just needed someone who can actually speak Elvish to converse with."

Pheldan glanced from his granddaughter to Glo and back again. "Kids these days." He shook his head.

Xelda laughed. It was a light, lyrical sound.

Glo found the whole encounter amusing. He also had to admit he was intrigued by the shop owner and his granddaughter. It had been some months now since he had spoken Elvish with anyone, and this brief encounter was a welcome change of pace.

While Pheldan fumed, Xelda gave them directions to the Charging Minotaur. The inn was only a few blocks over from where they were now. "They even have a stable." She nodded toward Lloyd's horse.

The companions said their farewells and started down the dimly lit street in the direction of the inn. Xelda waved after them. "Feel free to stop by anytime! I'm sure grandfather would enjoy lessons in Elvish!"

Glo chuckled softly to himself. This Xelda had quite the sense of humor. Maybe it wouldn't hurt to stop by Pheldan's store once in a while.

The foursome walked along the dark quiet side streets of the little town while Lloyd told them what he knew of Ravenford. It was a small village with about two hundred residents in and around the town. The towns folks were primarily fishermen and farmers. Being the only seaport between the cities of Dunwynn and Penwick, it was a typical stop for ships passing through as they made their way up the coast. The village and surrounding territory was ruled by a hereditary barony that for some reason never seemed to last more than a generation or so. The current baron, Gryswold, was the fourth son of the previous Baron of Penwick. He fought to win his own lands and titles and was a warrior of some renown in his younger days. Gryswold was awarded the titles to the town of Ravenford when he slew the dragon, Ullarak, who had slain the previous baron. Gryswold's wife, Gracelynn, was the only sibling of the current Duke of Dunwynn, who had yet to produce an heir. These circumstances made Gracelynn and Gryswold's daughter, Andrella, the object of every noble suitor in the surrounding area.

When Lloyd was done, Seth had to comment. "I was wondering how you knew all this, until you mentioned that Gryswold was from Penwick."

Lloyd smiled at his new friend. "I guess it's no secret that I am interested in anything that involves Penwick."

Glo could definitely see that, but was surprised by Lloyd's interest in politics. "Perhaps, but this business with the baron's daughter—Andrella was it—does not seem like something that would concern you."

Lloyd grinned sheepishly, his hand going to back of his neck. "Well, it's not that I'm interested in her in that way. It's just that I understand what it's like when things are expected of you just because of who your family is."

Thoughts of his father came unbidden to Glo, and he briefly relived one of Amrod's many lectures on 'The proper way for an elf from the House of Eodin to behave.' Glo did not believe that he should act like some pompous fool just because his family was one of the oldest and well known in Cairthrellon. Notions like that were what led him to leave home in the first place.

The group had grown silent. Glo observed the others; they all seemed lost in their own thoughts. Seth in particular had a dark expression. Lloyd let out a deep sigh. Glo felt a wave of empathy for this big human, who obviously had parental troubles of his own. Perhaps that was part of the reason he had left Penwick.

Glo reached out and placed a hand on Lloyd's broad shoulder. "Trust me, I understand."

Abruptly, the Charging Minotaur came into view. It was a fairly large building, two stories tall, with walls made from white painted stone and a red shingled roof. A covered porch wrapped around the front of the building, with a few chairs and benches on it. Above that hung a large sign with the picture of a minotaur's head. A couple of old-timers sat on the porch grabbing a late-night smoke. They nodded to the foursome as they approached the inn. Lloyd tied his horse to a hitching post out front and the four travelers walked through the front door.

They entered into a large common area, its center filled with a few rounded tables. Along the front wall were a couple of booths. There were two more booths along the left wall on either side of a large stone hearth. An inviting fire burnt inside, taking the chill out of the night air. On the right wall sat a long bar with a minotaur's head hanging over it. It seemed rather appropriate considering the tavern's name. On this side of the bar were two doorways, while past the bar was the entrance to a hall. Even at this late hour, there were a few patrons here, most with a glass of ale, but some with plates of hearty-looking food. Behind the bar stood a hefty man with short dark hair and a moustache, wearing an apron. Two barmaids carried trays in and out of a door, making the rounds between the kitchen and their customers.

Across the room stood a half-oval stage, raised up about three feet off the floor. A pair of stairs led up to it on either side. In the center stood a lavishly dressed gentleman with a lute, singing a lively tune about the Duke of Dunwynn. It appeared the Duke had caused a mess by introducing hippogriffs to the eastern seaport of Karajon. The magical beasts, a strange crossbreed of eagle, lion, and horse, were raining down excrements from the sky, inundating the poor town. The patrons of the inn roared with laughter as the bard continued describing the town's predicament, and how the rulers of Karajon were woefully inept in trying to handle the crisis. The foursome exchanged grins, then headed to the bar.

The bartender looked up from the mug he was drying. "What can I get you gents?"

Aksel motioned toward the group. "We'd like some rooms. We were told by Mr. Pheldan that Telpin could help us."

"Pheldan sent you, huh? No problem." He turned to a barmaid who was just exiting the kitchen. "Hey, Kailay! Can you tell Telpin that we have some guests to see him?"

Kailay turned out to be a young woman, with long, curly, strawberry blonde hair, and a shapely figure, which her outfit accentuated quite effectively. She turned toward them, surprise registering briefly on her face as she took in the newcomers. Her gaze lingered an extra moment or two on Lloyd.

"Sure, I'll go get him."

Kailay flitted by the companions. As she passed, she flashed a sweet smile at the tall warrior. Lloyd gave her a shy smile, his face turning almost as red as his outfit. When she reached the other end of the bar, Kailay glanced back over her shoulder, her eyes fixed on Lloyd. "Now don't you go anywhere," she said in a playful tone, then disappeared down the hallway.

The bartender grinned at Lloyd. "I think she likes you."

Lloyd did not respond, his face turning redder, if that was possible.

The foursome waited at the bar until Kailay returned with a short, fat, balding gentleman. The young barmaid smiled at Lloyd one last time. "Let me know if there is anything I can get you."

"S-sure thing."

Kailay smiled sweetly then disappeared back into the kitchen, long hair swishing behind her.

"So what can I do for you folks?" Telpin asked.

"We'd like some rooms. Pheldan told us to come here and ask for you," Aksel told him.

"Ah, Pheldan, my good friend. Yes, yes, of course. I can take care of you. Follow me."

Telpin led the travelers back down the hall. They passed the stage, nodding to the bard as he continued to sing his witty songs. The innkeeper led them down a long hall lined with doors on one side and windows on the other. The hall turned right and continued past another door and a set of stairs. Beyond that was a doorway labeled *Office*. Telpin ushered them into a small room, most of which was taken up by a large desk with so many papers covering it, they could hardly see the wood underneath. Telpin opened a drawer and rummaged around, finally pulling out two keys.

"These are for rooms six and ten. Those are the best rooms I have. Both on the second floor, with lots of space and two beds each. You should be very comfortable." His voice dropped low. "I'll rent them to you for two-thirds the price. That's only eighteen silver pieces per room, mind you."

"Also, my horse is out front," Lloyd added.

"Yes, yes." Telpin waved his hands. "We have a stable. It'll only cost an extra four silver pieces for your horse. Bring him around back, and my stable boy will take care of him."

Aksel nodded his appreciation. "Done." He pulled a purse from under his robe.

They were interrupted by a loud growling noise. Everyone turned and saw Lloyd holding his stomach, his face turning red. "Sorry. Is the kitchen still open?"

"Sure, sure." Telpin winked. "We'll get you settled into your rooms, and then I'll have Kailay and Morwen get you something."

The innkeeper led them upstairs. The first room was right at the top. Aksel and Seth decided to bunk there together. The second room was just across the hall. Telpin ushered Lloyd and Glo inside, and handed them the key.

"Hope you enjoy your accommodations." With that, the innkeeper spun on his heel and disappeared down the hall.

The rooms were spacious and comfortable as promised. The beds were overly large for Aksel and Seth, but just long enough for the tall Glolindir and Lloyd. The travelers swiftly dumped their gear and met back in the common room. Kailay served them a late dinner, more than happy to fuss over them, especially Lloyd. Starving after a long hard day, the companions dug in with relish. There was a hearty vegetable soup, whole chickens, corn, muffins, with ale and cider to wash it all down.

As they ate, Lloyd nodded to Glo. "I thought elves didn't eat meat."

Glo smiled between bites. "That's a myth. I think people came up with that story because my people are so respectful of the forests and the land. But they forget that elves are hunters as well as farmers. Trust me, when an elven party takes down game, we all share in the feast."

Seth tore off a second chicken leg and waved it around as if fending off a monster. "And everyone knows us halflings will eat anything put in front of us!"

Lloyd's expression was one of chagrin. "Sorry. I don't know very much about other races. As I told you before, there aren't very many in the Penwick area, other than a few dwarves."

Aksel came to his defense. "It's fine, Lloyd. Pay no attention to Seth. It's just that in the short time we've been traveling, we've heard a lot of myths about our various races. Sometimes it's rather humorous, and sometimes it's not."

Lloyd's expression grew serious. "Well, I meant no disrespect. Personally, I think that all people are equal and should be treated that way."

Glo looked at Lloyd with newfound respect—not many shared his viewpoint. In his travels, he had observed tolerance between the races, but their cultures and perspectives were so different that true understanding was difficult at best. Yet he believed that Lloyd meant what he said and would stand by those words.

Glo raised his glass. "A toast, then, to new friends. May our friendship be the beginning of a new understanding between the races."

Aksel and Lloyd raised their glasses as well. All eyes turned to Seth. The halfling gazed back at them with a cynical expression. "Really?"

"Come on, Seth," Aksel urged him.

Seth rolled his eyes, then raised his glass. "Oh very well—but don't expect peace to break out across the lands overnight."

The four clinked their mugs together and took a deep draft of ale. As they placed them down, Kailay walked up to the table. She held a steaming hot pie in each hand. "Well, that's what I like to see—good friends enjoying a good meal." She placed the pies on the table one at a time. "The fruit in these are from our own orchards just outside of town; this one's apple, and this one's cherry." She winked at them and flashed Lloyd a big smile, making the young man blush all over again.

As Kailay walked back to the kitchen, Glo observed Lloyd's discomfort with her attention. It was hard to believe that he was the same human that just faced a dozen or so orcs in combat. Glo turned back to the table just in time to see a knife appear in Seth's hand out of thin air. The halfling's blade flickered over the pies, challenging the eye to keep up. When he was done, they were both cut into four large slices. Seth helped himself to a quarter of the apple pie.

The four of them dug in, swiftly finishing both pies. Their appetites sated, they sat back, exhaustion setting in after a long, arduous day. They stood up as one, left a generous tip, then headed upstairs to their rooms. The four agreed to meet in the common room first thing in the morning.

Lloyd stripped off his boots and armor, lay in bed, and was asleep almost immediately. Glo sat motionless on his bed for a while, the events of the day playing through his mind. It had been fraught with danger, but the worst was when he froze as that huge orc attacked. Still, thanks to teamwork, they had survived and even saved most of their fellow travelers. Perhaps his father was wrong after all. With his new-found friends, they had made a difference this day. Glo felt they had started something important here, and he was determined to see it through.

More than that, he liked these three fellows: Seth with his cynical view of the world, Aksel with his desire to save lives, and Lloyd with his belief that all people were equal. He was certain his mother would like them. His father, of course, would not approve of any of them, but that was his loss. A grim expression crossed Glo's face at the thought. *Elves can be friends with other races, no matter what Amrod says.*

Glo glanced over at his sleeping companion. He appeared so relaxed that Glo envied him. Elves did not need sleep like the other races; some in fact would point to it as a human weakness, but Glo found it fascinating. Their differences made them stronger, as evidenced by their victory today. With that final thought, the young elf closed his eyes and entered a restful trance.

5
MALTAR

The next morning, Glo, Seth, Aksel, and Lloyd met in the common room as planned. During breakfast, a number of folks entered and exited the tavern, many smiling and nodding to them. Two even called out, "Good job!" and "Nicely done!"

Lloyd wore a confused expression. "I wonder what that's all about."

"Word of your exploits has gotten around town." Kailay approached their table with a pitcher in hand.

Glo found that hard to believe. "Already?"

The barmaid smiled at him as she refilled their mugs. "It's a small town. News travels quickly."

"What are they saying?" Aksel asked.

She gave them a coy smile, mostly aimed at Lloyd. "Not much—just that you took down about fifty orc bandits along with a giant, and saved the caravan from Tarrsmorr."

Seth's lips formed into a half twisted smile. "A giant, huh? Are you sure it was only one? I seem to recall two…or three."

"Everyone looks like a giant to you," Glo retorted.

Seth turned toward him and without missing a beat said, "Well, at least my trigger finger didn't freeze up."

Glo gave the halfling an acid look.

Aksel stepped in, staring first at one then the other. "Okay, okay, that's enough, you two." When neither replied, he turned back to Kailay. "It was more like twenty, and one was really huge. We were just happy to help."

Kailay put down the pitcher and put her hands on her hips. "I don't care if there were giants or not. You four are heroes, and the whole town is talking about it." Her attention swept across each one, her eyes finally settling on the handsome warrior. "Now that that's settled…is there anything else I can get you?"

"No, thank you," they all responded.

"Okay." Kailay turned and slowly walked away, her curls swaying behind her. "If you need me, I'll be in the kitchen," she called over her shoulder, flashing Lloyd one of her delightful smiles.

Seth folded his arms, a smug smile crossing his lips. "Sounds like we have a reputation already."

Aksel nodded. "I say we take advantage of it. Seth, why don't you poke around town and find out what's going on in the area."

Lloyd pushed back from the table, stretched and yawned. He patted his stomach, now full of pancakes, eggs, and potatoes. "While he's doing that, I need to get in my morning exercise."

Glo also had things to do. In particular, he needed ingredients for his spells. Aside from a caster's will, spells required two or three physical triggers to manifest them. The first trigger was the arm and hand motions, the second the spoken word, and the third a symbol representing the spell's effect. For example, the sleep spell he used required a fine pinch of sand. *Maybe I'll check out Pheldan's. Xelda might even be there.* He brushed any remaining crumbs from his robe and stood up. "I'm headed down to the shops. I could check to see if anyone knows anything."

Aksel wiped his mouth and cleared his throat. "And I'll check out

that temple we saw up on the hill. Let's meet back here for lunch."
Everyone agreed.

The rest of them got up, left a nice tip, and went their separate
ways.

It was around noon when the small company met back at the
Charging Minotaur. Seth had checked out the two other taverns in
town—*Falcon's* down by the docks, and the *Tavern of the Winds* a few
blocks over. He discovered that any trouble in the area was usually
brought before the baron during town meetings held up at the keep.
The meetings were open to everyone and were held every few days,
but the next one wasn't until three days from now. Still, he had heard
rumors of strange happenings in the area, including the caravan attacks, trouble at the farms north of here, and folks disappearing in
the woods to the southwest.

Meanwhile, Aksel investigated the temple and met with the town
Abbot, one Qualtan Berric. The Abbot had already heard of their exploits and alluded to the fact that he was good friends with both the
baron and the baroness. He told Aksel he would introduce them if
the occasion arose. While there, Aksel was given permission to setup
a shrine to his gnomish goddess, the Soldenar. He spent the rest of
the morning doing so in the small alcove allotted to him.

Lloyd had worked up a healthy appetite after a fierce workout
in the clearing behind the inn. The young man had an audience as
both Kailay and Morwen took turns watching him sweat. Kailay even
brought him a towel when he finished. It turned out that the young
woman was also a pretty good source of knowledge. She told Lloyd
all about the town meetings and the same rumors Seth had heard
while he was drying off.

Glo had gone to Pheldan's shop as planned. It turned out the old
half-elf did indeed have a small area where he kept spell ingredients.
Xelda had studied the basics of magic with the town wizard, Maltar, and ever since, Pheldan kept those ingredients in stock. Glo had
spent most of the morning talking with Xelda and thus learned more
about the irritable Maltar. He had also heard the rumors.

Seth rapped the table impatiently with his fingers. "What do we do for now?"

Glo wondered the same thing. "Well we've already taken care of the caravan problem. That leaves the farms north of here, or the woods to the south."

Lloyd chimed in eagerly. "I'm up for either."

Seth stared around the table, his expression incredulous. "Without being paid for it?"

Aksel faced the halfling. "Much as it would benefit us to be paid for our work, we could still poke around the farms or the woods to see what's going on."

Seth cocked his head, as if thinking it over, then sighed. "I suppose it couldn't hurt our reputation any."

Aksel opened his mouth to reply when the tavern door swung open. The room abruptly went silent, everyone turning to stare at the entrance.

Glo's back was to the door. "What's going on?" he whispered to the others. When none of them answered, he gazed over his shoulder toward the door.

In the doorway stood a man garbed in deep purple robes. He had short-cropped hair and a thin beard under a determined chin. Both were dark colored but with vague hints of grey. There was an air of power about the man that practically screamed the word mage. His sharp eyes scanned the room, abruptly stopping when they found Glo and his companions. The mage paused as if mentally evaluating the little group, then walked over toward them.

Glo leaned in close to the others. "That must be the town wizard. Careful. He can be touchy."

Maltar reached their table and stopped. His dark eyes scanned across each of them in turn. "An elf, a gnome, a halfling, and a human. You must be the band that rescued the caravan yesterday."

Aksel nodded. "Indeed we are. And you are…"

The man's lips upturned slightly followed by a short *humph*. "You are obviously not from around here. *I* am the Wizard Maltar—and I need some work done, immediately."

If nothing else, this Maltar is to the point.

Aksel leaned forward. "And what can we do for you?"

Maltar's eyes lifted and he gazed around the room; Glo followed suit. Everyone was staring at them, those closest quite obviously straining to hear what they were saying. The mage glared at the nosey patrons, causing them to blanch and turn away. Satisfied that any on-lookers were warned off, Maltar leaned in close and began his story.

"There is a scroll of moderate importance that I would like to have for my collection. My sources tell me that it has come to reside in the former keep at Stone Hill, in the woods southwest of here. I do not have the time to search the place right now, thus the need for hired help such as yourselves. I do not expect you to find the scroll, but could usea good map of the keep for later. I will pay 500 gold for you to scout out the area and provide me with such a map."

"And what if we do find the scroll?" Seth eyed the wizard with caution.

Maltar responded with that same humph. "*If* you are able to find the scroll and return it to me in pristine condition, I will reward you with 5,000 gold."

Glo raised an eyebrow. He glanced at his companions and saw a glint in Seth's eye. Aksel's hand went to his chin, but was otherwise silent. Lloyd's expression had not changed; he appeared just as eager as before the wizard's offer.

"So what say you?" Maltar shifted his weight from one foot to the other and glared at them.

Aksel looked around the table. Glo nodded his agreement, as did Lloyd and Seth. Aksel turned back to the mage. "Done."

"Very good." He pulled a small pouch from his belt and dropped it on the table. It made a metallic clinking noise as it landed. "There's a small down payment. When you have the map, or the scroll, bring it to me at my house, and you will get the rest." With that, Maltar spun on his heel, and left the tavern.

Seth reached for the pouch. "Agreeable fellow there."

Aksel was quick to respond. "Agreeable or not, we can do this job and check out those woods at the same time."

Seth opened the pouch and dumped the contents onto the table—a small pile of gold coins. He began to count them.

"The two might even be related," Glo mused aloud.

"Well, I'm up for it either way." Lloyd stretched his large frame and flexed his arms to emphasize the point.

"200 gold here," Seth told them.

Glo glanced from the halfling to the pile on the table. "That was quick."

Seth shrugged. "What can I say? I'm a fast counter."

Aksel stroked his chin as if deep in thought. "Well, if we're all agreed, I think we'll need a few more hands to pull this off. We'll definitely need someone who knows the area, who can lead us to this Stone Hill." He paused a moment. "And another warrior wouldn't hurt either. No offense, Lloyd, but good as you are, you are only one man."

"None taken," Lloyd responded evenly, "as long as there are enough monsters to go around." All eyes turned to him. Lloyd sat there with a broad grin on his face.

Glo chuckled. "Seth, I think you're beginning to rub off on him."

The halfling gave a short closed-mouth laugh. "What can I say? I just have that effect on people."

Aksel glanced at Seth. "Okay then, we'll need provisions and horses. Actually, riding dogs for you and me. You and Lloyd go see to that. Meanwhile, Glo and I will search out a guide."

Seth nodded, not taking his eyes off the pile of coins in front of him. He had split it in two, and now pushed the smaller pile across the table toward Aksel. "You're probably going to need this."

"More than likely," Aksel agreed. He pulled an empty pouch from his belt and started to fill it.

Meanwhile, Seth pocketed the rest of the coins and pushed back his chair. "Come on, big guy," he said to Lloyd. The tall warrior got up, nodded to Aksel and Glo, then followed the halfling out of the tavern.

Aksel had just finished stowing the coins away when Kailay came over to them. "Did I just see the Wizard Maltar at your table?" she said in a hushed voice.

Glo responded to her question with a question. "Why do you ask?"

She leaned down close, her voice taking on a conspiratorial tone. "We never see him in here. He mostly hides in his house. Occasionally he'll head up to the castle, but that's rare. Usually only if the baron calls for him." She briefly glanced around then continued. "You see, the baron and Maltar used to be good friends. They adventured together before they settled here, but they must have had some kind of falling out a couple of years ago. Maltar had a tower in the keep, but after that moved into his own house. He and the baron almost never talk anymore."

Aksel's eyes fell on Glo. "Interesting."

"Indeed." Glo had heard some of this from Xelda already, but not all. He turned back to Kailay. "Thank you for the information."

Kailay stood back up, a satisfied smile on her face. "You are most welcome."

This young woman appeared to know quite a lot about what went on in the town. It gave Glo an idea. "By the way, you wouldn't by chance know where we could find a guide?"

Kailay's face took on a quizzical expression. "You mean a tracker?"

Glo grinned. The girl was smart. "Exactly."

Kailay pursed her lips as she thought about it. She bent close once again and nudged her head toward a booth by the fireplace. "See those two over there, the thin one with the dark hair and the tall blonde woman?"

Glo and Aksel turned their heads, glancing in the direction Kailay pointed out. In a booth to the right of the hearth sat a dark-haired man in a brown leather outfit and a tall woman with blonde hair wearing a red cloak. Her chainmail-covered arms protruded from under the cloak as she raised her glass.

"That is Brundon and Titan. Brundon is a tracker. He's only been around a year or so, but he seems to know the area quite well. Titan grew up here. There's no one in town better with a sword except the captain of the guard, or maybe the baron himself."

Glo was impressed. This woman was indeed an excellent source of knowledge about the town and its occupants. He reached into his pocket and handed her a few copper coins. "Thank you very much, Kailay."

Kailay stood back up and curtsied. "You're very welcome." She pocketed the coins, then gathered up their dishes. As she walked back to the kitchen, she glanced back over her shoulder and flashed Glo a shy smile.

The young woman was positively delightful. On the surface she may appeared all bubbly and flirty, but underneath it all she had a keen mind. She was not at all like the pampered nobles he had known back home. Neither was Xelda for that matter. She was witty and smart with an appreciation for magic. Meeting the two was an eye opener for Glo. Prior to leaving home, he had led a rather sheltered life. Privately tutored, he had only met people his own age at social functions. Those he did meet tended to be superficial, with little awareness of anything that mattered. Neither Kailay nor Xelda were like that. Both showed great interest in the world around them. For the first time Glo saw how an elf could end up with a human or half-elf.

Aksel pushed back his chair. "Shall we then?" Glo wondered if his friend had any inkling of his thoughts, but Aksel's expression was unreadable.

Aksel, with Glo at his side, went over to meet the duo Kailay pointed out. The pair conversed softly, but stopped as the companions approached. The dark-haired man was tall and lean with a slim face, a hawk-like nose, and a thin beard and moustache. The woman appeared even taller, perhaps the size of Lloyd, with broad shoulders and well-muscled arms under her form-fitting chainmail. Her dirty blonde hair was braided on the sides and down the center in a warrior-like fashion. *Impressive,* he thought, feeling almost intimidated as the blonde woman's eyes took him in with mild interest.

"Good day to you," the woman said.

"Good day to you." Aksel gave a cordial bow. "May we join you?"

The lean man looked them over. "A gnome and an elf. Don't see that every day. Sure, have a seat." He got up and slid into the seat next to the tall woman. Aksel and Glo sat down opposite them.

"My name's Brundon, and this here's my friend Titan."

"I'm Aksel, and this is Glolindir."

"A gnome and an elf," Brundon repeated. "You must be with that group that saved the caravan yesterday."

Aksel nodded. "Yes, that was us; Glo and I and our other two companions."

Titan turned her steely blue eyes on Glo. "That was some nice work. Rumor has it that you've got a warrior with you who mowed down at least twenty orcs."

The corner of Glo's lips upturned slightly. "That might be just a bit exaggerated."

A thin smile spread across Brundon's face. "We kind of guessed that already. Folks around here love to stretch their stories. It keeps them *entertained*." He emphasized the last word, his voice taking on a mocking tone.

Titan gave her companion a sidelong glance. She did not appear thrilled with his attitude. "Either way, I'd love to meet this fellow you travel with."

"Well, that could be arranged," Aksel told her. This young woman was refreshing; she seemed genuine and straightforward, despite being a tad intimidating. Aksel found the half-truths and deceptions most people engaged in a waste of time. "In fact, the reason we sought you out is because we have another job—one with which we could use some help."

A spark lit in Titan's eyes; she leaned forward with an eager smile. She was about to speak, when Brundon put up his hand. Titan stopped, her mouth hanging open. She fixed her partner with a cool stare, then sat back and crossed her arms.

Brundon looked down at his fingertips and inspected his nails, as if totally disinterested. "A job you say? What does it entail?"

Aksel was no novice to negotiations. He had seen it all before in the markets at Caprizon. What Brundon was doing was a fairly standard tactic to drive up his price. Aksel kept his expression impassive. "It's not a hard job. We merely need someone to lead us to Stone Hill."

Brundon looked up, his expression remaining neutral. "Stone Hill, you say? Why would you possibly want to go there?"

Aksel did not answer immediately. He was certain Brundon knew the job was for Maltar. The entire room had seen the wizard talking with them. He cast a quick glance at Glo. The elf sat back, his fingers in a steeple, barely hiding the slight smile on his lips. Glo wasn't buying this act either. Aksel almost laughed, but caught himself. He didn't trust this Brundon and would only tell him what was absolutely necessary. "We were contracted to map out the old abandoned keep up there. So do you know the area?"

Brundon looked mildly offended. "I know it very well. You are looking at the best tracker this side of Dunwynn. If there's a place you need to find, or a trail you need followed, I'm your man."

Titan gave him a stern scowl. "Gods, Brundon, can you be any cockier?" She finished by jabbing him in the arm.

"Well, I am, love, and you know it." He rubbed his shoulder where she had hit him.

Titan shook her head and crossed her arms again, obviously still annoyed with her partner. Aksel had to stifle a laugh once more. He was starting to like this woman Titan.

Brundon leaned forward and lowered his voice. "But I must tell you that Stone Hill is not a safe place. It is surrounded by the Dead Forest, which, as you might guess by the name, is not a friendly wood. Travelers have seen and heard strange things there for the last few months. What's more is folks started disappearing there just recently." He leaned back, folded his arms, and gave Titan a strange grin. "No telling what you'll find up there."

Aksel cast a look at Glo, but this time the elf shrugged. Perhaps Brundon was exaggerating, but still there might also be some truth to what he said. Either way, he was tired of this back and forth. "Well, that may be, but we still have a job to do."

Brundon leaned forward, trying to sound casual. "So…what would the pay be?"

"Fifty gold pieces for the both of you," Aksel said firmly.

A smile crept across Brundon's face. He was about to say something when Aksel added, "Twenty up front, and the rest once we have safely returned from our journey."

Brundon opened his mouth, but Titan cut him off. She sat forward and put out her hand to Aksel. "Done."

Brundon's mouth hung open as Aksel reached forward and shook hands with Titan. The little cleric allowed himself a smile this time. "We leave within the hour. Meet us outside the inn."

Titan gave them a definitive nod. "We will be there."

Aksel stood up and dropped a few gold coins on the table. Brundon's eyes fixed on those coins. Before the tracker could say anything more, Aksel strode away, Glo beside him. Behind them he overheard Brundon and Titan arguing.

"I could've gotten us more," Brundon said.

"You know I was going up there anyway. Now we're getting paid to—so just deal with it."

Aksel nearly laughed out loud. He was really starting to like this Titan.

Once they were out of earshot, Glo said, "You handled that well."

"Thanks. I was beginning to lose my patience with that fellow."

"If it was me, I would have turned him into a toad."

Aksel glanced up at his friend, but the elf was smiling. "You know you can't really do that."

Glo grinned. "Not just yet I can't, but I will someday."

Aksel smiled in turn, picturing a toad with the tracker's face. Glo had an odd sense of humor; Aksel did not always know when he was kidding, but he was learning to read him. Either way, Glo made a good companion. Besides being a wizard, Aksel could trust him, and trust was really important to Aksel. He had lost his entire family and felt the weight of being alone ever since. Even when they took him in at the temple, he had not felt comfortable. Sure, the clerics were nice, trained him and all, but Aksel never really fit in. They still had families; he did not. Something had changed though in these last few weeks. Between Glo, Seth and now Lloyd, Aksel felt like he was part of something again—a family of sorts.

The two companions left the common room together, discussing the impending journey as they walked down the hall and climbed up the stairs to their rooms. Although neither could be certain what awaited them up at Stone Hill, they were both sure it would be an interesting trip.

6
INTO THE DEAD FOREST

Human and halfling disappeared into the woods, shadow-silent

About an hour later, the four companions met in front of the Charging Minotaur. Brundon and Titan soon joined them, leading two horses by the reins. The former wore a sour expression, but Titan appeared satisfied enough for the both of them—looking more than ready to use the longsword strapped to her side. The tall warrior no longer wore chainmail, but instead was dressed in full plate armor that gleamed silver in the midday sun. Glo noted the magical runes inscribed on the armor, put there to make the heavy metal lighter and easier to maneuver in. Across her brow she wore a metallic headband shaped like the letter 'M' with an attached piece reaching down to the jaw on either side of her face. In her left hand, Titan carried a large metal shield; on it was the likeness of a rearing lion over two crossed swords on a diagonally split backdrop of red and silver—most likely a family crest.

Glo watched as the impressive woman-warrior approached Lloyd.

She focused on the massive twin blades sheathed in cross-like fashion on his back, smiling at him with an almost child-like excitement. Aksel introduced the two, who shook hands and immediately fell into an avid conversation about weaponry. They continued talking as they packed their saddlebags and mounted their steeds—Lloyd on his paint and Titan on her quarter horse. Glo could not help but smile with amusement, listening to the two of them go on about weapons, battles and fighting techniques. Lloyd had found a kindred spirit in Titan. He almost envied the young warrior. The only one he had ever been able to share his craft with was his father, and that hadn't worked out so well.

Brundon rolled his eyes. "Titan can go on for hours like that."

"It's one of Lloyd's favorite subjects," Seth agreed.

"Good." Aksel gave a firm nod. "Then they can keep each other busy on the ride out to Stone Hill."

Glo finished with his own saddlebags, then mounted his horse and surveyed the rest of the group. Seth was dressed in his normal black silks and vest, his long dark hair pulled back into a tight ponytail. He had a knife strapped to his leg and a number of pouches on his belt, most likely filled with an assortment of throwing weapons and other equally dangerous or useful equipment. Aksel wore a white, high-necked robe with a diamond-shaped emblem on the chest—the symbol of his goddess, the Soldenar. A white cloak hung over his shoulders with the hood hanging down his back, its green lining visible around his neck. His copper hair tumbled over his forehead in front but was cut short in back, revealing his slightly pointed, gnomish ears.

Lloyd once again wore red leather armor. It covered his upper torso, but also had tassets which extended down to his legs. He wore a matching set of greaves, which covered his legs all the way up to his knees. Brundon was still dressed in brown leather, but now had a short sword strapped to his belt, a quiver full of arrows across his back, and a long bow over his shoulder. Glo himself had on his long, flowing purple robes. In his left hand, he carried a staff with the two crescents on the end, a present from his mother, and on his right shoulder sat his familiar, Raven. She was cawing, *"Nammë avánië, nammë avánië." We are leaving, we are leaving.*

They were just about ready to go when they heard a cry from the direction of the inn. Kailay rushed through the front door, down the steps and over to Lloyd, skirt swishing against the dusty road. She held up a basket to the surprised young man.

"Just a little snack for you while you're on the road," she said, looking breathless.

Lloyd's face reddened slightly as he dismounted. "Thanks. You didn't have to go to all that trouble."

Kailay handed him the basket. "It's no trouble at all." She glanced down at her feet with a shy smile, and waited while Lloyd secured the basket to his horse. When he turned back around, she stepped forward, reached up, and threw her arms around his neck, kissing him soundly on the lips. It only lasted for a few seconds, but Lloyd blushed through the whole thing. Kailay finally let go and took a step backward. She put a finger to her lips and said demurely, "That was for luck." She glanced around at the rest of them— "Good luck to you all!"—and ran back into the inn, a soft giggle trailing behind her.

Both Brundon and Titan wore amused expressions. "I've been coming here a year, and never got a goodbye like that," the tracker noted.

Everyone laughed while Lloyd turned even redder. The young man remounted his steed, his face still flushed.

Aksel glanced around at everyone, his eyes finally coming to rest on Lloyd. "Are we all ready now?"

The young man grinned sheepishly, his hand going to the back of his neck. "Yep."

"Okay then, let's get going."

⁂

The midday sun shone brightly overhead. From what Brundon told them, it would only take a few hours to reach the Dead Forest. The party headed southwest down the road, crossed the bridge over the Raven River, and passed the Temple of Arenor.

Townsfolk hurried about their business, but they were evidently not too busy to notice the strange group of travelers passing by on horseback. A number of folks stared as they went by, and a few even waved. Ten minutes later, the party had left the little town of Ravenford behind.

Once they were in open country, Glo turned to Raven and spoke a single word, "*Revia.*" It was the Elvish word for *fly*.

Raven replied in her small bird like voice, "*Lassuilye, Tura.*" *Thank you, Master.* She then went winging off his shoulder and up into the clear blue sky. The black bird spiraled higher and higher, riding the thermal currents, until she reached an altitude well above the trees. From there, she launched herself forward and flew down the road ahead of the little party.

Brundon took the lead, followed by Aksel and Seth. Next rode Glo, with Lloyd and Titan bringing up the rear—the two warriors still talking about weapons and battles. From the way they were going, Glo was sure they would talk for the next few hours, maybe even days.

The group followed the roadway southwest, the smooth cobblestone path paralleling the coastline. The road veered sharply northwest, skirting the edge of a forest directly in their path. According to Brundon, that was the Kelvan Woods—a very densely-wooded area that would not be easy to navigate on horseback. The road continued northwest for a few more miles until it reached a pass in the Kelvan Hills, and then it turned back southward. It would have been slow going through either the woods or hills; the road was still the fastest route to take.

The companions continued along the cobblestone roadway. After another mile or so, the forest disappeared, replaced by green rolling hills to their left. On their right, the land was flat and grassy. The blue glint of the waters of the West Raven appeared off in the distance. The day remained clear and sunny with only a couple of puffy white cumulus clouds in the sky. Birds winged their way through the air, both solo and in flocks. Every once in a while, Glo's raven came into view high up overhead, paralleling the party's progress, then flying off to scout ahead.

The road was smooth, and before the travelers knew it, they were turning southwest, entering Kelvan Pass. It was really not so much of a pass as a flat area between the rolling Kelvan Hills. The small company left the West Raven behind them and were now surrounded on both sides by the lush green hillsides. Patches of forest occasionally cropped up. It remained a beautiful spring day, and the ride was easy so far.

Glo thought about how peaceful it had been in the Bendenwoods before they were ambushed. This ride was equally pleasant, but that previous experience reminded him that this was no casual ride. They were on a mission and needed to remain vigilant, no matter how serene their surroundings might seem. Glancing around, he noticed the serious air that had fallen over the party. Lloyd and Titan had gone silent, moving into rear flanking positions on either side of the party. Both rode along easily but maintained careful watch over the passing countryside. Brundon, a little ahead of the group, kept an eye on the road's horizon, while Seth quietly scanned their surroundings.

Glo did his part via his contact with Raven. The black bird seemed quite at ease; he could sense her enjoyment as she soared through the clear skies above. The party continued south until the Kelvan Hills fell away to their west. In their place was a large peak off to the southwest. That, according to Brundon, was their destination— Stone Hill. The top of the rise looked barren from this distance, yet those with sharp eyesight could see the outline of the keep at the top of the hill. As the travelers closed on their objective, a patch of wood loomed up ahead. It did not look very appealing to Glo; the tree line appearing more grayish than green. There was something decidedly wrong about it, but aside from the off-color of the trees, he was not sure what from this distance. Brundon, still out in front, called for the party to halt.

"That's the Dead Forest on the road ahead. Do you want to continue into it, or do you want to head straight to Stone Hill?"

His question was met with silence. Glo stared at the grey woods. *So that is the Dead Forest. No wonder it is so unsettling to look upon.*

Aksel spoke up after a few moments. "I think it might be best to stick to the road. On the off chance that the keep is occupied, anyone, or anything, on the hill will see us coming."

The lean man nodded. "Better safe than sorry. If we stick to the road, we will soon be under the cover of the trees. Then we should be able to turn toward the hill without worrying about being seen from Stone Hill."

"Sounds like a plan," Aksel agreed.

They spurred their mounts onward and continued down the road. As the group approached the Dead Forest, they began to see why it was so named. All of the trees were wilted and sick; vegetation was scattered half-heartedly as if it'd forgotten how to grow there. No animal sounds. Not even a bird chirping to ward off the chilling emptiness of the bony scraps of trees people referred to as a forest. A feeling of unease settled over them as they entered those pale trees. Luckily the forest was mostly devoid of leaves, allowing the blue skies above to seep through. It should have warmed them, but even the sun seemed less cheery as they plodded forward. A short way into the woods, Brundon called for another halt.

The base of Glo's neck tingled with a strange sensation. "This is eerie. There is a palpable heaviness in this forest. The trees seem barely alive. Not even in the great forest of Ruanaiaith, which is very dark in places, is there such an oppressive gloom as hangs over these woods."

Aksel's expression was grim. "Then let's not stay in them any longer than we have to."

Brundon nodded. "Very good. I'll scout ahead. I recall seeing a trail leading up to the hill."

The lean man rode ahead while the others waited. The oppressiveness of the woods continued to hang over them, making it feel like forever before they caught sight of the tracker again. Brundon reappeared on the road ahead and soon rejoined them, reporting his findings.

"Sure enough, just as I remember. There is a path leading off the main road about a half mile south of here. It does not look well-traveled, but it will be easier than trying to travel through all of this dead underbrush." He surveyed the forest floor.

Aksel nodded gravely to the tracker. "Lead on."

Brundon led the way down the road until they came to a break in the trees. A narrow path led them westward off the path and into the forest. It looked like it had not been used in years. Since the forest was mostly dead, there was not much overgrowth, just the occasional fallen branch.

The group had to follow single file, so Titan moved toward the front, between Brundon and Seth. Seth was followed by Glo, then Aksel, with Lloyd bringing up the rear. Brundon rode a bit ahead, scouting the path in front of them. The group continued through the dreary forest in silence, as if a wrong word would cause the woods to close in on them. Grayness completely surrounded them, making the feeling of oppression grow worse. It was as if all of the color had been sucked out of the world, except for themselves and the mounts they rode upon.

The path slowly rose upwards, but they were still in the forest when they reached the base of Stone Hill. The trees thinned out as they continued their ascent up the hillside. Abruptly, Brundon stopped ahead, quietly raising his hand for them to halt. The others heeded his signal and reined in their horses. He slid off his steed and walked back between the others, a half-twisted smile on his face.

"The path enters a pass through the hillside about three hundred yards ahead. It would be the perfect place for an ambush," Brundon explained, trying almost too hard to be nonchalant. "I think it's best for me to scout ahead off the path and see what's up there."

Aksel nodded. "That sounds like a good idea."

Seth jumped off his riding dog. "I think I'll go, too."

Brundon gazed skeptically at the halfling. "No offense, but this kind of thing requires stealth. Can you handle that?"

Glo nearly choked. Brundon had no idea who he was talking to. He expected an acid retort from Seth, but the halfling was surprisingly calm. He gazed up at Brundon and said, "Tell you what—you head out into the woods. I'll follow after a minute or so. If you can see me or hear me coming, then I'll head right back and wait with the others."

A smile slowly crossed Brundon's lips. "I like your style, friend. Very well—let's see what you can do." With that, the tracker turned and sprinted into the woods. He was soon gone from sight. Seth waited a bit over a minute, then took off after him.

Glo could not contain his amusement any longer. "I think Brundon's in for a bit of a surprise."

"Don't underestimate him," Titan said to them. "He's pretty good in the woods."

"You don't know Seth," Glo responded.

They waited in silence after that. The woods around them were deathly still, a body without a heartbeat. Finally, after about ten minutes, Seth reappeared.

"Where's Brundon?" Titan asked, a slight edge in her voice.

Seth was rather nonchalant. "Oh, I'm sure he'll be along any minute now."

About five minutes later, Brundon appeared as well. He sauntered up to Seth, the corner of his mouth upturned outrageously. "Guess you gave up without even trying."

Seth folded his arms across his chest. "Did I?"

Brundon expression grew uncertain. "What do you mean?"

It was Seth's turn to smirk. "Oh nothing—but you might want to check your belt."

Brundon gazed at the halfling as if he were crazy, but then began running his hand around his waist. He reached back behind him, and his eyes suddenly went wide. "No..." he drawled. The tracker brought his hand out from behind his back. In it sat a familiar-looking black throwing knife. "How in the world..."

Seth wore a twisted grin as he stepped forward and swiped the knife back from the tracker. "I'm just that good. Now, can we get back to scouting out the trail ahead?"

Brundon shook his head in amazement. "Very well. I'll take the left flank, and you fan out to the right. Let's plan on meeting back here in about twenty minutes."

Seth nodded once, then took off. Brundon briefly caught Titan's eye, shrugged, then also took off. Human and halfling disappeared into the woods, shadow-silent.

Once they were gone, Glo heard a soft laugh from Titan. "That was priceless."

They waited once more, but somehow the forest no longer seemed quite as oppressive. Still, Glo could not help wonder what had happened to make them this way.

Glo whispered to Aksel, "It is unnatural for an entire wood to be like this."

The young gnome grimaced. "Probably some dark magic was used here at one time. But nothing I have ever heard of."

"Nor I."

Seth and Brundon reappeared out of the woods almost exactly twenty minutes later. The tracker signaled for the others to gather around. Seth spoke first, keeping his voice low.

"I think there is a trap up there inside the pass. I saw something lying across the path between the two cliffs. Whatever it is, it is crudely covered with underbrush."

Brundon then added his findings. "And I came across some large footprints. Two-legged and five toed, with clawed feet. *Bugbear* would be my best guess, from the shape and size." He looked knowingly at the others, his eyes finally resting on Titan.

7
BUGBEARS

Glo had read all about bugbears in his father's library back home. He had been required to read an entire book series entitled *Races of the World* as part of his studies. Bugbears were two-legged creatures, somewhat larger and broader than a man, but with a bear-like face. Goblinoid, like their cousins the orcs, they would also eat people. They needed to be very careful if there were bugbears in these woods.

Brundon continued his report. "I followed the trail up to the edge of the tree line. I did not want to get too close, but there is definitely something large and brown lying up on the cliff south of the pass."

Glo's nerves started to rise. "Don't bugbears usually travel in packs?"

Brundon gave him a lopsided grin. "Yes, as a matter of fact, they do. But they also like to send out scouts and set ambushes for the unwary."

Seth snorted. "Bet if we follow the trail up to the keep, we'll find the rest of his clan."

Brundon pursed his lips. "Most likely, but there's no telling how many of them there are."

Aksel's head tilted slightly, a quizzical expression crossing his face. "Maybe we can take advantage of the situation. By any chance, does anyone speak bugbear?"

There was silence for a moment, then Glo answered hesitantly, "I do."

Seth gave him a sidelong glance, his expression skeptical. "Really?"

"Sort of. It was part of my studies," Glo replied. The halfling still looked unconvinced. Glo sighed as he thought back on all the hours he had put into what he had then deemed useless studies. His father had forced him to learn the basics of a number of languages in order to *earn* the right to be called a wizard. Glo ticked off each language he had learned on his fingers as he spoke.

"I know Common, Dwarven, Draconic, Orcish, as well as Goblin, which is what bugbears speak."

Lloyd gazed at him, his expression curious. "You had to learn Common?"

Glo had a sarcastic retort on his lips, but stopped himself when he realized that Lloyd was serious. "Well...I am an elf."

"And elves speak what, Lloyd?" Seth said, his voice thick with sarcasm. Lloyd stared back at the halfling, a foolish look on his young face. "Elvish!" Seth finished folding his arms across his chest.

Lloyd's face took on a sheepish expression as he placed his hand behind his head. "Sorry, guess I didn't think it through."

Glo gave him a sympathetic smile. "That's okay. At least *you* didn't question my knowledge of languages like some people."

The corner of Seth's mouth rose slightly. "Pardon me. I didn't realize we were traveling with a walking library."

Aksel cleared his throat. "Anyway, if there is only one of them, let's see if we can capture it. Maybe that way we can find out more about what we are dealing with."

Brundon's eyes narrowed. "So what do you propose?"

Aksel paused and stared at him for a few moments. When he finally responded, he sounded more formal than usual.

"First, you lead Seth, Glo, and me back to the spot where you saw the bugbear."

Brundon's face took on a smug expression. "As long as the rest of you can be quiet."

Aksel fixed the tracker with a stare. "We may not be as stealthy as you two, but trust me, we can manage."

"Okay. Then what?" Brundon prodded him further.

Aksel sounded more and more annoyed as the lean man continued questioning him. "Then you and Seth spread out and flank the creature."

Lloyd interrupted them, sounding quite eager. "What do you want us to do?" He pointed to himself and Titan.

Aksel's face visibly relaxed, a thin smile gracing his lips. "Provide distraction. Give us about fifteen minutes to get into position, and then you and Titan start slowly heading up the path on horseback. Try to make a bit of noise so that you keep the bugbear's attention."

Lloyd nodded, his face lighting up with enthusiasm. "Sure thing."

A gleam of excitement filled Titan's sharp blue eyes.

Aksel smiled at the duo then addressed the group in general. "So while the bugbear is focused on Lloyd and Titan, Glolindir will cast a sleep spell on it."

"That's all well and fine. What do we do if the wizard's sleep spell doesn't work?" Brundon said with thinly veiled amusement.

Aksel turned to face Brundon, exasperation quite evident on his face. He paused a moment and took a deep breath. "That is why you and Seth will be flanking the creature. If the spell doesn't work, then the two of you will pounce on it from both sides."

Brundon looked over Seth speculatively, then turned back to Aksel with a dubious expression. "You do realize that bugbears are quite large and very strong, don't you?"

Seth stared at the tracker, his arms folded across his chest. "What's the matter? Afraid you can't handle it?"

Brundon glared back. "It's not me I'm worried about."

"That's enough!" Aksel barked, his voice hard as stone. He stared Brundon in the eye, neither flinching nor blinking, his face completely devoid of emotion. Brundon returned the gnome's gaze, appearing quite self-assured at first; however, as Aksel continued to glare at him, the tracker looked more and more uncomfortable. Glo and the others watched the staring contest in stunned silence—all except for Seth, who had a wicked grin on his face. When Aksel finally spoke, his tone was very firm. "Then let's just hope that Glo's sleep spell works. Unless, of course, you have any better ideas?"

Brundon held up his hands in front of him. "No. No, not really."

Aksel's expression was triumphant. "Good, then let's move."

Brundon led Seth, Glo, and Aksel through the trees and near-dead brush. They moved parallel but to the south of the path. When they reached a point adjacent to the pass, the tracker stopped and began cautiously moving north. After a few dozen yards, they dropped down on their knees and crawled the rest of the way up to the edge of the tree line. The four adventurers ended up behind a thick fallen tree trunk, the open cliff just on the other side.

Brundon raised his head, peeked out, and then ducked back down again. He signaled to the others that the bugbear was still there. Glo raised his head and peeked over the top of the fallen trunk. He saw a large humanoid-looking creature with big protruding ears lying face down on the top of the cliff, his back toward them. It had brown skin, but was also partially covered with thick brown fur. Its torso was wrapped in some kind of cloth, with a piece of spiked armor strapped around its left shoulder. Lying next to it on the ground was a large, deadly mace.

So that is what a bugbear really looks like. It was larger than he imagined, and even at this distance, he found it intimidating. Glo was glad he was not facing this big creature alone. The bugbear turned its huge head to look down the path to the east, and Glo caught a glimpse of the ugly, bear-like face before he ducked back down behind the fallen tree.

Glo's heart was pounding in his chest. "That was close."

"Shhhh." Seth put a finger to his lips.

Glo clapped a hand over his mouth. Seth was right; there was no telling how sensitive this creature's ears were. Aksel motioned to Seth and Brundon, and the man and halfling moved out to the respective left and right of their current positions. They soon disappeared from sight. The two remaining companions stayed down and waited. A few minutes later, they heard voices drifting up the path from the east. It was Lloyd and Titan.

Right on time. Aksel nudged him and cocked his head in the direction of their target. He lifted his head again and saw that the bugbear was now staring down the path toward the sound of the approaching warriors. It was now or never. Glo reached into a pouch on his belt and pulled out a pinch of sand. Then he began to concentrate while moving his hands in a circular motion—slowly letting the grains of sand slip from his fingers. As the last of the sand fell away, he spoke the word, "*Somnus*" and gestured toward the unaware bugbear.

As the spell released, a faint purplish circle appeared around the creature. The light disappeared after a moment, and the bugbear's huge head slumped down onto the rock surface and lay still. Seth appeared off to his right, moving soundlessly toward the listless creature. He spied Brundon sneaking in from the left. Seth reached the bugbear first and stood quietly over the slumbering monster. He knelt down and examined it. It didn't move at all, except the gentle rise and fall of its massive chest. Seth stood up and gave the all-clear sign. Glo and Aksel climbed over the tree trunk simultaneously and joined the others standing over the fallen bugbear.

"It's asleep," Seth whispered. "And I didn't even have to sing him a lullaby."

A fleeting smile passed Aksel's lips. "Good, then let's tie him up."

Brundon pulled a thick rope from his pack, and he and Seth bound the bugbear and gagged it for good measure.

Seth rubbed his hands together. "Now that that's settled, I'll take care of that trap below." Before anyone could stop him, he launched himself off the cliff. The three companions hurried to the edge and watched as Seth caught the branch of a tree and swung to the ground, landing neatly on one knee on the path below. He then stood, looked up, and waved to the three figures on top of the cliff.

Brundon's voice was filled with awe. "Nice trick."

It was the second time now that the halfling had impressed the smug man. "That's nothing," Glo said to him. "I once saw him fall from a kite thirty feet in the air, bounce off the net below, and easily land on both feet."

Brundon turned to face him, his expression one of disbelief. "From a kite? Now you're just pulling my leg."

"It's true." Aksel smiled. "It's called kite riding. It's a big deal where I'm from."

Brundon raised an eyebrow at the gnome. "You can't be serious."

Glo snickered. "I thought the same thing at first, but trust me, I've seen it with my own eyes. They even tried to get *me* on one of those contraptions."

"Kite riding?" Brundon repeated, his expression still skeptical.

"Yes, it really is a big deal up in Caprizon."

Brundon stared from Glo to Aksel, then shook his head slowly. "I can't tell if you're trying to pull one over on me, but there's not many people that I can't read either. I will say this—there's definitely more to you folks than meets the eye."

"You've no idea," Aksel responded with an air of mystery, his expression unreadable. He whirled around, winked at Glo and walked back to their sleeping captive.

Brundon gazed after the gnome, looking completely puzzled. Glo suppressed a smile. *Good for Aksel. Maybe Brundon will think twice now before questioning everything he says.*

Glo shifted his gaze back to the pass below and saw that Seth had uncovered a pit trap. A pile of dead leaves and twigs still covered it somewhat, but the halfling had pushed a section to the side. *There is no way they are going to get the horses over that*, Glo thought. Seth must have thought the same thing. The halfling skirted the edges of the pit and headed back down the pass toward Lloyd and Titan. Ten minutes later, the three of them appeared atop the cliff.

The bugbear had already woken up and was straining at its ropes, but Brundon had pulled out his sword and held it to the monster's throat. It stopped its thrashing and sat still, glaring at them all. At Aksel's request, Lloyd and Titan dragged the big creature back to the fallen tree trunk and propped him up on it. Aksel then asked Brundon to keep an eye out at the top of the pass.

"Sure thing," Brundon replied, a hint of newfound respect in his voice. He turned and ran west through the tree line and up the hillside until he was out of sight.

Glo sat down on the ground in front of the creature, trying to figure out how to handle this situation. The bugbear was still quite ugly, but being all tied up and seated up against the tree trunk, it did not seem particularly threatening at the moment. Of course, it didn't hurt that Lloyd and Titan stood to either side of the creature, hands on their sword hilts, with fierce looks on their faces. Titan in particular glared at the creature, as if daring it to try anything. Glo was quite impressed with how intimidating she could be, but the bugbear didn't look scared in the least bit. It stared up defiantly at the two warriors.

Well, intimidation certainly was not going to work with this creature. Glo rifled through his mind, dredging up all he had read about bugbears. He knew their characteristics, enough of their language to get by, and even some basic culture. This creature was not afraid of them, so how was he going to get it to tell them what they wanted to know? As the wizard racked his brain, the answer came to him in a flash. *Culture! That's the answer.*

Glo began to speak to the bugbear in its own language. He was not that great at it, but he could get his point across. As he spoke, guttural sounds came from his mouth consisting of grunts and growls. "We worship...Gruel...the one...true god," he told the bugbear. Gruel was the chief deity of all bugbears. Though generally barbaric in nature, bugbears were extremely religious. The bugbear's eyes widened. *It's working.* "We are here...to test...your honor," Glo said haltingly. "We remove gag. If you scream...Gruel think... you weak. You understand?"

The bugbear gave a fervent nod. Well, this will be the test. Glo turned to Seth.

"Remove his gag."

Seth raised an eyebrow but walked over to the bugbear and took out his knife. The bugbear stared at the gleaming blade as Seth held it up to his huge bear-like face. He slid it under the gag and cut it off cleanly in one quick motion. The material fell away and landed on the creature's lap. Seth stepped back, and the knife disappeared from his hand.

The bugbear cleared its throat, a horrible rasping sound, and said to the elf, "You worship Gruel? How that be? You not bugbear. You meat."

"We…worship…Gruel," Glo said with a grunt, doing his best to sound fierce. He felt woefully inadequate next to the huge beast, but he continued to give it his best. "Gruel…one true god. He master of…blood and battle. He twelve feet tall…with great fangs…clawed hands…clawed feet. He carries…ten foot…mace. Other gods… cringe…before Gruel."

Glo thanked his lucky stars for his father's extensive library. There was a book there entitled, The Deities of All the Races. It even had pictures of each god in it.

"Yes, yes," the bugbear declared with clear passion, "that is Gruel. You do know him."

"Yes. What your…name?"

"I am Gilstench."

"What your…clan?" All bugbears belonged to a clan. It was the cornerstone of their society.

"My clan is *Ironfist*." The bugbear proudly raised his head.

"Ironfist," Glo repeated. "Good. Gruel…sent us…to test you. To test…Ironfist *clan*."

Gilstench glared at him suspiciously. This next step would be crucial. If the bugbear did not buy this then there would be no getting anything out of him.

"*Ironfist…now…weak!*" Glo cried with as much ferocity as he could muster. If only Lloyd or Titan could speak Goblin. At least they would have a chance of intimidating this huge creature; but he did not, and it was left to him. He pushed on, giving it his best.

"See…we caught you…easy. We do…same with…all Ironfist clan!"

Gilstench's face screwed up in anger. It was a fearsome sight, but he did his best to remain calm on the outside. Inside, his blood had turned to ice.

"My clan not weak!" the bugbear barked at him. "Gilstench stupid. Gilstench should die. But Ironfist clan strong!"

Glo was unnerved by the fierceness of the outburst. Luckily, the bugbear did not seem to notice. It was probably not used to reading expressions on the face of its prey. It took him a moment to find his voice again, but then he prodded the creature.

"You…sure?"

Gilstench snarled and then began spouting hotly, "We have three warriors, tougher than me. And two mages. We live in the great keep on top of the mountain. And we grow. We have families. Young ones get big and strong. One day we will have more warriors."

It is working! There were five more adult male bugbears, and they were living in the keep on top of Stone Hill with their families. Were there just the bugbears up there? He decided to push Gilstench just a bit more.

"That all?" he said, doing his best to keep his voice even.

"No," Gilstench said with a growl. "There is Wizard in keep. Telvar his name. He great wizard. He teach great magic to Bilehack and Curdlemung. They become great, too!"

Another wizard? That caught him by surprise. Glo felt suddenly uneasy.

"What…kind…magic?"

"Dark magic. Undead magic. Bugbears guard keep during day. Undead do job at night. Ironfist magic great."

Undead? That's not good. This "little job" of mapping out the keep had just become far more dangerous. Glo stood back for a moment, trying to think. He gazed around at the others, but except for some raised eyebrows and questioning looks, no one said anything. Well, there was no hope for it. Right now they needed to do something with Gilstench.

Glo stepped forward. "Maybe…Ironfist…great, but Gilstench… not. What we…do with…you?"

"Gilstench must die!" With a sudden great heave, he broke his ropes and launched his huge frame right at Glo.

The young elf froze in his tracks as the bugbear hurtled toward him. Suddenly, something hit him hard in the side, knocking him down. Glo slammed into the ground, the world spinning around him.

"You okay?"

Glo opened his eyes, his vision fuzzy. He turned his head and saw two familiar forms standing over him, one dressed mostly in black, the other in white.

"Sorry about that," Seth apologized. "I thought it better if I tackled you before the bugbear did."

Glo grimaced, his hand going to the back of his head. Yes, that was right. The bugbear had lunged at him, but something else had knocked into him first. Glo managed a partial smile. "Can't argue with that. So where'd he go?"

His vision finally cleared. He glanced around and caught sight of three figures running away from them. The lead figure was clearly ahead of the other two. It was Gilstench! Lloyd and Titan were in hot pursuit.

"They're almost to the cliff," Aksel said ominously.

Glo sprang up and took off after the others. At that point, the bugbear reached the cliff. Before anyone could stop him, the creature leapt off into midair and disappeared over the rim. Lloyd and Titan stopped short just at the cliff's edge. They stood there staring down into the pass. Glo, Seth, and Aksel reached them shortly thereafter. Neither warrior had moved, transfixed by what they saw below.

"You might not want to look," Titan warned them, but Glo chose to anyway.

At the bottom of the narrow ravine he saw a dreadful sight. Gilstench had landed in the pit trap the bugbears set up in the road. He'd fallen through and was now impaled on spikes at the bottom of the pit, his large body still convulsing. The onlookers stood there, aghast at the sight. Abruptly, Brundon appeared beside them.

"I heard the commotion…" he began, then stopped as he gazed down into the ravine. "Oooo, that's gotta hurt."

Seth's lips formed into a half twisted smile. "I guess he got the point."

Glo raised an eyebrow. Lloyd and Titan both groaned. Only Brundon seemed to find the comment amusing, responding with a short closed-mouth laugh.

Aksel could not help commenting. "Really?"

Seth merely stood there wearing a devilish smirk.

It suddenly dawned on Glo that the others didn't know what the bugbear had told him. He motioned for them to back away from the cliff and then repeated what he'd learned.

When he finished, Aksel was the first to speak. "It sounds like they have a little mini-army up there at the keep."

Brundon's face had gone somewhat pale. "And I'm really not thrilled with all this talk of undead."

Glo couldn't have agreed more, but he had further concerns. "What worries me more is this wizard, Telvar. If he is teaching the bugbears how to make undead, he is much more experienced than I. That could prove to be a problem."

The group fell silent as they contemplated their next move. Aksel was the first to speak once more. "Well, we've come this far. I wouldn't want to turn back now. Let's take a vote."

Lloyd immediately voted for going ahead, as did Titan. Seth said he would go if everyone else wanted to.

Brundon let out a deep sigh. "Might as well. There's obviously no stopping you, and without me to guide you, there's no telling what you might run into up there. Plus, I don't think I could tear Titan away from the battle now."

They all smiled at that. Glo felt he was starting to understand Brundon. He was smug and egotistical at times, but he would stand by you in a pinch. Now he could see why Titan stayed with him.

All eyes turned to Glo. Aksel cocked his head as he stared at him. "Well?"

Glo had mixed feelings about this. On the one hand, he didn't want to disappoint his friends. On the other hand, this wizard, Telvar, had him very afraid. He pictured his father, Amrod, giving yet another lecture about the dangers of the outside world. The vision suddenly shifted to the last time he saw his mother, Aerandir. They stood amidst the colossal roughhewn pillars that marked the perimeter of the city. The mystic runes engraved into the columns glowed with a soft light, signifying that the magic that kept the city hidden was still in place.

She had stood there, a forlorn look on her otherwise unmarred face. Her long black hair, blown by the gentle breeze, partially covered those piercing green eyes as she stared at her only child for the last time. "Remember to use what we have taught you," she had said to him.

"How so?" he responded, his own emotions threatening to get the best of him.

"Use your mind. It is your greatest asset. Think things through before running headlong into anything."

"I will." They clasped hands one final time.

The image faded, and Glo was again standing amongst his friends. They all still stared at him, waiting for his decision. He had indeed promised his mother he would be careful, but what they were about to do was exactly why he had left Cairthrellon in the first place. He had set out to befriend the other races and to use his magic out here in the world, where it was most needed. This was an opportunity to do both. Glo took a deep breath, his mind finally made up. "I'm in."

Aksel nodded his approval. "Then it's settled. We'll wait until nightfall. Maybe we can sneak into the ruins after dark. As Glo said, that wizard could be trouble. Facing undead might be the lesser of two evils."

Seth wore an impish grin. "I thought undead were more evil than bugbears."

Aksel glared at his halfling friend. "It's a figure of speech."

Seth's face took on an innocent cast. "Geez. Can't you take a joke?" When Aksel did not respond, he continued. "Anyway, I'm going to go down and cover up that pit with the bugbear's body in it. It's late in the day and with any luck, none of his clan will come looking for him before dark."

With that, Seth disappeared into the woods. Meanwhile, Brundon searched for a place to set up camp. He returned shortly, having found a glade a little ways south of the path. The party relocated there and had a short, cold dinner while they waited for night to fall.

8
STONE HILL

There's five of them…coming this way," Brundon said between gasps. He had been scouting ahead up the trail.

"Five what?" Seth asked the breathless tracker.

"Skeletons…"

"Animated skeletons…" Glo mused aloud. This little expedition was getting weirder and weirder.

Seth snickered. "I'd say that qualifies as undead."

Aksel ignored the halfling. "How far behind are they?"

"About…10 minutes. Figured, the faster…I got back down…the more time…we would have to…prepare."

Aksel nodded. "Good thinking."

Seth's voice grew concerned. "Do you think they saw you?"

"I don't…think so. They seem to be moving in…some kind of formation, almost as if it were a routine patrol."

Aksel's hand went to his chin as he mulled things over. "Then let's set up an ambush of our own."

The companions had already traveled halfway up the mountain. The tree line ended here, the upper half of the hillside mostly bare except for a few patches of vegetation. It was about two hours after sunset, the edge of the moon just rising in the east, casting its pale silvery light across the dark mountainside.

Glo half listened as the others outlined their plan. It took dark magic—Necromancy—to animate a skeleton. That dark art was not practiced by the elves of Cairthrellon, but Amrod made sure they covered the subject thoroughly. A necromancer used negative arcane energy to gather undead minions. The more powerful the practitioner, the more undead creatures they could gather to their side. Worse, any who fell in the necromancer's vicinity would become part of those undead forces. A powerful practitioner of this art could have a veritable army of undead to command. If there was a weakness to be exploited against them, it was in their minions. They were usually mindless, following their master's orders to the exclusion of all else. Also, different types of undead creatures had specific vulnerabilities. Skeletons, for instance, were very susceptible to blunt weapons like hammers and clubs that would crack and break their bones. Glo's mind snapped back to the present as he realized the others had finished their strategizing.

"…and Glo and I will hang back here," Aksel ended. "So, what does everyone think?"

"I think that just might work," Brundon agreed, a hit of approval in his voice.

"We'll be ready," Lloyd and Titan said simultaneously. The two warriors tightened their grips on their weapons, their eyes shining with childlike exuberance.

Seth sounded impatient. "Let's just get going already."

He was right; they really didn't have much time. Aksel nodded. Seth and Brundon took off immediately, disappearing into the night.

Lloyd and Titan doffed their backpacks and rummaged through them. When Lloyd stood back up, he held a war hammer in each hand. The weapons looked like two steel mallets with large square heads and long cylindrical handles. Titan withdrew a mace from her pack. It consisted of a long handle with a heavy-metal spiked ball at the other end. She hefted it in her right hand. "This should do the trick nicely."

The two warriors headed up the path about ten paces, admiring each other's weapons the entire way. At that point the pair spread out, giving each other room to work. Everyone was in position. Now it was up to their quarry to spring the trap.

The night grew still as they waited for the band of skeletons to appear. The only sounds came from the soft chirping of crickets. Stars twinkled fervently against the inky backdrop of the crystal clear sky. The moon, now above the eastern horizon, threw long pale shadows against the otherwise dark hillside. Had they not been awaiting the arrival of undead creatures, it would have been a beautiful evening.

What is taking them so long? Glo wondered. He stared up the hillside, but the trail disappeared around an outcropping of rocks. Nevertheless, the young elf continued to strain his eyes until he saw movement around the bend. A group of stick-like figures came into view, and as he continued to watch, they moved down the path toward them.

"There they are," he whispered with a nervous twitch of his eye.

"Let them come to us," Aksel said in a calm tone.

Not turning, Lloyd and Titan murmured in acknowledgement.

As the figures came closer, their features became more apparent. They were definitely skeletons, their white bones gleaming in the moonlight in stark contrast to the dark hillside. The skulls bobbed up and down on thin boney necks. The jaws opened and closed as they ambled along, as if having a soundless discussion. Their arms and legs swung in strange disjointed movements, resembling puppets held upright from some giant invisible master in the sky. Each skeleton wielded a wickedly curved sword, brandishing it about as they walked as if hacking unseen enemies to their left and right. The entire scene was eerie and unreal.

Despite all of his training and studies, the sight of actual undead creatures sent a shiver up Glo's spine. He glanced around at the others, but they were all staring up the path. Abruptly, the lead skeleton halted, the rest of the creatures stopping short behind it. It pointed its sword downhill at Lloyd and Titan, and a strange chattering commenced between the creatures, a ghostly conversation. No one moved. The chattering suddenly stopped, then as one the skeletons rushed down the hill, bones clattering and blades swinging wildly in the air.

The skeletons closed the gap.

"Wait for it," Aksel said.

They drew nearer.

"Wait for it."

When the skeletons were only a few yards away, a voice cried out in the night. "Now!"

A rope rose up across the trail in front of the charging monsters. It pulled tight across their path, the two lead creatures hitting the cord at full speed. They tripped and plunged headlong into the ground. The three remaining skeletons could not stop in time and also tripped, landing on top of the others.

That was brilliant! Somehow Seth and Brundon managed to lay out a rope across the path without anyone seeing them, and pulled it at just the right moment.

Glo glanced at Aksel. "Was that part of the plan?"

"No," Aksel said, his voice filled with astonishment.

Lloyd fell into a battle stance, adjusting the grip on his hammers, as the skeletons rushed forward. He had packed them for situations like these, when swords would be virtually useless. It was something he had learned from his father—every enemy, no matter how strong, always had some kind of weakness. For example, an enemy who could turn aside a sword might be bludgeoned effectively. To that end, he was instructed in many different types of weapons.

Lloyd stood his ground, hammers ready, as the skeletons closed in. A quick glance to his right showed Titan ready as well, mace in one hand, shield in the other. The warrior impressed him—she knew a lot about weapons and fighting techniques. He looked forward to battling beside her. He was also impressed with Aksel. The gnome's plan of drawing the creatures in and having Seth and Brundon flank them from behind was an excellent strategy.

Lloyd studied the skeletons as they rushed downhill. He had been taught to assess his opponents first, to study their movements and determine their weaknesses. He had done so against the huge orc in Bendenwoods and won him that battle. He observed that the skeletons were not skilled fighters. They held their swords too tightly, brandishing them about as if cutting down weeds. Their movements had no finesse or purpose, and as close as they stood, the skeletons could trip each other with a single misstep.

The skeletons were drawing near now. Aksel's voice rang out behind them. "Wait for it."

The skeletons drew even closer.

"Wait for it."

They were nearly on top of them. Lloyd prepared for his first blow when a cry rang out in the night. "Now!"

The lead skeletons suddenly tumbled headlong to the ground a few yards in front of him. The trailing skeletons went plummeting after them and ended up in a heap of tangled bones.

Lloyd hesitated for a split second then launched himself uphill toward the pile of fallen enemies. As he charged forward, he caught a glint of bright silver out the corner of his eye. Lloyd smiled grimly, knowing that Titan was at his side.

As the two warriors closed in, the fallen skeletons clambered around, trying to disentangle themselves. The creatures on top of the pile were just beginning to rise when Lloyd and Titan plowed into them.

Lloyd planted his feet and swung his twin hammers in two heavy blows, each smashing into a separate skeleton. The creature on his left went down in a heap of broken bones and lay there twitching on the ground. The skeleton on his right lost its sword arm, its blade flying along with it.

Lloyd drew back his arm and sent another devastating blow into the creature. The large hammer smashed through its torso, splitting the boney body in half. Only the bottom of the skeleton was still intact.

Lloyd was elated at first, but to his surprise, instead of falling over, the half skeleton began to walk around. It wandered aimlessly about the trail, still searching for an enemy to fight. The bizarre sight made the young man pause, but then he tore his eyes away, surveying the battlefield around him.

Seth and Brundon were up the trail watching the battle. Beside him, Titan bashed a headless skeleton to pieces with her mace and metallic shield. Abruptly, he heard a shout from downhill.

"Lloyd! Titan! Behind you!"

Lloyd pivoted sharply and found himself face to skull with another boney creature. The lead skeletons had regained their footing and were flanking them. Lloyd reacted just in time to block a scimitar swung at his head. He caught the creature with a glancing blow that sent it backpedaling away from him, completely off-balance.

At that same moment, he heard a voice beside him. "Don't worry! I've got this one!" The shout was followed by the clang of metal and the clattering of bones. Lloyd chanced a quick look over his shoulder and watched Titan block an attack by the other skeleton, then slam it in turn with her mace. *By the gods, she's good.*

Lloyd would have loved to observe further, but he had his own battle to fight. His opponent had recovered and was advancing on him again. He blocked its sword once more, and then smashed it with his other hammer. It did not take long after that. He rained down blows on the monster until only a pile of shattered bones remained.

His opponent demolished, Lloyd scanned the battleground. Titan stood a few feet away, over a fallen skeleton, pummeling it into pieces with her mace. A few feet up the path, he spied Seth sitting on top of a headless skeleton. The creature was completely tied up, its feet twitching, but otherwise immobile. A chuckle escaped Lloyd's lips. Seth never ceased to amaze him.

The halfling pointed up the trail. "I think Brundon could use a hand."

Lloyd followed Seth's finger and saw a strange sight. The bottom half of a skeleton stood in the middle of the path. He watched curiously as Brundon rushed up behind it and kicked it with his boot. The creature whirled around and began chasing him, but Brundon dodged and ended up behind it. The tracker kicked it and dodged again. It was like watching a strange dance.

A familiar voice came from behind him. "He sure is stubborn." Lloyd turned in time to see Titan walk up beside him, a thin smile across her lips. "I guess we should go help him."

Lloyd fell in beside her. They walked up the trail together as the crazy fight continued. They stopped a few feet away, watching as Brundon dodged the skeleton again.

Titan chuckled softly. "Would you like a hand?"

Brundon glanced their way and shook his head. "No, I got this."

Titan glanced at Lloyd and shrugged. "Like I said, stubborn."

Lloyd had a sudden idea. He held out his hammer and called over to the tracker. "Hey, Brundon, care to try it out?"

Brundon had just swung behind the skeleton again. He glanced over at Lloyd and his eyes fell on the proffered weapon. A broad smile spread across his face.

"Don't mind if I do."

"Sure, accept his help and not mine," Titan said with mock disappointment.

Brundon backed away from the sightless skeleton. "Only his weapon, love, only his weapon. Of course, if you want to hand me your mace…"

"No, no. I'd like to see you wield that hammer."

"Suit yourself." Brundon reached the two of them and accepted the hammer from Lloyd, attempting to heft it with one hand. Without warning, the head of the hammer dipped and began to fall. Brundon swiftly grasped it with his other hand, catching it just before it hit the ground.

A short laugh escaped Titan's lips. "Having some trouble there?"

"I'm…just…fine…" Brundon grunted. Slowly but surely, he lifted the hammer back up. He grasped it firmly with both hands, and after a few test swings was able to effectively wield the weapon. "See, piece of cake."

Titan chuckled under her breath. "Yeah, sure it is."

Brundon ignored her, turning and rushing the roving skeleton. In a couple of minutes he reduced it to a pile of cracked bones. Brundon stood over the pile with a grim look of satisfaction on his face. "Well?" he said, glaring defiantly at Titan.

"Oh yes, all hail *Sir Brundon*, the skeleton slayer."

Sharp snorts of laughter broke out from down the trail. Lloyd turned around in time to see Seth roll off the skeleton he had been sitting on and fall onto the ground. He lay there laughing until he couldn't breathe.

Titan taunted him further. "Well, *Sir Brundon*, there's another skeleton waiting to meet its end via your mighty mallet."

Brundon fixed his partner with an acid stare. It quickly faded though, replaced with a half-twisted smile. "Why not." He shrugged, then strode down the trail to finish off the last skeleton. While Brundon joyfully hammered away, Lloyd and Titan rejoined the others.

"Nice work, everyone." Glo's eyes drifted in the direction of the hammering tracker, the corners of his mouth upturning slightly.

Aksel looked from Lloyd to Titan to Seth. "Did anyone get hurt?" No one had. "Good. Now then, let's pack up and get moving. We still need to make it to the top of the hill, and there's no telling what we'll find when we get to the keep."

Lloyd and Titan went to gather their things. As they put away their spare weapons, Brundon joined them. He stood there, both hands out, proffering the heavy hammer to Lloyd.

Titan lips twisted slightly. "Get out all your pent-up aggressions?"

Brundon appeared unphased by the jab. "Absolutely, love." He looked at Lloyd and winked. "Free therapy works every time."

Lloyd took back the hammer, a slight smile crossing his lips as he watched the tracker head back up the trail. He was beginning to understand Brundon. He reminded him a lot of his older brother, Pallas. Smug and self-assured, his brother had always looked down on Lloyd, much as Brundon did with Aksel and Seth at first. His brother was also proud and independent, as was Brundon. But they were also alike in one other way—they appreciated talent.

Brundon obviously recognized that in Titan. A lot of men wouldn't work with a woman warrior; they'd be too intimidated by someone like her. Yet despite their verbal jabbing, he sensed a mutual respect between the two. Lloyd had little doubt that when things got tough, they would have each other's backs.

Titan grunted softly as she lifted her heavy pack onto her back. "That was a nice little warm up, wasn't it?"

Lloyd stretched his arms to work out some left over kinks. "Definitely. Nothing like a little sparring to get your blood flowing." Secretly, he thought the entire encounter bizarre, but he was not going to admit that aloud.

They rejoined the group near the pile of boney remains. Once everyone was gathered, the small company resumed its ascent up the trail to the top of Stone Hill.

Brundon went ahead, the rest of the company following slowly behind. After the run-in with the skeletons, stealth seemed warranted. The path gradually wound its way up the moonlit hillside. Dark shadows fell across the trail from rocky outcroppings and the occasional tree, but the night remained quiet and the route was otherwise clear. The group of adventurers made it to the summit of Stone Hill with no further incidents. Brundon met them down the path just below the hilltop. He motioned for the others to follow, leading them off the trail and across the slope a bit to the north. When they finally reached the summit, the entire group was well hidden by some large boulders.

Glo peered out from behind their rocky hiding place and saw the shadowy outline of the keep off in the distance. The summit was mostly flat and devoid of vegetation, giving him a clear view of the dark structure. The elven race could see fairly well in low light, and with the moon behind him, Glo could see much of the castle ruins.

He judged the structure to be roughly a quarter of a mile away. There was a long, high wall facing them with a tower rising well above it at the north end. A faint greenish glow radiated out from the parapet at the very top. Glo thought it strange, but there was nothing more to be seen at this distance. The main keep sat behind the castle wall, dark except for a single lighted window on the top floor.

Back behind the rocks, the party gathered in a circle. Brundon reported his findings from his brief venture onto the summit.

"I saw another roving band of skeletons go by. They were well out from the castle wall, but this group was headed south. I followed them a short way and then noticed them slowly turn west. My best guess is that they are patrolling the ruins in a circular pattern. As for the keep itself, it looked mostly deserted, but there was a light on the very top floor."

Aksel stroked his beardless chin. "Hmmm, so we have patrolling skeletons and someone, or something, awake in the keep."

Brundon nodded. "Oh, one more thing. On my way back, I got a closer look at those walls. They are definitely crumbled and cracked in spots."

Aksel smiled at the tracker for the first time since they'd met him. "Nice work. If someone is awake in that keep, and there are patrols, an alternative entrance might be our best bet."

Glo followed up on Aksel's train of thought. "If there is a crack in the walls large enough for us all to fit through, then that could indeed be our entrance into the keep."

Seth gave a casual shrug. "I could check it out."

Aksel mulled it over. "That would probably be best, but even if you do find a way in, we still need to know how often that patrol goes by."

"I'll go back out with him and time them," Brundon offered.

Aksel nodded. "Excellent. The rest of us will wait here and get ready to move as quickly and as quietly as possible."

Brundon and Seth both disappeared into the night. The rest of the group prepared for a silent dash across the hilltop. Lloyd and Titan made sure that all their straps and weapons were tightly tied down in order to reduce noise. Glo and Aksel rummaged through their packs, making sure nothing was loose. By the time they were done, half an hour had gone by. Shortly thereafter, Seth and Brundon reappeared. The two looked a bit somber.

"So?" Aksel asked the duo.

Seth spoke up first. "Well, there is a crack at the base of the tower large enough to crawl through. I checked it out and the other side was deserted."

"There's just one small hitch. There are two parties of skeletons circling the keep." Brundon sounded clearly embarrassed at his initial oversight.

"Two?" Glo said louder than he intended. He lowered his voice. "How far apart?"

"Ten minutes. Each group makes a full circle in about twenty minutes." Brundon shook his head, still annoyed with himself. "If only I hadn't followed the first group, I wouldn't have missed the second one."

Titan reached out and placed a firm hand on her partner's shoulder. "Don't be so hard on yourself. Anyone could have made that mistake."

Aksel was sympathetic as well. "I agree. There's no use blaming anyone now." He turned toward Glo. "How long do you think it would take us to reach the castle wall?"

Glo estimated the distance versus the speed he thought they could travel. "Assuming we're trying to be quiet, I'd say about six minutes."

"Brundon and I can be there in three," Seth chimed in.

Aksel stroked his chin as he silently thought things over. "We could go in pairs, but I don't like the idea of getting separated." He paused another moment or two, then laid out his plan. "Okay, here's what we do. Seth and Brundon go back out and keep a lookout for the next skeleton patrol. Take Raven with you. As soon as they've gone by, send her to us. The moment she gets back, we'll take off for the castle wall. We go as fast as we can while still being quiet. If Glo is right, we should be there in just about six minutes. That'll give us four minutes to sneak through the crack and into the tower before the next patrol comes through."

"Sounds like our best bet," Glo agreed.

Lloyd was raring to go. "Then let's do it."

Titan grinned. "Lead on and I will follow."

Brundon and Seth headed back out as planned and took Raven with them. A few minutes later, the bird came winging back and landed on Glo's arm.

"*Nantë desiel,*" she said in her small voice. *They are ready.*

The party took off toward the keep at a brisk pace. Lloyd held his hammers to minimize the noise they would make in his pack. Titan held her mace and did her best to not clank, which was no small task in full plate armor. Nevertheless, the warrior managed to remain relatively quiet during the rush toward the keep.

About halfway to the ruins, they met up with Seth. The halfling took the lead. The moon, now well up in the sky, cast its silvery light over the hilltop almost too well for Glo's liking. As the keep loomed closer, he mentally kept track of the passing minutes. So far they were making good time. Before long they made it to the base of the ruins.

Glo glanced upward at the dark outline of the large structure. He estimated the keep walls to be about twenty feet high. The tower was much taller, maybe four times as high as the walls. Seth ushered them to a spot at the base of the tower. At ground level was the vague outline of a large low crack. Glo gauged the opening to be about three feet wide and two feet tall—just enough for them to crawl through.

Aksel fired off directions, the words tumbling from his mouth. "Seth, go through first and check it out. Brundon stay here and keep a lookout." He turned toward Glo. "How much time do we have?"

Glo did a quick mental calculation. "About three minutes."

"Then let's move."

Seth was already in the crack. As soon as he disappeared, Lloyd got down on the ground and began crawling through. The young man's long form was soon completely gone.

"Glo, go next," Aksel whispered impatiently.

Glo got down flat on the ground. The hole in the wall looked very dark from here. The sides and top were jagged and rough, attesting to the fact that this crack was natural. Glo could barely make out a dim light at the other end of the cramped tunnel. He began moving forward on his elbows and knees. It seemed like a tight squeeze, but his thin frame never touched the walls or the ceiling of the small passage.

When he finally reached the other side, he got a quick glimpse of his surroundings. The inside of the tower was mostly dark, except for a sliver of light coming through a crack in a doorway to the left. He could barely see the outlines of his companions gathered around in the dim light. Glo swiftly stood up and moved away from the crack. He turned and watched a small shadow shoot through the opening and roll to one side. He heard Aksel's voice.

"Glo, how much time?"

"Just about a minute."

The sudden sound of metal scraping on stone came from the crack. Glo stooped down and thought he saw a glint of silver in the dark hole. He could barely hear Brundon's voice from the other side. "What's with all the bloody noise?"

They heard Titan's strained reply. "You try crawling through a hole this tight in armor."

"Lloyd, quick, help Titan!" Aksel whispered, his voice frantic.

A large form moved in front of the hole, cutting off Glo's view. "It's alright, I've got it." Titan's voice filled with fierce determination.

The large form backed away from the hole. There was another loud scraping sound and a silvery shadow popped out of the hole onto the floor in front of them.

"Glo?" Aksel's voice called out anxiously.

Glo had been counting down in the back of his mind. "No time left," he said with alarm. The skeletal patrol would have rounded the corner of the keep by now.

"Shhh." The soft sound wafted out of the hole in the wall. It had to be Brundon. He must have seen the patrol and dove into the crack. They waited in tense silence for the tracker to speak again. A few minutes passed until they heard his voice again. "It's okay. The patrol just went by."

They all breathed a collective sigh of relief as the shadowy form of the tracker climbed out of the crack and joined them inside the dark tower. "Not sure how they didn't hear us with all that racket."

Titan crossed her arms. "Next time, you wear the armor."

Brundon's voice took on a mock innocent tone. "You know I chafe, love."

"Alright you two, save it for after the wedding," Seth said to the pair. "Right now we have a job to do."

Glo nearly burst out laughing. Leave it to Seth to cut to the chase. He suspected the halfling wasn't that far from the truth. There was definitely more between these two than maybe even they realized.

There was a moment of silence, then Titan whispered, "Not in a million years."

Brundon's response was equally soft. "Make that two million, love. Make that two million."

9
INSIDE THE RUINS

I think it's time to shed a little light on the subject

Now that they were safe from the patrol, Glo took another look at their surroundings. It was too dark to see much of anything, even for sensitive elven eyes. The only thing visible was the large door hanging partially open at the south end of the tower. Through it he caught a glimpse of the courtyard beyond.

"Brundon, go check the courtyard. Make sure there is no sign of movement out there," said Aksel, now sounding far calmer.

"Sure thing."

One of the forms around them moved off toward the doorway. The door cracked open slightly wider, outlining a dark silhouette. The group waited in silence until the shadowy figure rejoined them.

"It all looks quiet. There's nothing moving in the courtyard, or the keep, from what I could tell. But there are torches in places along the walls, and it will be hard to sneak across if someone is looking."

Aksel sounded apprehensive. "Okay, that could be a problem. We need to find another way into the keep."

There was no way they were going to do that in the darkness, but Glo had a remedy for that. "Brundon, can you go back and close that door?"

"Sure…" The form moved off toward the doorway once more.

"What do you have in mind?" Aksel asked.

"I think it's time to shed a little *light* on the subject."

The south door slowly closed, making a slight creaking sound as it swung shut. Without the moonlight, the room turned pitch black. As the rest of the party stood still in the inky darkness, Glo reached into one of the bags at his waist and rummaged through it.

When he pulled out his hand, he held a mossy material with a slight phosphorescent glow to it. He reached out with it, touched the end of his staff, and spoke one soft word, "*Lux.*" The end of his staff began to glow like a torch, shedding bright light in a wide radius around the little crew. Beyond that, the light dimmed a bit, but it was enough to illuminate the entire room around them. Everyone shaded their eyes, adjusting to the change in brightness. When they could see again, they began looking around.

They stood in a wide circular room. Besides the large door to the south, there was a second door on the west side of the room. It hung open, and a stairwell appeared beyond it, leading both upwards and downwards. There were no other openings of any kind in the cold stone walls of the tower. The rest of the room was barren, except for some rotted wood against the north side.

Seth's expression was one of distaste. "Nice homey place."

Glo's mind was elsewhere. He had been hoping for another doorway, one that led toward the keep. Maybe it was on one of the other floors?

Aksel listed out their options. "Well, we have three ways to go: into the courtyard, up to the top of the tower, or down below the tower."

Seth appeared thoughtful. "There might be a way into the keep down below."

Aksel seemed uncertain. "Maybe, or it might just be a dead end."

"Top of the tower," Glo repeated. "When we were approaching the ruins, I thought I saw a faint greenish light at the top."

"I saw it as well," Brundon said.

Glo nodded to the tracker and continued his train of thought. "If it ends up that we have to cross the courtyard, we should probably check the top of the tower first. If there is someone or something up there, and we are seen, then they may alert whoever is in the keep."

Aksel shared his concern. "That may be a good idea." He turned to Brundon. "Can you keep an eye on the courtyard?"

Brundon nodded. He strode over to the door and opened it a crack.

Aksel turned toward Seth. "How about going upstairs and scouting out the top of the tower?"

Seth shrugged. "I will, but I still think we should check the basement first." When Aksel did not reply, Seth put away the knife he had been absently fingering and headed over to the other doorway. He stopped and looked beyond it, first to the left then to the right. He glanced back over his shoulder, winked, and then disappeared through the doorway.

Aksel asked Titan and Lloyd to keep an eye out for Seth's return, then turned to Glo. "Once Seth is done with the top of the tower, he can check out the basement."

Glo raised an eyebrow. "I don't think he was very happy with your decision."

Aksel sighed. "Maybe I should have sent him to the basement first—but when you mentioned that green glow, it made me nervous."

"You and me both," Glo agreed. With any luck, Seth wouldn't find anything too out of the ordinary atop the tower. He was still hoping for another passage into the keep, but if the top of the tower was vacant, at least they would have half a chance of crossing the courtyard without alerting that wizard.

Aksel started pacing, talking as he moved to and fro. "Well, if we are going to get anywhere mapping out this place, then we are going to have to do something about the rest of these undead."

"Not to mention the bugbears."

Aksel continued to pace, deep in thought. When he finally spoke, he did not sound very certain. "If we can continue to take them on in small groups, then maybe we can get rid of most of them before this wizard, Telvar, finds out we are here."

"And when he does?"

"Hopefully that won't happen for a while."

Glo remained skeptical. This Telvar could pose a real threat to them. An experienced dark mage could defeat all of them combined. They could all end up dead, or worse—part of this necromancer's undead army. Glo sighed. *There's no help for it.* They were in the ruins now and turning back would defeat everything they had strived for.

"I hope it is as you say, my friend."

Aksel's expression was solemn. "So do I. So do I."

Seth reappeared, descending from the upper stairwell. He had been so quiet and the stairwell so dark that both Lloyd and Titan missed him until he was almost right in front of them. As the halfling pushed past them into the circular room, Lloyd announced, "Seth's back."

Everyone gathered around to hear what he had found atop the tower, except for Brundon, who remained guard at the courtyard door.

Aksel turned to face his halfling friend. "What took you so long?"

Seth gave him his best innocent look. "Oh, nothing. I just took a little detour on the way up. It turns out there's a second floor to this tower and someone was nice enough to leave this lying around up there."

As he spoke, he unslung his backpack, opened the top and dumped out the contents onto the floor of the tower room. A distinct clinking sound could be heard as a pile of small circular discs fell to the ground, lying in a haphazard pile. The discs glowed with a golden color in the light of Glo's staff.

Brundon glanced over from the doorway. "Gold…"

Seth nodded. "About two hundred fifty coins, by my count."

Aksel glanced up from the pile of coins and stared at Seth with suspicion. "Just lying around, huh?"

"Well, I might have moved around a floor tile or two."

Aksel sighed.

"Oh, I almost forgot." Seth reached into his pocket and pulled out a pouch, holding it out to his gnomish friend. "This is for you."

Aksel checked out the bag, then reached out and took it. He slowly loosened the drawstrings, turned it over, and emptied the contents into his hand. Out dropped a silver-colored ring decorated with a sparkling blue gemstone. Aksel appeared amused by the gift, the corners of his mouth turned up slightly.

"Seth, you are incorrigible."

"I try my best."

Aksel turned to Glo and held the ring out to him. "Can you tell what this is?"

"I can try." Glo took the ring from his outstretched hand. He examined it for markings or inscriptions, only to find nothing, but Glo had other resources available to him. There was a specific spell for identifying the properties of an unknown object. It was one of the first spells Amrod taught him because it required deep concentration.

First, one had to precisely prepare a concoction which augmented the spell. It was a mixture of simple table wine, but needed to be stirred with an owl's feather. Glo thought that was some sort of joke at first, but as it turned out, it was not. The amount of wine had to be exactly five ounces, not a drop more or less. The owl's feather had to be fresh for potency. A preserved feather would also work, but the potion would lose its potency faster. The liquid needed to be stirred slowly, in a clockwise direction exactly fifty times. Once done, the concoction could be stored in a vial and used for up to fifty days. Anything beyond that, and it would be useless.

Glo opened another pouch on his belt and rummaged through it. He pulled out a small vial—it was the last batch he had made before leaving home. It dawned on him that was almost forty days ago. He removed the stopper and drank the contents. He then held the ring out once more and spoke a single word, *"Eandem."*

A faint glow appeared around the object but quickly faded. Glo closed his eyes and concentrated on the ring. Faint images played through his mind until one came sharply into focus. An owl flew by, a single feather dropping from its tail as it continued to wing away. The feather gently floated to the ground and lay at his feet.

Glo's eyes snapped open, a wry smile coming to his lips. He grasped the ring with his right hand and held it out to his gnomish friend. "It is a ring of a feather falling."

Aksel appeared delighted with the find. He took the ring and put it on the biggest finger of his right hand. It looked a little loose, but it stayed on nonetheless as he tugged at it.

Seth's voice was thick with envy. "Don't say I never gave you anything."

A thin smile crossed Glo's lips. A ring of feather falling would allow Aksel to jump from any height and float harmlessly down to the ground, like a feather. Had Seth known beforehand what the ring was, he probably would not have given it up so easily.

"So what are we doing with all the gold?" Brundon whispered from the doorway.

Seth knelt down and grabbed his backpack. "I'll just hold onto these until we have time to divvy them up." As he scooped up the gold coins, he noticed everyone staring down at him. "What? After all, you did name me treasurer!"

Aksel, Glo and Lloyd exchanged glances. A wry smile graced Aksel's lips. "We did do that, didn't we?"

"Yes, we did." Glo smiled in turn.

"The gods help us," Lloyd added with mock concern.

Seth stopped his gathering and glanced up at the three of them. "Very funny. Just for that, I'm splitting this between me, Brundon and Titan."

Brundon and Titan exchanged glances. "Sounds good to us," they said in unison.

There were mild chuckles all around.

Aksel cleared his throat. "Well then, back to business." He glanced down at Seth. "So did you scout out the top floor?"

Seth got up off his knees. "Yep," he said, re-shouldering his pack. "And?"

"There are five skeletons up there—four of them scattered around the parapets and armed with bows. We're lucky they didn't see us cross the mountaintop earlier."

Glo's eyes narrowed. "What about the fifth one?"

Seth's expression turned serious. "Ah, yes. That one. That could be a bit of a problem."

Glo's brow furrowed. "How so?"

"The fifth one carries a staff and is standing over a large cauldron in the center of the tower. Oh, and did I mention that it radiates a green glow a few yards in all directions?"

Glo raised an eyebrow. That sounded like a skeletal mage. He glanced at Aksel—he also had an eyebrow raised.

Lloyd wore a curious expression. "So, what kind of skeleton is that?"

Glo couldn't blame him for not knowing—this was not your everyday monster. In fact, Titan and Brundon appeared equally mystified. Glo only knew about it from a volume in his father's library aptly titled *The Book of Undead Monsters*. "Basically, it's an undead wizard. The green glow around it is known as a *death aura*. It is a sphere of negative energy that will harm any living creature that steps inside it. Worse than that, it heals all undead enveloped within it."

Brundon did not sound thrilled with the prospect of facing this monster. "So let me get this straight. Just getting close to this thing can hurt you?"

"Yes."

"Not to mention that it constantly heals itself," Seth reminded them.

Aksel turned to Glo, his voice grave. "It would probably be best if you handled this thing."

Glo felt a sinking feeling in the pit of his stomach. He knew Aksel was right; letting anyone else get close to that creature was probably too dangerous. Still, it didn't make him any less nervous.

Aksel must have read his thoughts. "What? After all, magic is your forte."

"Wonderful. My first wizard's duel, and it's with an undead skeleton."

"Could be worse." Seth pointed out. "At least it's not with this Telvar guy."

Glo fixed Seth with an acid stare. He immediately regretted it. "Sorry, Seth, you were right."

Seth put a hand to his ear. "Come again?"

Glo sighed. "I said you were right. Don't push your luck."

Seth responded with a half twisted smile.

The next question now was, what would he do? While he was lost in thought, the others continued planning their strategy. Aksel led the discussion.

"Okay, Brundon, wait down here and keep watch on the courtyard. The rest of us will quietly go upstairs to the top of the tower…"

Titan interrupted him. "Um, Aksel, quiet and full plate armor don't mix very well."

Aksel paused and glanced at the warrior, quickly realizing his error. "Right. Let me amend that. Brundon, you and Titan watch the door while the rest of us go upstairs."

He was met with replies of "not a problem," and "will do."

Aksel continued on. "Our best bet is stealth until we can get close enough to launch an attack. Once in position, we should distract this skeletal mage. That way Glo can get in the first strike."

Glo nodded his approval. He would take any advantage he could get against his undead opponent. The discussion continued until they hashed out a plan they thought would work. The foursome then bade Brundon and Titan farewell and began their climb up the tower stairs.

The stairwell wound up the side of the tower within the narrow space between the inner and outer walls. It was mostly dark, but light did stream in from the occasional window in the outer wall. Glo extinguished his staff to avoid alerting anyone to their presence in the tower, so the group climbed the stairs in relative darkness. Seth led the way, followed by Lloyd, Glo, and finally Aksel. They went slowly, trying to remain as silent as possible. Still, it only took them a few minutes to reach the top of the tower.

As they approached the top of the stairwell, moonlight streamed in through the open doorway, illuminating the small landing there. The foursome climbed onto the landing and spread out on either side of the open door. The night was silent, except for a slight rattling noise through the open doorway. Glo peeked around the corner of the door and saw the top of the tower bathed in moonlight. It was just as Seth had described it.

Four skeletons stood around the parapets at regular intervals, their backs to the door. In the center stood a tall skeleton covered in tattered robes, carrying a gnarled wooden staff. It stood next to a large cauldron, a sickly pale green globe of light surrounding it. It was an uncanny sight, the five skeletons standing in the darkness, the silvery light of the moon reflecting off their white bones. Luckily for the companions, their timing could not have been better. The skeletal mage stood in front of the cauldron, its back toward the door.

Seth motioned to Lloyd, and the two of them stole out onto the top of the tower. The halfling crept across the tower top toward the nearest archer on the left. At the same time, Lloyd tiptoed his way up behind the skeleton on the right. After what seemed like an eternity, Lloyd stood within striking distance of his archer. He stopped, hammers poised in either hand, and glanced back over his shoulder toward the doorway.

Glo and Aksel waited at the door until Seth and Lloyd were in position. At that point, Aksel nodded. Three things happened at once: Lloyd charged, Seth leapt into the air, and Glo began his spell.

Lloyd crashed into his opponent, hammers swinging with bone crunching effect. With two powerful blows, he smashed the creature apart.

Seth used his forward momentum to kick the archer directly in front of him with both legs. The force of the blow knocked the skeleton over the parapet. It went clattering over the side and disappeared from view.

At the first sounds of commotion, the three other skeletons whirled around. The skeletal caster pivoted toward Lloyd. It raised its staff, boney arms appearing as the sleeves of its cloak fell away. Before it could do anything more, Glo let loose his spell. A single word sent a purple missile flying from his fingertips, careening its way toward the skeletal mage. With a loud *thud* it impacted the skeleton's side.

The caster was caught by surprise. It reeled from the shock, nearly falling backwards into the cauldron behind it. As it tried to right itself, Glo sent a second missile hurtling towards it. The creature, still off-balance, managed to raise its staff and send a stream of green liquid spewing back at the elf wizard. It collided with the projectile in midair, causing it to disappear in a puff of smoke.

Glo and Aksel saw the greenish spray at the same moment and threw themselves back behind either side of the doorway. A moment later, it hit the tower walls, causing the stone to hiss and smoke. As the liquid clung to the stone it started to melt. *That was a stream of acid!*

His heart pounding in his chest, Glo stood flattened against the wall of the stairwell. If that had hit either of them, they would be burnt and writhing on the ground in pain.

Aksel's face flushed, his voice high-pitched with excitement. "That was too close!"

"Agreed."

This skeletal mage was far too dangerous to enter into a head-to-head battle with him. Either he or his friends were likely to get hurt if he didn't end this quickly. He needed a spell that would do the job in one shot. The elven wizard could only think of one.

The moment the acid stream stopped, Glo jumped out from behind the wall. Just as he thought, the skeletal caster was preparing another spell. This time it was aimed at Lloyd.

Glo did not hesitate. He lifted his hand, pointing a finger at the tall skeleton, and spoke the words, *"Ardens Manus."* In response, a cone of searing flame shot forth from the young wizard's hand and flew toward the skeletal mage.

The stream of fire engulfed the creature, setting its tattered robes aflame. Unfortunately, the cone of fire also caught the side of the large cauldron beside the creature. There was a sudden spark and then a loud *boom!* An explosion rocked the top of the tower. A ball of flame erupted from the cauldron and expanded outward a few yards in all directions.

The skeletal mage was instantly turned to dust by the ball of fire, but the force of the explosion extended far beyond that. It fanned out from the center of the tower, blowing the other two skeletons right off the top of the circular structure.

Seth's and Lloyd's quick reflexes were all that saved them. Both man and halfling dove for the ground just in time. They were buffeted against the parapets, but otherwise were not blown off.

Glo was not so lucky. The force of the explosion hit him full in the face. Had he been any closer to the blast, he would have been badly injured. As it was, he was thrown back through the doorway and into the stairwell. Glo lay on the landing, the world spinning around him.

After a short while, the whirling stopped. He slowly raised himself up on his elbows and looked around. A small crater stood in the center of the stone floor where the cauldron had been. It was surrounded by a huge burn circle, smoke still rising from that area. All five of the skeletons were gone.

Lloyd and Seth slowly rose to their feet. Glo sat up further, but his eyes blurred. His head pounded and his body felt sore. He blinked a few times and his vision finally cleared. He checked his arms and legs but nothing felt broken.

At that moment, a voice sounded from underneath him. "Do you mind?" He looked down and saw that he was sitting on top of his gnomish friend.

Glo quickly got up. "Sorry, Aksel." Unfortunately, the swift movement brought another way of dizziness with it. Glo felt a steadying hand grab him.

Lloyd stood next to him wearing a big grin. "Those were some fireworks!"

Seth sounded less enthused. "Yeah, way to go, Glo. It's a wonder you didn't wake the whole keep."

Glo leaned on Lloyd for support, his face flushing with embarrassment. "Guess there must have been oil in that cauldron,"

"You think?"

Aksel interrupted them, his tone even and calm. "Easy, Seth. There's no help for it now."

Seth continued to glare at Glo but said nothing more.

Aksel turned to Lloyd. "How's that shoulder?"

Glo noticed a small hole in the armor of the shoulder that he was leaning on. Lloyd must have been shot during the scuffle.

"It's fine. Just a scratch. The arrow barely made it through my armor. I already pulled it out, and it's not even bleeding."

"I'll check it later just to be on the safe side." Aksel peered around at the others with concern. "Is everyone else alright?"

Glo pushed away from Lloyd. His head was clear now, and he did not want to lean on the young man's shoulder any longer, especially if it was wounded. "I'm fine. Just a little sore is all."

"Okay then. Right now we have bigger problems. Everyone in the keep must have heard that explosion, and we're sure to have company soon. We need to get back downstairs as fast as possible."

Lloyd nodded. "Right." Without another word, he bounded back into the stairwell.

Seth shook his head. "Warriors." He took off after the young man.

Aksel shrugged. "Guess we're running."

He and Glo took off after the others. As they descended the stairs, Glo relit his staff. He sorely wished that his little stunt had not alerted the entire keep, but there was no help for that now. This little *mapping* expedition had suddenly gone way wrong. He prayed that they all would make it out alive

10
THROUGH A MIRROR DARKLY

When they reached the first floor, Brundon and Titan were braced against the door to the courtyard. It rattled fiercely, as if it was about to come off its hinges. Eerie moaning came from the other side. Lloyd rushed across the room, dropped his hammers, and pressed up against the door next to them. His added weight stopped the rattling.

"What's out there?" Aksel cried.

"Zombies. A lot of zombies," Brundon said between gritted teeth.

Zombies. Just great, Glo thought. Skeletons were bad enough; Zombies were worse. They were reanimated corpses, totally mindless and impervious to pain. You could hack at them all day, and they would just keep coming. Zombies also had a terrible hunger for living flesh; any living thing they caught, they would devour. As if that was not bad enough, some zombies carried a disease—those infected by it became zombies themselves after they died. All around, they were grisly enemies. The only way to truly stop a zombie was to either decapitate it, chop it into little pieces, or burn it to ashes.

Titan turned to look at them as she braced the door. "What happened up there? We heard an explosion, and the whole tower rocked."

Seth responded first. "Glo decided it would be fun to blow up a vat of oil."

Titan's eyes narrowed as she surveyed Seth and Glo. "You can't be serious."

"More or less." Glo bowed his head in chagrin.

Aksel fixed his eyes on the halfling. "That's enough, Seth. We need to concentrate on the problem at hand."

The halfling's lips twisted to one side, but otherwise he remained silent. Aksel's eyes remained fixed on him. "Now, do you think you and Brundon can pull off that rope trick once more?"

"Sure. Piece of cake." Seth swiftly removed his pack and pulled out a length of rope. He ran over next to Brundon. "Here, take this."

Brundon hesitated, casting a glance at Titan.

She nodded her approval. "Go ahead. We've got this."

Brundon reluctantly let go and grasped the rope. The door rattled slightly, but together, Lloyd and Titan managed to hold it in place.

"Just make it fast," Titan said through gritted teeth.

Seth gave Brundon quick instructions. "Lay it on the ground so the door passes over it."

Brundon knelt with the rope as Seth shot across the doorway underneath the two straining warriors. The halfling quickly scurried another door length along the wall. He turned, knelt and then called out to Aksel.

"Ready."

"Okay, when I say three, let the door go and step back," Aksel said to the warriors. They grunted in acknowledgment.

Aksel and Glo stepped back a few paces as Aksel counted down. "One…two…three!"

The two warriors let go at the same time, leaping back from the doorway. The door rattled violently, then flung open, nearly coming off its hinges. As it banged into the inside wall of the tower, a group of sickly-looking humanoid creatures came shuffling through the entrance. They spied the two warriors and headed straight for them.

"Now!" Seth cried. He and Brundon pulled on the rope. It came up taut, the first row of zombies tripping on it and falling face forward to the ground. The senseless creatures immediately behind them rushed onward and fell over their downed comrades.

The tenacity of these monsters was working in their favor. They had been so intent on reaching their prey that the impromptu trap worked. A group of zombies were now tangled in a pile on the ground.

Before any could get up, Lloyd dashed in, his blades aflame just like they had been back in the Bendenwoods. He sliced away with deft precision, his swords scorching the creatures with each blow. Still, he appeared to be favoring his right arm, using his left far less, and then Glo remembered. *That's right, that's the shoulder he took an arrow in earlier.*

Even so, Lloyd still managed to dismember a couple of the creatures before they could get up. At the same time, Titan tore into the zombies. With a great overhand swing of her longsword, she cleaved a monster right down the middle.

Yet even though a few had been destroyed, there were still more of them on the ground. As they began to rise, a couple more zombies shambled in from the outside courtyard. Heedless of their brethren, these new monsters climbed over the others, pushing them back down again.

Lloyd and Titan met this new charge with swords swinging. They sliced through the air in savage arcs that cut deeply into the mindless monsters. The zombies, unperturbed by their wounds, continued to push forward, and the two warriors found themselves hard pressed to halt the advancing tide. On top of that, the zombies on the ground were now getting up.

That's when Seth and Brundon entered the fray. Seth flew through the air, slamming into the nearest zombie with both feet. It was knocked off-balance and sent tumbling into the other creatures. Brundon had his sword out and hacked away at another of the monsters from behind.

A sudden rapid movement caught Glo's eye. It was Lloyd. The warrior had taken a step back, his arms moving in swift, intricate motions. He stopped suddenly, then winked out of existence, only to reappear a moment later behind the zombies!

With two incredible slices, Lloyd lopped off first one head and then another. The bodies fell, twitched for a few moments, then lay still on the ground.

Seth knocked over another zombie with a mid-air kick while Titan cleaved another. Brundon managed to cut off the head of a third. It was all over in a few minutes. The zombies lay on the ground in a putrid pile of rotting flesh. The smell made Glo want to retch.

Seth held his nose. "Ugh, these things stink."

"Did anyone get scratched or bitten?" Aksel said to the entire group. Miraculously no one had.

The warriors backed away from the pile to catch their breath. Titan clasped Lloyd on the shoulder. "That was some trick…disappearing and ending up behind them like that."

Lloyd grinned. "It's a spiritblade…technique."

Titan grinned back. "Think you can teach me?"

Lloyd never got to answer. At that moment, Glo felt a sudden wave of panic wash over him. This time he knew immediately what it was. He swiftly explained to the others. "We've got trouble. I sent Raven aloft to watch the ruins, and something just spooked her."

As if on cue, they heard shouts and growls out in the courtyard.

Seth's expression grew grim. "Sounds like they're coming this way."

Aksel waved everyone back from the door. "I think it's time we retreat. Another battle and someone might get seriously hurt."

Glo retreated with the others, listing off their options. "Well, up is a dead end. And there are still skeletons patrolling outside. That just leaves down."

"Then down it is." Aksel ushered everyone toward the stairwell.

Seth grunted as he led the way. "Would have been nice if I could have checked the basement out first."

"He's never going to let that go," Glo whispered to Aksel.

"Heard that," Seth called back over his shoulder.

There were more noises out in the courtyard as they filed into the stairwell. Seth and Brundon led the way downstairs. Glo followed, holding his staff high above his head to illuminate the dark stairwell. Aksel was next. Lloyd and Titan brought up the rear.

At the bottom of the stairs they found a single door. It was locked, but Seth quickly picked it. The door creaked as it swung open, exposing a circular room similar to the one above. The only difference was the dank smell and the stacks of old wooden crates and barrels that sat here. Glo stepped in behind Seth and Brundon, lighting the entire room.

Brundon swiftly scanned the room. "I'm not seeing any other doorways down here." The tracker moved further out into the room.

Aksel barked out directions. "Seth, search the walls. Lloyd and Titan, set up on either side of the door. Worst case we catch them coming through and bottleneck the doorway."

The two warriors nodded and positioned themselves on opposite sides of the door. Glo moved to the center of the room, spreading his light as far as possible.

Seth rushed forward and scoured the walls, knocking here and there, checking for airflow between large mortar blocks of the basement walls. Brundon, after observing Seth, began to do the same on the opposite side of the room. Shouts and growls echoed down the stairwell from above.

Aksel turned to Glo. "Can you make out what they're saying?"

Glo listened intently, his keen hearing picking up most of the conversation. "It's bugbear. They found the zombie bodies."

Glo continued listening. About half a minute later he heard the words he was dreading. "Get ready everyone, they're headed down here."

Aksel called out to the halfling anxiously. "Seth?"

"I'm going...as fast as I…" Seth suddenly stopped at a section of wall on the south side of the tower. "I found something!" he said in a semi-hushed voice.

Aksel strode over toward him. "What is it?"

Seth scanned the wall feverishly. "There's definitely a blank space behind this wall."

Aksel called out to Lloyd. "Shut the door behind us!"

Lloyd reacted immediately, pushing the heavy door shut. Titan picked up a barrel and placed it in front of the door. The two warriors continued to stack up crates and barrels. Meanwhile, Seth had focused on a specific stone, working his small hands intently around it.

Heavy footsteps sounded on the stairs outside. Lloyd and Titan backed toward the others, weapons drawn.

Aksel spoke between clenched teeth. "Seth, open it now please."

Seth didn't take his eyes off the brick he was trying to move. "Just a minute."

Aksel looked over his shoulder. "We don't have a minute."

The heavy footsteps had stopped just outside the basement door. After a few moments, the handle started to turn. *Click.* Something tried to open the door, but the crates and barrels blocked the way. There was some loud growling then the door began to slowly push inward.

"Seth!" Aksel hissed.

"Got it," Seth whispered, with a smug smile. There was an audible click, and a section of the wall slid open.

Everyone piled into the open space behind the wall. Lloyd and Titan grabbed the sliding door, pushing it closed behind them with a quiet thud.

Aksel elbowed Glo in the side and nodded toward his lit staff. Glo immediately understood—the slightest crack in the wall might give them away if the light seeped through. Glo reached up and extinguished the staff.

Through the wall, the companions heard the sound of cracking wood followed by a crash. Heavy footsteps entered the room they had just been in. Excited grunts and growls accompanied the noise of trampling feet as the bugbears moved around the basement.

Aksel whispered to Glo, "What are they saying?"

Glo listened intently, trying to decipher the guttural speech. The bugbears were extremely excited, and thus hard to follow. "They don't know what to think. It sounds like they're scared."

The grunts and growls continued for a while longer. Finally, the sounds stopped and the heavy footsteps receded. The companions waited a bit more, but the basement remained silent.

Someone sighed. "Phew. That was close."

Glo couldn't have agreed more.

Aksel tugged on Glo's robe. "Any idea what all that grunting and groaning was about?"

"I only caught some of it. If I heard right, they found the pile of zombies and the crater at the top of the tower."

Brundon's voice sounded behind him. "Do they know who's responsible?"

Glo turned around, although he couldn't see the tracker in the dark. "That's the strange part. They seem to think that they were attacked by a large angel-warrior with a huge flaming sword."

Seth snorted. "That sounds like Lloyd alright. Although the flaming part could be you too, Glo."

"Yeah, yeah, enough with the fire jokes already." Once Seth found something funny, he did not let it go.

Aksel cleared his throat. "So then, shall we find out where we are?"

"Certainly." Glo pulled out a piece of glowing material from his bag, touched the end of his staff, and said the word, "*Lux.*"

The tip of the staff began to glow once more, lighting the area where they stood. It took a few moments for their eyes to adjust. They were in a long, wide corridor, the walls of which were smoothly chiseled stone block, and the floor flat stone slab. It was impossible to tell how far it went—even with the light from his staff.

Aksel turned to Seth. "Care to scout out ahead?"

Seth shrugged. "Sure, why not." He crept down the passage and disappeared from sight.

The others waited in silence for Seth to return. Glo noted that the corridor was cool, but not musty like the tower basement; there was only a hint of dampness. The walls were smooth and dry to the touch. A short while later Seth returned.

"The corridor only goes about one hundred paces, then dead ends at another wall. I think there is a hidden door there, but it will be harder to find without any light."

Aksel glanced around the group. "Okay then, let's have a look, shall we?"

Seth led them down the corridor. Glo observed unlit torches attached to either wall at regular intervals, more evidence that this passageway was man-made. Once they reached the other end, Seth searched the wall and indeed found another secret door. After listening cautiously, Seth triggered a hidden lever and the wall slid open.

Glo stepped through the doorway with his staff. On the other side was a hallway perpendicular to the corridor they were in. It looked identical to the passageway they had just come through, with stone block walls and a slab floor. Based on the direction and the distance they had just traveled, the companions realized they were now below the main keep.

As a group they were eager to move forward, but they were also exhausted and had sustained some minor injuries. They reached a unanimous decision to close the door and stay in the secret corridor for the rest of the night. It was well hidden, and therefore as good a place as any to rest.

Aksel healed Lloyd, then checked out Glo and Seth, both of whom had been buffeted by the blast atop the tower. Once done, they all shared a cold meal, then bedded down till morning.

It seemed like no time had passed when Glo's eyes snapped open. They were drawn to a small flame dancing above a torch on the wall. It radiated a soft warm glow across the corridor, illuminating the forms of his still-sleeping companions.

Glo's eyes drifted down the passageway and fell on a solitary figure leaning against the wall. It was Seth; the halfling must have relieved Brundon from watch duty sometime during the night. Seth returned his gaze and nodded a silent greeting.

Glo nodded back, then slowly stretched his limbs. He felt fairly well rested, so more time must have passed than he realized. Before long, the others had woke, packed their gear, and shared a cold breakfast. Lloyd, Titan and Brundon were engaged in an avid discussion of yesterday's battles, with Seth adding in the occasional pointed remark.

Glo ate in silence, reflecting on his own missteps. That fiasco atop the tower could have gotten them all killed. He panicked and had made a rash decision, firing off a spell without thinking it through. On the bright side, he hadn't frozen up this time. Still, he needed to be more careful. He had to be logical and not allow his emotions to cloud his judgement, especially where magic was concerned. *That would be the last time*, Glo vowed to himself.

Aksel roused him from his musings. "Glo, have you had any contact with your familiar?"

"No, actually." The question caught Glo by surprise. He was used to his familiar's presence in the back of his mind, but Raven was fairly silent this morning. Perhaps it was because they were separated by the keep walls.

Glo closed his eyes and reached out with his mind. It took a bit longer than normal, but he was able to form a tenuous contact with her. "She seems relatively calm, so I believe it's safe to say things have quieted down up there."

"Good." Aksel turned to Seth. "What about down here?"

Seth had his ear up to the hidden door that led to the basement. "It still sounds quiet out there too."

Aksel adjusted his robe. "Then let's go."

Seth pulled the hidden lever and the section of the wall slid aside. The basement beyond was dark and silent.

"Seth…" Aksel said.

"Already on it." Seth slipped through the doorway and out into the darkness.

They waited quietly in the hidden passage for Seth's return. He reappeared a short while later, held a finger to his lips as he passed, then disappeared once more. He returned out of the darkness shortly thereafter.

"All clear. Both ends of the passage lead to rooms. There was no sign of anyone in either. The room back this way"—he pointed a thumb over his shoulder—"is kind of interesting."

"How so?" Aksel asked.

"It's some kind of storage area. There's lots of stuff in there covered with sheets."

"That might be interesting. Let's check it out."

Brundon grabbed the pair of lit torches from the wall, taking one for himself and handing the other to Aksel. Seth closed the hidden door behind them, then led the way down the hall. Lloyd and Brundon trailed behind, with Aksel and Glo next, and Titan bringing up the rear. At the end of the hall they passed through a doorway; Brundon and Aksel fanned out, illuminating the room. It was a fairly large area, nearly as big as the common room back at the Charging Minotaur. It contained dozens of large objects covered with white sheets. The companions spread out, peering underneath the cloths. They found a collection of old furniture, still in pristine condition.

Glo was examining a spinning wheel he had found when he heard a low whistle. He glanced up to see Seth and Lloyd standing over a luxurious, ornate couch. Seth plopped himself down, sinking deep into the cushions.

His face took on a dreamy expression. "Oooo, this is comfy." Seth snuggled further into the cushions and closed his eyes. "Lloyd, you have to try this."

Lloyd looked quizzically at Seth. He tentatively pushed down on a cushion. "Seems nice…"

"Grab a seat," Seth told him, still not opening his eyes.

Lloyd pointed at the twin swords sticking out of the scabbards on his back. "Kind of hard to do with these on."

Seth shrugged. "Your loss. Glo? How about you?"

"I'm just fine, thanks," Glo said with thinly-veiled amusement.

"You don't know what you're missing," Seth said in an enticing tone.

Aksel interrupted them. "Yes, yes, that's all well and fine. Now can we get back to our exploring?"

"Sure."—Seth made no effort to move—"but when we are done here, I'm taking this couch with us."

Aksel glanced at Glo, who merely shrugged in response. He honestly had no idea what was going on with the halfling. Seth did have an odd sense of humor though. This might just be some sort of elaborate prank.

Aksel sighed. "If you can carry it."

Seth reluctantly rose from his seat. "Oh, I'll find a way."

A short while later, Lloyd found something. "I wonder what this is doing here." The young man stood in front of a plain full-length mirror. He had almost a trancelike look on his face as his hand stretched forward to touch it.

"Lloyd! Don't…" Glo cried out, just a moment too late.

Lloyd's hand touched the glass. A bright light radiated from the point of contact, then spread with frightening speed, swiftly engulfing his entire body. One second he was there, the next he was gone!

They all rushed over, but there was no trace of Lloyd. The mirror stood there, reflecting back their images, as if nothing had happened.

Brundon gazed pensively at the mirror. "Where'd he go?"

There was really only one explanation. "The mirror must be magical," Glo said. "It teleported him to another location."

"Is there any way to know where he went?"

Glo thought it over for a few moments. "The way these items tend to work, it would have to be linked to a second mirror. It's not a long-range spell, so it would have to be somewhere else in the keep. Unfortunately, the only way to know for certain is to go through ourselves."

Aksel made a swift decision. "I don't think we have much choice. With everything we've seen so far in this keep, he could be in more trouble than he can handle."

Visions of a dark mage played through Glo's mind.

Aksel turned to Seth and Brundon. "I think it might be better if you two stay here."

Seth merely nodded. Brundon, on the other hand, sounded concerned. "I thought you wanted us to stick together."

"I did, but you two have a knack for moving around unseen. If we don't come back shortly, we're either dead already, or in need of rescuing."

Seth's face took on a grim cast. "No problem."

Brundon glanced at Titan with concern. The tall warrior reached out and placed a firm hand on her partner's shoulder. She then looked at Aksel. "I'll go first."

Aksel nodded thankfully at the brave warrior.

Titan drew her sword, strode up and touched the mirror with the tip. The glass flashed to life once again and in less than a second she was gone.

Glo walked up to the mirror next. He had no idea where he would end up, but he was determined to help his friends. He looked at the reflection in the mirror, but it did not seem inclined to give him the answers he needed. Glo grimaced then reached out and touched the glass. It initially felt cool to the touch, but warmed as soon as he made contact. There was a bright flash, followed by a feeling of disorientation, and then the world around him slipped away.

11
IN THE DUNGEON

*He was in a small room with three walls made of stone
and the fourth made of bars*

Aksel watched with quiet concern as Glo disappeared. Things
had gone from bad to worse ever since they entered the keep.
He felt keenly responsible—his companions looked to him
for leadership, and he had let them down. He let his curiosity get the
better of him, confronting those skeletons at the top of the tower.
Things would have gone far smoother if they had just checked out
the basement first like Seth had wanted.

Hindsight is twenty-twenty, Aksel reminded himself. There was no
way to know that vat was full of oil, or that Glolindir would use a fire
spell on it. There was also no way to warn them of every single magical item they could run into—like a mirror, for instance. They were
all so new at this; it was a rough business, full of danger and surprise.
He guessed he should be glad they were all still alive. Aksel stepped
up to the mirror and glanced over his shoulder at Seth.

"If we are not back in half an hour, you should probably come
looking for us."

Seth nodded.

Aksel half smiled, then reached out and touched the mirror. The glass flashed in response, followed by a feeling of disorientation, then the world shifted around him. When things came back into focus, he found himself in a small square room.

He let out a deep sigh. Lloyd, Titan and Glo stood there, completely unharmed. The room itself was rather cramped, its small space filled with a few tables and a couple of large bookshelves. Glass vials, metal pots, open books, and scattered parchments covered the table tops. The bookshelves rose from the floor to the ceiling, their shelves lined with books of various sizes and colors. Across the room from him stood a heavy iron-bound door. The opposite wall contained a glass-paned window, the rays of the early morning sun streaming in to light the room. A quick glance behind him confirmed the presence of another full-length mirror just like the one in the basement. Glo stood over one of the tables, examining the books and parchments spread across it. Lloyd hovered over another table, peering at a bubbling setup of glass vials with various colored liquids in them.

Titan stood at the window, gazing outside. "It looks like we're at the top of the keep."

Lloyd lifted the lid off a pot. "Makes sense." He sniffed the contents within, wrinkled his nose, and then swiftly replaced the lid.

Titan peered at him over her shoulder. "Why is that?"

"This is a wizard's lab. Best to keep this kind of stuff far away from any other rooms."

Glo glanced up from a book he was holding. "And how do you know this is a wizard's lab?"

Lloyd grinned sheepishly. "My mom has one just like it at home. Although hers is quite a bit bigger—and a whole lot messier."

Aksel was caught by surprise at the sudden revelation. "Your mother's a wizard?"

"Yeah. Did I forget to mention that?"

"Yes," Glo said, "you most certainly did."

"Sorry."

Aksel glanced at Glo. The elf cocked an eyebrow, but otherwise said nothing. *So Lloyd's mother is a wizard.* That was very interesting.

Lloyd had talked about the rest of his family, but never mentioned his mother before. He wondered what else they didn't know about the extraordinary young man.

Aksel mused aloud. "Well, this has to be the dark mage's lab. We probably shouldn't stay here too long, but on the other hand, we might find something that could help us against him."

"I'll keep watch at the window," Titan offered.

Aksel gave her a brief smile. "Thanks." He turned to Lloyd. "Can you go listen at the door?"

Lloyd replaced the lid to another pot he had been inspecting. "Sure thing." He strode over to the door and placed his ear up against it.

While the two warriors stood guard, Glo and Aksel scoured the books and parchments. There were far too many—it would take hours to go through them all. Unfortunately, they did not have hours. After only a few short minutes, Titan called over from the window.

"I think I see that wizard."

Aksel put down the book he was holding. "Where?"

"There's a man in robes below walking across the courtyard. He just came out of the tower and is headed toward the keep."

Glo looked up from a parchment on the table. "If he's anything like my father, then he probably lives in his lab."

Lloyd chuckled. "My mom's the same way. She would spend weeks at a time in her lab. I think Dad inducted her into the navy just to get her away from all those books and potions; but then she had a lab built aboard ship."

Aksel glanced at Glo. The wizard raised another eyebrow. "Your mom has a lab on a ship?"

Lloyd's smile turned into a wide grin. "Yeah. It drives my dad crazy."

Now that was eccentric. Aksel really couldn't say anything though. His own family had been just as odd. They were archeologists-historians and had scoured the world for artifacts and the like. Aksel's home had been filled with strange objects brought back from those journeys. In fact, that is how his family had disappeared, searching for such objects. Still, this was not the time to dwell on that. Glo and

Lloyd were right. This Telvar was probably on his way back to the very lab where they stood. Aksel placed the book in his hand on the shelf where he had found it.

"I think that's our cue to leave. Put everything back where it was. No sense announcing to him that we were here."

"Better hurry," Lloyd whispered from the door. "I heard grunts and growls coming from the hallway—and they're getting louder."

Titan stepped away from the window and turned toward Aksel, her hand going to her sword. "What do you want us to do?"

Aksel thought it over for a moment. The two warriors were well trained and they would have the element of surprise on their side, but there was no telling how many bugbears were out there or how soon Telvar would arrive. "I still think it best if we retreat."

"Back through the mirror then?" Glo asked.

"Back through the mirror," Aksel agreed.

The four of them all hurried over to the magic mirror and filed through, disappearing from the room.

Less than a minute later, Seth appeared in front of that same mirror. He scanned the room, quickly realizing it was some kind of lab. Seth glanced over his shoulder in time to see Brundon appear behind him.

Brundon cautiously surveyed the area. "Where is everyone?"

Seth shook his head uncertainly. He turned to look at the lab. It probably belonged to that wizard the bugbear told them about. It was also not the best place to be if one wanted to avoid the dark mage. He was about to say as much when the wooden door across from them burst open. An old man wearing black robes strode in. His dark eyes immediately focused on them, his hands lifting and pointing their way.

Seth reacted instinctively. He grasped a knife from his belt and let it fly at the dark mage. Not waiting to see if it landed, he spun around and dove for the mirror. As he flew past Brundon, he yelled, "Quick, back the way we came!"

Brundon began to pivot as Seth touched the glass. The world

dissolved around him and he lost sight of the tracker. A moment later the world reappeared, but he was not back in the basement. He was in a small room with three walls made of stone and the fourth made of bars. Beyond the bars was a torch-lit corridor, lined with more cells on both sides and ending in a large wooden door.

Lloyd and Titan were braced up against a door in the barred wall, heaving against it with their combined might. The stubborn door refused to budge. Leaning against a stone wall was Glo and Aksel.

"Nice of you to drop in." Aksel's face was emotionless, though there was a trace of frustration in his voice.

Seth snorted. "Yeah, nice to see you, too. Wish the circumstances were better." Seth gazed at the mirror he had just come through. It was full-length just like the other two, but the glass was dark with no apparent reflection.

"It's a one way mirror," Glo told him. "You can travel to it, but not from it."

Seth shook his head. "Wonderful."

"Where's Brundon?" Titan called out, staring at him with those steely blue eyes.

Seth had almost forgotten about Brundon. Guilt washed over him as he explained what happened back in the lab.

When he was done, Titan's face was grim. "I just hope that knife of yours found its mark."

Lloyd placed a comforting hand on her shoulder. "I promise you, we'll find him."

"If that wizard harms a hair on his head…" The tall warrior stopped herself, her voice cracking from anger and concern.

Aksel attempted to comfort her. "I don't think he will. This Telvar must know where that mirror in his lab leads. With all of us safely tucked away, he thinks he has the upper hand."

"Aksel's right," Glo added. "He'll want to know what we're doing here and who sent us. He's not going to dispose of anyone till he gets some answers."

Titan took a deep breath, her body visibly relaxing. "Thanks everyone. I hope you're right." She suddenly noticed all eyes fixed on her. The tall warrior began to blush. "Brundon is—like a brother to me. I would never forgive myself if something happened to him."

A thin smirk crossed Seth's lips. He wasn't buying it for a moment. "Well then," he said aloud, "let's make certain that it doesn't."

Seth strode toward the cell door. Lloyd and Titan moved out of his way. This was a dungeon cell they were in, after all, and the weakest part of any cell was always the lock. Seth knew how to handle locks. Lock picking, in fact, was one of the few useful things he had learned from his family.

Seth had the distinct displeasure of growing up surrounded by thieves. He learned to pick his first lock when he was only five. Originally he thought it was all a game. By the time he was ten, he could unlock any door and most safes. It was not until he was in his teens that he figured out that it was more than just a pastime; it was the family business.

Seth inspected the locking mechanism on the door. It was a standard pin-tumbler lock. It might take him a couple of seconds to fiddle with the pins, but he knew he could open it in under a minute. He wrestled with it all of ten seconds when the tumblers clicked into place. The halfling made a big show of pushing the cell door open with a single hand, something the two warriors couldn't do with their combined strength moments ago.

A smug smile crossed his face. "So, who wants to get out of here?"

Lloyd grinned at him, then proceeded through the door. Titan began to follow, then stopped and placed a steel-clad hand on his shoulder. Her eyes were filled with gratitude. "Thank you, my friend."

"It was child's play." Seth feigned indifference. Secretly, he was quite pleased with himself. He still felt guilty for leaving Brundon behind. Freeing them made up for that somewhat.

Seth exited the cell and moved up ahead of Lloyd. He swiftly checked the other cells. All were empty except for a grisly skeleton or two. Thankfully, these were not moving. When they reached the door at the other end, Seth found it locked. He put an ear up to it and listened. There was a sound coming from the other side; it was rhythmic in nature. A broad grin crossed his face when he realized what it was.

"What is it?" Aksel whispered.

"Snoring," Seth said with thinly veiled amusement.

Aksel waved everyone back down the corridor and laid out a plan. A few minutes later, Seth unlocked the door. He and Glo pulled it back as Lloyd and Titan charged past. It was over in moments. The two sleeping bugbear guards never even got the chance to cry out.

On the other side of the room was another door; this one was not locked. Seth cracked it open to find a well-lit hallway leading away from the dungeon. It was stone block on stone slab, the same as the other corridors they had seen. Seth led the way as they moved swiftly down the hall.

They had only traveled a short distance when he spied a junction up ahead. Seth motioned for the others to wait here and silently crept forward. He peeked around the corner and spied one lone bugbear guard patrolling the intersecting hall. Seth rejoined the others.

"There's a single bugbear guard," he whispered.

Lloyd reached over his shoulders to draw his swords. "That shouldn't be a problem."

Seth held up his hand. "Wait. Let's do this quietly."

Titan's eyes narrowed. "What do you have in mind?"

Seth outlined a quick plan, with himself acting as a distraction. A couple of minutes later, the bugbear lay at his feet, easily overpowered by Lloyd and Titan, who had caught it off-guard.

The companions moved swiftly down the hallway the bugbear had been patrolling. A short way further, Seth discovered a set of carved stone stairs leading upward. They followed them up and found themselves in a dark corridor.

Seth scouted ahead while the others waited. The hallway was completely black, but that was not a problem for him. He had been trained to rely not only on his eyes. He put those skills to use now, listening as he crept down the dark corridor. *Silence.* He felt the wall as he slowly took each step. Cool hard stone. He sniffed the air. *A hint of dampness.* He was still underground.

About fifty paces down, Seth felt a lessening in airflow. *There's an obstruction ahead.* He approached it carefully, still feeling his way along the wall. He came to a door. It was unlocked. He listened. *Silence.* Seth opened the door and walked through. By the free flow of air around him, he could tell he was in a large open area. He slowly felt his way around until he came across something against the wall. He reached out and carefully touched it. *Fabric.* He pulled on it and found it was loose. Seth bent forward and pushed against the object. *Soft and cushy.*

Seth slapped himself on the forehead when he realized where he was. He swiftly retraced his steps until he found the others.

"What did you find?" Aksel asked.

"You'll see soon enough." Seth liked being mysterious. It was intrinsic to his profession, and it was also fun!

When they reached the room a few minutes later, everyone groaned. Aksel held a torch aloft while Glo lit up his staff, illuminating the dark room. They had found their way back to the storage room with the magic mirror. Seth plopped himself down on the comfy couch.

"Let me know when you decide what we're doing next."

With that, he closed his eyes and let his body sink further into the soft cushions of the sofa. The others continued to deliberate. He knew they would talk things through for a bit, especially Aksel and Glo. Those two overanalyzed everything. He would let them handle the fretting while he relaxed. A short while later, Aksel roused him from his comfortable perch.

"We found another door."

"Where?" Seth asked.

"Behind one of the large cabinets."

"Oh very well." Seth grudgingly got up and strode over to the newfound door, putting his ear up to it.

Silence. Beyond the door was another dark corridor. Seth told the others to wait there, then went out to explore. He wandered around for quite a while, discovering more dark rooms and passageways. As he went, he began mapping it out in his head. Based on his calculations, he was probably near the back of the keep.

Seth turned a corner and saw light down the hall. He made his way down the passage, and found a dimly lit cross corridor. A few torches lined the walls at irregular intervals. The dancing flames left a number of shadowy areas along the passage.

At the far end of the corridor, he spied a strange greenish glow.

It reminded him of the undead mage at the top of the tower. His curiosity piqued, he crept down the passage toward it. As he drew closer, the green light grew brighter. It was a sickly color; something about it did not seem quite right. He also began hearing noises drifting down the hall—it was a rhythmic sound. As he got closer, Seth realized it was chanting.

He reached what turned out to be an archway and peered in. Beyond lay a large chamber, the walls hewn from stone just like the halls. The ceiling was shrouded in darkness, numerous columns disappearing into the shadows above. In the center of the chamber stood a large pool filled with sickly green glowing water, the source of the strange light. Sporadically-placed torches lit the rest of the chamber, but much of it was still bathed in shadow.

Seth's eyes were drawn to the other end of the pool. Two figures stood over a stone slab up a short flight of steps, their bodies covered with brown fur. Both figures wore horned helmets and carried long gnarled wooden staffs. They were bugbears; probably the two mages that Gilstench mentioned yesterday.

The mages stood over a stone altar with an unmoving body stretched across it. Their staffs raised as they chanted their hideous song. Seth peeked further around the corner and saw four pale bugbears standing beside the pool. They were unmoving, their eyes filled with vacant stares. They were zombies!

Bugbear zombies? Seth thought he had seen it all till now.

He had to tell the others about this. Seth backed quietly away from the arch and retraced his steps down the hallways and rooms to where the rest of the party waited.

12
NECROMANGERS

Three quarters of an hour had elapsed since Seth found the bugbear mages. Now he led the companions down the hallway just outside the large chamber.

They halted a few yards down from the entrance. Glo saw the strange light emanating from the archway. It bathed the walls and floor just outside the chamber with a sickly green color. Seth crept down to the arch and peered inside. After a few moments, he returned.

"They're still there."

"Not very surprising," Aksel whispered. "I am by no means an expert when it comes to the dark arts, but even I know that a Create Undead spell takes an hour to cast. And perhaps more importantly, in order for it to work, it must be cast at night."

Glo had to stifle a laugh for the first time since they entered the keep. They only escaped from the dungeons a couple of hours ago, and at that time it had been early morning. It couldn't be more than noon now.

He thought back to what Gilstench had told them. Telvar was teaching dark magic to two bugbears, Bilehack and Curdlemung. Bugbears were not noted for their intellect, but these two novices had made a huge blunder. All the better. He had been worried about facing two trained necromancers and four bugbear zombies. While this would still be dangerous, at least now they might have a chance.

The companions retreated down the hall and formulated a plan of attack. Seth described the layout of the chamber in detail. It gave Aksel an idea.

"If we can get Glo close enough to the mages, he can use his fire spell on them."

Seth wore a wicked grin. "Are we sure there's no oil up at the altar?"

Glo gave him an acid look. "Very funny. Perhaps you want to take them both on yourself?"

"Me?" Seth said with mock fear. "Nah. I'll leave the caster types to you. Anyway, those zombies need to be distracted as well."

A worried look crossed Aksel's face. "What did you have in mind?"

Seth reached into a pouch on his belt and pulled out a couple of small round objects. "How about smoke bombs?"

Glo raised an eyebrow. "And you yelled at me for calling you an assassin? Why don't you just announce it to the world with those things?"

Seth glared at him with a look that could have melted iron.

"Are you really an assassin?" Lloyd asked.

Seth shifted his dark gaze toward the young man. "Ninja," he answered, pronouncing the word carefully. "The term is ninja. And I really don't like to talk about it."

Aksel cleared his throat. "Alright, from now on the A word and the N word are forbidden." He glanced at Glo. "Right?"

Glo agreed. "Sure, as long as we can forget about that incident at the top of the tower."

Seth grinned impishly. "But we got such a bang out of it."

"Seth!" Aksel hissed.

"Fine. No more fire jokes." Seth had trouble wiping the smirk off his face.

Aksel sighed deeply. "Good. Now then, what about those smoke bombs?"

The discussion continued until they had come up with a reasonable plan. Seth went first, sneaking down the hall and disappearing through the archway. A few minutes passed before Glo started down the hall after him.

When he reached the archway, Glo peered around the corner. The chamber was indeed large, the columns rising up into the shadows as Seth had described. His eyes were drawn inexplicably to the pool. Something about the pale green water bothered him. It was more than just the color. The pool seemed...wrong somehow.

He ripped his eyes away and focused on the would-be necromancers. They still hovered over the altar, chanting horribly. He peered in a bit further and saw the zombie bugbears lined up next to the pool, facing the altar.

Try as he might, Glo could detect no sign of Seth. He had to admit, the halfling was good. Now it was his turn.

Glo tiptoed through the doorway and along the shadowed wall opposite the zombies. He kept his eyes trained on the bugbears, but luckily he went unnoticed. He stealthily inched his way across the chamber toward his goal—the first column.

It went painstakingly slow, and he stopped a number of times, warily watching the creatures, but none turned his way. After what seemed like an eternity, Glo made it to the column. He drew in a deep breath, calming his nerves.

Once they settled, he peered out into the chamber. There was a faint movement behind the column directly across from him. *There's Seth.* The halfling signaled he was ready.

Glo glanced toward the entrance. From this angle he could see Lloyd and Titan just outside the archway. The two warriors had their blades drawn, ready to charge.

Aksel stood beside the duo, waiting for Glo's signal that all was ready. Glo nodded, signifying that they were in place.

Aksel turned and motioned to Lloyd. The young warrior sprang forward and raced into the room, heavily stomping on the stone floor as he ran. Strangely enough, no one turned. The horrible chanting all but drowned out Lloyd's dramatic entrance.

The warrior stood between the archway and the pool, both swords drawn and reflecting green and orange between the light of the strange pool and flames surrounding his blades.

"Penwick!" Lloyd cried at the top of his lungs. That got their attention.

The zombies slowly turned around, mindless faces gaping at the red clad warrior. Even the two bugbear mages stopped their incessant chanting and whirled around.

Lloyd, with a look of satisfaction on his face, screamed his battle cry again and launched himself toward the waiting zombies.

At that same moment, two round grey objects flew out into the midst of the zombies. They clanked onto the stone floor and then exploded. Clouds of thick grey smoke billowed out from them, enveloping the four zombies.

The would-be necromancers turned toward the expanding cloud. They growled at each other excitedly as the smoke continued to cover their hapless minions. After a few more agitated grunts and growls, both casters turned toward Lloyd, their staffs raised.

Through all this, Glo had been on the move. He ran from pillar to pillar across the pool from the excitement, preparing his own spell as he went.

Glo rounded the last column just as the bugbears focused on Lloyd. They were so intent on the warrior that they did not see him coming. He stopped a few yards away, raised his arm and spoke the words, "*Ardens Manus.*"

A cone of searing red flame leapt from his outstretched fingers and fanned out toward the unsuspecting bugbears. Both necromancers paused and glanced over their shoulders, but it was too late.

Looks of dread crossed their brutish faces as they were engulfed by the cone of fire, then the bugbears disappeared from sight. Yelps of pain could be heard from inside the bright hot cone. It only lasted a few moments, then the stream of fire stopped. The cone faded away, and the two necromancers reappeared, their bodies scorched and their fur smoldering, little flames still dancing in spots.

The bugbears turned as one toward the source of the searing attack. Their dark beady eyes fell on the solitary elf. Horrible growls escaped their throats as they raised their staffs. It was a frightening visage. Glo took a step back and began another spell of his own.

The bugbears, so focused on retaliation, neglected to heed the clanking metal sound that crossed the floor. As the noise grew louder, Glo's nerves faded and a slim smile crossed his face. Their plan had worked. Once again, the bugbears were too late to realize their imminent danger.

They turned just as Titan slammed into them. The green light of the pool shown off the warrior's polished armor as she bowled into both bugbears shield first. She struck with such momentum that she sent the large creatures tumbling off the steps onto the floor below.

One bugbear had been hit so hard, it lay on the floor completely dazed. The other one scrambled to its feet and turned to run.

Titan turned swiftly, drew her sword and took a great swing. She caught the necromancer in the back, the gleaming blade slicing through the hapless creature, splattering its blood across the room. The bugbear fell to the ground in a heap, not to move again.

The second bugbear recovered and regained his feet. He growled as he raised his staff, training a spell on the warrior who had knocked him down. Before he could let it fly, two projectiles flashed across the room and hit the creature square in the chest. A pair of knives protruded from the necromancer's torso as he slowly slid to the ground in front of the altar.

Glo turned to see Seth standing there with a smug smile on his lips. Behind the halfling, Lloyd stood over a pile of zombies with a wide grin on his face, the last vestiges of the smoky cloud dissipating around him.

Behind him, Aksel strode into the room. "Did anyone get hurt?"

"No," they all said at once.

Their plan had worked! Both mages and zombies had been dealt with swiftly and painlessly.

Seth went to retrieve his knives from the bugbear mage. As he passed the altar, he stopped and stared. "Looks like they found Gilstench."

Aksel, Lloyd, and Titan ascended the steps to see for themselves. Glo started to follow, but then something caught his eye. From the steps, he could see the bottom of the pool. There was something down there. Glo strode over for a better look. He reached the edge of the pool and peered down. At the very bottom lay a large dark crystal about the size of a fist. Glo watched in fascination as the gem pulsed with a greenish glow, the steady beat of a crystalline heart.

His head began to hurt. In fact, his entire body began to tingle in a rather unpleasant way. The feeling abated momentarily but then reasserted itself once more. Glo realized that the strange phenomenon occurred in rhythm with the pulsing of the dark crystal.

He suddenly became aware he was not alone. Seth stood next to him and stared at the gem below. The halfling had a strange look on his face. Seth spoke slowly, as if mesmerized, "It's…rather… pretty…"

"Don't stare at it," Glo warned him in a raspy voice. He too was finding it difficult to speak.

Seth shook his head and glanced up at him. "What do you mean? It's not like it's…"

"Alive?" Glo finished for him. "No, not exactly. But it radiates evil…" It was getting harder to think. Glo realized he needed to do something now, before the crystal completely clouded their minds. He struggled to lift his hand, feeling as if it were made of lead. Glo finally managed to raise a finger and point it at the bottom of the pool. He found it difficult to speak, but finally managed to croak out two words. *"Nullam…Telum…"*

A purple projectile lanced out from his fingertips and sliced through the water toward the bottom of the pool. Time seemed to slow as the missile approached its target. The projectile finally reached the pulsing crystal.

Sloosh! The waters shuddered from the impact, and the dark crystal shattered. A dark green light fanned out in all directions from the now-empty space.

Glo heard an eerie high-pitched scream. It was not in his ears, but in his mind! The sound faded away, receding as if sucked to a faraway place. The dark green light abruptly vanished. The water was now clear, the sickly green color completely gone; there was no trace left of the crystal.

Glo noticed Aksel hurrying down to the edge of the pool. "What was that?"

"I am not completely sure."

Aksel had a haunted look in his eyes. "I thought I heard a scream, but there was no sound. It was as if it was in my mind."

Lloyd and Titan came up behind the little cleric. "We heard it too."

Glo paused a moment as he thought it over. "I have read of things like this in my father's journals. There are ancient artifacts that can act as receptacles of magical energies. The energy contained by such a relic can be positive or negative—good or evil, as we would term it."

He paused and took a deep breath, still feeling the after-effects of the strange encounter.

"Some of these items accumulate so much energy, they almost take on a life of their own. I believe that this crystal was one of those relics."

Aksel's voice was soft and there was a faraway look in his eyes. "My family used to research such things. In fact, the last time I saw them, my parents were leaving on an expedition looking for such an artifact."

An uncomfortable silence fell over them. Glo had always wondered what became of Aksel's family. He had never really talked about it. All he knew was that Aksel had been taken in by the clerics at the Temple of Caprizon in his early teens.

Titan placed a hand on Aksel's shoulder. Her voice was very soft as she spoke. "I lost my mother when I was two. The only recollections I have of her are vague flashes of her face and smile."

The tall warrior and little cleric gazed at each other, a shared expression of sympathy passing between them. Glo was deeply moved; both had experienced so much loss. Perhaps he had been too quick to judge his own parents. Maybe he was lucky just to have them. The silence that fell over them was interrupted by a shout from across the room. It was Seth.

"Hey, look what I found!"

Glo almost jumped. He could have sworn the halfling was right next to him a few moments ago.

Seth stood next to an open doorway in the wall behind the altar. The door had not been there a few moments ago.

Aksel appeared astonished. "Another secret door? Who built this place?"

Lloyd and Titan grabbed torches as they walked over to join Seth. When they reached the door, they held the lights aloft.

Glo peered through the doorway; it opened to a small room. A thick layer of dust covered the floor as if it had been undisturbed for a long time. A round table stood in the center with a skeleton seated at it. Glo, momentarily startled, noticed the skeleton was covered with cobwebs. He peered closer and spotted some objects on the table, a dagger and a book. The dagger had a jet black handle with an inky sheen to it. The book was thick and leather bound, its cover blank.

Glo cast the identification spell and the dagger began to glow. A vision formed in his mind of the dagger superimposed on a snake's head, its mouth wide open and fangs protruding. The vision then changed. The dagger remained, but now there was a large spider crawling over it. It opened it jaws displaying two black fangs. The visions faded. Glo opened his eyes. He reached down, picked up the knife by the handle, and held it hilt-out toward Seth.

Seth glanced at him curiously. "It's a dagger of venom. Stab your target and say '*Venenum*' to invoke the spell."

A broad smile spread across Seth's face. "Nice." He took the dagger and hefted it gently. "Good balance, too."

"And now he is twice as deadly." Lloyd grinned from ear to ear.

Titan wore a wry smile. "Deadly, and on our side. I can live with that."

Seth's mouth twisted sideways. "You know it."

The halfling removed one of his other knives from its sheath, and slid the new dagger into it. Meanwhile, Aksel had opened the book and was leafing through the pages. A low whistle escaped his lips.

"What is it?" Glo asked.

Aksel motioned him over and pointed to the page he had been reading. Glo raised an eyebrow when he saw the contents.

"Well?" Seth said impatiently.

Glo glanced up and saw Seth standing with his arms crossed, glaring at them. "Oh, sorry. It's a manual of golem creation. Stone golems, specifically."

It was Seth's turn to whistle. "What's something like that doing here?"

Aksel glanced around them. "It does make you wonder who built this place."

Could this be one of Larketh's hidden lairs? Glo wondered.

Lloyd and Titan were having a side discussion. "Do you know what they're talking about?"

Titan shook her head. "Aside from golems, no, not really."

Glo let out a short laugh. "I'm sorry. I forgot not everyone knows about this stuff."

Seth folded his arms across his chest. "Speak for yourself."

Glo just shook his head. He turned back to Lloyd and Titan. "Well, you know that golems are magical constructs…"

"…created by wizards," Lloyd finished for him.

"Yes. And there are four types, the first three made from clay, stone, and iron."

Titan eyed him curiously. "What's the fourth?"

Glo hesitated a moment. "They're called flesh golems and they're made from the remains of living creatures."

"Eww." Titan grimaced.

Lloyd looked puzzled. "How's that different from a zombie?"

Glo opened his mouth to respond, but Aksel cut him off. "Let's not go into that."

Titan's expression was one of disgust. "I think I'm with Aksel on that."

Lloyd still appeared puzzled. "So we've all heard of golems, but what's a manual of golem creation?"

Glo took a deep breath. "It's a complex process, the secrets of which were only known to a few. That's why there are not that many golems. On top of that, not all golems are created equal. The most powerful were made by the Golem Thrall Master, Larketh, but that was well over one hundred years ago."

"During the Thrall Wars?" Titan asked.

"Yes."

Lloyd wore a thoughtful expression. "I've heard my mother mention Larketh. Wasn't he killed at the end of that war?"

Aksel answered this time. "Yes. And all of his research was lost with him. That's what makes this manual so valuable." He leafed through some pages. "It contains step-by-step instructions on how to make a stone golem."

Glo nodded in agreement. "Further, the detail in this book is astounding—only a great master like Larketh could have written it."

Aksel closed the book with a resounding thud. "Unfortunately, we may never know exactly who wrote it, but for now let's move on. We still have that wizard to deal with, not to mention finding Brundon."

13
UNEXPECTED REUNION

In the ceiling above him was a small rectangular hole

The small company retraced their steps, following the dimly lit corridor beyond the point where Seth had found it. The lights signified frequent use, and with any luck it would lead to a way out of the basement. Seth led the way through a maze of rooms and passages. It was a crazy mix of hallways. Some ended in secret doors, others opened into rooms with yet more hidden doors and passages beyond. The only saving grace was that all these were illuminated by torches.

At one point, Lloyd halted, his frustration quite apparent. "Who built this crazy place? Couldn't they have just built a single hall that leads to a staircase or something?"

Titan placed a hand on the young man's shoulder. "Don't worry, Lloyd. I'm sure we'll find our way out of here."

Glo gazed at him sympathetically. "I think that whoever built this place did so on purpose."

"It's actually a typical design for a thieves' den," Seth chimed in.

Aksel looked at the halfling. "How's that?"

"Well…most thieves live in fear of discovery, so they design their hideouts to be mazelike. It makes it hard for newcomers to find their way through. It's also a great design to fill with traps."

Lloyd squinted at Seth. "You seem to know an awful lot about thieves."

"Yeah, well there's no denying ninjas, thieves and assassins have a lot in common. And no, I was never either of those things. I just… know too many people who went down the wrong path."

It was quite evident how uncomfortable Seth was with this conversation. Glo swiftly changed the subject to avoid embarrassing him further. "Yes, well what you said before makes a lot of sense. Whoever designed this keep was definitely paranoid."

Aksel caught on as well and played along. "I quite agree. You could be lost down here for days without finding the way out. Based on that, I suspect the actual path out of here is very well hidden."

Glo glanced at Seth. The halfling merely nodded at him without as much as a smirk or sarcastic remark.

After another hour of traversing the seemingly endless maze of halls and chambers, they came upon a small room lined with shelves. It appeared to have been once filled with foodstuffs, the only remains of which were some nearly disintegrated bags and containers.

They were about to move on when Seth called out, "Hey, look at this."

He stood in a corner staring upward. Glo followed his gaze. In the ceiling above him was a small rectangular hole with wood molding frames on all four sides. Glo judged it to be about a yard long and nearly as wide. By the light of his staff, he could see a few feet beyond the opening. It appeared to be a shaft with smooth stone walls on either side, but strain as he might, he could only see blackness beyond where the light faded.

Titan came up beside them. "Is that what I think it is?"

Seth was bent over sideways gazing up into the darkness. "Considering this room was used for food storage…"

"…then this could have been a dumbwaiter…" Glo continued for him.

"…which means it may lead to an upstairs pantry," Titan said, sounding rather hopeful.

Lloyd's voice rose in excitement. "So there might be a shortcut out of this crazy basement?"

Glo gave the young man an encouraging smile. "It may very well be."

Titan hit Lloyd in the arm. "See, what did I tell you?"

Lloyd grinned back at her.

Aksel was also bent backwards, gazing up into the darkness. "Seth, do you think you could climb up it?"

Seth straightened and turned toward Aksel. "Not a problem. Just hand me your torch."

Aksel did so. Seth took it from him and put it out. He then tucked the piece of wood behind his belt and turned to Lloyd. "Give me a boost."

Lloyd stepped forward and positioned himself under the hole. He clasped his hands together and bent down, making a foothold for the halfling.

Seth lips twisted sideways. "Here goes nothing."

He stepped onto Lloyd's interlocked hands and nimbly scrambled onto his shoulders. Lloyd stood up and then so did Seth, reaching as high as he could. He was just able to grab hold of the wood frame around the hole. Seth hoisted his body up and managed to wedge himself inside the chute.

Glo watched in amazement as he began slowly inching his way up the shaft. Seth had his hands pressed against one smooth stone wall while his feet were firmly planted on the opposite wall. He slowly moved one hand, then one foot, then the other hand followed by the other foot. It was an incredible feat of strength and agility, the likes of which Glo had never seen.

Aksel called up the chute, his voice thick with concern, "Are you sure you're okay?"

"Piece…of…cake…" Seth replied through what must have been clenched teeth.

They watched the halfling disappear up the chute beyond the light of Glo's staff. They waited in silence after that for some sign that their friend had made it to the top. Finally, a faint light appeared far up the shaft.

"He made it!" Aksel cried.

Lloyd, Titan, Glo and Aksel all cheered, clasping each other in congratulations. A brief image popped into Glo's mind of Seth taking a deep bow. A minute later a rope dropped down from the hole in the ceiling, dangling a few inches from the floor.

A broad smile spread across Aksel's face. "Guess he wants us to climb up. Who wants to go first?"

"I will," Lloyd said perhaps a bit too enthusiastically.

Titan let out a short laugh. "Had enough of this basement maze?"

Lloyd grinned sheepishly at her. "Kind of."

The young warrior grabbed the end of the rope and gave it a hard tug, but it held fast. Flashing a quick smile, Lloyd hoisted himself up and swiftly climbed into the shaft, disappearing into the darkness.

Glo watched the rope sway and jerk as Lloyd continued his climb. Up in the shaft, the dim light at the top was now blocked by a dark shadow. Finally, the cord stopped moving. Glo gazed upward and saw the light had reappeared at the top of the chute.

"Looks like he made it," Titan said.

Aksel turned to Glo. "You go next."

Glo nodded and grasped the waiting rope. He gave it a gentle tug, but realized it was unnecessary. If the line could hold Lloyd, it would certainly hold him. He smiled wanly, then pulled himself upwards. Thankfully he was in fair shape. Practitioners of the arcane arts tended to concentrate on their minds and neglect their bodies. Glo thought that foolish; it was one of the few things he and his father agreed on.

"A weak body leads to a weak mind," Amrod would say.

As Glo shimmied up the rope, he heard Aksel talking with Titan.

"I'll go next, then you follow."

Her reply was rather skeptical. "It's not exactly easy climbing in full plate."

There was a momentary pause, then he heard Aksel's voice again. "Not a problem. Tie the end of the rope around your belt, then wrap it under your arms like a harness. When you're ready, give it a tug, and we'll haul you up."

That was smart. Secured like that, there was little chance of Titan falling.

Glo continued his ascent, his eyes fixed on the dim light above. The chute was fairly dark, but when he neared the top of it the shaft grew brighter. He was surprised to see that the chute was actually wider up here. The outline of two heads abruptly appeared above him, one smaller than the other.

"What's taking you so long?" Seth asked.

"I'm moving as fast as I can!" Glo grumbled. "This isn't as easy as it looks!"

"You should try it without a rope," came the immediate retort.

Glo chuckled in spite of himself. Seth had a point. He redoubled his efforts and was just about to the top, when two red-clad arms reached down and grabbed his own. They hauled him up the rest of the way with little effort.

Glo landed with a thud against a tiled stone floor. Next to him stood Lloyd and Seth. However, behind them was a third figure.

"Brundon…" The word tumbled from his mouth. "How? Where?"

An ironic smile crossed the lean man's face. "I don't remember much. One minute I'm in that lab. This old man bursts in and there's a flash of light. Next thing I know, I'm locked in this dark room. Then, about ten minutes ago, Seth pops his head out and says, *'How you doing, Brundon?'* I tell you, my friend, life is full of surprises."

The corner of Seth's mouth lifted somewhat. "Just wait until Titan sees you."

Glo noted a slight flush in Brundon's complexion at the mention of his partner. He silently agreed with Seth. It would be an interesting reunion. For the moment, he had an idea of what might have happened to the lean tracker. "Anyway, it sounds like you were charmed."

Brundon's eyes narrowed. "You mean a charm spell? So what you're saying is my body continued to function but my mind was put to sleep?"

Glo nodded. "More or less."

Seth snickered. "I know people who go through their whole lives like that."

They all turned to stare at the halfling.

Seth put up his hands in defense. "No one here of course."

Glo raised an eyebrow.

Lloyd turned to face Glo. "Anyway, we were just filling Brundon in on all the fun he missed."

Brundon let out a short laugh. "Heh, with fun like that, I'm glad I missed it."

Glo glanced around the room. It was a small space, the size of a single bedroom, lined with shelves. Some barrels stood against the wall with the rope he had climbed tied around one of them. There was a single door on the other side of the room.

Brundon noticed him looking around. "It's a pantry. You definitely won't starve in here."

Sure enough, the shelves were filled with foodstuffs, and unlike the room below, these were fresh. He heard a noise back by the shaft. Lloyd reached down and pulled Aksel up into the room.

Aksel was as surprised as the others to see Brundon, but the dark-haired man was looking beyond the little cleric. Aksel explained that Titan was reluctant to climb the rope wearing full plate.

Brundon appeared amused. "Sounds just like her. Give her ten orcs to fight, and she'll charge in without question. But ask her to scale a wall, and she'll give a look that would melt iron."

The rope by the chute jerked a couple of times. "I believe Titan is ready," Aksel announced.

Brundon offered to help Lloyd haul her up. The duo grabbed sections of the rope and pulled in unison, the thick cord piling up in front of the barrel. It wasn't long before a tuft of dirty blonde hair appeared at the top of the chute, followed by the gleam of torchlight off steel.

Brundon braced himself against the barrel and held the rope as Lloyd let go. He knelt down and offered an arm to his fellow warrior. Titan clasped arms with him and then Lloyd heaved hard. The tall warrior came out of the chute, landing rather solidly on one knee.

"I think...you've put on...a few pounds," Brundon huffed.

Titan looked up, her eyes widening as they fell on him. "Brundon? How?"

"Oh, you know, love, I get around." He casually stepped forward and extended a hand to her.

In one swift motion, Titan got up and swept him into her arms. She practically lifted him off the ground, grasping him in a steel bear hug. "I thought I'd lost you for good this time!" Her voice filled with emotion.

Brundon gasped at the firm embrace. "I'm…fine…love, but I won't be…if you squeeze me…to death."

Titan suddenly froze. She glanced around and saw that all eyes were fixed on them.

"Sorry," she murmured, dropping Brundon like a hot potato. Her face turned all shades of red as she took a step back. Without warning, her fist lashed out, catching Brundon square in the arm.

"Ouch, what was that for?"

"For making me worry, you jerk!" she said, mixed emotions playing across her face.

Brundon was speechless. He glanced around at the others, clearly confused at her reaction. No one said a word until Seth finally broke the awkward silence.

"Okay, okay, get a room, you two."

Glo nearly choked. Aksel raised an eyebrow, and Lloyd broke out into a wide grin. Brundon stared from the halfling to Titan, his expression incredulous. Titan said nothing. She folded her arms and glared at Seth.

Seth was not phased in the least. He brushed by them all and strode to the door. "Now then, how about we get out of here."

The halfling examined the door. "Locked, huh? Not for long." He went to work on the door mechanism and in a few seconds they heard a click. Glo heard Seth mutter under his breath. "Child's play."

Glo was impressed. He was beginning to think there wasn't a locked door or chest that was safe with Seth around. The halfling now had his ear to the door.

"Quiet," he said to them, even though no one was talking. "I hear something. It sounds like pacing. Heavy-footed, whatever it is."

Brundon dropped his voice into a hush. "Yeah, I heard it too. Whatever it is, the footsteps get softer for a bit, then get louder again. It repeats every three minutes."

"You sure?"

"Yeah, I'm sure. Timed it for about an hour. Didn't have all that much else to do." Brundon's face took on a comical cast as he glanced around the small room.

Seth cocked his head to one side. "Well then, a three minute round trip means that whatever it is will probably have its back turned for a good minute and a half—easily enough time for me to have a look around."

"Okay, but be careful," Aksel cautioned.

A mock innocent expression crossed Seth's face. "Aren't I always?"

"Not really." Glo barely suppressed a smile.

Seth glared at the wizard. Before he could fire off a retort, he was interrupted by Brundon.

"Um, before you go, you wouldn't happen to have a spare knife?" He pointed to his empty scabbard and quiver. "All my weapons appear to be gone."

"Sure." Seth pulled a knife from his belt and tossed it, hilt first, over to Brundon.

The tracker caught the dagger with ease and hefted it in his hand. "Thanks."

Seth merely nodded and went back to listening at the door. Shortly thereafter he announced, "And there it goes."

Seth turned the knob and cracked the door open. Daylight streamed into the room, confirming that they were indeed above ground. Seth opened the door a bit more and stuck his head through the doorway.

He pulled his head back in and whispered, "I might be awhile."

With that, he stepped through the doorway and closed it soundlessly behind him. Glo and Aksel exchanged glances, silently hoping their friend would be cautious this time.

14
STONE GOLEM

A true warrior makes due with his surroundings

Seth eased his way into the hall, closing the door behind him. He stopped and surveyed his surroundings, listening carefully. The only sound that reached his ears was those heavy receding footsteps.

The afternoon sun streamed through a small window high up on the wall, lighting up the hall. Directly across from him was another door. The hallway extended a few yards to the left, before making a sharp turn. At that end of the hall was another door.

Seth crept forward, making no sound as he moved. He reached the corner and peered around it. A long corridor stretched before him with many doors on either side. In the center of the hall, perhaps ten yards away, stood a huge grey creature. Thankfully, the monster's back was to him as it lumbered down the hall.

So this is the source of the footsteps. A stone golem!

The thing was huge. It was nearly twice the size of Lloyd, maybe nine or ten feet in height. Its broad shoulders were almost half as wide as it was tall. Massive arms hung down either side reaching to its knees. They ended in blocky fists as thick as those arms. The monster was quite intimidating, but Seth was not easily frightened.

It must be patrolling this hall. The question is why? All Seth could see were those doors. Since golems only did their master's bidding, it stood to reason that there was something of value behind one of them. His curiosity got the better of him. He needed to find a way out of here anyway, didn't he? He could easily duck through one of those doors before the golem turned around.

Convinced he was taking a reasonable risk, Seth crept down the hallway toward the pacing creature. He passed a few doors along the way, but something told him to keep going. He was used to trusting his instincts; they hadn't failed him yet. Halfway down the hall, he came across a flight of stairs. Ahead of him, the golem had almost reached the end of the hall. It would turn soon.

Seth made a swift decision. He darted toward the stairs, reaching them just as the golem began to turn. He flew down the stairwell to the landing below and stopped. More stairs led to a hallway below. Seth climbed down until he had almost reached the bottom. Leaning forward, he peered around the corner. The hall opened into a wide room that ended in an archway with two large doors—most likely the entrance to the keep. A huge grey figure stood between him and those doors. It was *another* stone golem! Thankfully, it was facing away from him.

Okay, this is starting to get serious. The huge rock monster was nearly identical to the one upstairs, but this golem was stationary. There were two more archways on either side of the foyer, but there was no way to get to them without passing the golem. On the other side of the stairs was a door barely hanging on its hinges.

Seth watched the stone creature for a minute or so, but it did not move. *It must be standing guard.*

Keeping one eye on the golem, he crept over to the broken door and peered inside. It was a large room with a long table surrounded by chairs, all rotted now. This must have once been a dining hall. There was another doorway leading off of it. Seth went over to that door and peeked into the next room. This was a smaller chamber with cabinets, a counter, and a large hearth at one end. It must have been the kitchen. There were no other doors in here. So much for that.

Seth stole back out into the foyer. The golem still had not moved. With nothing more to do down here, he headed back up the stairs. He stopped at the landing and waited until the heavy footsteps went by, then hurried up the second flight. Peering out into the hall he saw the first golem heading toward the end with the pantry, where his friends were hidden. Directly across from the stairs was a door. Seth silently crept over to it and tried the handle. It wasn't locked. He opened the door just enough to slip into the room, then gently pulled it closed behind him.

This room was also rather large. There were at least a dozen cots in here. Backpacks and gear were strewn all over the floor. Across the room he spied a fire pit—it had been hacked out of the solid stone floor. Seth snorted. *Leave it to bugbears to make a pit inside. Why use a kitchen when you can ruin a perfectly good floor?*

Seth stole between the cots. Without warning, something grabbed his leg! He heard a high-pitched squeal from underneath the cot next to him. He looked down and saw a small furry hand holding onto him.

Seth bent down, grabbed the arm, and gave it a hard yank. A young bugbear came tumbling out from underneath and sprawled on the floor in front of him. He almost laughed, but was stopped by the sound of sobbing. It was coming from under that same cot. *There must be another little bugbear under there.*

Seth had to silence them. If the golem heard the noise, he would be done for. He jumped on top of the bugbear, pinning it down with his knees. Seth nearly reached for his knife, then stopped himself. He was no assassin; that was his family's way.

He glanced up and spied a stray cooking pot just within reach. In one smooth motion, he grabbed the pot and conked the little bugbear on the head. It went silent. The second bugbear stopped crying, staring out at him from under the cot. Abruptly, it began to wail again, this time louder.

No help for it. Seth reached under the cot and dragged the second little bugbear out. He banged it on the head, and it too went silent, slumping down next to its companion. *That should keep them quiet for a while.*

Seth stared appreciatively at the pot in his hand. It was a handy little weapon, but he preferred his knives. He got up, threw it onto the cot and continued sneaking across the room.

Brundon sat on a barrel, ostensibly inspecting the knife Seth had given him. He preferred his bow and arrows, but if push came to shove, he was fairly handy with one of these. Every once in a while he would glance over at Delara, or Titan as she preferred to be called these days. Delara leaned silently against the wall, arms folded across her chest, her eyes straight ahead. Her expression was stony, as if wearing it would erase her outburst from before.

Brundon had gotten used to that look. It was her *talk to me and I'll break your face* expression. It meant Delara was livid about something, though he wasn't sure what. One minute she was hugging him, the next she had punched him—rather hard, too. Still, for the life of him, he couldn't figure out what he had done wrong. The wizard was the one who had captured him. He had no control over that. The fact was, he was lucky to be alive…

Oh. It finally dawned on him—she'd thought he was dead. He knew now what he had to do. He had to apologize to her, but not while she was in that mood. No, he knew better than that. He would wait till later, when Delara had finally calmed down.

In the meantime, Brundon gazed around the room at this odd little group they had fallen in with. They were not your run-of-the-mill mercenaries. On first glance, Lloyd might fit that bill, but certainly not the others. Yet they exhibited a wealth of hidden talent, including phenomenal fighting techniques, creative spellcasting, imaginative battle tactics, and strategic planning.

Of course Brundon was no novice at spotting hidden talent. That is how he met Delara, in fact. No one in Ravenford would take her seriously. She would have ended up as some low-rank guard up at the keep. Brundon saw her true potential. She was tall, strong, and could handle a blade better than any man in town. It didn't take much prodding for her to enter the mercenary business with him. They had done alright for themselves this last year. Even Delara's father begrudgingly acknowledged their success.

Aksel broke the silence. "He should have been back by now."

"The gods only know what trouble he could have gotten himself into," Glolindir agreed.

Aksel looked over at Brundon. "Can you go out there and find him?"

"Me?" Brundon feigned disbelief. "You want me to go out there?"

The little gnome's expression was one of genuine concern. "Please, Brundon? Seth could be in real danger."

"I think you underestimate your friend. From what I've seen, Seth can handle himself."

Delara spoke up for the first time in a while, "Oh go ahead, Brundon. Can't you see how worried they are?"

Brundon turned to face her. Good, she was speaking to him again. Her expression was still somewhat flinty, but maybe if he did this for them, it would put him back in her good graces.

He gave her one of his best smiles. "Very well, love, since you asked so nicely…"

He noted a flicker of amusement in Delara's eyes. Pleased with himself, Brundon sheathed the dagger in his boot, then jumped off his barrel.

"Thank you," Aksel called after him as he strode to the door.

Brundon turned and nodded. "Now, if I can have a bit of quiet? It wouldn't be good to walk out there without timing it just right."

The room fell silent as Brundon pressed his ear up to the door. The heavy footsteps were getting louder. He continued eavesdropping until they began to recede. When the footfalls had grown soft enough, Brundon pulled the door open. With a nod to the others, he slipped out into the hallway. It was bright out here. He noted the window high up on the wall and the sharp turn in the corridor opposite.

His eyes focused on the door directly in front of him. He crept over to check the knob. It was not locked. Brundon put an ear up to the door but heard nothing from the other side. He slowly opened it and eased his way in, gently closing the door behind him.

This was a well-lit room with a number of shelves. They were lined with swords, maces, lances, chainmail vests, and even full body armor, all rusted through. He had found the armory. With nothing of value left in here, Brundon went back to the door and listened.

The footfalls were still rather faint. He quietly opened the door and slipped back into the hall. There was another door where the hallway turned. He crept toward it, but when he reached the corner, his heart skipped a beat.

That is one big golem. The stone creature was near the end of the hall. It would soon turn around and head back his way. Brundon zipped across the hall and tried the other door. Luckily it was not locked. He hurriedly opened it and stepped inside, shutting the door behind him.

Brundon breathed a heavy sigh, then surveyed his surroundings. There was a large four-poster bed on the opposite wall with a night table next to it. A dresser and wardrobe stood against another wall, and a desk with a chair was against the wall next to him.

He stepped further into the room. The bed had relatively new sheets on it, but the covers had been thrown aside. It appeared as if it had recently been slept in. The door to the wardrobe hung open. Brundon glanced inside and saw some long black robes there.

So this is the wizard's bedroom. Yet there was no sign of the wizard or Seth. Brundon shrugged. *Onward then.* He placed an ear to the door. From the sound of it, the golem was right outside. Brundon gulped. He waited until the footfalls began to recede, then he opened the door a crack. The large golem trudged back down the hall away from him once more. Brundon stepped lightly out into the corridor and closed the door behind him.

There were more doors further down the hall. He had some time; he could probably get to the next door and back again if it was locked. He crept down the corridor and was almost to the next door when he heard a creak behind him. He spun around, his hand going to the knife hilt in his boot. The door to the bedroom stood open. He could have sworn he shut it. Maybe he didn't close it tightly enough, and it had swung back open. Either way, he had to close that door. If the golem saw it open, there would be trouble.

Brundon hurried back to the door, grabbed the handle and pulled it shut. He sglanced in the direction of the large stone golem. It had reached the end of the hall and was just about to turn around. Brundon scurried across the hall and slid the last couple of feet, making it behind the corner just in the nick of time. Brundon let out a long sigh, then strode over to the pantry door. He would hide back in here until the golem made another round and then try farther down the hall.

Lloyd had watched the door since Brundon left. They had been cooped up in this little room for too long now, and his nerves were on edge. He was not normally like this, but that maze in the basement had made him anxious. Lloyd did not like confined spaces. He was far more comfortable in open spaces where it was easy to wield his swords. He knew he was being foolish—he could just hear what his father would say.

"A true warrior makes do with his surroundings. One must adjust their fighting style and even weaponry. To depend on the sword and fancy maneuvers is a sure fire way to get yourself killed."

Lloyd took a deep breath and calmed himself. He *was* a warrior. He had earned the right to be called a spiritblade. Feeling more settled, Lloyd began assessing his surroundings.

These were close quarters. He and Titan would have to fight side by side to defend it. That meant no spin attacks or wide counters on his part. He would stick to simple slashes and parries. His eyes fell on the barrels at the back of the room. They might make a good blockade if need be. He strode over and tipped it slightly. It had some weight to it.

"What are you doing?" Aksel asked.

"Just being prepared." Lloyd rolled the barrel toward the door.

"Good idea," Titan said.

He glanced over as she tipped the second barrel and rolled it across the room behind him. They had just deposited both barrels on either side of the door when the knob began to turn.

Lloyd and Titan stepped back and drew their weapons. When the door opened, Brundon stepped inside.

Aksel was the first to speak. "Did you find Seth?"

Brundon put a finger to his lips, then closed the door behind him. He said in a soft voice, "There's no sign of him. But you're not going to believe—"

His statement was cut short. Lloyd heard a shout from outside the room. It was followed by the sound of heavy thumping. It sounded far away at first but swiftly grew louder. "What is that?"

Brundon slowly backed away from the door. "A stone golem!"

"A stone golem?" Aksel's voice rose in pitch.

Brundon nodded vigorously. "A big one. Think ten feet tall."

Lloyd should have been terrified, but his instincts kicked in. He grabbed his pack and rifled through it for his warhammers. Swords would be useless against stone. He glanced over and saw Titan doing the same. When they stood up, they held hammers and maces in their hands.

At that same moment, the thumping stopped. The companions listened in silence. A moment later, a scream sounded through the door. "Knock down the door! Kill them all!"

Lloyd and Titan exchanged a quick knowing glance. As one, they dropped their weapons and lunged for the barrels. Each rolled a barrel in front of the door. As the duo stood back, something heavy crashed against the door. The wood shook violently, but the barrels held it in place.

That is not going to hold for long. Lloyd braced himself against a barrel, adding his weight to it. Titan did the same. The doorway was struck a second time and the entire frame shuddered. He felt the reverberations throughout his body.

That golem can hit! One punch from that creature could kill a man. It was going to be hard to fight such a monster in these close quarters. Titan flashed him a quick smile as they prepared for the next strike.

Aksel began barking orders. "That door won't hold for long! Our only chance is escape. Brundon, quickly, down the chute. Glo, you follow him."

The door was struck. Lloyd felt his entire body shaking. Behind him the wood of the doorway was splintering and cracking. Dust fell from the stone wall surrounding the entryway. A few more blows and the whole thing would split wide open.

A voice cried out from the hallway, "Harder! Harder!"

That had to be the mage, Telvar. Lloyd glanced over his shoulder but couldn't see anything. Brundon and Glo were now gone. Aksel stood over the chute and called out to the two warriors, "I'm going next. Lloyd, you follow. Then Titan."

"I'll never make it down that rope in full plate!" Titan cried. The golem struck again. The door shook and more splinters flew, but somehow it held. It would not be long now though.

Aksel vaulted across the room and held out his hand to Titan. In it he held a ring. "Here, take this."

It was the ring of feather falling. A grim smile graced Titan's lips as she took it from him. "Thank you."

"Thank me later." Aksel sprang back toward the chute. He disappeared just as the golem struck again.

Lloyd glanced over his shoulder as a big chunk of wood splintered off the door. Sunlight streamed through the hole, and he caught a glimpse of something big and grey outside the door. *That must be the golem.*

The golem struck the door once more. This time the entire top splintered apart. The knuckles of a large grey fist protruded through what was left of the door. They could no longer hold it without getting pummeled.

Lloyd and Titan stood back, grasping their weapons and taking a defensive stance side by side. He could clearly see the golem through the top of the doorway. It pulled back one huge fist, winding up for another blow.

"Go, Lloyd! I'll hold it off until you get down," Titan yelled.

"But Titan…"

"My friends call me Delara," she whispered. "Now go!"

The golem slammed into the door. The frame cracked, and the rest of the wood pushed in against the barrels. Still the barrels held.

Lloyd did not want to leave Delara alone to face the golem. Every instinct in his body screamed for him to stand and fight. Deep down, he knew it was not a battle they could win, especially not in these close quarters, maybe not at all.

"Alright!" he said finally, "but you better be right behind me."

Delara glanced over her shoulder and winked.

Lloyd ran for the chute but did not grab the rope. Instead he jumped straight into the hole feet first. He reached for the rope as he fell, finally managing to catch hold of it. His gloved hand skidded a moment then held fast, but he didn't wait. He began a rapid, hand over hand descent downwards.

From the top of the shaft, he heard a loud crash and splintering of wood. The barrels must have finally given way. There was no time left. Lloyd loosened his grip and half slid, half fell the rest of the way to the bottom. If not for his gloves, his hands would have been stripped raw.

He reached the bottom in a matter of seconds, barely maintaining his balance as he landed. He immediately yelled up the shaft, "Titan, jump!"

Lloyd heard more crashing noises coming through the shaft. That was followed by a resounding metal clang. *Titan must have been hit!*

Anger flowed through his veins. *I should never have left her!*

Caution to the wind, Lloyd grasped the rope and began to climb back up. He heard a second metal clang then something fell into the chute above him.

A light flashed behind him, and he heard Glo's voice.

"Wait, Lloyd! Look!"

Lloyd stared at the thing falling down toward him and spotted a gleam of metal. A moment later he caught a glimpse of blonde hair. It was Titan! She had made it into the chute after all and was slowly floating down toward them.

Lloyd jumped back down and out of the way as Titan floated down from above. She landed softly on her feet and grinned at them. "See, everything is fin…" All of a sudden, her knees gave out.

"Delara!" Lloyd and Brundon cried at the same time.

Lloyd lunged forward, catching her just before she hit the ground. Brundon was immediately at her side. The two men lifted her back up while Aksel examined her. There was a huge dent in the side of Titan's armor.

"You…should see…the other…guy," she gasped, forcing a smile.

"Hold her steady." Aksel placed his hands over the dent and brilliant white light flowed forth. The reflection mirrored off Titan's armor, lighting up the entire room.

"You had us all worried for a second there, love." Brundon tried to sound casual, but there was a trace of anxiety in his voice.

She attempted a grin. "Nah, I've had worse."

Aksel grunted. "Maybe, but if you hadn't been wearing full plate, you'd probably be dead right now."

"Why do you think I wear full plate?" Titan began to laugh, then abruptly halted. "Ow, ow, ow."

Aksel glanced up at her. "You might want to refrain from laughing, at least until I fix these cracked ribs."

Titan smiled wanly at the little cleric. "Now you tell me."

Boom. The ceiling above them shuddered.

"What was that?" Brundon asked.

Lloyd looked up and saw dust falling down out of the chute.

Boom. The ceiling shuddered once more.

He caught a glimpse of movement in the shaft. More dust fell down on them.

Brundon sounded incredulous. "It's the golem. It must have jumped into the chute."

Glo came closer and held his staff up to the chute. Something large and grey blocked the shaft. "It must be stuck. Wedged in tight between the stone walls."

Brundon laughed. "Guess that thing won't be going anywhere anytime soon."

A brief wave of panic struck Lloyd. Their escape route had been cut off. "So what do we do now?"

Titan was the first to answer. "How about moving me from under all this dust? I'm going to need a bath after all this." She tried unsuccessfully to brush herself off.

Brundon grinned. "I'm sure there's one around here somewhere, love."

Lloyd and Brundon helped Titan away from the chute. Aksel insisted she lay down until he finished healing her. She begrudgingly complied.

Once she was settled, Lloyd brushed off his hands. "So then, how do we get out of here?"

Glo shrugged his shoulders. "It's not going to be easy, especially without Seth."

15
THE ANCIENT SCROLL

This would give him all the power he needed

Seth rifled through the bugbears' belongings, looking for anything of use. Unfortunately, there was nothing. Abruptly, he heard a shout in the hallway.

"Come here!" the voice cried. It was followed by heavy thudding. It swiftly grew louder, then receded.

Seth rushed to the door and opened it a crack. He saw the golem at the end of the hallway, down where the pantry was. He heard a voice yell out. "Knock down the door! Kill them all!"

Telvar! It had to be the wizard. Seth scanned the hall, but could not see anyone. Either he was around the corner or—he was invisible!

That isn't good. If this wizard could make himself invisible, then he was far more experienced than Glo. In a straight out duel, Telvar would easily kill him. Their only chance was to take this wizard by surprise. Luckily, surprise was Seth's specialty.

Bang! The sound reverberated down the hall.

The golem's trying to break into the pantry! Seth had to hurry. He pulled out a grey cloak from his pack and swiftly wrapped it around him. The color was close to the walls of the keep, and would help him blend into the background.

Bang! There was the sound again.

The door will not hold long. Seth crept out into the hall and down toward the pantry. The banging continued, now accompanied by the cracking of wood.

Seth strained his ears, hoping to hear the wizard's voice again. *If I can just pinpoint Telvar's location…*

A disembodied voice cried out, "Harder! Harder!"

The wizard was definitely nearby. Hopefully he would remain focused on the golem, but Seth had to be careful. He would only get one chance at this, and he needed to make it count.

Bang!

Seth reached the corner. The golem stood in front of the pantry door, hammering away at it. It was a mindless creature and would strictly follow its master's commands. Seth halted, straining his ears for any sign of the wizard.

Bang! Crack!

The golem smashed through the upper part of the pantry door. Seth heard Titan's voice from inside. "Go, Lloyd! I'll hold him off until you get down."

Then a disembodied voice screamed right in front of him, "Kill them all!"

Got him! Venom dagger already in his hand, Seth inched forward. He needed to be within quick stabbing distance to be sure.

"But Titan…" He heard Lloyd protest.

There was a momentary pause and then Titan yelled, "Now go!"

Seth tried his best to remain detached, but it was difficult. These were the first friends he had in, well, ever. The stone golem kicked in the bottom of the door. Wood went flying everywhere. He chanced a quick peek inside and saw Titan, shield up in front of her, mace in her other hand.

Now that's brave.

The golem inserted its bulk into the doorway and blocked his view. Seth wrenched his eyes away and listened again for the wizard.

Where was he? He forced himself to ignore the crashing and banging coming from the pantry. *There! He could hear heaving breathing right in front of him.*

A loud *clang* resounded in the pantry. *That sounded like stone on metal!* A cold chill ran up Seth's spine.

The breathing began to move. Seth followed.

A second *clang* came from the pantry, and then all sounds stopped. Telvar's voice screamed out—right in front of him, "Don't let them escape! Go after them! Down the basement! Kill them all!"

Seth had caught a glimpse of Telvar when he burst in on them in the lab. He estimated the mage to be about five and a half feet tall. With that in mind, he guessed where his heart should be. Bracing himself, he stabbed at an upward angle as hard as he could.

He was rewarded with the feeling of his dagger sliding into something. That was followed by a shrill scream. Seth ignored the cry and invoked the dagger's magic with a single word, *"Venenum."*

He must have guessed right. There was a loud groan, and whatever he had stabbed slumped down. It fell forward and hit the floor. A body materialized on the ground in front of him. It was indeed Telvar. Seth withdrew his knife and checked the mage's pulse. He was dead.

Seth heard more banging sounds from the pantry. He looked up but saw nothing there—the golem had disappeared.

Seth entered the room. The noises were coming from the chute. He went to the edge and looked down. There was something in the shaft. The obstruction began to move, thrashing around and banging against the walls.

It was the golem! It had tried to climb down and was now stuck.

Seth laughed. The mindless creature followed its master's last command faithfully. It tried to follow his friends down into the basement. When Seth finally stopped laughing, he yelled down the chute, "Are you guys down there?"

"Seth? Is that you?" It was Aksel.

"No. It's the Soldenar. Of course it's me!"

There was a slight pause, then Aksel yelled back, "Where were you?"

"I was searching the rooms. How did the golem find you?"

There was another pause, then Brundon said, "I think it was the wizard. I went looking for you and found his bedroom instead. Watch it though—I think he's invisible."

"He was," Seth yelled back, "before I killed him."

"You did what?" This time it was Glo.

"I killed him!" Seth shouted, feeling rather pleased with himself.

His enjoyment was cut short though when he heard Brundon cry. "We got trouble! It's another golem!"

Blast! The other golem was still following its master's last command. It went down to the basement to kill his friends.

Seth's mind raced. Golems were controlled by their master; that control was exerted through an item. Since Telvar was commanding the golems, he must have been carrying those items.

Aksel's voice traveled up the shaft. "Quick close the door. Lloyd, Brundon, try to hold it!"

Seth rushed back out into the hall and bent over Telvar's inert form. Fortunately, he also had some skill with magic. He normally didn't need to use it, but now his friends' lives depended on it. Seth concentrated while moving his hands over the mage's body. When the magic built enough, he said the words, *"Nullam Deprehendere."* The two rings the wizard had been wearing began to glow, as did the cloak he was wrapped in. *The spell had worked!*

The cloak could wait. Right now he was concerned with the rings. They had to be the control items, one for each golem. He bent down and slid them off the dead mage's fingers, then ran back into the pantry.

Seth heard pounding coming up the chute, followed by Brundon's frenzied cry. "We can't hold it. It's gonna break through!"

Seth yelled down the chute, "Telvar had two magical rings. I have them now."

Glo cried frantically up the shaft, "Destroy them. Quickly!"

Of course. Destroying the rings should destroy the golem!

"I'm on it!"

Seth glanced around this way and that, looking for something to smash the rings with. In the corner lay a twisted piece of gleaming metal. It was the remains of Titan's shield. It was all bent up, but Seth could still use it to crush the rings. He held them out, one in each hand. They were both plain ribbons of gold.

A crash resounded up the chute followed by Brundon's desperate cry. "It's breaking through the door!"

There was no more time. He placed the ring in his left hand down on the ground, then grabbed the heavy metal shield. He lifted it high over his head and with a swift heave brought it crashing down on the ring. There was a crunching sound as the metal slammed into the stone floor.

Down below everything went still. Seth stood frozen, listening. All at once, he heard screams.

Gods! I smashed the wrong ring.

Then he heard Aksel's voice. "You did it, Seth! You did it!"

A wave of relief washed over him. Those weren't screams of agony; they were cries of joy! "What happened to the golem?"

Glo answered this time. "It turned to dust."

The other golem started thrashing around inside the chute. Seth laughed. That one wasn't going anywhere. He looked at the second ring, still in his right hand, then pocketed it.

"I'll be right down," Seth called to his friends.

"Okay," Aksel yelled back.

Seth returned to the hall and removed the magical cloak from Telvar's corpse. *This could come in handy.* He also searched the mage's pockets and found a small book. He flipped through a couple of pages—it was a book of spells. *Glo should be able to make good use of this.*

Seth's mouth curved to one side. Things had turned out just fine after all. He was still smiling as he walked down the hall and descended the stairs to find the others.

It was midafternoon when Glo, Aksel, and Seth reentered the wizard's lab. Seth found the entrance to the basement easily from the first floor. Once down there it was only a short distance to the storage room where his friends were holed up. If they had just proceeded a bit farther in the first place, they would have stumbled across the exit. It was probably just as well. If they had taken the stairs up, they would have run into the golems out in the open, and things might not have gone so well.

Once they made it back upstairs, Seth and Brundon went to scout out the upper levels. Before he left, Seth presented Glo with Telvar's spellbook. Glo had been rather surprised; Seth could be extremely generous when he wanted to be. While they waited, Glo leafed through it.

All wizards had spell books. Glo himself had one, though it was not very full. His father had more than one. There was a particularly thick one in his father's study and a pocket-sized one his dad carried with him. Glo had not been allowed to see either. Whenever he brought up the subject, he received a lecture about the dangers of magic he was "not ready to handle". Once Glo began his arcane studies, his father gave him a few scribed pages of spells that he deemed safe. It was a very limited list.

Thus the recovery of Telvar's personal spellbook was an amazing find. Unfortunately, Glo would not be able to use most of those spells; there were many that were beyond him. Those would require far more study to master. Yet there were a few spells that he could probably teach himself, so it was not a total loss.

When Seth and Brundon returned, they announced that the place was deserted. The bugbears were nowhere to be found. They must have packed up and left while the companions were busy with Telvar and the golems.

Titan was now fully healed, thanks to Aksel. The little cleric sent Brundon, Lloyd and Titan to bury Telvar's body and retrieve their mounts. Meanwhile, Seth had led Glo and Aksel up to the top floor—the one that contained Telvar's lab. They had mapped out the first and second floors of the keep, and a good portion of the basement, but there was still no sign of Maltar's scroll. With any luck, they might find a clue in the lab.

Glo and Aksel went through the bookshelves and parchments, while Seth swept the lab for secret doors and compartments. It wasn't long before Aksel called to the others, "Look what I found." The gnome held a small book open in his hands. "It appears to be Telvar's journal."

Glo went to peer over Aksel's shoulder as he leafed through the book. "It seems that Telvar came here looking for the secret to golem creation. There are a number of references in here to scrolls and manuals that he was searching for."

"Hmmm," Glo murmured, "that's interesting. I wonder if one of those scrolls is the one Maltar wants."

"Bet Telvar would have loved to get his hands on that manual we found in the basement," Seth called from across the room. "Too bad he'll never see it now."

Glo pointed to a passage in the book. "Look here." He began to read out loud. "I've found two of the old golem master's stone golems and their control rings."

"Interesting," Aksel mused. "So Telvar did not create the golems, but rather found them."

"Doesn't surprise me," Seth remarked. He was now on the floor examining the stone tiles.

Aksel's brow furrowed. "So Telvar came here looking for the secrets to golem creation. He finds two stone golems and refers to the old golem master. Is that starting to ring any bells?"

Glo and Aksel exchanged a knowing glance. "Larketh," they said simultaneously.

Glo nodded. "It makes sense. I was leafing through that manual we found in the basement. It is highly detailed."

Aksel put down the journal. "So basically we've uncovered one of the Golem Thrall Master's old strongholds."

"I'd say so," Glo agreed.

"I found something!"

Seth knelt over a hole in the floor, a stone tile resting next to him. There was a box hidden in the space below which he ran his nimble fingers around. He stopped at one point and twisted something. There was an audible click.

"Child's play," Seth murmured softly. He reached down and lifted the box out of the hole. It was locked, but Seth swiftly picked it. He lifted the lid and whistled softly.

Glo could see a gilded scroll case inside. Seth gently lifted it out of the box and popped the lid off. The three of them peeked inside and saw the edges of a scroll. The paper looked brand new, neither yellowed with age nor frayed in the slightest. It was either a new scroll or it was indeed old with some kind of preservation spell cast on it.

Aksel was the first to speak. "I assume this is what Maltar is looking for."

Seth held the case up to Glo. "There's only one way to be sure."

Glo took it from his hand, then walked over to the nearest table. "Help me make some room."

They cleared out an area, then Glo pulled out the scroll and unrolled it onto the flat surface. To his surprise, the scroll did not contain written instructions, instead it was covered with symbols. *These are runes.* Glo was familiar with runes, but he had never seen ones like these before.

Seth grew impatient. "Well? Is it the one?"

Glo was too absorbed to answer. There was something strange about these runes, as if they exuded—*power.* That was it! *These are runes of power. This scroll must have been written by an ancient wizard.* It was a magic so far beyond Glo that it made the spells he knew look like children's toys. And look at how much damage he had done with those.

The explosion atop the tower replayed through his mind. This time he did not flinch. He accepted it for the mistake it was. Glo needed to be far more careful with magic from now on. A spell like the one now in front of him belonged with someone who could handle it, someone like his father or Maltar. Having made up his mind, Glo picked up the scroll and rolled it up.

"Is everything ok?" Aksel asked.

"Oh, yes, everything's fine," Glo assured him. "This is indeed the scroll Maltar is looking for." He slid it back into the case and closed the lid.

"That's great, Glo, but are you sure you're alright?"

Glo turned to face his friends. He noted the worried expression on Aksel's face. Much to his surprise, he also saw something bordering on concern in Seth's eyes. A genuine smile crossed his lips. "Let's just say that I'm learning not to play with fire."

Seth snorted. "That'll be the day."

The sound of horses' hooves reached them through the open window. They looked out into the courtyard and saw Brundon, Titan and Lloyd leading a string of horses and dogs through the open entrance where the main gate used to stand.

"Let's head back down," Aksel said. "If we leave now, we can be back in Ravenford before dark."

The wizard Maltar was sitting in his lab when he heard a quiet knock at the door. "What is it?" he yelled, not bothering to get up.

"There are some travelers to see you, Master," a voice said from the other side.

Maltar grew angry. "Tell them to go away!" *Stupid apprentices. They should know better than to bother me while I'm busy.*

"But, Master," replied the fawning voice, "they say they've found the scroll you were looking for."

Travelers? What travelers? Oh, yes, he remembered. *That table of common buffoons I found at the inn yesterday. They found the…*

Maltar paused in mid thought, sprang up and rushed to the door. He swung it open and stared into the face of his disciple.

"Did you say they found the scroll?"

"Yes, Master," the apprentice said nervously.

This he had to see for himself. If these charlatans were trying to pass off a fake scroll to him, he would fry the lot of them.

"Where are they?"

"Downstairs, Master. In the parlor."

Maltar dashed down the stairs, half annoyed and half excited. When he got to the parlor, he found four young people sitting there—a human in red leather armor, an elf in bright purple robes, a halfling dressed in black, and a gnome in white cleric's robes. Yes, now he remembered. These were the riffraff from the tavern the other day. He had sought them out after hearing about their success fending off a band of orcs. He thought perhaps they might not be too inept to map out the keep on Stone Hill for him. Was it possible that they found the scroll?

The travelers all rose as he entered the room.

Calming himself, Maltar addressed them congenially, "Welcome. I hear that you have completed the errand I bestowed on you."

The gnome spoke for the group. "Yes, we have, Wizard Maltar. We have been to Stone Hill. Here is a map of the ruins, as you asked." The little gnome walked over and handed him a packet of parchments.

Maltar took the papers and looked them over. This was not what he was interested in. *If they're wasting my time…*

The elf stepped forward. In his hands, he held a gilded scroll case. "And here, I believe, is the scroll that you were looking for."

Maltar reached out and took it from the elf. With trembling hands, he opened the end and peered inside. The parchment appeared brand new. He emptied the contents into his hands, handing the case back to the elf. He unraveled the scroll just enough to see the writing.

Those runes. This is it! It was the scroll he'd been looking for. This would give him all the power he needed. Now they would have to accept him!

Someone cleared their throat, breaking Maltar out of his revelry. It was the gnome.

"There is the matter of our reward?"

"Yes, yes." Maltar waved a hand to his apprentice. "Pay them. Five thousand gold, I believe."

"Five thousand, five hundred," the halfling corrected him. "Five hundred for the map, and five thousand for the scroll."

"Yes, that's right," Maltar said absently. "Pay them five thousand, five hundred gold," he ordered his apprentice.

He could not believe they found the scroll. Maybe this little band was not as useless as he originally thought. The old wizard grabbed the case and placed the scroll back inside. He then turned to leave the room, but someone cleared their throat again.

"Yes?" Maltar asked, over his shoulder, his eyes fixed on the scroll case in his hands.

"Please let us know if we can ever be of service to you again," the gnome said.

Maltar pursed his lips and nodded. "Yes, indeed I will."

With that he hurried out of the room and back upstairs. He had much preparing to do before he would be ready. But he had the scroll. Finally!

Lloyd, Seth, Glo, and Aksel strolled down the road away from Maltar's cottage. Seth held a satchel full of coins in his hands that jingled as he walked.

Seth appeared quite satisfied. "Well, that was profitable."

"Yes. Not so bad for our first team mission," Aksel agreed.

"So what's next?" Lloyd asked.

Seth responded almost immediately, "I for one would like to return to Stone Hill. If we could figure out how to work that ring, we could control that Golem."

Glo gazed at him, his expression skeptical.

Seth shrugged. "What? It could come in handy. And, of course, I still want my couch."

Glo, Aksel, and Lloyd all turned to stare at the halfling. Seth wore a wide grin. The three of them burst into laughter. Still chuckling, they continued on their way toward the inn.

16
WIZARDS' DUEL

You seem to have a habit of killing wizards, young elf

The common room of the Charging Minotaur had been abuzz since the companions return from their excursion to Stone Hill. Brundon sat at the bar, relating a somewhat embellished version of the story to any and all who cared to hear the tale; and in a small town like Ravenford, that was pretty much everyone.

Lloyd, Seth, Aksel, and Glo sat quietly at a table in the center of the room. Folks at the bar would occasionally raise a mug in their direction. A couple of them even bought them drinks.

The effervescent Kailay waited on them. She circled around the table and laid out their dinner plates, making an extra fuss over Lloyd. "Is all that really true? Did you actually fight off an army of bugbears, skeletons and zombies; plus five stone giants *and* an evil wizard?"

The companions exchanged brief smiles, then Aksel spoke for the group. "Let's just say that Brundon has a tendency to stretch the truth."

"There weren't that many monsters or golems," Lloyd said inbetween bites. The young man was ravenous from the exertions of the last two days and dug into his meal as if he hadn't eaten the entire time.

Kailay placed her hands on her hips and gave them all a stern look. "Either way, this town is grateful to you for clearing out that den of monsters." She leaned over and placed a hand on Lloyd's arm. He stopped mid-fork full and glanced up at her. "And I for one am very grateful," she added in a soft voice.

Lloyd dropped his fork and sat back, his face reddening. Glo and Aksel tried hard not to laugh. Seth wore a half-twisted grin.

"It…was nothing…nothing at all," the young man stammered.

Kailay slowly stood up, obviously pleased with the effect she was having on him. "Well, I think you should be rewarded," she continued in a sultry voice. "Let me know if there is anything else I can do for you."

Lloyd turned positively scarlet, his face nearly as red as his armor. Kailay flashed him an impish smile then slowly sauntered away.

"I'd say you're going to have to do something about that one."

Glo turned and saw Titan standing behind him. She wore an amused expression.

Lloyd, still flustered, responded in a quiet voice, "Ummm…yeah, I guess."

Titan shook her head and smiled. "Lloyd, you are something. You're not afraid of monsters, mages, or even stone golems; but one small blonde girl frightens you to death."

The entire table burst into laughter. Even Lloyd grinned, albeit sheepishly. Titan pulled up a chair and sat with them. "It's alright my friend. We all have our weaknesses." She leaned forward. "Brundon actually has two of them—fame and fortune."

Glo glanced over at the bar. Brundon was still telling stories, his arms waving around, the audience wrapped in his ongoing tale.

Aksel shrugged. "As you said, everyone has their weak points."

She nodded. "True enough. Still, as a whole, I think we made a pretty good team."

"I'll second that." Lloyd held his mug aloft. "To teamwork."

Titan, Glo, Seth, and Aksel raised their tankards as well. "To teamwork." The five of them knocked mugs together and downed their ales.

When they were done, Titan put her hands on the table and rose. "Gentlemen, it has been a pleasure. If you are ever in need of help…"

"Thanks, Titan. The same goes for you," Aksel said.

A genuine smile crossed Titan's lips, her face softening dramatically. "My friends call me Delara," she said in a voice only they could hear.

Glo had never seen the warrior let her guard down before. Her blue eyes danced, lighting up her face, revealing her to be a striking young woman.

"Delara, then." Aksel's face softened.

Delara's smile lasted a moment longer, then faded, her face assuming its normal stony mask. Glo was amazed at the transformation. The lovely Delara was gone, replaced with the warrior Titan. She bid them goodnight and strode back to the bar.

"She is some warrior," Lloyd declared.

Glo nodded. "Indeed. They don't come much braver. She almost got herself killed holding off that golem."

Aksel stroked his chin. "I could definitely see hiring her again."

The side of Seth's mouth rose ever so slightly. "Even if it means bringing along Brundon?"

Aksel shook his head, the corners of his mouth upturning.

Lloyd threw down his fork and knife onto his empty plate. "Speaking of work, what do we do next?"

Seth was the first to speak up. "Well, I would like to go get that golem."

"Hmmm," Aksel murmured, "I think we should figure out how to control the golem first. It wouldn't do to set it free and have it try to kill us again."

Seth leaned back in his chair, his hands folded behind his head. "I'm working on that."

Aksel appeared skeptical. "Really? How's that going so far?"

"Well, Glo and I found some hints in the golem creation manual.

It said the control item needs a password to make it work. We also found a passage in Telvar's notes. It alluded to the control item and mentioned something about Telvar's first love."

Aksel raised an eyebrow. "Please continue."

Seth stared up at the ceiling as if the answer was written up there somewhere. "I looked over the ring itself, but there were no markings of any kind on it." He shrugged and looked at Glo.

Glo picked up where Seth left off. "So, considering that Telvar is dead, we were thinking Maltar might have known him. If he did, he may be able to tell us something about the man."

Aksel folded his hands in front of him on the table. "Okay, assuming we do gain control of the golem, the next step would be to get it out of the chute."

Lloyd opened his mouth, but Aksel held up a hand. "The thing probably weighs a ton. I doubt even you and Titan together could lift it."

"It was worth a shot," Lloyd murmured.

So how would we get the golem out of the chute then? Glo thought. As Aksel just pointed out, it was too heavy to lift. So if it could not go up, then it had to go down; but it was far too big to fit through the chute. Too bad it was made of stone. If it wasn't so solid, it could just slide down the chute. *Wait, that's it!*

"Stone to Mud," he said aloud.

"Stone to Mud," Aksel repeated. "You mean, change the golem from solid earth to liquid earth?"

Seth nearly jumped out of his chair. "That would do it! The golem would practically drip out of the chute into the basement."

Aksel stared at Glo dubiously. "But isn't that a complicated spell? I mean, no offense, but aren't you a bit inexperienced to cast that?"

"Oh yes, that spell is definitely beyond me…"

"…but it wouldn't be beyond Maltar." Seth finished for him. He could hardly contain his excitement.

"No, it certainly wouldn't." Aksel leaned back and stroked his chin. "However, I am fairly certain it would come at a price. We would need a scroll inscribed with the spell, and then a second scroll to change it back. A mud golem would be pretty useless."

Glo pressed his fingers together in front of his lips. "So two scrolls: Stone to Mud, and the reverse spell, Mud to Stone. I agree, he isn't just going to give them to us for nothing."

Seth grinned impishly. "Doesn't hurt to ask."

Glo shook his head. He knew Seth would continue to pester him till he agreed. "Very well. I'll go talk with Maltar in the morning, but Aksel is right. This is all moot if we can't figure out how to use the ring."

Seth stretched and yawned. "Don't worry so much. I'm sure… we'll figure…it out."

It was getting late, and they were bone weary from a long, strenuous couple of days. They got up, left Kailay a generous tip, and headed to their rooms for a well-deserved rest.

After breakfast the next morning, Glo left for Maltar's cottage. He was deep in thought and missed the tavern door quietly opening and closing behind him as he stood outside the tavern.

Maltar had quite a reputation in these parts. He was quite adept with arcane magic, but was equally well known for being a recluse, and a bit short tempered. A number of young people had studied with him, including both Xelda and the Lady Andrella, only to quit due to his lack of patience. All in all, he was not the most ideal person to be asking for anything. Just how was he going to approach the old mage?

Glo was so preoccupied that he was in front of Maltar's cottage before he knew it. It really was a homey place, with its dark brown exterior, green shutters, and white picket fence, but the pleasant exterior belied the temperament of its primary inhabitant.

Oh well, here goes nothing.

Glo opened the gate and strode up the narrow walkway to the front door. He hesitantly raised a hand and knocked. There was no response. Glo waited in silence, doing his best to appear calm; inwardly, he was still nervous about this whole encounter. When the front door finally opened, a thin, pale young man in grey robes stood there. Glo did not recognize him. He must have been another one of Maltar's apprentices, one they had not seen yesterday.

The lean apprentice glared. "What is it?"

Glo tried his best to be polite. "Is Maltar home?"

The apprentice made an unpleasant face. "Who wants to know?"

"My name is Glolindir. My friends and I had done your master a service yesterday. I was wondering if I could ask him a couple of follow-up questions—"

"The master's busy and cannot be interrupted. Now go away." He stepped back and swung the door shut.

"Wait!" Glo cried. He stepped forward before the door completely closed, but the apprentice did not stop. The door slammed on Glo's foot.

"Ouch!" Glo's foot was now wedged in the doorway, caught between the door and the frame. He tried pulling back, but his foot was firmly stuck. He nearly lost his balance trying to get free, barely keeping himself from falling backwards.

Glo was not quite sure what happened next. It wasn't the pain; the door hadn't been slammed that hard. Nor was it the feeling of foolishness as he stood there with his foot caught in the door. Perhaps it was an instinctive reaction after having been in life threatening situations over the last few days. Either way, whatever the reason, Glo lost control.

He lifted a finger and spoke the words that sent a magical projectile careening from his hand. It passed through the crack in the door, followed by a *thud* and a low groan. A second later, the door swung wide open. The apprentice stood there, a scorch mark on his chest from where the missile had exploded. The anger drained out of Glo, replaced with guilt over what he had done.

Unfortunately, the apprentice was now enraged. The lean man opened his mouth as if to scream, but then instead raised his hands in a familiar pattern. *He is going to cast a spell!*

Glo stepped back and threw up his hands. "I'm sorry!"

The apprentice ignored him. His hand pointed at Glo and he uttered the words, "*Ardens Man—*"

Glo knew full well what was coming. He was about to be burnt, just like those bugbear mages. He cringed, waiting to be engulfed in a cone of flame. Luckily, it never came.

The apprentice stopped mid-word. His eyes widened and his face twisted. He stared at Glo and tried to say something, but nothing came out but gurgling sounds. The wizard's apprentice fell to his knees, then keeled over onto his face. His body lay still across the open entryway.

Glo spied a small figure standing in the foyer just behind the fallen apprentice. It was dressed all in black with the exception of a green cloak. A dagger gleamed in one hand. Recognition slowly dawned on him.

It's Seth! Where did he come from?

Glo stared from his friend down to the body on the ground and then back up again. "Seth? How did you—"

Glo stopped short; this was not the time for questions. He bent down and checked the man's pulse but couldn't find one. He gazed up at Seth woodenly as the full weight of what just happened hit him. Glo spoke in a hushed voice, "He's dead."

Seth dropped the dagger, his eyes misting over. His voice broke as he stared back at Glo. "He was going to…I didn't mean to…" Seth's face contorted into a look of anguish. "I am not an assassin!" he hissed.

Glo immediately understood what had happened. Seth was merely trying to protect him. Unfortunately, the halfling was just a bit too good with his knives. He was about to tell Seth that very thing when they heard a commotion from inside the house.

"What's going on out there? Who's disturbing my work?" It was Maltar.

This is not good. If Maltar found them with his dead apprentice, he might just blast them out of existence. *It's my fault. I'll accept the consequences alone.*

His voice was harsh as he hissed at Seth. "Quick, hide!"

Seth was frozen in place. "But…"

"There's no time. Get out of here."

Seth stood there for a moment longer, then snatched up his fallen dagger. He grabbed his cloak, said a single word, then disappeared from sight.

Glo was startled. *Seth can turn invisible?* There was no more time to think about it. The next moment, Maltar entered the foyer.

The master wizard stomped toward the nervous elf. "There better be a good explanation—" He stopped in mid-sentence, staring at the grey-robed body draped across the open doorway. Maltar's eyes narrowed. "What's this? Flibin, get up! Don't just lie there!"

"I'm afraid he can't," Glo said softly.

Maltar turned his gaze on Glo. "And why not?"

Glo tensed himself for the inevitable response. "Because he's dead."

Maltar stared at Glo, his expression uncomprehending. "Dead? Did you say dead?"

Before Glo could respond, Maltar did something he would never have expected. He stepped close to the body of the hapless apprentice, pulled back a leg, and then kicked the corpse. When the man did not respond, Maltar kicked him a second time, and then a third.

Glo's eyes widened in disbelief. Just what kind of man was this Maltar?

Maltar finally stopped kicking the corpse. His voice was devoid of emotion as he spoke. "Yep, he's dead alright." Maltar peered up at him. Glo could feel his skin crawl as those dark, penetrating eyes bore their way into his soul. The mage then spoke in a commanding voice, "Tell me exactly what happened."

Glo gulped at first, then related what had transpired between him and Flibin, including the apprentice's rude behavior and his own lapse in judgement. He finished with Flibin's demise but left Seth out of it, claiming complete responsibility for the apprentice's death. He had been the one who lost his temper. If anyone deserved to be punished for the crime, it was him, and him alone.

Maltar's gaze did not waver, his face a grim mask as he stared at Glo. The young elf expected at any moment to see the mage lift his hands and send him spiraling into oblivion. Then, without warning, Maltar threw back his head and let out a frightening cackle.

"Ah ha ha!" The mage let out a shrill laugh. It was a hideous sound. Glo thought the man might be dying.

Maltar gasped in-between cackles. "Serves…him…right! I told him…he needed…to be faster…with his spells." The mage paused a moment to catch his breath. "So you got the drop on him, huh?

Ha, ha, ha." Maltar continued to chortle, doubling over and slapping his knee. He went on like that for a good while. Finally, the mage straightened up, tears of laughter streaming down his face. He wiped his eyes with his sleeve, then produced a handkerchief out of nowhere and blew his nose. When he was done, the kerchief magically disappeared.

His eyes settled on Glo once more. When he spoke, his tone was almost jovial. "Very good, very good. Come on in." Maltar motioned for him to follow.

Glo was stunned. Maltar's reaction was unfathomable. It was as if he had no regard for the life of his apprentice. Glo felt numb from head to toe. He woodenly obeyed the mage, as if watching his body from the outside as it stepped over the corpse of the fallen apprentice and followed Maltar into the hallway.

Down the hall past the mage, Glo spied a man and woman in robes. Maltar called out to them, "Flibin's gone and got himself killed. Go fetch the body from the foyer and bring it over to the temple. This young wizard will be over shortly with the money to raise him."

Maltar turned around and looked Glo in the eye. His tone was deceptively mild, but the intensity of his gaze was frightening. "You will raise him, won't you?"

Glo realized that he was being tested. Maltar's crude display had caught him off-guard, but the old mage hadn't totally written off his apprentice. The temple would have experienced clerics, ones that could restore the life of a recently departed soul. It was a spell of divine magic, commonly termed "Resurrect the Dead". It was similar to what Aksel did with healing, but this spell required ingredients to cast—rather costly ingredients. Furthermore, there was no guarantee the spell would work. It greatly depended on the state of the body and the willingness of the spirit to return to the world of the living.

Still, Maltar's test was a no-brainer for Glo. If there was a chance to atone for his mistake, to pay for the hapless Flibin's restoration, he would take it. It would cost quite a bit of money, but it was worth it. This was not some flesh-eating orc, bugbear, or undead creature. This was the life of a human being.

Glo stared back at Maltar unflinching. "Of course. As soon as we are done here, I will get the money and bring it to the temple."

Maltar held his gaze for a moment more, then nodded with approval. "Very good. Now that that's settled, we can get down to business."

The mage turned and led him into the parlor, the room in which they met yesterday. It was furnished with a long brown couch, a couple of red padded chairs, a coffee table, and two end tables on either side of the couch. Long red drapes framed the windows on the exterior walls. Maltar motioned Glo to have a seat on the couch. The mage unceremoniously plopped himself down in a padded chair across from him.

"What can I do for you?" Maltar said.

Glo cleared his throat, still not sure where to begin. He decided to just lay it all on the table and hope that Maltar's good mood would make him amenable to their request. "I was with the group that procured that scroll for you yesterday."

"Yes, yes, I thought you looked familiar. Go on, go on."

"Well, at the ruins we ran into another wizard. He was the one who had possession of the scroll."

Maltar's eyes narrowed. "Another wizard? Had possession of my scroll?"

This was not going the way Glo had hoped. He needed to quickly allay Maltar's concerns. "He's dead now. He was a dark mage, and we had no choice but to dispatch him."

Maltar continued to stare at him. "Hmmm, you seem to have a habit of killing wizards, young elf."

Glo was not sure how to react. Maltar's face was unreadable; he could not tell if the mage was getting angry. There were a few moments of uncomfortable silence.

"Did you ever find out this dark mage's name?"

Glo was still nervous and the words came tumbling out of his mouth. "Yes. His name was Telvar. He had taken up residence at the keep."

A smug smile crept across his Maltar's face. "Telvar? That hack!" He paused a moment, then leaned forward. "And you killed him?"

Glo smiled back wanly at the wizard. "Yes. He gave us little choice."

Maltar gave him an approving nod. "Good, good." The mood in the room lightened considerably after that. "He was more of a nuisance than a wizard. He was always trying to compete with me, not that he could even come close, mind you. So, I don't suppose you know what Telvar was up to in those old ruins, nor how he came across my scroll?"

"Well…" Glo hesitated, deciding what to say. The mage looked pleased at the moment, and he did not want to say anything that would change his mood. "…we did find his laboratory. He appeared to be researching the process of golem creation, best we could tell."

Maltar raised an eyebrow. "Golem creation? Interesting. Go on."

"He also had two stone golems with him in the ruins."

Maltar stood up suddenly. "He had two stone golems?" The mage began to pace around the parlor. "Now how would that third rate hack come by stone golems?" Maltar whirled on Glo. "You did say two golems."

Glo nodded. Maltar was turning out to be quite an unpredictable character. His emotions vacillated wildly from one extreme to the other. Glo felt like he was walking on eggshells around this mage. Even his father, Amrod, was not this temperamental. He continued with the story, hoping his explanation would mollify the irascible wizard.

"Yes. His notes indicated that he found the golems and their control items in the ruins. And although he was researching the golem creation process, there was no indication that he actually discovered how to make one on his own."

Maltar visibly relaxed. His shoulders dropped, and he stopped pacing. "Very good. That was a very thorough piece of investigating there." He looked at Glo appraisingly for a few moments, then sat back down across from him. "So tell me, where are these two stone golems now?"

Glo eyed the old mage carefully. "We had to destroy one of them."

Maltar's eyes grew wide with disbelief. "You…destroyed…a stone golem?"

Glo threw up his hands. "No, no, not me alone. It took the combined efforts of our entire party."

Maltar glared at Glo with suspicion. "Really? Your entire party?" Maltar pointed down at the floor. "The entire group that was here yesterday?"

Glo's nerves had returned, and the words spilled out quickly. "The four of us and the two mercenaries we hired to help us. They're regulars around town."

Maltar shifted in his seat. He continued to stare at Glo as he digested what he had told him. After a long pause, he began to speak again.

"I would know if there was anyone in this town who had the power to destroy a stone golem. Therefore, I can only assume that you and your companions were primarily responsible for its demise. Though I will say, I am surprised." The master wizard stared at Glo as if he saw him anew. "And the second golem?"

Glo fumbled for the words. This was the tricky part. "Um, yes… that is the reason I am here. The other stone golem is still intact. However, it is stuck in a shaft between floors in the keep."

Maltar sat forward in his chair. "Come again?"

Glo explained as quickly as he could. "We were in a pantry. There was a chute in one corner that led down to the basement. We figure it must have been a dumbwaiter for carting up food from storage. When the stone golem came after us, we all retreated down the chute and into the basement. Telvar ordered it to follow us, but the shaft narrowed farther down, and the golem got stuck."

Maltar eyes grew softer as he began to grasp the truth of the tale. Glo realized this next part was crucial. He needed to be very careful how he phrased it.

"After Telvar's demise, we found the control item for the second golem on him. We were thinking, if we could figure out the password to it and then free the golem, it might be handy to have around." Glo watched the mage apprehensively, not sure how the man would react to his statement.

Maltar sat back in his chair and seemed to consider his words. "Yes, yes, a construct like that could indeed come in handy. To free it, you would need a spell of Stone to Mud. Then to repair it, you would need a spell of Mud to Stone."

The mage sat forward again. "I can make up scrolls for you, but those are not cheap." Maltar paused a moment as if to calculate the price in his mind. "It will cost you 4000 gold pieces each."

Glo nodded. "Understood." The price was actually a bit steep, but there was nowhere else they were going to get them around here. Frankly, Glo was just relieved that the mage was willing to make the scrolls for them.

Maltar got up from his chair. "Excellent." He paused and looked down at Glo with those piercing eyes. "You are very to the point, young wizard. I can work with that. I seem to have an apprentice spot to fill at the moment. Tell me, would you be interested?"

Glo's eyebrow shot up. Apprentice? To this volatile human? That would be worse than studying with his father. At least with Amrod he knew what to expect. He had known his father all his life and was aware of what the older elf's limits were. This Maltar was a loose cannon that could go off at any second. Still, if he did not accept the mage's offer, he was just as likely to be offended. If that happened, they would get nothing out of him. It looked like he had little choice. Glo swallowed hard. "Why, I would be honored."

Maltar nodded with approval. "Very good. Now as far as the control item password, that could be anything."

Glo sat forward in his seat. "Yes, but there was a hint in Telvar's notes. It mentioned something about Telvar's first love."

Maltar let out a short laugh. "Heh. Telvar's first love, you say? Well, I knew the wretch for a long time, and I can tell you, Telvar never loved anyone but himself."

Glo was about to respond when the two other apprentices entered the parlor. Maltar turned and gazed at them expectantly. "Well?"

The woman was the one who responded. "Flibin's body has been taken to the temple as you instructed. The clerics are preparing him to be raised. They will start the ceremony as soon as they receive their fee."

Maltar appeared pleased. "Good, good." He motioned the duo to join them. "Abracus, Gristla, this is Glolindir. He is my new apprentice."

Gristla's eyes widened and Abracus's mouth fell open. They swiftly recovered, most likely used to Maltar's ever changing temperament. Both apprentices reached forward and grasped Glo's hand in turn, welcoming him to their small group.

Maltar seemed rather pleased. "Glolindir here is quite resourceful, as you have seen. He will keep you on your toes." He turned to face Glo. "And, Glolindir, if either of these two gives you any trouble, you have my permission to give them the same treatment you did Flibin."

The other two apprentices stared at their master with expressions of disbelief. Glo was about to assure them that he would never do such a thing, when the mage turned and slapped him on the back.

"That'll keep them on their toes!" Maltar chortled wildly. The unpredictable mage then spun on his heel and strode out of the room. "This audience is over," he called back over his shoulder. "Abracus! Gristla! Provide Glolindir with what he will need to perform his duties as my apprentice."

With that, Maltar disappeared, leaving the three young mages staring at each other in astonishment.

17
RAVENFORD KEEP

The keep proper stood in front of them, reaching high into the blue skies above

Glo returned to the Charging Minotaur and found his companions waiting for him in a booth near the hearth. Seth had returned earlier and told them what had happened with Flibin. By the time Glo arrived, they had already put two and two together and figured they would have to pay for the resurrection. Aksel and Lloyd both thought it was the right thing to do. Seth, still mortified over what happened, raised no objections.

Glo had discussed the details of the resurrection with Gristla and Abracus. Originally it would have cost them 5,000 gold pieces just for the spell ingredients, but Maltar had some kind of deal with Abbot Qualtan. It turned out that he was another of Maltar and Gryswold's traveling companions from back in their adventuring days. Thus, the total charge for resurrecting Flibin was only 4,000 gold. Seth insisted on walking the fee over to the temple. It was obviously something he needed to do.

Meanwhile, Lloyd, Glo and Aksel discussed their options. They now had only 1,000 gold pieces. They would need at least 8,000 gold to pay for the scrolls to free the golem. Three days had passed since they left on Maltar's quest, so that meant there would be a town meeting today. With any luck, they could get hired out for a job. That would meet both their goals: lending their skills where they were most needed and making some money toward acquiring the scrolls. When Seth returned, they agreed to head up to the keep.

Aksel glanced around the table. "We should dress in our best clothes…"

"Why?" Lloyd said suddenly.

Seth looked at Lloyd as though he were crazy. "We're going to court. What else would you wear?"

Lloyd flushed. He gazed down at the table and mumbled, "I don't know." Just as suddenly, he looked up, his face alight. "Maybe we should show up in our battle gear. It will look more like we mean business."

Seth stared incredulously at Lloyd. "Why that's the stupidest idea…"

Aksel raised a hand, cutting him off. "They don't know us up at the keep. Showing up in full battle gear might make them think we are looking for trouble."

Lloyd let out a deep sigh. Something was definitely wrong; this was not like Lloyd at all. Glo glanced at Aksel and Seth. Both just shook their heads. Glo turned back to Lloyd. "Are you alright?"

The young man gazed at Glo with an almost pleading look in his eyes. It was only there for a moment and then it was gone, replaced by an embarrassed smile. "I'm fine. You're right. We should dress our best." Before anyone could respond, he slid out of the booth. "No use sitting around. Let's get ready." With that, he crossed the common room toward the back hallway.

When he was out of earshot, Seth turned to the others. "What was that all about?"

"I have no idea," Aksel replied.

Neither did Glo. There was definitely something Lloyd was not telling them. He had been skirting around it since they had first met.

Still, whatever it was, it was his business. For now, they all needed to get changed. The trio followed him upstairs. When Glo reached their room, Lloyd was sitting on his bed. His armor was off, and in its place he wore a plain white shirt. On the bed lay a fancy red tabard. Lloyd looked sullenly at the sleeveless coat as if loathing to put it on. Glo spoke tentatively to him, "That's a nice looking tabard."

Lloyd glanced up. "Thanks."

"Well, are you going to put it on?"

"Yes." Lloyd stood up, grabbed the tabard, and pulled it over his head, straightening it out as it fell over his tall frame. There was a large insignia on the front; the shape of a majestic lion with two swords crossed underneath it against a black and red background. Farther down was another smaller symbol, this one of a sailing ship on a blue and red background. There was a smaller lion next to it, and two more swords crossed underneath. Once again, Glo was hesitant to comment.

"That's an interesting insignia."

"It's the symbol of Penwick," Lloyd said proudly, smoothing out the cloth. All traces of doubt were suddenly gone. Lloyd stood tall and majestic in his fine attire.

Glo was thankful to see his friend no longer sullen. "It looks good on you."

Lloyd smiled back at him. "Thanks."

Glo went to his dresser and rummaged through his own clothes. He had dress robes in here somewhere. He continued to talk as he searched. "So the symbol of Penwick is both a lion and a ship?"

"Well, umm, not exactly. The ship is…the symbol of the Penwick Navy."

"That's right. You said your dad was in the navy."

Glo finally found them. He pulled out a silky purple robe of much finer material than his travel robe. It was emblazoned with three interlocked white triangles. He shook the robe, trying to get the wrinkles out.

Lloyd came closer and bent down for a better look. "Is that the symbol of your town?"

"No, it's the crest of my family."

Lloyd's face took on a strange expression. "Are you a noble?"

"Um, I don't know if it translates exactly. My family belongs to the House of Eodin. It is one of the seven major houses of Cairthrellon."

"So that would make your family one of the most respected in your city."

Glo raised an eyebrow. "You could say that."

Lloyd's expression turned thoughtful. "I am sure that position comes with a lot of responsibility."

"It has its share."

An ironic smile crossed the young man's face. "It's kind of funny, you know. Most people think of nobles as lucky. They see it for the money, the power and the fame. What they don't get is the obligations that go along with it. It's less about what you get than what you give."

Glo was amazed. That was a very profound observation. Up till now, he had thought of Lloyd merely as a warrior, but the young man had surprising depth. He was about to ask Lloyd how he knew so much about nobility, when someone pounded on the door.

"Hurry up in there! We don't have all day." It was Seth.

"Just a minute!" Glo yelled.

He flashed Lloyd a quick grin then doffed his regular robes and pulled on the dress ones. Meanwhile, Lloyd went to open the door. Seth walked in with Aksel trailing behind him. The former wore a fancy green dress jacket over his black outfit. The latter was garbed in bright white robes with the symbol of his faith on them.

Aksel stopped in front of Lloyd. "You look nice."

"Yeah, I don't know what you were so worried about," Seth added thoughtlessly.

Lloyd shrugged his shoulders. "It's no big deal."

Glo finished straightening his robes and glanced around the room. "Alright then, let's go."

The four companions headed downstairs and through the tavern. Kailay dashed over as they passed the bar. She looked them all over appreciatively, though her eyes lingered a bit longer on Lloyd once again. "Wow! Don't you all look nice. What's the fancy occasion?"

"We're off to the town meeting," Glo confided. "If we're lucky, maybe we'll find some work."

"That's a great idea," Kailay whispered back conspiratorially. She looked them all over once more and then stepped closer to Lloyd. She placed a hand on the young man's chest. "That looks like very fine material."

Lloyd froze where he was, clearly embarrassed. Kailay ran her hand over the material. "My mom is the town tailor. I've learned a few things by watching her."

Lloyd's face reddened further. Aksel came to his rescue. "Ahem. I'm sorry, Kailay, but we really need to get going. I'm sure we'll see you when we get back."

Kailay was clearly disappointed. Nonetheless, she dropped her hand and stepped back, her eyes still fixed on Lloyd. "Okay, but promise to come and see me later."

Lloyd managed a nervous, "Okay."

"Great!" Kailay flashed him a bright smile, then whirled around and ran back to the bar.

The four companions exited the tavern and headed in the direction of the keep. As they strode along, Glo stole a sidelong glance at Lloyd. The young man wore a troubled expression, as if wrestling with some internal conflict. Perhaps it had to do with Kailay. Lloyd had been rather hesitant to act on her advances. Or maybe it had nothing to do with her at all. Maybe it had something to do with their earlier discussion about nobility and responsibility. Lloyd seemed awful passionate about that.

The little band reached the base of the hill below the town keep. A road led up the hillside, ending at the entrance. High walls enclosed the grounds, capped with parapets at regular intervals. A tall, rounded tower stood in one corner. Only the top of the main keep was visible beyond. The front entrance consisted of a wide archway; the black iron base of a thick portcullis hung suspended in the top of the arch. Two guardsmen stood on either side of the entrance. They wore black and white tabards over chainmail suits with an insignia emblazoned in the center of their chest—a black dragon on a background of white red and blue. Above the dragon stood two smaller symbols, a sword and a pouncing eagle. As the companions approached, one of the guards signaled them to halt.

"State your business," he said in an officious tone.

Aksel spoke for the group, "We're here for the town meeting."

The guard looked them over carefully. "A human, an elf, a gnome, and a halfling? Wait here one moment." He turned around and strode through the gate. Less than a minute later, he returned with a third guard. "Aren't these the folks you were telling us about?" the first guard asked the third one.

This new guard looked them over and nodded. "This is definitely them; the crew that went up to Stone Hill with Titan."

"That would be us," Aksel admitted.

Glo raised an eyebrow. "I take it you know her?"

An ironic smile crossed the guard's face. "Titan and I go way back. We grew up together."

"Well, you'll not find a more valiant companion," Lloyd stated fervently.

The guard's smile broadened into a grin. "Ain't that the truth." He turned to the other guard. "It's okay, I've got this." The gate guard nodded and fell back to his post. The new guard introduced himself.

"I am Francis Valas of the Ravenford town guard."

Lloyd extended his hand. "My name's Lloyd."

Francis took his hand. "You're that spirit…blade?"

Lloyd nodded. Francis turned next to Glo. "And you're the wizard."

"Glolindir."

Francis shook his hand as well then faced Seth and Aksel. "And you two must be the ninja and the cleric."

Seth pointed a thumb toward Aksel. "He's the cleric. Not sure where you got ninja from, though."

Francis looked baffled by the reply. Aksel shook his head wearily and explained further. "I'm Aksel and this is Seth. Ninjas don't like to be pointed out as such. It is part of their way."

"Oh." Francis nodded as if he understood. The wan smile on his face said otherwise. He turned to Seth and said, "My apologies, good sir."

Seth shrugged. "No problem."

Francis still appeared confused but pressed on anyway. "I've heard the story about what happened up at Stone Hill a few times since yesterday. In all honesty, most accounts sound exaggerated, but like I said, I've known Delara for years. From what she told me, Stone Hill was infested with a small army of monsters and a dark wizard."

Aksel nodded. "That is pretty much the way it was."

"Well then, this town owes you a vote of thanks." Francis stepped closer and lowered his voice. "There have been rumors around town of all kinds of monsters cropping up here and there; bandits as well. But to have a nest of those creatures so close to town—now that could have been real trouble."

Glo was starting to like this Francis. He was both friendly and forthcoming.

"We're just glad we could help out." Lloyd gave him a warm smile.

Aksel cleared his throat. "Which brings us to why we are here. We've come to attend the town meeting. We'd like to help out more if we can."

A grin spread across Francis's face. "I think that can be arranged. Normally hired help isn't allowed at the town meetings—the captain of the guard contracts them out separately, but in your case I think we can make an exception." He paused a moment as if thinking it over. "Let me take you to see the lieutenant. He will know how to handle this." Francis motioned them to follow. "They're with me," he told the gate guards.

They proceeded under the portcullis and entered a large courtyard. A number of guards performed various duties here, anything from grooming horses to practicing archery. The keep proper stood in front of them, reaching high into the blue skies above. It consisted of a massive stone structure with two huge wooden doors and many glass windows above the first floor. Glo counted three stories in general but saw that it rose to four and even five stories in some smaller sections and towers. The building itself was composed of light grey stone, but the midday sun gleaming off the walls of the keep made it look almost white in spots. In some of the low-lying sections, thick masses of greenish moss and clinging ivy vines covered the sides of the structure. Over to their right stood an entrance to what looked like gardens populated with large sculpted bushes, multicolored flowers, and even a flowing fountain in the center.

They were led through the front doors and into a large foyer. From there they went through the main hall, a room as large as the tavern area of the Charging Minotaur. It had a two-story vaulted ceiling with columns along its length and multiple balconies off to the sides. The entire expanse was covered with plush red carpets, tapestries, and various portraits along the walls. On one wall in particular there was a large mural. It depicted a knight in full armor, along with a wizard, a cleric, and two more people faced off against a large black dragon. Glo assumed it represented the battle between the baron, along with his former traveling companions, and the dragon, Ullarak.

Glo spied the entrance to another hallway at the other end of this hall. Two large shield-shaped banners hung high on the wall on either side. The one on the left displayed the same symbol as the tabards of the castle guards; the symbol of the Barony of Ravenford. The shield on the right had a background of white, red, and black. The symbol on this one was the same fierce-looking golden eagle that was portrayed on the other shield. There were two more symbols above that, but these were a crown and a lion. The lion looked quite similar to the one on Lloyd's tabard. Glo pointed to the shield on the right.

"That's an interesting coat of arms. It bears some similarity to Lloyd's. What house or place does it represent?"

Lloyd answered before Francis, "That's the symbol of the House of Avernos. The Baron of Penwick is head of that house."

Francis nodded. "Yes, indeed it is. I see by your tabard that you are from Penwick as well."

"Yes...I am," Lloyd responded tentatively. Francis completely missed the young man's discomfort.

"Did you know that our Baron Gryswold is also from Penwick?"

Seth answered before Lloyd could reply, "Of course he did. Lloyd knows everything about Penwick."

Francis appeared impressed. "Really?"

Lloyd gave Seth a warning glare. "Well, not everything."

Seth snickered softly as Francis motioned them to follow. "We'll have to let the baron know there's another Penwick expert in town. It's actually one of his favorite subjects."

Lloyd sounded less than enthused. "That's okay, don't go to any trouble on my account."

There was no dampening Francis's enthusiasm. "No trouble at all."

The group exited the main hall and entered a long hallway at the back of the keep. They passed a few closed doors on either side of the hall and stopped in front of a large, ornate doorway at the other end. Francis bade them to wait there then opened the door and entered the room. Inside someone was speaking. They caught a glimpse of people sitting on long benches. Francis walked over to another guard and had a brief conversation. After a short while, they both strode back to the doorway. The two guards exited the room and closed the door behind them. The second guard wore the same uniform as the others, except that he had two stars in the upper left corner of his tabard. Francis introduced them.

"This is Lieutenant Relkin. Lieutenant, this is Aksel, Lloyd, Seth and Glolindir."

Lieutenant Relkin gave them a curt bow. "An honor to meet you gentlemen. I understand it was you four who cleaned up that mess up at Stone Hill."

"Along with Titan and Brundon," Lloyd added.

A pained look crossed Lieutenant Relkin's face. It quickly disappeared. "Ah yes, Delara and her companion Brundon. They are quite able in their own right."

Glo thought the reaction strange. He glanced at Aksel, but the gnome's expression was unreadable as he responded, "We found them so."

Relkin merely nodded. "Be that as it may, mercenaries are not usually allowed in town meetings."

Glo raised an eyebrow. He found the term 'mercenary' distasteful. It implied an interest purely in profit. Perhaps that described Brundon, but certainly not Titan. He also wondered if he and his friends would be turned away from this meeting. Relkin paused for a moment as if deliberating that very point before answering.

"However, considering your accomplishment up at Stone Hill, I think we can make an exception in your case."

Aksel executed a curt bow. "We are most grateful."

Relkin nodded. "Very good. Francis, you are dismissed. The rest of you follow me." He opened the door and led the four of them inside.

18
THE TRUTH ABOUT LLOYD

Gods, the man could swing a blade!

The companions found themselves in a long room with rows of benched seats facing toward the front. There was a pathway up the middle very much like a temple. The seats were filled with people, all of whom were watching a man at the front of the room. He was currently speaking about fishing rights in the nearby Merchant Bay. Behind him, up a few steps, stood two thrones. On the left throne sat a powerfully-built man. He appeared to be in his mid-forties with piercing blue eyes, darkish brown hair, and a beard and mustache that same deep color.

That must be Baron Gryswold. Even though the baron was seated, Glo could tell he was tall. Gryswold wore simple finery of a military cut with a longsword strapped to his side. The Ravenford symbol was emblazoned on it in the upper left corner. On the throne to the right sat a tall, regal woman with long chestnut hair, bright amber eyes, and porcelain skin. Something about her carriage reminded Glo of his mother, Aerandir.

And that would be the Baroness Gracelynn. The baroness wore a pale blue gown with the symbol of the God Arenor, the god of sun and light as well as strength and healing, emblazoned on it—a golden circle with six rays spreading outward from them. Glo remembered Xelda telling him that the baroness was a proficient cleric, although that was not her primary calling.

Below the symbol on the baroness's dress, Glo observed a second symbol—the heraldic of the House Avernos. As the man up front droned on, Lieutenant Relkin motioned them toward an empty bench in the back. They quietly shuffled down the row and sat down, Relkin joining them. Glo gazed around the room. There was a man in guard's uniform, standing to the baron's right, though a few steps down.

"That's Captain Gelpas," Relkin whispered.

A young woman sat off to the right of the baron and baroness in an ornate chair. She had long strawberry blonde hair and cream-colored skin, but her most prominent feature was her electric blue eyes. While perhaps not quite as tall as the baroness, she carried herself with the same regal air. Her lavish green dress furthered her majestic appearance, accentuated with finery that was more in line with a lordly court than a simply barony.

"And that's the Lady Andrella. She will be eighteen in just a few weeks," Relkin whispered to him once more.

The fisherman finally sat down, and a court herald took his place. The man began reading from a long parchment, announcing further news from around the barony. Lieutenant Relkin stood up and whispered to them, "You'll excuse me. I must inform Captain Gelpas of your presence."

"Thank you," Aksel whispered back. "You have been most kind."

Lieutenant Relkin nodded, then strode away. He circumvented the pews and pulled Captain Gelpas aside. The two men briefly exchanged words, then Relkin pointed over to where the companions sat. Captain Gelpas gazed over, giving them a curt nod. The men talked a bit more, then Lieutenant Relkin exited the room, leaving them on their own. The herald finally finished his announcements. The meeting continued with more talk about town businesses, including the needs of the farming community, tax collections, and the state of the royal treasury.

Seth yawned. "Wake me when it's time to go." He feigned falling asleep in his seat.

Aksel gave the halfling a disapproving look. "Seth, behave yourself."

Seth did not open his eyes. "I always behave myself," he responded, "just not always that well."

Glo had to stifle a laugh. Seth was not all that wrong; the meeting was terribly boring. The details of running the town were tedious at best. Glo marveled at the baron and baroness, how they put up with even the most monotonous of their subjects. He gazed toward the Lady Andrella, curious if she was handling it as well as her parents. Surprisingly, the young lady was staring in their direction. At first he thought she was looking at him. Perhaps she had never seen an elf before? Glo soon realized she was staring at Lloyd.

He gazed over at the young man, but Lloyd was totally unaware of her attention. His eyes were riveted on Baron Gryswold. He watched him with a fierce intensity, studying his every move, hanging on his every word. It was as if he was an actor, learning to play a part. It truly made no sense. Why would Lloyd care how a nobleman acted in court? Glo felt a nudge in the side. It was Aksel.

"What?" he whispered to the gnome.

"Did you hear that?"

Glo shifted his focus to the conversation up front. The subject was trade with other towns. A merchant was talking about the orcs they had encountered.

"I've lost three shipments now from Tarrsmorr to these bandits in the last three months."

That voice belongs to Pheldan. Glo shifted in his seat until he got a better view of the speaker. Sure enough, it was the half-elf, Pheldan. He caught a glimpse of a woman with long dark hair sitting next to the merchant. That had to be Xelda. Pheldan continued to speak.

"The only caravan we've seen in the last few months just narrowly made it through a few days ago. And that was only by the grace of some gifted passengers and a passing warrior. I tell you, Baron Gryswold, if something isn't done soon, I will go out of business."

The baron sat forward, his expression one of concern. "I'm truly sorry Master Pheldan, but I just don't have the men to send out and search for these brigands."

The Lady Gracelynn also sat forward. She was very poised, but her tone was deeply sympathetic. "Who were these passengers and this warrior you speak of?"

"I don't exactly remember their names," Pheldan replied, "but I can tell you that one was an elf, one was a gnome, one was a halfling, and the last was a giant of a man, all dressed in red."

Seth's eyes snapped open. "That's us!"

Aksel put a finger to his lips. "Shhh, I can't hear what they're saying."

Xelda's voice rang out across the room. "If I may speak, your Ladyship?"

The Lady Gracelynn smiled at the young woman. "Go ahead, my dear."

"The elf is Glolindir. He's a wizard from the west. He's been at our shop a few times since. The gnome is Aksel, and I believe he is a cleric. The halfling is named Seth. I am not sure what his vocation is. And the tall human is Lloyd. He is most definitely a warrior."

It was the baron's turn to speak. "Do you by any chance know where these folks can be found?"

"I think they are staying at the Charging Minotaur, my Lord," Xelda responded.

Captain Gelpas chose that moment to step up to the throne. The baron bent forward as the captain whispered into his ear. Gryswold straightened up and gazed toward the back of the room. At the same time, he cleared his throat and made an announcement. "Ahem. It has come to my attention that the group of whom you speak is in this very room."

Murmurs broke out amongst the crowd. People turned this way and that. The baron raised his voice to be heard over the din.

"I've also been told that this same band cleared out a horde of monsters and a dark wizard from Stone Hill only yesterday, all at the request of our good friend, Wizard Maltar."

More murmurs swept through the crowd. A townsperson right

in front of the foursome stood up and cried, "They're back here!" Everyone stood up and turned around to look at them. The entire assembly was thrown into an uproar. Glo could hardly hear anything over the din. The captain of the guard pushed his way through the crowd and motioned for them to follow him up front. Meanwhile, the town herald tried to settle down the crowd.

"Quiet! Quiet please! Everyone be seated!"

The townsfolk slowly settled down and took their seats. A hush fell over the crowd as Glo and the others were presented to the baron and baroness. The Lady Andrella now stood by her mother's side.

The baron addressed them in a formal tone. "Your service to our town is greatly appreciated." The baron looked them over, his eyes narrowing as they fixed on Lloyd. "Did I hear right before? Is your name Lloyd?"

Lloyd bowed to the baron and baroness. "Yes, your Lordship."

"Lloyd," the baron repeated as if trying to remember something. Abruptly, he snapped his fingers. "A warrior named Lloyd in a *Penwick* tabard. And not just any tabard, but a tabard from the House of Stealle!" The baron rose from his chair, his excitement apparent. "You must be Krato's son."

Lloyd's response was rather subdued. "Yes, your Lordship. I am."

Gryswold stepped closer, looking Lloyd up and down. "So you're the young Lord Stealle. I can definitely see the resemblance."

Lord Stealle? Lloyd? Glo looked at Aksel and Seth. Both seemed equally surprised. *Kratos Stealle?* Wasn't that the hero of Penwick Lloyd spoke about—the one who defeated the Pirate Eboneye and helped save the city? The one who was now a Lord and Admiral of the Penwick Navy? Suddenly it all made sense. Lloyd was the son of the famous Lord Kratos Stealle. He was a noble of Penwick. That was how Lloyd knew so much about nobility and responsibility. It also explained why he was reluctant to come here in his Penwick tabard. Lloyd didn't want anyone to know who he was. He must have set out from home to make a name for himself on his own merits. He did not want to depend on his family name. Glo felt a sudden bond with his new friend. They had both set out from home without any support from their families.

Baron Gryswold continued on exuberantly. "Your father is a fine man and a noble warrior. Did he ever tell you the stories about our fight with the Eboneye?"

A knowing smile spread across Lloyd's face. "Many times, your Lordship."

Gryswold threw back his head and laughed. He proceeded to speak in a voice loud enough for everyone in the chamber to hear. "Those were glorious times! It must be, oh, about twenty years now. The scoundrel Eboneye had taken over Penwick. The baron had been slain, and the town forces were scattered."

Gryswold's voice grew louder, his eyes ablaze. "Your father and I rallied those forces, and together we routed the invading horde. It was a bloody war, but street by street, we took Penwick back until the entire city was once again ours. Eboneye tried to run, but Kratos and I gave chase. We cornered the cur on his ship and a great battle ensued. Gods, the man could swing a blade. Slew Eboneye himself! The ship went down in the harbor, and the pirate's reign of terror ended."

The entire assemblage cheered as the baron finished his story. Gryswold stood there with a wistful look on his face. He shook his head and gazed down at Lloyd once more.

"And you are Kratos's son. Kratos was always a striking figure of a man. The women of Penwick were always fawning over him. I see the apple doesn't fall far from the tree." Gryswold turned toward his wife and daughter. "What say you, Andrella?"

Glo turned in time to catch the young lady staring at Lloyd. As all eyes fell on her, she swiftly shifted her gaze toward her father. The young lady faltered a moment, but recovered expertly, although there was a slight reddish tinge to her cheeks.

"Oh, um, I think that…any son of your old comrade is a friend of the court of Ravenford."

Glo turned to gaze at Lloyd. The young man's eyes were locked on the Lady Andrella. His face lit up, and his mouth hung open ever so slightly. Lloyd was obviously taken with the young noble woman, and Andrella appeared to return his interest.

Gryswold sounded rather amused by Andrella's response. "Ah, well said, my daughter."

Gracelynn interrupted the baron's fun. "Although Mistress Xelda was nice enough to tell us your names, I believe that formal introductions are in order."

Aksel stepped forward. "Ahem. This tall elf is the Wizard Glolindir Eodin from the fair city of Cairthrellon. Glolindir is also the newest apprentice to the Master Wizard Maltar."

Gryswold was clearly surprised by that bit of news. "Really? My old friend Maltar is very picky about his apprentices. You must have impressed him greatly."

Glo bowed to the baron and baroness. "One does one's best."

The Lady Gracelynn responded graciously, "If my knowledge of geography is right, Cairthrellon is a long way from here."

"It is indeed, your Ladyship."

The Lady Gracelynn's expression turned sympathetic. "Well then, please consider this your second home." Her smile was so serene that Glo did indeed feel quite welcome here. The lady then turned to Lloyd. "And the same to you, young Lord Stealle."

Lloyd was still staring at the Lady Andrella. He swiftly shifted his gaze to the baroness. "You are most kind, your Ladyship."

Aksel, as stoic as ever, continued with the introductions. "And this is our comrade, Master Seth Korzair, from the city of Ilos. He is…well…he is…" Aksel paused as he tried to find the right words.

Seth stepped forward and addressed the nobles directly. "Your Lord and Ladyship, let's just say that I am a jack of all trades. An expert in those areas that might confound the warrior or the mage." He gave a quick smile to all and then stepped back.

Gryswold exchanged a quick glance with Gracelynn, both with a trace of a smile on their lips. Gryswold then turned back toward Seth. "I see."

Aksel cleared his throat. "Thank you, Seth. And I, your Lord and Ladyship, am the Cleric Aksel Alabaster from the temple of the Soldenar in the city of Caprizon."

Lady Gracelynn's voice was filled with reverence as she responded, "Well met, fellow cleric. It is not often that we get to see clergy of the other races here in Ravenford. And I must confess, I do not know a lot about the Soldenar. Perhaps you would be kind enough to instruct me during your stay in our fair town?"

Aksel bowed low to the gentle lady. "It would be my honor."

The baron was obviously a strong leader, but the Lady Gracelynn seemed to be the heart of the small town. She had a way of making everyone feel both important and welcome.

Baron Gryswold returned to the subject of the orc bandits. "As you already know, our merchants' caravans are falling prey to a group of bandits on the road west of here. You four have already fought off these thieves, but there may still be some at large. I don't have the men to hunt them down, so I would ask if you could get rid of them for us."

"It would be an honor, your Lordship," Aksel said without hesitation.

Lloyd answered him as well, "Don't worry, your Lordship. We'll be sure to take care of every last bandit."

A broad smile crossed Gryswold's face. "Spoken like a true Stealle! Captain Gelpas here will fill you in on the details and outfit you with anything you may need."

With that, the foursome were dismissed from the throne room. They followed the captain down the center aisle toward the doorway. Glo cast one last glance back toward the throne room as they exited. The baron and baroness were engaged in conversation with Pheldan, Xelda, and some other folks whom he did not know. The Lady Andrella, however, gazed in their direction. She immediately turned away when Lloyd glanced back at the throne. A brief smile crossed Glo's lips. There was definitely something between these two, and he was curious to see where it would lead.

Once outside the throne room, Gelpas addressed the group, "All of the caravans that disappeared were traveling along the west road from Tarrsmorr through the Bendenwoods. We sent out a small contingent to search for them a few weeks back. Every train made it to the town of Bendenwood, but once leaving there, they were never seen again. Not a trace."

Aksel's hand went to his chin. "So you think these orc bandits were attacking the wagon trains somewhere between the town of Bendenwood and the eastern edge of the forest and that, somehow, they managed to make each caravan disappear."

Gelpas appeared impressed with his quick appraisal of the situation. "That is what we believe. If you can find their hideout, take care of any remaining bandits, and possibly recover any of the goods they have stolen, it would be a great service to Ravenford."

"We'll do our best, Captain." A solemn look crossed Lloyd's face.

Gelpas nodded approvingly. "Good. Now, will you need any weapons or supplies? I have been instructed to give you access to our armory."

Seth cleared his throat. "And how much will we be getting paid for this job?"

The captain shifted his gaze toward the halfling. He was about to answer when a voice called out from behind them.

"Wait, wait!" It was Pheldan. Xelda accompanied him.

"Hail, Pheldan. Hail Xelda," Glo pronounced formally. Then he spoke in Elvish, "*Elen sila lumenn omentilmo.*" That roughly translated to *a star shall shine on the hour of our meeting.*

Both grandfather and granddaughter gave him a warm smile. Xelda replied in kind, "*Cormamin lindua ele lle.*" It was another formal elven greeting that meant *my heart sings to see thee.*

Glo felt his face flush slightly. Xelda's eyes danced with amusement. She appeared quite satisfied with the effect her reply had on him.

"We just talked it over with the baron and the other merchants and I will be funding this mission. All except Haltan that is. He wouldn't part with a copper piece if his life depended on it." Pheldan paused to cackle at his own joke. "Anyway, they are ruining our businesses and must be stopped. Five thousand gold once you've routed the bandits. Also, please stop by my shop before you head out. I will supply you with whatever you need. The other merchants said the same. Anyway, don't forget." With that the old half-elf bid them farewell.

"Goodbye, Glolindir," Xelda said, her eyes alight as she strolled past him.

Glo wore a bemused expression as Pheldan and Xelda walked away arm in arm. Xelda intrigued him. Her Elvish had improved since the last time they talked. It was now nearly flawless, yet her choice of greeting, while formal, could be taken quite personally as well. Did she realize what she had said, along with the implications?

Gelpas interrupted his train of thought. "You seem to have made quite a number of friends in your short time in our town."

"We're just friendly people," Seth responded innocently.

A thin smile spread across the captain's lips. "Umm, yes. Anyway, I trust that answers your question about payment, Master Seth?"

"Yep."

Glo glanced at Aksel. The gnome just shook his head.

Luckily, the captain did not appear to mind. "Well then, now that that's settled, the armory is this way."

19
TROUBLED HEARTS

No one is that smart

The four companions gathered back at the Charging Minotaur. News of their meeting with the baron and baroness must have traveled all over town. When they entered the common room of the inn, the patrons were all abuzz with talk of it. When Kailay saw Lloyd, instead of running over to them, the young woman's face screwed up and she began to cry. She brought her apron up to her face, then turned and ran into the kitchen.

Lloyd was mortified by what had just happened. "What'd I do?"

Glo put his hand on the young man's shoulder. "As we have already seen, news spreads quickly around this town. I'd wager that Kailay found out you are nobility, my friend."

"So?" Lloyd said, clearly not realizing the implications.

"You're too good for her now, your highness," Seth said with a wicked grin.

Lloyd's face flushed with anger. "I am not!"

Aksel grasped the young man's arm. "Whoa. Easy there, Lloyd."

Lloyd, his face flushed, stared at the little cleric for a few moments. He took a deep breath, visibly calming down. "This is one of the reasons I didn't want anyone knowing who I was. It just… complicates things."

Glo truly empathized with him. There were times that he wished he could just forget who he was and who his family was. Lucky for him it made little difference out here on the east coast. Lloyd did not have that luxury. He spoke to him in a soft voice, "Believe me, Lloyd, I understand."

Lloyd turned to look at Glo. A variety of emotions played across his face, until finally a slim smile appeared on his lips. "I guess that you would."

"Look, Lloyd, who you are doesn't really change anything between us. Right, guys?" Glo glanced at Aksel and Seth.

Aksel nodded. "Not to me."

"Is your family wealthy?" Seth asked.

Lloyd gazed at the halfling with a puzzled expression. He paused a moment then replied, "All of my family's money is tied up in rebuilding Penwick. So no, we are not really wealthy."

Seth's face twisted into a half-smile. "Then nothing has changed between us."

A smile slowly spread across Lloyd's face. The smile then turned into chuckling. Glo and Aksel both found themselves joining in. *Leave it to Seth to make light of a sticky situation.* When the laughter died down, Glo reached out and grasped Lloyd's shoulder once more.

"Seriously, it is not your fault. She's the one who believes your lineage puts a wedge between you two. If you just leave her be, I'm sure she'll be fine in a few days."

Lloyd gazed over at the kitchen door, then shrugged. "I guess you're right."

Aksel suggested they sit down and discuss the details of the hunt for the orc bandits. The four companions adjourned to the booth they had used earlier in the day. They had only been seated a minute or so when the other barmaid, Morwen, came over to wait on them. Morwen was a few years older than Kailay, perhaps in her mid-twenties. She had long straight raven hair, dark brown eyes and a tan complexion. Her tight barmaid outfit over-accentuated her comely figure. She was very friendly, but not in the flirtatious way that Kailay could be sometimes.

When she walked up to the booth, Lloyd asked her, "Where's Kailay?"

Morwen hesitated a moment before answering, "She…had to go home. She…wasn't feeling well."

"I'm sorry to hear that. I hope she feels better soon," Lloyd replied. He did his best to be cheerful, but the pained expression on his face belied the attempt.

Once Morwen took their orders, they went back to planning. They reasoned that the bandits must have a hideout in the area. The key was finding it. According to Pheldan, the next caravan was due in sometime later the next day. That gave Lloyd an idea based on his previous experience with bandits. He suggested catching them as they lay in wait for the next caravan. They would route the bandits but then let one escape. That way they could follow the bandit back to its hideout. They would need a tracker to follow the orc they let go. Despite Seth's protests, Brundon was the most likely candidate. They would also get the chance to work with Titan again—a choice everyone could agree on.

Lloyd spied Brundon and Titan sitting in their usual booth. He went over and brought the duo back with him. They slid into the booth and the six of them discussed the new job and their various parts in it. Brundon had experience with bandits as well. He agreed that their plan was the best approach to routing them all. Titan's eyes gleamed at the chance to fight orcs.

It was now late in the afternoon, and there were still preparations to be made before starting this journey. It was decided that they would leave first thing the next morning. Fees were agreed upon and coins changed hands, then the entire group headed to the shops to pick up provisions. Pheldan was as generous as he had promised. The companions and their mercenary friends were well-outfitted for almost no cost.

Glo ran into Xelda at the back of the shop. She spoke to him in

Elvish. Her speech was a bit slow, but her pronunciation was excellent. He gathered that this was the first time she had a conversation in a while and not just recited ritual greetings or farewells.

"*When do you…leave?*"

"*First thing in the morning.*"

"*How…long will you be…gone?*"

Glo chuckled softly. "*That depends on our quarry.*"

"*I wish you good…hunting.*"

"*I thank you for your well wishes.*"

"*Return…safely. I will be…waiting.*"

Glo raised an eyebrow. Once again, Xelda had said something which could be taken as personal. Her choice of words and inflection would typically be used between promised couples. Glo immediately dismissed the idea. She was still learning the language. Proper inflection took regular usage to perfect. There was no way Xelda really knew what she had said.

Glo finished saying goodbye to Xelda and her grandfather, then moved on with his companions to the other shops. True to Pheldan's word, the other merchants were equally supportive; stops at the local fletcher, the armorer, the cobbler, the smith, and the tailor rounded out their needs for supplies and repairs at quite low prices.

The only surprise they received was at the tailor. When they walked in, Kailay stood behind the counter. As soon as she saw Lloyd, she turned and fled into the backroom. Glo could have kicked himself. Kailay had told them her mother was the town tailor. He should have remembered and sent Lloyd somewhere else. Lloyd was upset by the girl's reaction, but there was nothing that could be done about it.

A minute later, a woman wearing a seamstress apron came out of the backroom. Glo did a double take. She looked just like Kailay, with the same strawberry blonde hair, shapely figure, and a smile that could light up the room. However, this woman showed traces of age around the edges of the eyes and corners of the mouth. She introduced herself as Arwel, Kailay's mother. Glo got another surprise when Gristla also stepped out of the backroom. Gristla was Arwel's oldest daughter and Kailay's sister. *This was definitely a small town.*

Once everyone finished gearing up, they went their separate ways.

Glo went to study the new spells that Maltar had given him. Aksel headed to the town temple to pray for some new spells of his own. Lloyd went to train at the back of the inn. Brundon and Titan went with him. Seth was enigmatic about where he was going. The others came to expect this of him. They knew he was going to study or train in secret.

Later that evening, the six of them met for dinner. They were all tired after a long day, but were well-provisioned and better prepared for the upcoming journey. When they finally adjourned for the evening, Lloyd went straight to bed. Unfortunately, the young man did nothing but toss and turn. Glo sat on his own bed, quietly leafing through the new entries in his spellbook. He was a bit nervous about the coming mission, and wanted to be extra careful about what kind of magic he would have prepared the next day.

A voice roused him from his studies. "Are you busy?"

Glo looked up from his book. Lloyd sat up, a troubled expression on his face.

Glo put his book down and closed it on his lap. "I can talk a bit. What's on your mind?"

Lloyd gave a deep sigh. "Women, I don't really understand them."

A wry smile crossed Glo's lips. "What makes you think I do?"

"You're really smart."

Glo chuckled. "No one is that smart."

"So you are telling me that even with your brains you don't understand women?"

Glo let out a derisive snort. "Heh. I don't even understand Seth most of the time."

Lloyd hung his head as if in defeat. He obviously needed some kind of encouragement, but Glo had no idea how to explain it to him. He finally decided the best thing to do was to share his own experiences. Maybe if he heard someone else's troubles, he would not feel so alone.

"Growing up in a noble elven household, I was privately tutored. The few people my age I met were at social functions, and they were mostly pampered nobles. I never had anything in common with them."

Lloyd gazed up at him, his eyes filled with sympathy. "I'm sorry to hear that."

Glo responded with a wan smile. "So what about you?"

"Most of my time was spent either on the family farm or studying to be a spiritblade. We were always too busy for parties or anything like that. I really didn't know anyone my own age back home, other than my sister's friends."

So Lloyd is just like me, Glo realized. Neither of them had any real social experience. That being the case, what could he possibly say to ease his friend's mind? Glo finally decided to address what he thought was really bothering him.

"You know, you never led Kailay on. She was the one who chased you. And honestly, if you gave in at all, I think she would have been hurt far worse when someone of your own station came along."

Lloyd's face flushed. "What do you mean?"

Glo couldn't help smiling. "Let's just say that a certain lady at court took quite an interest in you today."

The young man's face reddened further. "You don't mean the Lady Andrella?"

Glo laughed. Lloyd positively wore his heart on his sleeve. "My good friend, the young woman could hardly take her eyes off you."

Lloyd grew so excited, he nearly jumped off the bed. "Really?"

Glo nodded. "Absolutely. She was watching you whenever you weren't looking."

Lloyd's expression suddenly turned anxious. "So what do I do about it?"

That is an excellent question. Unfortunately, Glo was the least likely person to give him the answer he sought. Still, he had to tell him something. Lloyd was far too distraught, and needed a clear head for the next few days. "The best I can tell you is to be yourself. She seems to like you already anyway. Maybe that is all you need to do."

Lloyd appeared skeptical. "You think so?"

"Honestly, Lloyd, I hope so. Life is tough enough just being yourself. I can't imagine how hard it would be trying to be someone else."

Lloyd gazed at him for a few moments, then finally smiled. "Thanks, Glo. You're a true friend." With that, the young man launched himself back into bed and was asleep in a matter of minutes.

Glo sat up for a while, pondering the whole subject of relation-
ships. He was no expert on the matter, and he quite frankly doubted
that one existed. His own mother and father had been married for
nearly one hundred and thirty years, yet neither seemed to completely understand the other. So what hope was there for someone like
Lloyd or himself, neither of whom had even been in a relationship?
Well, at least Lloyd seems at peace for now.

His mind wandered back to the coming mission. He believed
that they were far better prepared than they had been on their trip
to Stone Hill. Back then they had no idea what they were getting
into; they merely reacted to situations as they arose. This time they
knew exactly where they were going and who they were facing. There
would be no surprises. With that thought, the young elf closed his
eyes and drifted into a restful trance.

Early the next morning, the small company gathered in front of
the Charging Minotaur. It was fairly quiet outside the inn this time
of day. Most townsfolk were either working their farms or out on the
bay fishing. The six travelers were all busy packing their saddlebags.
Every once and a while, Lloyd would glance over toward the inn, his
expression pensive. Glo eventually realized that the young man was
looking for Kailay.

They had not seen the young barmaid during breakfast that
morning. She had always been there before, with her bright smile and
perky attitude, cheering them on. Glo sincerely hoped that she would
return to work soon. He would hate to think that her embarrassment
over a harmless flirtation would keep her away indefinitely.

Glo finished securing his packs, then climbed up onto his mount.
He trotted over next to Lloyd and Titan, both of whom waited on
their steeds.

"Is everything okay?"

Lloyd wore a wan smile. "I'm fine."

Titan shook her head and sighed. "Ah, he's worried for no reason.
I heard what happened with Kailay. Most of the town knows, which
is really why she's so embarrassed." She leaned closer and lowered

her voice. "Trust me, I've known Kailay since we were kids. This is not her first crush. She used to have one on my older brother, Bret. That ended way worse."

Lloyd's expression changed to one of concern. "Really? What happened?"

"That is a long story. Let's just say that Bret is not the gentleman that you are, Lloyd."

Lloyd's face turned ashen. "I had no idea."

Titan threw up her hands. "Oh, no, no. It wasn't that bad. My dad caught them before things got too far out of hand, and afterwards Bret couldn't sit for a week!" That broke Lloyd out of his mood. He, Titan and Glo all laughed at her story. "And anyway, from what I've heard, you've got another young blonde to worry about."

Lloyd's face reddened significantly.

Glo glanced at Lloyd. "See, didn't I tell you?"

Titan leaned in close and lowered her voice once more. "I've known Andrella a long, long time. She's been inundated with suitors since she was about twelve, and she hasn't given any of them the time of day. You're the first young man to have caught her eye."

A wide grin broke out across Lloyd's face. "Thanks, Delara."

A second later, Aksel's voice rang out, "Are we ready to go?" The little cleric sat astride his riding dog, glancing around at the gathered riders.

"Yeah," "Yes," "Sure," came the multiple replies.

"Then let's move out."

Aksel spurred his dog forward and the others fell in behind him. This time, they turned north then west, following that road out of town. As they passed Ravenford keep, Glo spied three riders waiting up by the front gate. One of them had long blonde hair and was garbed in a green riding outfit. The other two wore the uniforms of castle guards. When the riders saw them, they headed down the hill.

Aksel held up his hand and called the company to a halt. They waited at the base of the hill for the riders to reach them. The center rider was the Lady Andrella. Accompanying her were Francis and Lieutenant Relkin. Each of the men carried a large basket in one hand. The young lady addressed the group of riders.

"Good adventurers, we would like to wish you the best of luck on your upcoming endeavor. The Barony of Ravenford greatly appreciates your efforts in the name of our town and as such we would like to present you with this small token of our esteem."

The young woman snapped her fingers, and Francis and Relkin dismounted. They strode forward and presented the baskets to Lloyd and Titan.

Titan dismounted and took one of them. "Why thank you, Francis."

Francis seemed a bit flustered around the tall warrior. "Ah… you're welcome, Delara…but it was Andrella's idea…"

Titan opened the top and peered inside. Her eyes opened wide. "Andrella! You shouldn't have. There's enough food in here for a small army."

The Lady Andrella smiled warmly at the tall warrior. "Nothing's too good for old friends, Delara. Or new ones," she added, glancing around at the other riders. Her eyes finally settled on Lloyd.

"Thank you, sir. This is more than kind," the young man said as he accepted the other basket from the lieutenant.

There was a trace of a smile on Andrella's face.

Aksel cleared his throat. "Ahem, good Lady, we very much appreciate this token of esteem from the First House of Ravenford. Please rest assured that our efforts will be strengthened measurably by your kind support."

"You are most welcome," she replied, though her eyes drifted once more to Lloyd. The young man smiled shyly at her and her cheeks reddened slightly. As Francis and Relkin remounted their horses, the Lady addressed them one last time. "Good luck then. May the gods keep you safe, and may you return to us soon." She whirled her mount around and spurred it up the hill. Francis and Relkin followed.

Once the riders were out of earshot, Brundon spoke up. "Well, my friends, this little group certainly has earned the favor of the House Avernos." He glanced at Lloyd. "Perhaps some of us more than others."

"Jealous, Brundon?" Titan taunted.

Brundon feigned surprise. "Me? No, love. Quite the contrary in fact. I like knowing someone in favor with the baron's family."

Glo found his statement puzzling. "Delara, forgive me for asking, but didn't you say you were old friends with the Lady Andrella? She seemed to refer to you as such."

A pained expression crossed Titan's face. "Andrella and I are most definitely old friends. It's just…complicated…"

As Titan faltered, Brundon spoke up for her. "What Delara is trying to say is, sometimes being friends with the first family of Ravenford isn't enough. There are others in the keep who can make things difficult, especially for mercenaries."

Glo raised an eyebrow. Brundon must have been referring to Captain Gelpas. After all, the captain was the one in charge of contracting out work. Gelpas seemed like a fair man though. So why would he have a problem with Brundon and Titan? He was tempted to ask more, but the duo had gone silent. It was obvious they did not want to talk about it further.

20
BACK TO THE BENDENWOODS

They call him the one-eyed god

The riders resumed their journey down the west road and the little town of Ravenford was soon left behind. They followed the roadway northwest alongside the Raven River until the river branched off into two tributaries, the Berribrun and the West Raven. The road then continued to parallel the West Raven, past the Kelvan hills to the south and the Dwimmer Forest to the north. It was another beautiful day, the sun still low in the sky behind the travelers. Morning dew covered the grass, and the leaves glistening with residual moisture. Glo's familiar flew overhead. She appeared over the party, circled for a minute or two, then shot out ahead of the little band over the treetops. The party crossed over the Berribrun and now traveled on the north side of the West Raven. They skirted the fringes of the Dwimmer Forest.

The woods were a stark contrast to the Dead Forest. The trees rose high above the travelers, their boughs full with lush greenery.

The floor of the woods was blanketed with dark, thick underbrush. The sweet smell of pine and the strong odor of cedar wafted on the gentle breeze that reached the roadway. The sound of birds singing their early morning songs filled the air—the avian creatures flitting from tree to tree. Occasionally an entire flock would rise up from one tree, make a huge airborne circle, and wing their way to another tree a short distance away, landing as a group. Squirrels danced among the branches, chasing each other, playing tag. They heard the rustle of an animal moving through the brush, often followed by a deer or fox sighting.

Glo gave a heavy sigh. "Now that is what a forest should look like."

It had been almost two months now since he had left his woodland home of Cairthrellon. He had not thought about it at the time, but he was beginning to feel homesick. These last few days in the cramped town of Ravenford and the awful Dead Forest had taken more of a toll on him than he realized. The sights, sounds, and smells of the Dwimmer Forest drove the point home most poignantly.

Aksel dropped back to ride beside Glo. "Are you alright?"

He turned to Aksel and smiled. "I'm fine. Just a momentary bout of homesickness is all."

"I know what you mean," Aksel confided in him. "I can't believe how flat everything is out here. It just seems…unnatural."

Just then, a small black form winged out of the sky. Glo turned his head and spied Raven, angling down toward him. The wizard raised his arm, and the bird landed on his wrist. She hopped up onto his shoulder and perched there saying, "*Ikotane vanima, ikotane vanima.*" *So beautiful, so beautiful.*

"Well, at least Raven is content," Aksel said.

"Yes, she is." The bird's happy mood raised Glo's spirits as well. He sighed as tranquility washed over him for the first time in quite a while. "She is merely happy to be out among nature."

The little band continued to follow the road as it wound alongside the West Raven. Soon they passed the Dwimmer Forest and were back in open country. They saw a group of hills to the south of the river. Those were the Kelvan Hills, according to Brundon. They had passed through them on their previous journey to Stone Hill. North of the road, the Vogel Hills rose lazily to meet the sky. The rolling green hills were a familiar sight to the companions and would accompany them all the way back to the Bendenwoods.

As the day wore on, the weather stayed clear. The riders continued westward, making good time on the smooth paved surface of the roadway. It was just shy of midday when they caught their first glimpse of the Bendenwoods. The edge of the forest spread out before them, reaching far to the south of the West Raven and all the way north to the foot of the Vogels. Aksel called a halt, and the riders drew together on the road.

"Whew," Lloyd whistled. "That is one large forest."

"The Bendenwoods is one of the largest forests on the east coast," Brundon told him.

"But not the largest," Glo said. "If this little wood impresses you, then you should come with me one day to Cairthrellon. The great forest of Ruanaiaith puts Renesnyn to shame."

"Renesnyn?" Lloyd repeated.

"The elven name for the Bendenwoods."

The young man stared at him skeptically. "And this Ruanai…"

"…aith," Glo finished for him.

"Ruanaiaith," Lloyd repeated.

Glo nodded.

"Is it really that large of a forest?"

"Oh, most definitely. Ruanaiaith stretches from Cairthrellon in the west to Kai-Arborus in the east, easily thrice the length of Renesnyn. And it is home to some of the largest and oldest trees in Thac. They grow to enormous size. Some of them support the elven city of Kai-Arborus, sections of which rise high above the forest floor. Arcarion and Giant Oak, they dwarf anything you might see here in this forest."

"Well then," Aksel chimed in, "now that we've had our lesson in elven forestry for the day, we should probably stop and have lunch."

"You can never know too much," Glo responded. "As my father loves to say, *knowledge is power*."

Aksel nodded. "I couldn't agree more. Speaking of which, maybe

Raven can do some scouting for us and improve our knowledge of what's ahead?"

"Touché," Glo conceded.

He turned to the black bird currently perched on his shoulder and said, *"Iquista ernthye de ale'quel." Please scout up front.*

"Vee'lye iest." As you wish, Raven replied. In seconds, she was winging skywards toward the rambling forest in front of them.

A short way off the road stood a small grove of pine trees. Brundon scouted around the grove and found a small clearing in its center. The company left the road and set up there for lunch.

They unpacked the two baskets the Lady Andrella had given them—each one filled to the brim with food, including breaded chicken cutlets mixed with slices of ham and cheese, sliced potatoes baked with some kind of cheese sauce, buttered corn giblets, apple and cherry pies, and some spiced apple cider to wash it all down.

Brundon licked his lips. "Looks like a meal fit for a king, though I would have preferred ale."

Titan jabbed him in the arm. "Maybe Andrella wants us to keep sober on this mission."

Brundon gave her a hurt look. "Where's the fun in that, love?"

"Hey, food we didn't have to catch ourselves, and pie! No complaints here." A knife appeared in Seth's hands and he began to cut into his lunch.

Everyone ate heartily. The main meal was soon gone, and Seth handily sliced up the pies. That was soon gone as well, and the group began to clean up the remains. As they packed what little food was left, Raven returned from her scouting mission. Seth spotted her circling high above, and they all watched as she spiraled down and landed on Glo's extended arm.

"Ilyana tín," she told her master.

"All is quiet, she says," Glo happily relayed to the others.

Aksel looked pleased. "Excellent. Let's finish up here and move out."

Brundon put down his plate and stood up. "I'll go ahead and scout out the ground."

"Shirking clean up duties again?" Titan taunted him.

Brundon feigned offense at her remark. "Me? I would never do that, love. Besides, there is too much that cannot be seen from the air." He cast a quick glance at Glo. "No offense to your raven, mind you."

Glo shrugged. "None taken."

Seth wiped off his plate and got up as well. "How about we both go. You can fan out to the north and I'll take the south."

Brundon gave him a lopsided grin. "Less work for me."

"Go ahead," Aksel said.

The duo took off ahead of the others. The rest of them cleaned up, packed everything away, then headed back out of the grove. Once back on the road, they continued their westward trek. The Bendenwoods drew closer, the trunks of individual trees now visible in the distance. It was early afternoon, the sun directly overhead. The travelers felt the heat of the orb beating down on them. The riders continued their advance but were still a couple of miles from the edge of the forest when Seth and Brundon returned. Seth had not seen anything to the south, but Brundon had quite a different story to tell.

"I found some shoe tracks north of the road. Three of them to be exact; a bit larger than your average man, from what I could gauge. So we're either talking Lloyd-sized men, or…" He gazed around at the others knowingly.

"Orcs," Titan finished for him. "Where do the tracks lead?"

"Into the forest; I followed them about a quarter mile in. There they met up with four more sets."

Aksel stroked his chin. "So there are seven of them all together."

"So it would seem. The four tracks come down from the north, meet these three, and then all seven of them head south from there."

"From the north? What is up that way?" Glo asked.

"Nothing but the Vogel Hills," Titan said.

Aksel continued to stroke his chin. "If they are headed south, they might very well be setting up another ambush."

Lloyd had been quiet up to that point. "I'll wager they set up not too far from the last ambush, probably on the north side of the road. They might even have some scouts down the road, or up in the trees."

Brundon gazed at Lloyd with approval. "That makes a lot of sense."

"Indeed it does," Aksel murmured. He gazed past Seth and Brundon, toward the forest. "If Lloyd is right, we should leave the road now. Any closer to the woods and we risk being spotted."

Brundon nodded. "I can take you to where I spotted those tracks. Then we can follow them south till we find the orc camp. If we're lucky, we can sneak up on them."

Seth snorted. "Luck has nothing to do with it. Whoever is there will never see me coming."

Brundon grinned at the halfling. "Even I can't even see you coming, and I'm no slouch at spotting things."

"No, you aren't," Seth admitted.

Glo glanced at the halfling with feigned disbelief. "Seth? Did you just pay Brundon a compliment?"

"Did I?" Seth responded glibly. "Guess I must be going soft." He wagged a finger at Brundon. "And don't let it go to your head. You still make as much noise as a boar crashing through the woods."

Lloyd let out a short laugh. "Now there's the Seth we've all come to know and love. Don't take it personal, Brundon. If he thinks you're too loud, just imagine what he must think of me!"

Brundon shrugged. "Frankly, I don't care what he thinks of me as long as I'm getting paid."

Aksel raised his hands. "Gentlemen, fun as this all is, we have work to do." He turned to Brundon. "Now please lead us to those tracks."

Brundon nodded. "Will do." The tracker wheeled his horse around and headed back the way he came.

Seth looked at Lloyd. "And you sound like a lumbering ox." He then wheeled his dog around and took off after Brundon.

Lloyd, Aksel, and Glo glanced at each other and grinned.

Titan gazed at them with a bewildered look. "Am I missing something?"

Glo turned to her and explained, "You have to understand, Seth always has to have the last word."

"Ah." Titan nodded, then grinned as well.

The party filed off the road and followed Brundon back to where he first spied the tracks. There they turned west and traced the footprints into the Bendenwoods. They continued a short ways into the trees before stopping. At that point, the tracks met a second set of tracks from the north. All seven tracks headed south from there, as Brundon had indicated.

The riders dismounted and set up a perimeter. Aksel sent Brundon and Seth on foot to follow the trail south. The two of them were gone the better part of an hour before they returned. The group huddled together as Brundon reported, "It's a party of orcs alright. They're camped right where we guessed, about a hundred yards north of the road."

Seth added his findings. "As we guessed, there are scouts up in the trees; two of them keeping an eye on the road."

"Well, they obviously know that the next caravan is coming soon," Titan said.

Seth's voice was thick with suspicion. "Kind of makes you wonder who is supplying them with that information. Maybe someone in Ravenford even?"

"Hmmm, you may have a point," Aksel murmured. "We might want to look into that when we get back."

Seth and Brundon mapped out the orc camp in the dirt. The two orcs in the trees were on either end of the encampment. The other five orcs were gathered in the center of the campsite, preparing for a raid on the next unsuspecting caravan. Four of the orcs carried curved swords, but the fifth had a staff.

"Probably some kind of cleric then," Aksel observed.

Lloyd appeared surprised. "Orcs have gods?"

"Yes, as a matter of fact they do. I believe orcs worship the god Krieg."

"That is correct," Glo said. "They call him the one-eyed god. According to legend, Krieg lost his left eye in an epic battle with the chief of the elven gods, Elwynd Cor'lessian. Of course, the orcs dismiss the tale, saying that Krieg always had one eye."

"I think I like this god of the elves!" Lloyd declared. "You will have to tell me more about him when you get a chance, especially about this fight with the orc god."

Glo grinned at the young man. Lloyd was interested in anything to do with battle, even legendary ones. "Sure thing, but for the present, I think I can help with the orcs scouts. If I put them to sleep, they should be easy targets."

"Then I can climb up and take them out, one at a time." Seth fingered the sharp point of a knife that had appeared in his hand.

Lloyd clasped Titan on the shoulder. "We can handle the warriors."

Titan's eyes gleamed with anticipation. "Just leave them to us."

Aksel glanced around the group. "Well then, that covers everything except for the cleric. It wouldn't do to have him casting spells about during the fight."

Glo had to agree. Clerics could do more than heal with divine magic. There were other spells they could cast which would paralyze or blind their foes. Aksel chose not to do so, saving his powers for healing, but there was no telling what this orc cleric might do.

Aksel turned to Brundon. "What if you stay hidden back in the trees? As soon as you hear Lloyd and Titan charge in, start pelting the camp with arrows. Once they engage the enemy, change your focus to that cleric. That should keep him occupied."

"Sounds like my kind of fight." A wicked grin spread across Brundon's face as he unslung his bow.

"Okay then, let's move out."

Brundon and Seth led the way through the forest toward the orc encampment. The others followed behind them, making as little noise as possible. They covered a couple of miles until Brundon called a halt. He and Seth dismounted and disappeared into the woods. The two reappeared a short while later.

"They're about five hundred yards south of us," Brundon said.

"And are basically in the same positions," Seth added. "The two sentries are still in the trees. The warriors are shuffling around a bit, but seem to be sticking to the general area of the encampment."

"Sounds like they're getting restless," Glo said.

Aksel turned toward Seth. "Can you get Glo close enough to those sentries to put them to sleep?"

Seth crossed his arms. "No problem."

"Then you finish the job." Aksel's tone was grim.

Seth just nodded. The two of them got up and headed out into the forest, leaving the others behind.

21
ORC AMBUSH

Suddenly the world rushed past him

With Glo and Seth gone, Aksel turned to Brundon. "We'll leave the mounts here. Get us within fifty yards of the encampment, then you can move out and get into position. Start firing as soon as Lloyd and Titan charge."

Brundon's mouth rose on one side. "Will do."

They secured their mounts, following Brundon through the trees. The companions went slowly, being as silent as possible. After what felt like forever, Brundon held up his hand. He motioned for the others to wait, then disappeared into the woods.

The forest around them had gone quiet. Lloyd scanned the woods ahead. He couldn't see anything other than trees, but the silence was a dead giveaway that something was amiss. The young warrior closed his eyes and began to meditate. He slowed his breathing and cleared his mind. When his eyes snapped open, he felt completely calm and ready for battle. Lloyd's eyes rested on Titan. Her face was set for battle—grim countenance and firm jaw characterized by her steel blue eyes. Lloyd admired her. She wielded her sword and shield with expert precision and power. While not flashy, her methods were both effective and direct.

Lloyd's style was more flamboyant, but that didn't make it better. The combination of parries, counters and spins he used worked well with two weapons, especially when fighting multiple opponents. Being a spiritblade is what made that viable. Strangely enough, Lloyd hadn't even touched a blade for the first year of his training. That time had been solely dedicated to physical conditioning and meditation. Once he did pick up a blade, it was strictly one-handed. It took him five long years and many hours of sweat, cuts, and bruises to master the sword. Even then, he could not have pulled off his current fighting style without mental and spiritual training.

His first real breakthrough came after years of deep meditation when he finally made contact with his inner spirit. Once he found that spark, he was able to call forth the power from within. Lloyd could suddenly move faster, hit harder, and withstand more punishment than ever before. It was then that he adopted his current two weapon style, but his studies didn't end there. With his newfound skills he learned to combine body, mind and spirit—to execute quick, precise movements and envision clear mental images, all while calling forth his spirit energy. He had become a blade adept—a spiritblade.

A sudden movement caught Lloyd's eye. A small black figure flew down from the tree tops toward them; it was Glo's familiar, Raven. The bird landed on a nearby tree branch and cawed briefly at Titan, Aksel, and himself, *"Tana carina, tana carina."*

"That's the signal," Aksel whispered. "The sentries are gone. Now it's your turn. Go!"

Lloyd glanced at Titan. They exchanged a quick nod, then took off through the trees. Titan fell a bit behind, but not far, considering she was running in heavy armor. Lloyd heard shouts through the trees ahead. He burst into a clearing and found five orcs ducking and dodging as one arrow after another flew at them. A brief smile crossed Lloyd's lips. Brundon was doing an excellent job.

Lloyd charged forward, his blades igniting as he closed in on the two nearest bandits. He swung his swords in wide sweeping arcs, catching both orc warriors with a burning blade. A battle cry sounded beside him and a glimpse of shining silver flash passed. Titan entered the fray and engaged the other two orcs, but Lloyd was too busy for more than a fleeting glance.

He continued to move, allowing his body to flow with his blades. Lloyd spun his twin swords in unison with his body, deftly parrying the curved blades that came at him. He had just finished off one of his foes, when a scream rang out across the clearing. Lloyd parried a strike and threw back his opponent, chancing a quick glance around the battlefield.

The orc cleric had dropped its staff and was clutching an arm with an arrow protruding from it. The briefest of smiles flitted across Lloyd's lips, for at that same moment, Titan's shield bashed a foe and sent it careening back into the orc Lloyd had been fighting. The two orcs slammed into each other and went tumbling to the ground.

There was one orc still standing. As it rushed Titan, Lloyd quieted his mind, the world slowing around him. He struck a well-practiced pose, his arms moving in swift, intricate motions. He reached down deep inside, searching for that spark of inner spirit, and at the same time envisioned his body rushing forward with incredible speed. The whole effort took just under a second—and suddenly the world rushed past him.

As Titan parried the orc's assault, Lloyd was suddenly behind it. He swung with all his might, lopping the head clean off the unsuspecting monster. Titan flashed him a quick grin and then the two of them rushed the remaining warriors. The fight was quickly over.

Lloyd surveyed the clearing. He just caught a glimpse of the enemy cleric as it disappeared through the trees at the other end of the glade. At the same time, a dark figure skirted the clearing in hot pursuit of the retreating orc.

"Brundon's got him," Titan said with just a trace of pride.

Lloyd was amazed at how fast the tracker wove through the trees after his prey. He turned back toward Titan and saw the satisfied grin on her face.

"It'll never get away from Brundon. He'll track it from here to Tarrsmorr if need be."

Lloyd grinned back at the warrior. "Of that I have little doubt."

Aksel entered the clearing from behind them. "Where's Glo and Seth?"

A voice rang out behind them. Lloyd spun around and saw Glo enter the glade. "Seth took off after Brundon and that orc priest."

"Did you see which way they were headed?"

"North."

Aksel's eyes swept the glade. "I think we're done here. Let's get back to our mounts and follow them."

Lloyd led the way, followed by Glo and Aksel, with Titan bringing up the rear. They had only gone a short way when Lloyd spied a small black figure winging its way down from the treetops. It was Raven. He watched her land on Glo's arm and listened as the wizard spoke to her in Elvish. Glo then held out his arm and the black bird took off again, propelling herself up and away. She spiraled up to the treetops and then flew off toward the north. "If she spots them, I can get a sense of where they are."

Lloyd was impressed. "My mom's familiar never does much other than lay around the lab—and occasionally light things on fire."

"Really? What kind of familiar is it?"

"A mini-dragon."

Glo was silent for a moment. "Do you mean pseudodragon?"

"Yes. That was the word for it."

Aksel called forward, "Lloyd, what's your mother's name?"

"Lara. Lara Stealle."

Both Aksel and Glo fell silent. A puzzled expression crossed Aksel's face. "Does she have another name?"

She did in fact. She had a number of them. Names and titles from all the various roles she played in Penwick society. "Well, her maiden name is Hault. That is the name she used for the school. But she is also known as the High Wizard of Penwick."

"High Wizard? As in the top wizard in the city?" There was a note of surprise in Glo's voice.

"Yes." Lloyd had thought that rather obvious.

Aksel's hand went to his chin. "Um, Lloyd—what school were you referring to?"

"The Hault School of Magic. It's the school she founded to train magic users."

"Interesting," Glo said. "A school devoted to training wizards? We have nothing like that in Cairthrellon."

"Perhaps elves prefer training alone?" Titan called out from the rear.

"Unfortunately, that is more accurate than you know," Glo said.

Aksel addressed Lloyd again, his tone somewhat strained, "So your mother's maiden name is Hault? As in Lara Hault; the only wizard to ever turn down a seat on the Wizard's Council?"

Lloyd started to feel embarrassed. This is why he didn't like talking about his parents. "That's her."

Glo's tone was incredulous. "Let me get this straight. Your mom is High Wizard of Penwick, runs a magic school, and turned down a seat on the Wizard's Council; the same council that rules over the entire magical community of Thac?"

Lloyd let out a deep sigh. "Yes." This is exactly what he was afraid of. He didn't want his new friends to start treating him differently just because of his parents' fame. "Look, it wasn't all that big of a deal. She just didn't want to be away from Penwick. Between her research, the school, and the reconstruction projects, she just doesn't have the time. Anyway, according to her, '*The council is just a bunch of stuffy old men and women who wouldn't know the truth about magic if it jumped up and bit them.*'"

Glo, Aksel and Titan all broke out in laughter. Lloyd felt suddenly relieved, the tension in his shoulders dissipating. Glo was still chuckling when he spoke up again, "It sounds like your mom is not afraid to speak her mind."

Lloyd shrugged. "Yeah, that's my mom alright. She's not very tolerant of nonsense. She thinks other wizards are full of themselves." Lloyd suddenly realized what he had said. "Sorry, Glo. No offense intended."

Glo let out a short laugh. "None taken. In fact, I quite agree with your mom."

Lloyd thought about that for a moment. Glo really wasn't like other wizards. He was neither stuffy nor did he act self-important.

"You know, I have a feeling my mom just might like you, Glo. You're not exactly a typical wizard."

Glo's tone was ironic. "I'll take that as a compliment."

A short while later they recovered their mounts. Lloyd continued to lead the way, Titan bringing up the rear. They soon picked up the trail of the fleeing orc. The companions followed the tracks for nearly an hour. Night had almost fallen when Glo announced, "We're very close. Raven's only a few hundred yards away."

Lloyd scanned the forest ahead. "It looks like the trees are thinning out. We must be near the north end of the woods."

"About five hundred yards ahead," said a disembodied voice. It sounded like Seth, but there was no sign of him anywhere. Abruptly, the halfling appeared out of thin air.

Glo rode up and fixed an eye on Seth. "Playing with that cloak again?"

The corner of Seth's mouth lifted slightly. "Wouldn't you?"

"Yes," the wizard admitted, his tone somewhat wistful.

Aksel rode up next to them. "Where's Brundon? And where's that orc priest?"

"The orc left the woods and headed up the hillside into a cave. Brundon is waiting at the forest's edge, keeping an eye on the entrance. I circled back to stop you from charging on ahead and making a ton of noise."

Glo glared at Seth. "Elves do not make a ton of noise."

"No, but you can hear Titan's armor clanking from a mile away."

Titan rode up next to them. She fixed Seth with a steely-eyed stare. "I do not clank. Jingle, perhaps, but not clank."

Seth held up his hands. "Ok, maybe not that bad, but we have no idea how many orcs are up in that cave. We need to be as quiet as possible."

Titan nodded. "Point taken."

They dismounted and led their mounts from there. At the forest's edge, they tethered their steeds and hiked the rest of the way. Brundon waited at the tree line, nestled behind a group of boulders. Beyond there, the trees opened up, revealing a gentle, grassy slope. It receded perhaps another hundred yards, then ended at the base of a hill, part of a range of hills that rose up beyond that point.

Everyone gathered around Brundon, and he brought them up to speed. "The orc entered the cave a short while ago. I haven't seen anything move in or out of the cave since."

"Perhaps it leads farther back inside the hills," Aksel mused. He turned to Seth. "Would you like to do a little scouting?"

Seth shrugged. "Sure, why not." He wrapped himself in his cloak and said a single word in a language Lloyd did not understand. Seth then vanished into thin air.

Lloyd was impressed, but it was not the invisibility that amazed him. Lloyd's mother could do that just as well. It was that once Seth disappeared, he was so silent that he was near impossible to detect.

There were a few trees up the slope, so Glo sent Raven to keep a closer watch over the cave entrance. Now there was nothing to do but wait. It was all up to Seth, but at the first sign of trouble, Lloyd would be ready.

22
THE CAVE GUARDIAN

These creatures were extremely hard to kill

Seth left the forest behind and climbed the grassy slope toward the cave. Night had fallen, shrouding the earth in darkness. It would be hours before the moon rose. The shadows of the rolling hills rose into the sky before him and the tall trees of the Bendenwoods behind. Directly above, a star-studded strip stretched across the sky. He stole through the grass, the night quiet around him. The only sounds that reached his ears were the soft chirping of crickets, the rustling of leaves, or the occasional hoot of an owl. A gentle breeze brushed against his skin, bringing the scent of pine from the forest below.

Seth moved slowly, making no noise as he closed in on the cave. He was perhaps two dozen yards away, when he spied a faint glow coming from inside.

Thump.

Seth froze in his tracks. *What was that?*

Thump.

There it was again. *That came from the cave.*

As the thumping grew louder, a shadow appeared inside the cave. It grew in size until it blotted out the dim light emanating from the cavern. The thumping grew louder, finally punctuated by a low growl.

Seth felt a chill run up his spine. He thought about backing away, but then told himself he would be fine; after all, he was invisible. He watched with fascination as a creature emerged from the cave. The hulking shadow was man-shaped but hunched over. The silhouette slowly expanded upwards, two giant arms stretching out toward the sky above. One of those arms held a long cylindrical object—most likely a club. There was a deep groan, then those thick arms fell to hang low at the creature's side. The beast was huge, nearly as large as one of those stone golems they had seen back at the keep. A broad, square-shaped head stood above its wide shoulders, supported by a short, thick neck. Seth caught a momentary glimpse of mottled green skin.

Troll. That's what this thing is. He felt another shiver run up his spine. If he was not invisible, he would be in immense danger.

Trolls were brutish creatures that ate almost anything alive. Their great size and strength made them formidable opponents. They were also quite agile, despite their ponderous frames. Still, that was not the worst thing about fighting one. These creatures were extremely hard to kill. If you sliced a troll, the wound would immediately start to heal. The regenerative powers of these monsters was legendary. Even if you cut off its head, it would start to grow one back. The only way to defeat a troll was to use fire or acid. That would cauterize the wound and stop the creature's body from regenerating.

Seth stayed completely motionless, carefully watching the silhouette of the troll. The creature stood at the cave entrance, its large head swiveling from side to side. Abruptly the head stopped. Seth heard sniffing sounds. The head began to move again, back and forth, the monster still sampling the air.

It must have caught some scent.

Abruptly the head turned in his direction. It lifted slightly and sniffed once, then twice.

The thing smells me!

The troll lowered its head and growled, then slowly lumbered forward. Seth's blood turned to ice. He fought the instinctive urge to run. It might smell him, but if it heard him too, he'd be a goner for sure. Seth forced himself to slowly back away. The troll was moving faster now, advancing at a pace that belied its large frame.

I've got to do something quick, or it'll be on top of me in no time.

He glanced around and spied a tree behind him and to the right. He altered his course toward it, backpedaling as silently as possible. The troll continued to close the gap between them till it was only a few yards away. It towered over him, the fetid odor of its unwashed body assaulting his nostrils.

And I thought orcs smelled bad.

A few more steps and it would trample him, invisible or not. Seth chanced another quick glance behind him. He had almost reached the tree. Just a few more steps was all he needed.

Abruptly, the monster halted. It sniffed the air.

It was now or never. Seth bolted for the tree. A loud roar sounded behind him and he felt the ground shake as the troll thudded after him. Not stopping, he ran with all the speed he could muster. The thudding grew closer and he could feel the whoosh of the monster's great club as it swung through the air behind him.

With a mighty leap, Seth launched himself at the trunk of the tree. He grabbed on and scrambled up the side. Just as he reached the lower limbs, something slammed into the trunk below him. He heard a loud *crack* and the entire tree shook.

Seth almost lost his grip, but somehow he managed to hang on. He scrambled up into the tree limbs and did not stop until he was halfway up the tree. Another roar sounded from below. He looked down and saw the troll, its blood red eyes searching the branches for him. He was out of its reach for the moment, but he was far from safe. Trolls were extremely strong. If it couldn't find him, it might just decide to uproot the entire tree.

A sudden movement caught Seth's eyes. A black bird sat a few limbs over, staring at him oddly.

Is that Raven? If it was, then Glo would know he's in trouble.

At that moment, a faint sound reached his ears. It was hard to hear over the growling of the troll below, but it sounded like…clinking. The troll must have heard it too. Its red eyes suddenly disappeared from sight; its heavy footsteps receded from underneath the tree.

Seth stood up and parted the branches, searching for the source of that sound. Five shadows moved up the slope from the forest below, the lead shadow a bit ahead of the others.

That must be Lloyd! The clinking would be Titan right behind him. Seth felt a brief moment of relief, but it quickly passed. The others were coming to his rescue but had no idea what they were up against. Thankfully, the troll was most obliging in that area. It stood out in the open, lifted its arms and roared.

As if in answer to its challenge, a bright red beam of light lanced across the night from down the slope. It pierced through the darkness and caught the troll straight in the chest. The beam illuminated the creature as it hit, making its features momentarily visible to the naked eye.

The huge, ugly, flat face winced as its chest smoldered from the impact of the fiery beam. The troll's mouth opened wide as it roared in pain, exposing a row of wicked pointed yellow teeth.

Seth had to stifle a laugh. The monster had practically asked for that one. Luckily, Glo had a new fire spell with which to answer.

With the troll's attention firmly fixed on the others, Seth was now free to move. He leapt to the ground, tumbled gracefully, and rolled to a squatting position. He spun around just in time to see Lloyd engage the troll.

The warrior's blades burst into flames as he launched into the monster. He dodged under its huge club, then sliced into it with both swords, cutting deep into the monster's hide. The troll yelped in pain, taking another wild swing at the warrior. Lloyd easily dodged out of the way.

The clinking had grown loud now, the starlight shining dimly on Titan's armor as she closed in on the fierce battle. She was mere moments away from entering the fray. Meanwhile, Seth circled around the troll, trying to get directly behind it. He had no weapon that could harm the big creature, but a wild idea came to mind.

Lloyd was back to slicing at the troll. Two more cuts gashed the creature, sizzling and scorching its mottled green skin.

The troll swung its huge club at the red-clad warrior. Lloyd twisted out of the way, but this time the edge of the club caught him in the back. It was a glancing blow, but the force of it knocked him onto his face.

As the troll advanced on the downed warrior, Titan was suddenly there. She inserted herself between Lloyd and the monster, her shield ready for the impending blow.

The troll raised its huge arm to swing, but flinched as two arrows embedded themselves in the side of its head. A moment later, another red beam of light lanced through the night and caught the monster in the chest. The troll roared in response, beating its torso and trying to put out the smoldering fires on its chest.

Seth was now behind the troll. He unslung his backpack, knelt down and pulled out a torch. When he looked back up, Lloyd was on his feet. He and Titan split up, flanking the troll from opposite sides.

They began a staggered set of attacks on the monster. First, Lloyd charged in, slashing with those burning blades. As the troll tried to retaliate, Titan rushed in from the other side, attacking with her gleaming sword.

All the while, Seth continued preparing his wild scheme. He found some flint in his pack, then laid out some twigs. He used the flint and a small stone to start a fire.

The battle with the troll continued on. The monster seemed confused, flailing its massive club around, back and forth, but not connecting with either foe. The two warriors kept up the dual-pronged attack, the troll's hide now crisscrossed with scorched gashes.

Meanwhile, Seth had been fanning the flames. He now had a decent fire going and stuck the end of his torch in the burning fire. A savage roar caused him to glance up again.

The troll was enraged, flailing wildly about with its club. Lloyd somehow managed to get around it and slash the troll with his fiery swords, but as he backed away, the troll caught him with a quick backswing. Lloyd took the hit full in the chest and was sent flying backwards, his blades careening out of his hands.

The troll roared in triumph and rushed in to finish the downed warrior. Titan chased after it, brutally slashing at the creature from behind, but to no avail. The monster was intent on murdering the foe who had burned it so badly.

Two more arrows embedded themselves into the troll's head, but the creature completely ignored them. It hulked over the stunned Lloyd, its massive club lifted, preparing for the killing blow.

At the last moment, two purple projectiles arced through the air, catching the troll directly in the face. There were two mild concussion sounds, the monster's head snapping back with each one. The troll shook its head, momentarily stunned by the unexpected onslaught.

Titan took advantage of the momentary pause, running past the shaken monster and once again placing herself between it and Lloyd. The warrior held up her shield, bracing for the heavy blow that was sure to come. Lloyd was still on the ground. He had begun to stir, but there was no way he would recover in time.

A sudden rage erupted inside Seth. *No. Not again. Never again.*

The torch was now burning nicely. Without a second thought, Seth grabbed it and darted up behind the troll. The massive form towered over him, but Seth was too livid to care. He grasped the end of the torch with both hands and thrust upwards with all of his might. It wedged itself into the troll's posterior, embers scattering in all directions.

The troll let out a loud grunt, then screamed in pain. It dropped its club, reaching behind with both hands to grab at the torch. Seth tumbled out of the way, swiftly putting as much distance as he could between himself and the monster.

His distraction worked. While the troll pulled the torch from its painful perch, Lloyd rose back to his feet. He recovered his blades, then joined Titan in a renewed assault.

The monster had just plucked the torch from its rear end, when the two warriors drove into it. They hacked away with rhythmic precision; one, two swings from Lloyd, a third swing from Titan. They continued to slash away, driving the troll slowly backwards.

The monster desperately tried to fight back, but no longer had its club. It flailed around wildly with its huge fists, but Lloyd dodged them and Titan blocked them with her shield.

The fight went on for a few more minutes, then finally the troll went down. The two warriors continued their onslaught until the troll lay in an unmoving heap.

The companions regrouped a short distance away from the body. Aksel went straight to Lloyd's side. "You took a heck of a beating. Let's make sure you're alright."

Lloyd must have been in great pain. He sat down without protest, not even bothering to sheath his swords. Aksel held his hands over him, running them up and down the length of Lloyd's body. About a minute later he stopped. "This could take a while, Lloyd. Please sit still."

Lloyd merely nodded.

Once again, the little cleric stretched his hands over the battered warrior. This time he chanted softly as he did so. Healing white light began to pulse from his hands and slowly engulf Lloyd's body. The rest of them stood a short distance away, their faces bathed in Aksel's healing light.

Seth glanced around the group. "Thanks for the assist, guys."

Titan let out a short laugh. "I think we should be thanking you."

Glo appeared rather amused. "Yes, that was a very interesting technique that you used on that troll. I don't think I've ever seen anything like that before."

Brundon's mouth twisted into a half grin. "Yeah, Seth, what do you call that move?"

"Oh, it's just something I made up on the spot." He really had not given it much thought. It had been funny though, and it worked to boot. Perhaps he should name it.

Glo, his expression completely deadpan, had a suggestion. "How about calling it *Fire in the Hole?*"

Seth and the others snorted, breaking out into short fits of laughter. *Fire in the Hole?* That was actually funny. Even more so that it had come from Glo.

Glo met Seth's surprised stare with a thin smile. Then, much to his surprise, Glo winked at him!

Wow. Would wonders never cease? Glo was developing a sense of humor. Now that was unexpected. Seth grinned wryly at his elven friend. Perhaps there was hope for him yet.

23
THE ELVEN BARD

Strange night for a stroll in the woods

Elladan had not seen the first volley of arrows. He might have heard them if he had not been gaily strumming his lute. Without warning, the driver next to him slumped down in his seat. The young elven bard dropped his lute and reached for the man.

"Are you alri…" As Elladan touched him, the driver toppled over off the wagon.

"What the…" Elladan immediately slid over and grabbed the reins, pulling the wagon to a halt. As he jumped down, he heard a whizzing noise.

Thunk.

Elladan glanced up. An arrow protruded from the side of the wagon, right where he had been sitting moments ago. He immediately hit the dirt.

That was way too close. Elladan tried to see where the arrow had come from, but it was nighttime and the surrounding woods were way too dark. He suddenly remembered the driver. Elladan got up on his hands and knees. The driver still lay in the road a few yards back, an arrow protruding from his chest.

As he crawled over to the man, screams erupted from down the road. A group of figures burst from the forest and charged the wagon behind his. They growled and snarled as they bore down on the caravan.

Orcs!

Crack! The sound of a whip rang out behind him, followed by the sounds of horses' hooves. He looked behind him and saw the lead wagon take off down the road. Elladan turned back and crawled like mad over to the driver. When he reached him, he found that the man was dead.

More cries came from the wagon behind him. The attackers had stopped their charge and were exchanging arrows with its occupants.

Aw heck, what do I do now? I'm no fighter.

As if to answer his question, one of the orcs turned in his direction. Elladan had no choice; he ran for his own wagon. If he got it moving, maybe the others could still get away.

He heard whizzing once more as he leapt up onto the wagon. A sharp pain lanced up his left arm as he landed on the wagon seat. He glanced down to see his shirt torn and a stripe of red welled up through the hole, but luckily no arrow.

Ha. Missed me!

He'd take care of the arm later. The young elf grabbed the reins and gave them a hard tug. It didn't take much. The horses were already nervous and bolted down the road. Elladan checked behind him and saw the besieged wagon also jerk forward.

It's working! We're going to get away.

He flew down the road at break neck speed, the wagon jolting all over the place threatening to shake apart. Elladan pulled back hard on the reins, but the horses fought him and kept running at top speed.

"Hold on there!" he cried.

He leaned back and tugged as hard as he could.

Snap!

The reins suddenly came loose in his hands—he almost fell backwards into the wagon. Elladan somehow managed to right himself and then held on for dear life. The horses ran wild now, completely out of control.

The dark forest flew by on either side, everything a blur. They hit something in the road and the wagon jolted up in the air. It came down hard, jarring his teeth. If that happened again, the whole wagon would come to pieces!

I've got to do something.

The other half of the broken reins lay just out of reach, resting on the long wooden tongue that separated the two animals.

If I can just reach them.

Elladan stood up, precariously balancing himself on the jerking wagon. He slowly bent forward, stretching for the reins.

Just a little more.

The forest continued to flash by in a blur.

Almost there.

Crack!

The wagon jolted underneath him, then swayed to the left. Elladan teetered precariously as the horses raced on. Abruptly, the wagon overturned and he was sent flying through the air, the forest floor whooshing by underneath him. Something large and dark loomed up before him. Elladan covered his head, sure he was going to die. By the grace of the gods, he missed whatever it was. He let out a sigh but tensed up immediately as he hit the bushes. His clothes tore and something sharp raked against his skin as he flew through the brush. Moments later he slammed into something and everything went black.

Elladan's eyes snapped open. All he could see was darkness.

Where am I?

He tried to move but found he was tangled up in a thick bramble. He thrashed around, trying to free himself, then suddenly remembered how he had gotten there. Elladan froze, not daring to breath.

He listened carefully to his surroundings but heard nothing. The forest was quiet. He counted out a full minute before moving again, slowly this time. He found that he ached all over. Elladan carefully extracted himself from the wooden thicket. When he finally got free, he gave himself the once over. He was bruised and scratched up, but luckily nothing was broken. That bramble he had got stuck in had saved his life.

My lute!

It was nowhere on him. Elladan turned around and crawled back into the brush. He found the instrument right next to where he had landed. By some miracle it was still intact.

Elladan carefully rose to his feet and got his bearings. He could just make out the road through the trees. It was probably a good ten yards away. He silently crept to the edge of the forest and looked out from behind the bushes. A broken wheel lay in the middle of the road. Off to his left he spied the remains of the wagon, completely turned over on its side.

Beyond that he saw the lead wagon stopped in the middle of the road. Figures scurried around it, some carrying torches. In the dim light he could see their faces: monkey-like, with two short tusks protruding from the lower jaw, and greenish-hued skin.

Orcs!

The lead wagon hadn't gotten away after all. That's when he noticed the bodies strewn all over the ground. Elladan stifled a reflex gag.

This is no time for queasiness.

He glanced down the road the other way. Three more wagons were lined up there. There were more bodies and more orc bandits looting the remains of the caravan.

The thieving scoundrels! They killed everyone.

It took all of his restraint to keep from dashing out and attacking the murderous fiends. Reason took over as his anger cooled.

It will do no good. I'll just get myself killed. He was no warrior. He was just a bard.

The best thing he could do now would be to make it back to civilization. Folks needed to be warned that there were orc bandits in these woods. They could send an army out here to rout the fiends, and he would come back with them. He would play magical tunes on his lute and encourage the warriors to roust the bandits and send them to their graves for what they had done. But first he needed to make it out of these woods alive.

With orcs to the east and west, he could not take the road. No, it would be better to head north and find his way out of the woods that way. Elladan was a student of geography. He knew this area, or at least on paper. There were hills north of here—the Vogels. He would make it to those hills and then follow them east to Ravenford. There he could report what had happened. His mind made up, the bard took one last look at the hapless caravan.

Those poor souls. I will write a song to honor them someday. With that thought, he turned and backtracked into the forest.

After wandering around the forest for a couple of hours, Elladan was no closer to finding his way out. Sure he was an elf. His home of Kai-Arborus was a city in the trees in the great forest of Rua-naiaith—for all the good it did him. He was a city dweller with no tracking or survival skills. Thus Elladan was totally lost out here in the forest. He continued plodding his way through the never-ending brush, when suddenly he found himself on a wide dirt path.

Finally! The first signs of civilization he had seen in hours.

Elladan followed the path, a spring back in his step. It was far easier going now that he was out of the underbrush. Another hour passed and his resolve began to waver, when he caught sight of the trees parting ahead. With renewed vigor, Elladan sprinted forward until he reached the edge of the forest.

He breathed a sigh of relief. *I made it!*

The moon was out, casting a silvery sheen to the surrounding landscape. Ahead of him rose the shadow of a group of rolling hills. The road wound across a grassy slope all the way to the base of those hills. The edge of the forest continued to either side of him as far as the eye could see. Elladan paused, trying to decide what to do next.

As he stood there, a sound reached his ears from the trail behind him. Still unnerved from the night's events, he ducked back into the woods, burying himself in a deep wood thicket. He peeked out and waited. He watched with growing uneasiness as a line of wagons appeared on the trail. His gut twisted as he got a good look at the drivers.

Orcs!

These were the wagons from his caravan. One of them rode lopsided on a badly patched wheel. Elladan held his breath as they drove past. He continuing to watch as the orc caravan followed the path up to the hillside, till one by one, each wagon disappeared.

Elladan's curiosity got the better of him. He left the woods and crept through the grass, paralleling the dirt path. When he got within a hundred yards of the hillside, he saw a darker area illuminated by the moonlight.

There's a cave! That was where the wagons had disappeared to. Well, now he knew where the scoundrels' hideout was. He would get back to civilization and report this and then return with an army.

These bandits' days are numbered. With that last thought, the young elf headed back toward the forest's edge and then turned eastward.

Perhaps an hour later, the weary bard still trekked eastward. His progress was slow as he sought camouflage from the woods. That second encounter with the orcs had spooked him, and he was not going to travel out in the open, even if it delayed his long journey. As he picked his way through the underbrush, he called up a mental image of a map of this area. If he kept moving east, the Bendenwoods would eventually end and he would find the road east toward Ravenford. It was probably still another day's journey by foot, and he was already exhausted from having been up all night. Still, there was no hope for it. He had to let folks know what had happened out here.

"Strange night for a stroll in the woods."

Elladan nearly jumped out of his skin. He froze in his tracks, glancing around furtively for the source of the voice. His eyes finally fixed on a dark figure standing off to his right, well hidden by the forest's vegetation. Whoever this was, they spoke the common tongue. Also the frame was lean, not bulky like an orc. It was perhaps a bit taller than he—most likely a human.

"Who…who are you?" he finally managed to say.

The figure answered in a rather nonchalant tone, "Just a tracker. The more important question is, who are you, my friend?"

Elladan was not fooled. That statement was deceptively mild. This human was obviously the suspicious type. He could respect that. *Trust no one* was one of his own mottos. Still, whoever this human was, he was certainly not in league with the bandits. Orcs considered humans food. If the man was indeed a tracker, then running into him was a stroke of luck. Elladan decided to confide in this shadowy figure, if only just a little.

"I am a mere entertainer, separated from my caravan by chance misfortune."

The figure moved closer. "Separated from your caravan, you say?"

Moonlight shone through the trees, illuminating the man. He was dark-haired with a slim face and a hawkish nose. He sported a mustache and a thin black beard. Elladan also noted a bow and quiver across the man's back as well as a sword hanging at his belt. The man's hand rested gently on the hilt.

Elladan felt a bit more comfortable now that he could see the man's face. "Indeed. We were attacked."

The man's eyes narrowed. "Attacked? By whom?"

"Orcs."

The man's expression grew skeptical. "Orcs? But how could that be?"

Elladan found his reaction strange. It was almost as if he already knew about the orcs, yet was surprised they had attacked his caravan.

"Trust me, friend, we were all taken by surprise."

The man stepped closer, gazing at him with keen eyes. Elladan also observed his hand had dropped away from his sword hilt. "Tell me, when did this attack happen?"

"Just after sunset. The caravan was running late, and we hadn't quite made it out of the woods yet."

"Just after sunset," the man repeated slowly. "How many of them were there?"

"I'm not sure…" Elladan thought back to the assault and tried to count the attackers in his mind. "Probably about seven or eight."

The man stepped back, his face taking on a resolute expression. "We have to warn the others."

"Others?"

"The group I'm traveling with," the man clarified. "Follow me, and I'll explain along the way." He turned around and headed toward the edge of the woods.

Elladan hesitated for a split second, then took off after the man. "Wait!" he called in a semi-hushed voice. "What's your name?"

"Brundon," the man replied softly, not slowing down in the slightest.

The sun had just crested over the horizon when Brundon led Elladan up the slope toward the hillside. The tracker was very agile, and the exhausted bard struggled to keep up with him, but somehow managed. In the early morning light, he could clearly see the chain of rolling hills rising up in front of them.

Those are definitely the Vogels, Elladan thought. He was not sure why the tracker was leading him this way, but he decided not to question the man. It was then Elladan spotted the cave mouth looming up ahead of them. That was the tracker's destination. Elladan breathed a sigh of relief. Finally, a place to hide out in this accursed wilderness, even if it was a dank cave.

As they drew up toward the cave's entrance, Brundon stopped and scanned the countryside around them. Elladan followed his gaze, his eyes stopping as they fell on what appeared to be a body. The young elf's eyes narrowed. It was a body—a rather huge body in fact. He immediately recognized it—the green mottled skin and huge flat face were a dead giveaway; that was a troll!

Brundon followed his gaze. "Cave troll. We had a run in with it last night."

Elladan's eyes grew wide. "You took down a cave troll?"

Brundon snorted. "Not alone, I assure you. No, we are traveling with some rather impressive folks."

Elladan could only nod his agreement. Cave trolls were nasty creatures. It would require a considerable amount of power to take one down. Brundon shook him out of his musings.

"Shall we?" The tracker turned toward the cave's mouth and motioned him to follow. The entrance to the cave was dark, though he could see a dim light farther in the back. They had not taken two steps inside when a large figure loomed in front of them. Elladan was momentarily startled, but then the figure stepped into the light of the morning sun.

Elladan raised an eyebrow. It was a woman, a tall human woman. A warrior in fact, outfitted in full plate armor with a longsword strapped to her side. She was easily a head taller than Elladan, her shoulders broader than his. Her hair was a dirty blonde, braided on both sides and down the center in a warrior-like fashion. She gave him a steely-eyed stare, a thin smile across her lips.

"Picking up strays, I see."

Brundon's response was equally laced with sarcasm. "Very funny, love. Actually, I found him wandering in the woods. Says his caravan was attacked by orcs."

Her expression swiftly changed, replaced with a look of surprise. "How can that be? I thought we had driven them off."

"Obviously there's more of them."

"More of whom?" came another voice from inside the cave.

Elladan peered around the warrior and saw a tall, thin form outlined in the dim light. He squinted, trying to make out the stranger's features in the darkness. He found he could not, but the figure swiftly stepped into the morning light. Elladan had to do a double take.

It's an elf! The lithe form and the pointed ears were unmistakable. *The chances of running into another elf so far from home…* The bard stopped in mid-thought. There was something off about this elf. For one, he was way too tall. Elladan was one of the tallest elves back home, but this elf was a good head taller than he. What's more, he had pale blonde hair. No elf he had ever met had hair that color.

What kind of elf… It hit him. This was a Galinthral elf, one of the subjects of the great elven king, Galinthrae. But that was impossible! The Galinthral had disappeared with the legendary city of Cairthrellon over five hundred years ago. Since then, many had searched the Ruanaiaith where Cairthrellon was purported to have been. None had ever found it. Many searchers had not returned at all. Still, standing here in front of him was clearly a Galinthral elf. There was no mistaking it.

A less sophisticated elf might have been rendered speechless, but not Elladan. He was a consummate performer and not easily rattled. After only a momentary pause, he executed a deep bow and introduced himself.

"Elladan, of the House of Narmolanya. *Elen sila lumenn omentil-mo*," he added in formal Elvish. In the common tongue, that roughly translated to *a star shall shine on the hour of our meeting*. It seemed rather appropriate, given the circumstances.

The corners of the other elf's lips upturned slightly. He bowed in turn. "Glolindir Arshatheriat of the House of Eodin. *Saesa omentien lle*," which meant *a pleasure meeting you*.

Brundon cleared his throat. "Ahem. Wizard Glolindir, our new friend Elladan here seems to have had a run in with more orcs last night."

"More orcs?" said a high-pitched voice from inside the cave.

Three more figures appeared behind Glolindir, two rather small, but the third taller than all of them. They stepped into the light and Elladan saw that the smaller figures were a gnome and a halfling.

The former wore white cleric robes with the symbol of a diamond across the chest. Copper hair tumbled over his face but did not completely cover his pointed gnomish ears. His expression was grim, his eyes intense as he regarded Elladan. The latter, in stark contrast, was dressed almost completely in black with the exception of the green cloak wrapped around his shoulders. He had a knife strapped to his leg and a pouched belt around his waist. He was rather lean, his thin face topped with jet black hair pulled back tight into a pony tail. The halfling also eyed Elladan intently, a clear expression of distrust on his face.

A tall figure loomed behind the duo, capturing Elladan's attention. It was probably the largest man he had ever seen—broad shouldered, but not stocky, garbed in red leather armor from the neck down to his thighs and from his knees down. His youthful face was rather handsome, framed with a shock of tousled brown hair. The young man regarded Elladan rather pleasantly.

Brundon pointed at the gnome, then the halfling and ended with the tall man. "Elladan, this is Aksel, Seth, and Lloyd. Everyone, this is Elladan."

The gnome, Aksel, replied with a very formal, "Welcome, good traveler."

The halfling, Seth, just nodded and continued to eye him with suspicion.

Lloyd stepped past Glolindir and extended his hand, a smile on his youthful face. "Pleased to meet you."

Elladan grasped the young man's hand and immediately regretted it. His grip was like iron! "Likewise," Elladan managed. The big man released his hand, and Elladan pulled it back, rubbing it to try and get the feeling back in it.

"So what was this about more orcs?" The gnome spoke with authority.

Elladan immediately recognized that tone. Aksel was the leader of this group. That was surprising. He would have thought that Lloyd or possibly Glolindir would be the head of this strange little group. "It is a rather long story, and I've been on my feet all night. You wouldn't have some refreshments for a weary traveler?"

"Of course," Aksel responded with a polite nod. "Please join us." He ushered Elladan inside the cave. The others made room for him to pass, though the halfling continued to eye him with suspicion.

The cave was rather deep. Elladan guessed it went back about thirty yards before ending in a blank wall. The last ten yards opened up into a wide area with a fire pit and a well near the back wall. There was a small fire going in the pit, a number of blankets scattered around it in a circle. A ring of stones encircled the entire area. Aksel provided Elladan with a canteen of water, and the bard quenched his thirst. Everyone gathered around and grabbed a seat, except for the tall woman warrior. She remained guard by the cave entrance.

Elladan then relayed the story of the ill-fated caravan. As the tale unfolded, he kept a sharp eye on his audience. Their expressions were grim. Aksel in particular was mortified by the massacre. Elladan expected that reaction from a cleric, but he was surprised to see a trace of moisture in Lloyd's eyes as well. Everyone showed deep concern and sympathy except for Seth. The halfling was quite difficult to read, his face a stony mask as he listened to the account.

When Elladan finished, Aksel let out a deep sigh. "You have my deepest sympathies; that should not have happened."

"If it actually did," Seth said, his tone skeptical.

Elladan could not help smiling. Here was someone as cynical as he. Elladan admired that trait in others. "I do not blame you, friend. You do not know me. It is usually my own policy to trust no one, but these are unusual circumstances. And it is times like these that force us to look beyond our normal distrust of one another and band together to face a common foe."

Elladan paused briefly, gauging his audience once more. He definitely had their attention. His voice rose in force as he continued to speak. "These orcs killed everyone in my caravan and made off with their wagons. They must be hunted down and made to pay for their crimes!"

Lloyd jumped up from his seat and cried, "I vow to you that these orcs will pay."

"Shhhh," Seth hissed. "Why don't you just warn them we're coming?"

Lloyd's hand went to the back of his head. "Sorry," he said in a soft voice.

Elladan was puzzled by the halfling's reaction. "What do you mean?"

Aksel looked from Seth to Lloyd and let out a sigh. He then turned back to Elladan and explained further. "Yesterday, we caught a group of orcs laying in ambush along the road. We let one escape and followed it back to this cave. It never came back out, so it must have gone down there." He nudged his head toward the well at the back of the cave.

"It most likely is connected to the orc's lair. So it would be best to refrain from loud noises," Glolindir said.

Elladan nodded. "That makes sense."

He was rather impressed with this group. It was a sound strategy, following the orc back to its hideout.

Glolindir addressed him once more, "Your story is quite plausible. The orc we were chasing made it up to the cave just around sunset. Assuming the well leads to their lair, he could have easily alerted the bandits in time to gather a second party. They could have rushed back down to the road in time to ambush your caravan. Especially if you were running late, as you said."

Aksel cleared his throat. "Well, I for one am interested in this other cave you mentioned." He turned toward Brundon. "Would you mind checking it out?"

"Sure," Brundon agreed. "Right after a bit of breakfast."

Elladan's stomach chose that moment to growl. He put his hand over his abdomen and smiled wanly.

Lloyd let out a short laugh. "I think you're not the only one who's hungry."

Aksel peered around the group. "Very good then. Elladan, would you care to join us for breakfast? When we are done, we can discuss our next steps."

Elladan bowed to the little cleric. "I would be most delighted. In fact, if you don't mind, I could prepare a little something for you."

Seth stared at him skeptically. "Are you any good?"

"Even if he is mediocre, I'll take his cooking over yours," Glolindir needled the halfling.

"At least I don't burn everything in sight," Seth retorted.

Glolindir grimaced.

Aksel glared at Seth. "I thought we agreed we weren't going to mention that anymore."

Seth folded his arms in front of him and shrugged. "He started it."

Elladan was sure he missed something in that exchange. *Ah well, it can't possibly be that important.*

He had lost his own cooking gear in his rush to escape the massacre, but these folks had more than enough for him to borrow. As he prepared breakfast, Elladan peered around at this strange group he had happened upon. He had never heard of such a mixture of the races coming together like this. It was almost like an omen.

Elladan, Elladan, he admonished himself, *I think you've been listening to too many of your own stories.* The bard smiled and hummed a little tune as he bent over the cooking fire.

24
DOWN THE WELL

As Elladan prepared breakfast, Glo thought about the events of the previous evening. While Aksel healed Lloyd, Seth had gone to investigate the troll's cave. When Seth returned, he reported that the cavern was empty. There was no sign of the orc priest that they had followed there. When Aksel suggested they camp in the troll's cave, everyone balked. Trolls ate everything and anything. Worse, they left the carcasses lying around, and according to Seth, this troll cave was no exception. Aksel argued that it was far safer than camping out in the open. In the end, the gnome won out.

Glo involuntarily shuddered at the thought of what they saw on first entering the cave, but the companions proved to be resilient. They dragged the remains outside and buried them there. Afterwards, they started a fire and cooked a stew. Between the light from the fire and the smell of dinner, the cave appeared much less forbidding. Any residual unpleasant odors were soon masked.

The well in the back of the cave was the only place the orc could have gone. There was a wooden beam affixed to the top, but there was no rope. Further, the well was so dark that it was impossible to see the bottom. It was rather late when they finished dinner, so they decided to explore the well first thing in the morning. Brundon went to scout the surrounding area. According to Titan, he could go for days without sleep. The rest of the party set a watch and bedded down for the night. They only woke a short while ago, roused by the return of Brundon with the elven bard.

Glo watched Elladan prepare the morning meal. He seemed quite at home, singing a merry little tune as he hovered over the cooking pots. Had Glo not heard his smooth voice, he would have still guessed he was a bard—the bright outfit was a dead giveaway. Dressed almost completely in white, Elladan wore a white tabard over a white coat with spangled trim open at the bottom, a white shirt, and white trousers. The only non-white parts of his outfit were the brown leather boots, brown fingerless gloves, and the green cloak that hung over his shoulders. The hilt of a short sword hung in a scabbard at his side.

Elladan appeared to be quite the charmer. The decidedly handsome elf had thick black hair, dark soulful eyes, high cheekbones, and a prominent chin. From his youthful face, Glo guess him to be somewhere between 100 and 110 years old, just a bit younger than he. The bard also had a way with words. That little speech he had given was rather rousing. His curiosity getting the better of him, Glo went to join the young elf.

"Elladan, what brings you out to these parts?"

Elladan glanced up from his pots. "I was actually on my way to Lukescros. The fair there is next month. I took runner-up in last year's bard competition. This year I intend to win." Elladan winked, an impish grin spreading across his face.

Glo found himself smiling back. This Elladan's bubbly attitude was infectious. "So where is this Lukescros?"

"It's just north of Penwick," said a familiar voice. Glo cast a glance over his shoulder and saw that Lloyd had joined them.

Elladan looked at the young man. "So you've been there I take it?"

"Once or twice," Lloyd admitted. "The fair really is a big deal. People come from all over to see it."

Elladan stirred the contents of a pot. "I'm guessing from that red armor you're from Penwick."

Lloyd grinned self-consciously. "Guilty as charged."

"Maybe when this is all over, you can join me at the fair?"

"That might be fun," Lloyd agreed.

Elladan flashed them a brilliant smile. "Excellent, but first things first." He brought up the spoon to his lips and tasted its contents. "Ahhh, perfect. Breakfast is ready. Let's eat and then we'll teach these bandits a lesson."

Breakfast turned out to be excellent. It was easily the best Glo had had since leaving home. Afterwards, Brundon set out searching for the second cave while Titan resumed her guard duty. The others gathered around the fire to discuss the next steps. Aksel began by recapping the goals of their current mission.

"We've been sent to the Bendenwoods by the Baron of Ravenford to track down the orc bandits that have been attacking caravans. Until last week, no wagon train had made it through to Ravenford in months."

Elladan let out a low whistle. "I had no idea."

Aksel went on to describe their first encounter with the orc bandits and their subsequent disruption of the second ambush. Based on the attack on Elladan's caravan, they realized that the orc bandits' numbers were dwindling, but their exact numbers were still unknown. Aksel turned his eyes to each of the group. "So we need to figure out the extent of what we are dealing with here."

Seth unfolded his arms. "Finally. Now can I get down that well, or what?"

Glo snorted. "Do you want to climb down, or should we just have Lloyd drop you on your head?"

Seth glared at the wizard. "A rope will be just fine, thank you."

Aksel shook his head then took a deep breath and exhaled slowly. "Okay then. Seth, go ahead, check out the bottom of the well. And be careful. Pure reconnaissance, nothing more."

Seth's mouth twisted into a lopsided smile. "Aren't I always?"

"Orcs, golem, troll," Glo ticked off in answer.

Seth's smirk widened. "And if I hadn't gone ahead in all those cases, where would we be now?"

Lloyd let out a short laugh. "Can't argue with him there."

Seth nodded to the young man. "Thank you, Lloyd. And anyway, I now have this." He grabbed the end of his cloak and brandished it around.

Elladan watched the display with a curious expression. "What does it do?"

Seth turned toward the bard, his smile turning smug. "You'll see…or then again, you won't."

Glo shook his head. Seth was having way too much fun with this. "It's a cloak of invisibility," he explained to Elladan.

The bard's eyebrow shot up. "Really? Handy little thing to have there."

Seth glared at the wizard. "Thanks, Glo. Next time I want a secret kept, remind me not to tell you."

Aksel once again interrupted their banter. "Okay, you two. Back to the matter at hand." He arched an eyebrow at Seth.

The halfling folded his arms across his chest, but said nothing more.

Aksel continued to stare at him. "So, once you and Brundon both get back, we'll have a better idea what we are dealing with. Then we'll decide what to do next."

Elladan cleared his throat. "May I join you? Aside from being an entertainer, I know a few songs that can be useful in a battle."

He was not exaggerating. Bard songs were laced with magic, having all kinds of effects on those around them. They could do anything from bolster comrades to distract or enchant enemies. Thus, a bard could be a valuable ally in battle. Aksel glanced around the group. Lloyd and Glo were fine with Elladan accompanying them.

Seth merely shrugged. "Whatever."

Elladan appeared sincerely grateful. "Thank you. I promise, you will not regret it."

Seth glared suspiciously at the bard. "We better not."

The meeting broke up. Seth, Lloyd, and Aksel headed toward the well. Meanwhile, Elladan pulled Glo aside. "Testy little fellow there, isn't he?"

Glo chuckled. "You have to get to know Seth. He's a bit gruff, but his heart is in the right place. He was not exaggerating earlier. On our last mission, he saved everyone's life."

Surprise registered on Elladan's face. "Really? That must have been quite some adventure. I'd love to hear the story sometime."

Glo regarded the bard curiously. It was true that bards were entertainers, but they also were responsible for recording a good portion of written history. It amused Glo to think that one day their adventures might end up in a book. "Perhaps when this is all over, but for now"—he held up his spellbook—"I have some brushing up to do."

"And I have a lute to tune," Elladan replied with a smile. "As you say, we will talk more another time." With that, the bard chose a nearby rock to sit on and began tuning his strings.

What an interesting character, Glo thought. He could go from absolutely cheerful to deadly serious at the drop of a hat. A brief smile crossed his lips, then he turned his attention to his spellbook.

There's a light down here. Seth dangled upside down at the end of a rope. It was secured to the wooden beam across the top of the well. He was about a hundred feet down, hanging from the ceiling in a small underground cavern. Seth expected it to be pitch black, but there was a large crack in the wall. Light streamed through the opening, dimly illuminating the small cavern.

He dropped down, landing catlike on the rocky floor. He stayed motionless for a while, making certain that no one had heard the slight noise he made on landing. Once he was sure it was safe, Seth crept over to the fissure in the wall. The crack was vaguely triangle-shaped, maybe two feet wide at the base and roughly six feet in height. It was not exactly a roomy hole, but an orc, or human, could definitely fit through it if they turned sideways.

Seth flattened himself against the wall and listened. Faint sounds drifted through the crack. He touched his cloak and whispered the word, "*Invisibilitate.*" Instantly, he disappeared from sight. Seth pushed off the wall and entered the fissure. He crept through about six feet of craggy rock before emerging into a wide tunnel beyond.

The walls and floor here were rocky, though lighter in color than at the bottom of the well. It was most definitely a natural structure, leading into the interior of the mountain beyond. However, someone was living down here. There was a lit torch, fastened to the wall, a few yards down the tunnel where the passage wound out of sight. Seth could hear voices drifting around that corner. It was definitely Orcish. He had not told the others, but he knew the language somewhat. It was not something he was proud of—a side product of his questionable upbringing.

Seth continued down the passageway till he reached the bend and then peered around the corner. This passage was also lit by torchlight. Maybe thirty yards down, two orcs leaned lazily against opposite sides of the tunnel wall. Beyond where they stood, the tunnel opened up into a wide cavern. He could not see much from here other than it was also well lit. The two orcs carried those wickedly curved swords sheathed at their sides. They grunted at each other in their guttural tongue, not paying much attention to their surroundings. Seth crept quietly down the tunnel until he could hear some of their conversation.

"Can't believe…stuck guard duty…back exit…"

"Narthos scared…humans…elves…"

"Ha ha…Narthos almost…troll food…"

"Ugh…Narthos lucky…nothing get past troll…"

"Ha ha…humans…elves…now troll food…"

"Now I hungry…can't wait…get back to camp…"

That clinched it; they had definitely found the orcs' lair. This Narthos was most likely the orc priest that got away. Sounds like they had made him nervous. He had placed these sentries here, but the orcs didn't expect anyone to get past the troll. The cave that Elladan found was probably the main entrance. If that was true, it would probably be watched more closely than this one. This just might be their best way in, but first he needed a better look at the cavern beyond the sentries.

Seth crept closer. Behind the two orcs, the tunnel opened out onto a wide ledge. The cavern beyond was quite large, but his view of the floor was blocked by that ledge. He could hear noises drifting up from the cavern, but they were faint. Seth had seen enough. He had no doubt they could get in this way. They would just need to handle the sentries quietly.

He left the two orcs, silently making his way back toward the well. As he went, his mind drifted back to this new elf, Elladan. Seth did not trust him. Everyone had some kind of angle—he had seen far too much dishonesty and greed in his short life. More often than not, it led to someone getting hurt, or worse.

When he first met Glo, Seth was certain he had some kind of hidden agenda. They had crossed paths on the road to Caprizon. Seth had been on foot, and Glo in a caravan. For some reason, the elf invited him aboard and even paid his passage. Seth's curiosity got the better of him; he decided to go along and figure out the elf's game.

It turned out Glo's only agenda was getting to know the halfling. He had never seen one before. It seemed Glo's people were secluded behind some sort of magical barriers, hidden away from the rest of the world. Seth was taken aback by the elf's desire to help people. He had never met someone so idealistic. He initially thought Glo a fool, but the elf was so genuine and kind that Seth found that he actually liked him. Still, he thought the elf one of a kind until he met Aksel and Lloyd. These two turned out to be just as idealistic.

Still, Aksel was no fool. And Lloyd, just like Glo, was sincere in his desire to help others. Despite everything, Seth found himself caring about these three. He decided to stick with the trio despite their naïve viewpoints; after all, somebody had to watch out for them.

Seth reached the fissure and reentered the dim cavern beyond. He would keep a close eye on this Elladan. If the bard was who he claimed to be, then he might indeed be an asset to them with this job. However, if there was the slightest hint that he was deceiving them, then Seth would deal with the fraud swiftly.

Seth now stood beneath the well opening. He leapt upward and caught the bottom of the rope hanging from the ceiling. Seth then shimmied back up the rope to report to his companions who waited for him in the cave above.

Aksel appeared anxious. "You found them? Are you certain?"

Seth folded his arms, fixing the cleric with a hardened glare. "No. I've never seen an orc before."

Aksel let out a sigh. "You know what I meant."

Seth smirked at his gnomish friend. "As I was saying…there are two sentries, although they were doing more talking than guarding." Seth went on to tell them about the discussion he had overheard.

Lloyd jumped to his feet. "Then we've found them!"

"We also now know that Seth speaks Orcish," Glo pointed out.

Seth fixed the tall elf with a withering look.

Aksel ignored them both, waving Lloyd to sit back down. "Yes, yes, but we still have no idea of how many are down there."

Lloyd remained standing. His expression grew thoughtful. "True, but we do have the element of surprise. From what Seth just told us, they are not expecting us to come down through the troll cave. So all we need to do is quietly take out the guards." He folded his hands across his chest, an expectant look on his face.

Seth was impressed. Up till now he had thought Lloyd the *charge first, ask questions later* type, but it seemed the warrior had some understanding of strategy after all.

"That is an excellent point," Aksel conceded. "However, before we make our move, I'd like to see what Brundon finds at the main entrance. After that, we can formulate a plan of attack."

Everyone agreed. They all went back to preparing for the upcoming assault.

"I found the cave." Brundon had just returned from his scouting mission. "There was a trail from the forest to the hillside, just as Elladan said. It was covered with wagon tracks."

Elladan nodded to the group. "Just like I told you."

"The cave opening itself is fairly large, easily big enough for wagons. It looks like it goes fairly deep back into the mountain, but it was also quite dark. If there are any sentries in there, they'd see us way before we'd see them."

Seth coughed loudly.

Brundon glanced at the halfling, the corner of his lips rising. "Correction, they'd see most of us."

Aksel nodded to the tracker. "Thank you, Brundon. It appears that they are not trying to hide the main entrance. Either they are extremely stupid, or…"

"…they expect to be followed that way," Seth finished for him. "Sounds like a great place to set a trap."

Aksel's hand went to his chin. "That makes a lot of sense. I guess you were right, Seth. The well is our best bet."

Aksel turned to Brundon. "Can you wait up here and keep watch?"

Brundon appeared strangely relieved. "Will do."

✳

Seth went down the rope first. He landed in the small cavern and stood watch by the crack in the wall. A soft crunching sound made him glance back over his shoulder. Lloyd crouched down in the center of the cave just below the well. The spiritblade waited a few moments, then crept over to where Seth stood. A few seconds later, Titan dropped down into the cavern. The warrior made surprising little noise as she landed, no more than Lloyd in fact.

Seth had been against her coming at first, but when she showed him the specially-made chainmail she would wear, instead of her standard plate armor, he relented. It was actually quite ingenious; every link was sewn into a cloth outfit. Titan had come up with the idea herself and had Kailay's mother, the tailor, purposely sew it for her. What resulted was a form-fitting chainmail outfit which made no noise when moving at a normal pace.

Titan crept over to join them. Glo dropped down next. The elf made virtually no noise as he landed. The four of them listened carefully, but no sounds came through the fissure. Seth motioned for them all to follow, then crept through the crack in the wall. He slowly led the way down the tunnel, calling a halt just before the bend.

Seth turned invisible then peered around the corner. The two orcs were right where he left them, lazily leaning against opposite walls. They were still grunting and growling at each other, paying little attention to the passage they were guarding. Seth swung back around and tugged on Glo's robe twice. That was the signal to go ahead with their plan. He then stole back out and down the passageway toward the two orcs.

All Seth needed to do was get passed them. Glo would do all the heavy lifting. Seth was merely there to finish the job. Lloyd and Titan were there for insurance, but if the two warriors had to get involved, they could kiss their plan of a quiet entrance goodbye. Step by step, Seth inched closer to the two orcs.

"Getting hungry…"

"You…always hungry…"

He was only a few yards from them now.

"…brought back…meat last night…"

"Narthos keep all…himself…"

Seth realized they were talking about the caravan from last night. He fought hard not to gag.

"Narthos…greedy…"

"…be his…downfall…"

There was about a yard between the two orcs, easily enough for him to slip through undetected. Seth carefully wound his way in-between them. As long as neither orc decided to move, he should be fine.

"Hope…demon eat him…"

"Ha ha…as long as…not eat us…"

Demon? Seth froze in his tracks. He glanced up at their ugly faces, but he could not read their expressions. Seth was not certain he heard right, but that reference to a demon was not good. Still, there was nothing he could do about it now. He slowly crept forward once more. Finally, after what seemed like forever, he was through. The orcs kept chattering, but he was no longer paying attention. He continued a few feet past them, then turned and waited.

Less than a minute later, the top of a pale blond head appeared around the bend in the tunnel. It was followed by a robed arm. A moment later, a faint purplish circle appeared on the floor of the tunnel, just catching the two orcs in its radius. Both their heads nodded, then drooped, followed by their bodies slumping down the walls and sliding to the floor of the passage. Luckily, they made little noise.

Seth rushed forward and quietly dispatched the guards. It had the unfortunate side effect of breaking the invisibility spell, but it could not be helped. He was the best at this kind of quiet work.

Once done, Seth stood back up and let out a deep sigh. He glanced up and saw Lloyd and Titan slowly moving down the passage toward him. Both were taking great pains to be silent. Seth had to admit, they were not doing a bad job. He could see Glo behind them back by the bend in the tunnel. Seth gave him the all's clear sign. Glo nodded, then disappeared back around the bend. He would head to the well and get the others.

Seth waited until Lloyd and Titan joined him. He signaled for them to wait there, then went ahead to scope out the cavern. He would have to wait a while before he could turn invisible again. Magic was funny like that. In the meantime, he would have to do this the old fashioned way. Seth crept to the end of the ledge, then got down on his belly. He inched forward till he could just see over the edge.

The first thing that hit him was the smell. The overpowering odor of orc wafted its way up from the cavern floor below. He fought the urge to clasp his hand over his nose. The floor of the cavern was maybe thirty feet down. The area was well lit, torches flickering at regular intervals along the walls. There were orcs everywhere, dozens of them. Some sat around fires, others moved about the cavern floor, and yet others appeared to be asleep. As he glanced around, Seth noticed something strange about these orcs. They were mostly women and children. *This is the bandits' base camp!*

Seth continued to scour the room until he spotted four full-grown male orcs. Two of them wore armor with those wickedly curved swords strapped to their belts. The other two sat around a fire. One wore armor like the others. The other was garbed in robes.

There's that orc priest. They'd let him escape last time. This time he wouldn't be so lucky. Seth spied a small path that ran along the cavern wall. It rose up from the floor and ended at the ledge he was on. He had seen enough.

Seth slid back and checked behind him. Everyone was now here, waiting for him at the end of the tunnel. He crept back to join them and filled them in on what he had found.

Aksel's expression was troubled. "It would be best if we don't harm the women and children."

Seth grimaced. He understood Aksel's concern. In fact, it was one of the things he respected most about his gnomish friend—his belief in the sanctity of life. Still, it was not always realistic to think that you could always save everyone. "There's a lot of them down there."

Aksel appeared unphased by his statement, the gnome's jaw firmly set. "All the more reason to try."

Seth heard the sound of soft whispering. Lloyd and Titan had their heads together and were speaking in a rapid, hushed conversation. The two warriors must have realized all eyes were on them. Lloyd spoke for the duo. "What if we draw the warriors to us?"

Aksel's hand went to his chin. He rubbed it furiously. A few moments later he nodded. "That just might work."

Seth silently agreed. In fact he might be able to help. A wicked smile spread across his lips. "If you give me a few minutes head start, I can get close to that warrior and the priest. "I should be able to keep them occupied for a bit."

"I could probably help you with that, too," Glo said. He pointed his fingers and made a weaving motion in the air. "My projectiles hone in only on the specific target. No one else would be hurt."

Elladan cleared his throat. "I may be able to help as well. There's a song I can play which will not only boost morale, but will also make the sword arm more accurate and deadly."

Seth's eyes narrowed. "Why don't you just step out on the ledge and scream, 'We're here!'"

Elladan flashed him a half smile. "Don't worry, I can play so softly you'll barely hear it. The magic will still work." To emphasize his point, he plucked a string.

Seth heard the barest of sounds. He glanced at Aksel. "Did you hear that?"

Aksel nodded slowly. "Just barely."

Lloyd's expression was puzzled. "I didn't hear anything."

"Neither did I," Titan said.

Glo appeared amazed as well. "I think it was just outside the range of the human ear. I heard it, as did Aksel and Seth, only because of our racial tendency toward improved hearing."

"Very well. Do it," Aksel instructed the bard.

Elladan went ahead and played his song. When he was done, Seth did notice a lifting of his spirits. Still, he was not about to admit that out loud.

Aksel nodded to Elladan, then turned to Seth. "Go ahead. We'll give you fifteen minutes to get in position."

Seth's mouth twisted sideways. "More than enough time." He grasped his cloak and turned invisible once more, then headed for the ledge that led down to the cavern floor below.

A little more than ten minutes later, Seth was in position—about a yard away from the orc warrior and priest. The pair were still sitting next to the fire, close to the other end of the cavern. A few more minutes went by, then a loud voice echoed across the cavern.

"Hey ugly!"

Seth glanced up and saw both Lloyd and Titan standing at the top of the ledge, swords drawn and ready for battle. Not his most original line, but it was quite effective. The two orc warriors closest to the ledge drew their swords and rushed up to attack the two humans. The warrior in front of Seth stood up and drew his sword.

"You know, you should never turn your back on a wizard," Seth said aloud.

The warrior half turned, looking for the source of the sound. He took a swipe through the empty air in front of him with his wickedly curved sword. At that same moment, Seth glimpsed two purple blurs winding through the air toward them. They slammed into the orc's back.

Thud. Thud.

The warrior convulsed, momentarily stunned by the dual concussive strikes. Seth, knife already in hand, rushed forward and stabbed the orc straight in the heart.

"*Venenum,*" he spoke the single word.

The orc glared down at him as he became visible. It clutched its heart, then collapsed to the ground. Around him, the entire cavern had erupted in confusion. Shouts and screams sounded from all sides. Seth glanced over and saw the orc priest was gone. Behind him, a robed figure disappeared down another tunnel.

Dragon dung! The priest had gotten away again.

Seth glanced back the other way. Lloyd and Titan had easily dispatched the two remaining orc warriors. The rest of the cavern occupants swiftly gathered against the cavern wall between Seth, Lloyd and Titan, cowering away from the three of them.

Aksel's voice rang out across the cavern, "Lloyd. Seth. Chase after the priest!"

Seth nodded and raced for the tunnel the priest had disappeared into. Within moments, the tall figure of Lloyd was at his side.

25
CAPTIVE AUDIENCE

I seem to have misplaced my torch

Seth and Lloyd disappeared into a tunnel at the other end of the cavern. The three orc warriors were dead, and the rest of the orcs, all women and children, cowered together against a wall of the wide cavern.

Aksel turned to Glo. "Can you speak to these folks?"

Glo nodded. "What would you like me to tell them?"

"Tell them we won't harm them as long as they don't give us trouble. Tell them to sit down against the wall and be still."

Glo strode up in front of the remaining orcs. Titan joined him, her sword sheathed at her side. Glo stole a quick glance at the warrior. She gave him a brief, reassuring smile. The orc women pushed the children behind them and eyed the wizard and warrior cautiously. Glo kept his hands at his sides and spoke calmly in Orcish to the crowd. "Sit down and no harm will come to you."

At first the orcs just stood there, then one older woman stepped forward. "How do we know you speak the truth?"

Glo kept his voice even. "Are you an elder of this tribe?"

She held her head up proudly. "I am."

"We have no quarrel with you, only with your priest. Sit down, and we will not harm you."

The elder orc did not move. She stared from Glo to Titan then back again, as if measuring the truth of his words. Finally, she turned around and motioned for her people to sit down. All the orcs obeyed her without question. The elder then sat herself down.

"Thank you," Glo told the elder, relieved that she had listened. He looked over his shoulder to see Aksel staring at him, a thin smile on his face.

"Nice work."

Elladan drew up beside Aksel. The bard gazed around the large cavern, his eyes finally falling on the sitting orcs. "So what do we do now?"

"Now, we wait." Aksel sat down on a nearby rock, clasped his hands together and began to pray.

"Very well," Elladan replied. The bard chose another rock nearby to sit down on and pulled out his lute. He began to play a tranquil tune.

The orc women and children grew silent, all eyes fixed on the bard. A partial smile graced Elladan's face as he continued to play.

A short while later, Seth and Lloyd reappeared. Their frustration was quite evident. Aksel rose up from his rock to greet them. "Well?"

Seth responded for the duo, "We lost him. The tunnel splits a few hundred yards down, and there were too many footprints to track which way he went."

"Dragon dung," Aksel swore.

Glo was surprised. It was the first time he had heard the little cleric say anything profane.

Seth glanced around at the scene behind them, a thin smirk on his lips. "Captive audience, Elladan?"

"The best kind," the bard said without missing a beat.

Titan still stood over the crowd of orcs, keeping a watchful eye on them. The orcs, however, still appeared rapt in Elladan's performance. Glo nudged his head toward the crowd and spoke softly.

"So what do we do with them? We can't just sit here and babysit them all day."

Elladan must have heard him. "Don't worry. I've got it covered." The bard's tune changed subtly and took on an even more soothing tone. The crowd of orcs began to yawn and one by one fell asleep. Within a few minutes, every orc woman and child was out cold.

Elladan rose and slung his lute back over his shoulder. "There you go. Problem solved."

Glo had to admit, he was impressed. At best, he could only put four creatures to sleep at a time. "That does come in rather handy. How long will they be out?"

Elladan cocked his head to one side. "Hmmm, about an hour, give or take."

Aksel stroked his chin. "That should be good for the moment, but I don't like leaving them alone here like this."

The cavern grew silent. Glo was not sure what to do with the orc families either. Aksel was right. The gods only knew what was down here in these caves. Leaving them alone, defenseless was unconscionable. Unfortunately, leaving Lloyd or Titan behind to guard them was not an option either. They might need both warriors, depending on what they ran into themselves.

Seth was the first to break the silence. "Hm. I wonder…"

The halfling strode over toward a thick canvas draped across a section of the cavern wall. He lifted up a corner. Behind it was the entrance to another tunnel.

"I wonder where that leads," Glo mused aloud.

"You all go check it out. I'll stay here and keep an eye on the women and children," Titan said.

Glo looked at the tall warrior. Her expression was strangely soft.

"Good idea. Thanks," Aksel told her.

The rest of them joined Seth.

"That priest was camped out right in front of this tunnel," Seth explained. "I thought it odd at first that he was over in this corner, but maybe he was protecting something inside."

Glo peered past the canvas. The tunnel beyond was pitch black.

Seth nudged him. The halfling wore an impish expression. "A little light please? I seem to have misplaced my torch."

Glo could not help chuckling, and he was not alone.

Elladan appeared puzzled. "You do know there are dozens of torches in this cavern."

Seth's mouth rose to one side. "Yeah, I know. I just couldn't resist saying that."

A quasi-smile crossed the bard's lips. "Guess I must have missed something."

Glo clasped Elladan on the shoulder. "Long story. I'll tell you later."

He lit the end of his staff and held it aloft. Lloyd held the canvas aside for them, and Seth and Glo entered the tunnel. The passageway only went a short way back before ending in an alcove. It appeared to be empty except for a small altar.

Seth motioned for the rest of them to wait, then crept ahead. He only went a few yards, then stopped and knelt down. After a few moments he called back to them, "There's a pit trap here. Glo, can you bring that light closer?"

"Sure," Glo said. He walked down to join Seth, still holding his staff aloft.

There was indeed a pit trap in the floor here, lined with sharp spikes. The trap extended the width of the tunnel and maybe three dozen yards back. Glo swept the passageway with his keen elven eyes. He spied a wooden board lying against the wall of the tunnel behind him. It appeared to be fairly long, probably long enough to reach the other side of the pit.

Seth walked past him and knelt next to the board. "Yeah, I saw this already." He gave it a tentative heave. "It's kind of heavy though."

Glo reached down and tried to heft the board with one hand. He budged it slightly, but it was too long and unwieldy. He glanced back toward the others. "Hey, Lloyd. Care to give us a hand with this?"

The young warrior strode down to join them. He easily lifted the board and laid it across the pit. Seth crossed over and entered the alcove. From here Glo could see a copper idol on the altar. It had one eye.

"Is that Krieg?" Lloyd asked. From his tone it sounded as if he was sizing up a would-be opponent.

Glo found it amusing. "A replica, yes. The real Krieg is supposed to be twelve feet tall and weigh over two thousand pounds."

A broad grin spread across Lloyd's face. "Now that's more like it."

Seth had disappeared behind the altar. They heard his voice ring out. "There's a chest back here."

Glo continued to hold his staff aloft while Lloyd went to join the halfling. They returned about a minute later, Lloyd carrying a medium-sized chest in his hand. He brought it back out of the tunnel and opened the lid for the others to see. The chest was filled with gold, silver, and copper pieces along with some jewelry, although nothing magical.

Aksel bent close and perused the contents. "This is probably loot from those missing caravans."

"It's about a thousand gold, a little more than two hundred silver, and just under three hundred copper," Seth said.

"You counted it that fast?"

Seth shrugged. "What can I say? I'm good with money."

Glo eyed the coins pensively. It seemed like an awful lot of coins, even if the bandits had waylaid a few caravans.

Elladan also bent over the chest, his expression thoughtful. "I wonder…maybe not all of this is from the caravans." He glanced over at Aksel. "I'd like to try something."

Aksel's eyes narrowed as he stared back at the bard. "Sure, go ahead."

Elladan motioned to Lloyd. "Here, help me with this." The bard began scooping out the copper pieces. He walked them over and dumped them in a pile in front of the still-sleeping orcs. Glo wondered what the bard had in mind, but decided to wait and see. They all pitched in, except for Seth, who watched with a stony expression, his arms folded across his chest. Once they were done, Elladan motioned for Glo to join him.

"Come translate for me."

Glo raised an eyebrow but followed Elladan over to the sleeping orcs. The bard stood over the elder woman who had spoken for the tribe before. He bent down, and gently shook her. She roused slowly, but nearly jumped when she saw the two elves standing over her.

"It is alright elder," Glo said in Orcish. "We only wish to speak with you."

She nodded slowly, still eyeing him suspiciously.

Elladan put a hand on Glo's shoulder. "Ask her if the priest collected 'offerings' from them."

Glo raised an eyebrow. He suddenly realized where Elladan was going with this. A thin smile crossed his lips as he translated the question.

The elder's expression was still distrustful, but her eyes were filled with curiosity. "Yes. Narthos takes everything from us. Why do you ask?"

Glo turned to Elladan. "She said yes."

Elladan stepped aside, revealing the pile of copper coins lying on the cavern floor. The orc elder saw the pile and her eyes widened.

"That's our money!" she declared.

Glo translated for Elladan.

"Tell her they can have all of it back if they pack up and leave these caves for good."

Brilliant. Glo looked upon the bard with admiration. Elladan merely winked. Glo translated for the orc elder. Her suspicion wavered as she eyed the pile of coins. Finally she agreed. They helped her gather the coins and dump them in a pot. When they were done, the elder roused the rest of the sleeping orcs. They had a brief conversation, then all of them began packing. In a very short time, they had gathered up their belongings and filed out of the cavern down the same tunnel where the orc priest had disappeared.

Aksel motioned to the others. "Let's follow them and see where they go."

The companions kept pace a short distance behind the crowd of orcs. They reached a three-way split in the tunnels. The orcs all headed down the left branch. They followed them a few hundred yards beyond and came to a cross tunnel. The orcs turned left and headed down that passage. It was dark, and rather wide, but unlike the others the ground here was dirt-packed and it sloped upwards. Sunlight shone at the other end.

"Looks like we found the main entrance," Seth said.

About halfway up the tunnel, Glo spied alcoves on either side. They were filled with boulders stacked up on logs. Cross logs stuck up like levers behind them. Seth had been right—this entrance was indeed booby trapped. Luckily there were no orc warriors here to man them. Glo wondered where they had gone. Based on Elladan's account of the last caravan attack, there should be a least a couple more.

The passageway abruptly ended, opening up to the hillside beyond. It was close to midday, the sun shining brightly overhead. The forest stood down the slope below them, about a few hundred yards away. The companions watched the orcs trudge away. They traveled down the trail and were soon swallowed by the forest.

Aksel let out a deep sigh. "Well that's done."

"So what about that orc priest? Think he came this way?" Lloyd sounded pensive.

Aksel stroked his chin. "Somehow I don't think he would have left all his money behind."

Glo agreed. *There had been an awful lot of gold coins in that chest. Too much, in fact. Most folks don't travel with that much on them.* "I have a nagging feeling there is more to this than just the caravan attacks."

Aksel's expression was thoughtful. "Interesting. So you think someone was paying them to attack the caravans?"

"Wouldn't be the first time," Seth interjected. His tone was rather cynical.

Glo glanced at the halfling. Seth's expression was bitter. "Is that from experience?"

Seth nodded. "What can I say? My family was horrible."

Glo grimaced. He couldn't imagine what it must have been like for Seth growing up. It made Glo think twice about his own family. Maybe they weren't so bad after all. All his father was guilty of was being overzealous.

"Anyway," Seth continued, "there are wagon tracks here. What say we follow them back into the caves?"

Everyone agreed.

Seth led them back down to where the two tunnels crossed. The tracks continued north from there. They followed them a few hundred yards more until they came to a wide cavern. There they found the remains of the wagons. They were smashed into pieces. There was no sign of the wagoneers. Glo shuddered. He was afraid they had all met a grisly fate.

The only saving grace was that Elladan found his backpack. It was thrown to one side. His money was gone, but he found a few of his personal belongings and some books that he deemed priceless. His expression was ironic. "Guess I'm lucky most orcs can't read."

When they were done searching through the wreckage, Aksel spoke to them in a subdued tone, "I think we've seen enough here. Let's head back to that split where you lost the priest. Now that we're all together, we can explore those other tunnels." He turned to Seth. "Care to lead the way?"

"Sure," Seth replied with mock enthusiasm. Without another word, the halfling turned and headed back the way they came.

26

LOST IN THE CAVES

A demon lord is an entirely different matter

The companions retraced their steps back to the intersection where they had lost the orc priest. Two tunnels split off from the main one. The first side tunnel headed off at an angle to the northwest. The second tunnel went off at an angle roughly northeast. Glo peered down each passageway; they were both pitch black. "So which way do we go?"

No one spoke at first. They eyed each tunnel speculatively. Finally, Seth broke the silence. "I think we should try the northwest tunnel first."

Aksel gazed at the halfling curiously. "Any particular reason?"

Seth shrugged his shoulders. "Call it…a hunch."

Seth took the lead down the northwest passage. The tunnel sloped downward, marking their descent farther underground. After a few minutes, the passageway turned to the north then leveled off. Glo noted a damp smell in the air. He looked at the tunnel walls; he could indeed see moisture on them. They covered a short distance till Seth held up a hand.

"What is it now?" Aksel whispered.

Seth nodded toward the tunnel ahead. "Another pit trap."

Sure enough, another pit trap stretched across the tunnel in front of them. Glo searched around, but this time there were no wood planks nearby to lay across the hole.

"We could go back to the main cavern and bring those boards down here," he suggested.

Aksel paused a moment then shook his head. "No, that would take too much time. We have been wandering around down here for a few hours now, and the day is more than halfway over already."

A sudden gurgling noise made them jump. Lloyd held his stomach, a guilty smile on his face. "Sorry."

"Well that confirms it," Seth observed in an exaggerated tone. "Lloyd's stomach is never wrong."

Aksel half-smiled at the halfling's joke. "Well then, we better get a move on."

"I can probably jump the pit," Lloyd offered.

"So can I," Seth added, not to be outdone.

"I could if I wasn't wearing chainmail," Titan said wistfully.

Glo smiled at the warrior. "That's okay. Two boneheads are more than enough."

Titan grinned back.

Meanwhile, Aksel glanced speculatively from Seth to Lloyd. "Well, if you're sure…"

Lloyd nodded. "Absolutely."

"No problem," Seth agreed.

The duo glanced appraisingly at each other as if this were some kind of competition. Aksel looked at one, then the other. Finally, he turned to Seth. "You go first."

"Ha!" Seth cried in triumph.

The others moved to either side of the tunnel to make room. Seth backed a few paces down the corridor, then ran forward. By the time he reached the edge of the pit he was running full speed. Seth leapt into the air, easily soaring over the spike-filled trap. When he reached the other side, he tucked his body into a ball. Seth hit the ground rolling, then sprang up into a crouch.

"Agile little fellow there, ain't he," Elladan said, clearly impressed.

Glo merely nodded. Elladan hadn't seen half of what Seth could do—or Lloyd for that matter.

Aksel called over to Seth, "Go ahead and see what you can find."

"Okay," came the response as the halfling's small form disappeared into the darkness ahead.

Meanwhile, Lloyd backed up away from the pit. The warrior started swiftly, his long legs taking him to the edge of the hole in just a few strides. He too went soaring over it. When he hit the ground, he did a forward roll, coming up on one knee.

Once again, Elladan was impressed. "He practically flew through the air."

Glo let out a short laugh. "The first time we saw him, he leapt off his horse, a sword in each hand, did a mid-air somersault, and landed right in the middle of a pack of orcs. They were all dead in minutes."

"Wish I had been there to help," Titan declared. She had that same glint in her eye as when she was about to enter battle.

Across the pit, Lloyd got up and brushed himself off.

Seth reappeared and said something to Lloyd, then the two of them disappeared down the tunnel. They reappeared a minute or so later, Lloyd carrying a long board. He slowly lowered it across the gap. Titan caught it on the other side and finished laying it down.

The rest of them easily crossed the board, then continued down the passageway. Seth moved out ahead. They went another few hundred yards farther when Seth held up his hand. They all halted.

"What is it?" Lloyd hissed.

Seth paused a moment. "I'm not sure. Glo, can you bring that light up here?"

Glo moved to the front and raised his staff. There was definitely something at the very edge of the light. Glo strained his eyes. Whatever it was, it appeared translucent with a greenish hue. Glo angled his staff around. The thing blocked the entire tunnel. Abruptly it began to wobble. A chill ran up Glo's spine as he realized what it was.

"Cube!" Seth hissed.

A gelatinous cube; a giant type of ooze known to inhabit underground areas. They were shapeless creatures with no head, hands, or feet. Their entire bodies were some kind of sensory organ that could detect prey from many feet away. Cubes lived to eat; in fact, that's all they did. Furthermore, there was no easy way to kill a cube. Its entire body was a weapon that they'd slam into their prey. Cubes used their formless mass to entangle their victims, secreting a slime which paralyzed their prey so they could be slowly digested. Since cubes were mostly transparent, it was said that one could see the remains of whatever they'd engulfed still encased in their bodies. It would remain there until totally digested. Glo shuddered at the thought. It was a nasty way to go.

From Aksel's tone, he was well aware of what they were facing. "Quick, back across the pit."

Lloyd began to protest. "But…"

"Now!" Aksel cried.

Lloyd still hesitated. Titan reached over and placed a hand on the young man's shoulder. Her voice was cool, but understanding. "This is not a fight we can win with arms."

Lloyd glanced at her then sighed. "Very well."

They began to retreat toward the pit. If they could reach the other side, they should be safe. Unfortunately they had hesitated just a bit too long. The cube was moving forward fast. Glo knew if it wasn't slowed down, they would never reach the pit.

"Go ahead," he called to the others. "I'll be right behind you."

The cube closed in on him. It towered over him, reaching all the way to the ceiling, maybe fifteen feet up. Glo nearly lost his nerve, but somehow managed to hang on.

No. I will not panic. I've let my friends down once too often. Not this time. Glo calmly began his spell. The incantation only took a second, but the cube had covered a surprising amount of distance in that time. Glo gulped hard, then lifted a finger and spoke two words.

"*Nullam Telum.*" Instantly, two purple missiles leapt from his fingertips and careened their way across the cavern. Glo did not stop to watch them. Instead, he turned and went running down the passageway after his comrades. He had taken not two steps when the projectiles connected with the cube.

Thud. Thud.

He chanced a quick glance over his shoulder. The cube had slowed down. Concussive waves rippled through the creature, making it difficult for it to move its massive form. Glo ran, almost careening into Lloyd and Titan. "What are you two doing back here?"

Titan wore a thin smirk, but her eyes were filled with admiration. "I couldn't stop him. He's almost as stubborn as Brundon!"

Lloyd grinned at her. "I couldn't leave him alone with that thing!"

Glo's heart was filled with sudden warmth. These two had the hearts of lions. They were true warriors and true friends. He smiled at the young heroes. "Okay then, let's go!"

The warriors each grasped an arm and rushed him back down the passageway. When they reached the pit, everyone else was already across. Glo glanced over his shoulder. The cube was on the move again and closing fast. They wouldn't all make it across in time.

"Come on!" Aksel cried waving them to cross.

Glo turned to face the cube. "You two go ahead. I'll keep this thing at bay."

Lloyd began to protest. "But…"

Titan cut him off. "Let him do this, Lloyd. He's the best one for the job."

"Go. I'll be fine." Glo wished he felt half as sure as he sounded.

Lloyd sighed. "Okay, but, Titan, you go first."

"Lloyd…" she began.

"I left you behind with the golem, I'm not doing it again."

Titan's eyes filled with warmth and her face visibly softened. "Very well." With that the woman warrior spun around and sped across the board.

"Good luck," Lloyd yelled, then he too took off across the pit.

Glo only half heard him. He had already sent two more projectiles at the approaching cube.

Thud. Thud.

Once again, the cube slowed down. Concussive waves rippled through the creature once more and it had trouble controlling its movements. It was still coming though. The cube was nearly on him.

One more time. Glo wove his arms around ending the movement with a lifted finger. He again spoke the two words, *"Nullam Telum."*

Two more missiles leapt from his fingertips. This time they only had a few feet to travel. As soon as they were off, Glo turned and ran. He vaulted across the board almost too fast, precariously balancing as he sped along. Somehow he did not fall. Both Lloyd and Titan grabbed him when he was within arm's reach and pulled him off the board and onto firm ground. Glo glanced back at the cube. It had stopped at the edge of the pit, its body quivering in the light of Glo's staff.

Aksel cried out in excitement, "Look at that! Something's happening to it."

Aksel was right. Not only had the cube stopped, but it was wiggling more than before. It began to jiggle like crazy.

"Man, look at that thing go," Elladan drawled.

Without warning, the cube began to dissolve. It started from the top and slowly shrank down. There was a loud hissing noise as the creature grew shorter and shorter. Green smoke rose from its insides. A strange, acrid odor reached the companions.

They all held their noses. Elladan waved a hand in front of his face. "That smells worse than the swamps back home."

Finally it was over. All that remained of the creature were a few pools of green liquid. The pools smoked for a few moments, then those too faded.

Everyone gathered around Glo. They pounded him on the back amid cries of "You did it!" and "Way to go, Glo!"

"Tha...nks," Glo managed to reply. "I...think..."

He was a little sore from where Lloyd and Titan had struck him, but he shrugged it off. His friends were right. He had done it. He had remained calm in the face of danger. It was a new feeling for Glo. He actually felt proud; not in the pretentious way he had before, when he thought he knew everything. He now knew the world was dangerous; you could literally die out here. Yet he stood his ground and faced that danger. He had done so for his friends. Their courage inspired him. He was a better person because of them.

While Glo came to terms with his new feelings, Seth crossed back over the pit and examined the remains of the cube. After a short while, he called over to the others, "I found something."

"Careful. It could still have traces of acid on it," Aksel said.

Seth's response practically dripped with sarcasm. "Do I look stupid?"

Glo could not stop the grin that spread across his face. He glanced at Aksel and saw the gnome react the same. The companions crossed back over, careful to avoid the lingering pools of acid. In the center of one pool lay what turned out to be a hammer, but not just any hammer. It was larger than the warhammers that Lloyd carried around with him. Glo bent down for a closer look. There was a lightning bolt carved on one side with lettering under it.

Seth knelt next to Glo. "What does it say?"

Glo could not quite make it out. "I'm not sure. It's a language I've never seen before. The words read *Marteau Foudre*."

Elladan knelt next to them. "I've run across a lot of languages in my travels. Never heard those words before, though."

Glo stared at it a bit longer, then gave up. "Well, let's get this cleaned off and take it with us." He took out a cloth and wiped down the hammer. When he tried to pick it up though, it wouldn't budge.

Glo panted as he tried to heave it. "This…thing is…really heavy." He let go. "Lloyd, Titan, perhaps one of you should try."

The two warriors exchanged glances. "You go ahead," Titan told Lloyd. "You're the hammer wielder. I'm comfortable with my mace."

Lloyd grinned at her. "You sure?"

Titan merely nodded. As Lloyd stepped forward to grasp the hammer, Glo swore he heard her say under her breath. "Boys and their toys." He looked over at the women warrior, but her expression remained innocent. Still, her eyes danced with amusement.

Lloyd reached down and tried to lift the hammer with one hand. He could barely budge it. He shook his head, then rubbed both his hands together. Lloyd reached down, grasped the handle with both hands, and gave a mighty heave. The hammer slowly lifted off the ground. Once off the ground, he was able to carry it, but wielding it as a weapon would be a whole different matter.

Aksel glanced around the group. "I doubt the priest made it past that cube. My guess would be he went the other way."

The companions decided to backtrack and try the other tunnel.

They swiftly retraced their steps and soon were headed down the northeast passageway. Once again, Seth led the way. A few hundred steps after the intersection, the tunnel turned north, just like the northwest passage. This passageway did not slope down, nor were there any signs of moisture. After a while, Seth called a halt. He turned to face them and held up a finger to his lips.

Glo listened carefully. There was a faint rhythmic sound coming from somewhere up ahead. It sounded like…chanting.

"I think we may have found our priest," Elladan whispered.

Aksel nodded. "Seth, can you check it out?"

The halfling did not reply. Instead, he wrapped his cloak around his body and disappeared from sight. About ten minutes went by, when they heard his disembodied voice. "There is a cavern up ahead."

Glo nearly jumped out of his skin. He hissed at the halfling. "Seth! A little warning would be nice."

He heard a disembodied chuckle. Glo glanced at Aksel. The gnome just shrugged. Glo took a deep breath and calmed himself. *Oh, well. Seth is Seth. He's not going to change on anyone's accord.*

Seth suddenly reappeared in front of them. He wore a wicked smile as he continued his report. "There's some kind of weird stone circle in the middle of the cavern. Our orc priest is there with a second orc priest. They're standing on either side of the circle and chanting. There are also two orc warriors."

Elladan gave them a quasi-smile. "That's the rest of them by my count."

"Plus one extra priest," Aksel said.

Glo half-heard the conversation. He was lost in thought. Two casters standing around a circle chanting could really mean only one thing; they were trying to summon something. Summoning magic could be used to bring forth many types of monstrosities—creatures from other locations or even different planes of existence. The power of the creatures summoned depended on the expertise of the summoner. However, magical devices such as summoning circles could control monsters far more powerful than the summoner. It was a dangerous business, and more than likely would blow up in the summoner's face. If this was the same orc priest they had been chasing all along, he was probably desperate by now. There was no telling what he might try.

"What does the circle look like?" Glo asked.

Instead of answering immediately, Seth knelt down and drew a picture in the dirt. Glo studied it for a few moments, till his fears were confirmed. "Just as I thought. It's a summoning circle."

Aksel murmured to himself as he stroked his chin. "I wonder what they are trying to summon?"

Seth's face went ashen. "Um, guys. You know those first two guards back by the well—one of them mentioned a demon."

Glo's eyebrow shot up. "A demon? Are you sure?"

Seth shook his head. "I don't know. My Orcish is not that great."

"What was the exact word they used?"

Seth paused for a moment, then repeated the word he had heard. "Dagul."

Glo blanched. That was indeed the orc word for demon. Demons were evil creatures from another plane of existence. Their sole purpose was to destroy, but first, they would feed off of mortal pain and suffering. That was what sustained them. His countenance grew grim as he confirmed Seth's translation. "I'm afraid you heard right, my friend."

The side of Seth's mouth upturned somewhat. "Most of the time I like being right. This is not one of those times."

Elladan glanced around the group. "I say we put a crimp in their plans."

They decided that Seth would sneak in and work his way behind the orc priest on the other side of the circle. The others would wait five minutes, then Lloyd and Titan would charge in and take care of the orc warriors. Seth would waylay the one priest while Glo took on the other. The plan went like clockwork. It had barely begun when it was over. All four orcs lay on the ground, their souls on the way to meet their god, Krieg.

Glo examined the summoning circle. He recognized the markings immediately. He hated to admit it, but one day he would have to thank his father for all the tedious hours of study he'd forced upon him. Glo's voice was hushed as he spoke, "They were most definitely trying to summon a demon. And not just any demon. I think it was a demon lord."

His voice grew even softer as he uttered those last two words. They all fell silent, as if a palpable darkness had fallen over the chamber.

Lloyd was the first to break the silence. "I know demons are bad, but is a demon lord that much worse?"

Aksel was the one to answer him. "Yes, well, a demon lord is an entirely different matter. They are the strongest of demons, risen to the top through sheer ferocity and destruction over the multitudes of other demons. Thus, a demon lord has an entire host of demons subject to it, and they are at its beck and call."

Aksel paused and drew in a deep breath. "If you bring a demon lord forth and can actually control it, you will have an entire army of demons at your command. However, unless the summoner is very powerful and skilled, it is more than likely that the demon lord will consume him or her, and then it will be free to call forth its armies and wreak havoc on the mortal world."

Lloyd's face had gone ashen. Titan reached out and placed a firm hand on his shoulder. Her expression was grim, but her words were soothing. "It's a good thing we put a stop to them, then."

Lloyd caught her eye and a small amount of cheer returned to his face. He clasped her hand and nodded. "Yeah. Good thing."

Aksel had begun to pace back and forth. "The real question is, where would simple orcs like these come across the knowledge to summon a demon lord?"

Glo had been thinking along the same lines. First there was all those gold coins, and now this. Someone else was behind all this. The question was who? "There is obviously more going on here than we know, but either way, we cannot leave this circle here. It must be destroyed."

Elladan had an idea. "Maybe Lloyd can smash it with that big hammer." Elladan made the motion of swinging the heavy object down on the platform in front of them.

Lloyd shook his head, his expression crestfallen. "I wish I could, but I don't think I can swing it hard enough to do any real damage."

A sudden idea came to Glo. "That can be fixed," he told the young warrior. "Take out the hammer."

Lloyd glanced at Glo, his expression uncertain, but he retrieved the hammer from his pack anyway. At the same time, Glo reached into a bag on his belt and pulled out some brown hairs. He held them in one hand and began his spell. He made the appropriate hand gestures, then reached out and touched Lloyd on the shoulder while speaking the words, *"Taurus Vires."*

Lloyd's body began to glow with a dull golden color. Those around him saw the brief image of a bull's head appear over him. The young man suddenly straightened, lifting the hammer well above his head and swinging it with ease.

Lloyd was elated. "Wow! I feel ten times stronger."

A broad smile spread over Glo's face. The spell hadn't really increased his strength all that much, but it was just enough to be effective. Lloyd grinned as he walked over to the stone circle. He climbed onto it and stood in the very center. Hoisting the hammer over his head, he brought it down with incredible force.

Bam!

The tremendous bang was followed by the sound of cracking stone. The ground beneath the companions' feet trembled.

Elladan cheered Lloyd on. "That was one heck of a blow!"

"I'll say," Titan agreed. There was the slightest trace of envy in her eyes.

Lloyd lifted the hammer high over his head once again and brought it down heavily onto the stone circle.

Bam!

Another huge bang rang out, followed by more cracking stone. Again the ground trembled beneath their feet. This time, something small hit Glo on the shoulder. He looked up and saw tiny bits of rubble falling from the cave's ceiling. It subsided after a few moments, but it gave Glo an uneasy feeling.

Seth scowled at the exuberant warrior. "Lloyd! Be careful with that thing. Do you want to bring the whole ceiling crashing down on us?"

Lloyd looked down at him, the sweat now openly streaming

down his face. "Just one more should do it." His expression was determined as he hefted the hammer high above his head.

They braced themselves as he brought the heavy weapon down one more time on the stone platform.

Wham!

There was a resounding crash, followed by a deep rumbling. The entire stone structure fragmented and broke into pieces. Tiny bits of rubble fell from the ceiling above but thankfully subsided. Lloyd slowly waded out of the remains of the stone circle, a look of satisfaction on his face. They all gathered around the young warrior.

As he climbed out of the rubble, Elladan reached forward and clasped him on the shoulder. "I knew you could do it."

Titan grasped his other shoulder. "Yes, that was very impressive."

Seth was not quite as enthused as the others. His tone was scathing. "We never had any doubts. Not only did he destroy the circle, but he almost took the whole cave down with it."

Lloyd's face turned red. "It wasn't that bad, was it?"

Elladan patted Lloyd on the shoulder. "Never mind him. He's just testy."

Seth glared at Elladan, then turned around and stormed away.

Glo found it interesting that Elladan had come to Lloyd's defense, but that was the effect he had on people. Lloyd was so genuine and honest, it was hard not to like the young man.

While Lloyd packed away the hammer, Aksel spoke to the group in general, "I'm guessing it's about midafternoon now. We've accomplished what we set out to do. Let's grab a quick bite, then rendezvous with Brundon and head back to Ravenford."

27
BRINGING DOWN THE HOUSE

The force of her blow echoed up and down the passage

After a quick cold lunch, the companions set out toward the main entrance. It would be easier than climbing back up the well for most of them. As they approached the cross tunnels, the sound of voices reached their ears.

"Seth…" Aksel began to say.

"On it," Seth replied before he could finish.

The halfling wrapped his cloak around himself and disappeared from view. Five minutes later Seth reappeared amongst them, his expression uncharacteristically worried. "There are three figures in black robes back there. They're headed this way."

Glo raised an eyebrow. Figures in black robes? That sounded an awful lot like that dark mage, Telvar. "Did you get a good look at them?'

"No, their faces were covered the entire time, but I did hear them say they were looking for Narthos. They were also wondering where the orc sentries were."

Glo's eyes narrowed. "Did you say Narthos? That's the name the elder used to describe the orc priest."

Seth nodded. "Yeah. The two well sentries used that name too."

Titan's voice suddenly rang out across the tunnel, "Look out!"

Glo glanced up to a frightening sight. A fist sized ball of flame hurtled out of the darkness toward them.

That's a ball of fire! If that hit, they'd all be burnt to a crisp. It would be on them in seconds; it would expand and explode into a storm of flame. There was no time to do anything but cringe. Suddenly, Lloyd was there; he appeared out of thin air in front of them. The warrior brought up his blades just as the flame ball hit. It exploded into an arc of fire flaring out all around him. The flames grew longer and longer, threatening to engulf the young warrior. Yet somehow Lloyd held his ground. His arms visibly shook as they strained to hold back the flames.

As suddenly as it appeared, the ball winked out. Lloyd stood there, blades still crossed, tendrils of smoke rising all around him. Glo was in awe. Somehow, Lloyd had managed to stop the fireball. He caught it before it expanded and held it off until it burnt itself out. The young warrior had saved them all from a painful death.

Clap, clap, clap.

The sound came from the same direction as the ball of fire. A voice rang out in a snide tone, "Very impressive, young man." A figure in black robes suddenly appeared. It was flanked on either side by two more figures dressed the same. "I did not think that possible. Maybe we should try that again."

Smoke still rose from Lloyd's body. His armor and skin were somewhat singed. Somehow Glo didn't think he would last through another attack like that. Still, the young warrior did not back down. He squared his shoulders and met the man's challenge. "Go ahead if you want. It will do you no good."

An evil laugh erupted from under the black hood.

Aksel stepped forward. "Who are you?"

"Who we are is of no importance."

"Then what do you want?"

"We are looking for a friend of ours, Narthos. You wouldn't

happen to have seen him, would you?" The mage's tone was deceptively mild, but his words were laced with malice. Glo realized that unless something miraculous happened, they weren't getting out of this alive.

"Glo," a voice whispered his name. "Don't look."

Out of the corner of his eye he saw Titan standing next to him. Glo nodded slightly to indicate he had heard her.

"Can you make me stronger?" she whispered.

He nodded faintly once more. He wasn't quite sure what she was up to, but at this point it didn't matter. It might be their only chance.

"Wait for the dark," he whispered back. Glo had to be careful. If the mages saw any hint of him casting a spell it would be over. Thankfully, their attention was fixed on Lloyd and Aksel. To help matters, Elladan had stepped forward as well.

"Narthos? You mean that orc priest. Yeah. Last we saw him, he was down at the summoning circle. He was still there when we left."

"Then you won't mind leading the way down there?" the dark mage said. It was more of a command than a request.

Glo had managed to extract what he needed from his pouch unnoticed. In one swift motion, he extinguished the light on his staff. The tunnel was plunged into darkness. As he rushed through the appropriate gestures, a voice rang out, "Falder! Give us some light."

Glo quickly reached out and touched Titan's shoulder. "*Taurus Vires.*"

As soon as the spell went off, Titan pulled away. A few seconds later, light flared across the cavern, emanating from a mage's hand. Titan now stood behind Lloyd, the giant hammer held firmly in her hands. The two other mages caught sight of her and began to weave deadly spells. Glo started one of his own, but then Titan bolted toward the tunnel wall. She pulled back the hammer for a mighty blow while shouting, "Get back!"

Everything happened at once. Titan swung the hammer. A mage let loose with a red hot ray. Lloyd rushed after Titan. Glo and the others backpedaled away. Two arrows whizzed past their heads. Seth threw a knife.

Bam!

The hammer slammed into the wall just as a red hot beam caught Titan in the side. The tall warrior flinched as the force of her blow echoed up and down the passage. A moment later, two arrows embedded themselves into one mage, a knife into the other. The mages' cries were drowned out as a deep rumbling filled the passage. The ground beneath them began to shake and the roof started to collapse. Large rocks began to rain down all around. Lloyd had just reached Titan's side when Glo lost sight of them. Desperate cries of "Lloyd" and "Delara" sounded amidst the crashing of rocks.

Suddenly, the air shimmered in front of Glo. It coalesced into the form of Lloyd, the young warrior tightly gripping Titan in his arms. Shouts erupted from all around. "Wa-hoo!" "They made it!" Lloyd and Titan both grinned, but then the young man collapsed in her arms. Everyone rushed forward. Titan pulled him back up while a familiar figure slipped under his other arm.

Titan's eyes went wide. "Brundon, what are you doing here?"

Aksel cut off his response. "Now's not the time! Fall back!"

The companions fled down the passageway, Titan and Brundon carrying Lloyd. They made it all the way back to the main cavern. The rumbling around them had subsided somewhat, though mild tremors continued sporadically. Aksel bade them lay Lloyd down, then immediately knelt at his side. Healing white light began to pour from his hands over the warrior's burns.

Brundon fixed Titan with a hard stare. "You do know what you did was crazy?"

The corner of Titan's mouth twisted upward. "It beats the alternative. And you never told us what you are doing here."

Brundon winked. "What, love? Did you really think I was going to leave you down here to have all the fun?"

At that moment, Lloyd's eyes snapped open. He gazed all around.

Elladan gave the warrior a partial smile. "Welcome back."

Glo grinned. "That was some stunt you pulled there."

Seth's comment was a bit more pragmatic. "Lloyd, don't take this the wrong way, but why aren't you burnt to a crisp?"

Lloyd managed a wan smile. "Spiritblade skill...flame resistance..."

Titan stepped forward and regarded Lloyd with a warm smile. "I never got to thank you for saving my life."

Lloyd smiled back. "You saved us…I just returned the favor…"

The tremors around them began to get worse. The rumbling grew louder, the sound of crashing rock emanating from the tunnel behind them. Tiny bits of rubble fell from the ceiling above.

Aksel's healing light faded. "That will have to do for now." He stood up and glanced around the cavern. "We need to go."

Lloyd sat up slowly. Titan bent down and lent him a hand. As soon as he was on his feet he waved her off. "I'm fine."

She narrowed her eyes but then let go.

"What about you?" Lloyd asked. He pointed toward Titan's side. A wide circle of chain links were melted, the fabric underneath scorched.

She stared back at him, steely eyed. "It's nothing."

Aksel cut off any further discussion. "I'll look at it later. For now let's move!"

As the companions raced across the cavern, the sounds of rumbling grew louder. They vaulted up the path to the ledge, then filed one by one into the passage leading up to the well. Loud crashes sounded behind them. Glo cast a quick glance back. The ceiling of the cavern was coming down! They redoubled their efforts, swiftly reaching the fissure and ending up beneath the well. Seth leapt up first and scrambled up the rope out of sight. Elladan went next. Aksel waved Brundon on, but the tracker turned to Titan.

"Go! I'll be right behind you."

She raised an eyebrow. "You sure?"

"Yes! Go!"

Titan gave him a brief smile, then vaulted up the rope, the heavy hammer tucked firmly in her belt. The small cavern was shaking now. Down the passage they heard more rocks falling. Brundon shot up the rope, then Aksel waved Glo on next.

Glo looked at his friend with concern. "What about you?"

"I'll carry him on my back," Lloyd declared.

Aksel nodded. "Yes. Now go!"

Glo nodded back then leapt up the rope. He climbed as fast as he could, his hands turning raw from the quick ascent. As he reached the top, two chainmail clad arms reached down and pulled him out of the well. He found himself back in the troll cave, everyone gathered there except Lloyd and Aksel. As he got to his feet, the ground trembled again. Glo glanced around the cavern. Tiny cracks began to appear in the ceiling. Small pieces of debris began to fall. "The whole place really is coming down."

Brundon gave Titan an ironic smile. "Well, love, I always said you didn't know your own strength."

Her lips twisted into a half-smile. "Never caused an earthquake before though."

Seth snorted. "I don't think you can take all the credit. Lloyd's hammering didn't help."

Further retorts were cut off as Lloyd, with Aksel on his back, climbed out of the well. The cave around them was rumbling now, the cracks in the ceiling widening. The companions rushed to the entrance and out into the open air, swiftly putting as much distance between them and the hillside. The ground around them still shook. Behind them the cave entrance began to crumble. The entire hillside came down around it, plumes of dust rising high into the sky. After a few minutes, the shaking subsided, only minor tremors sporadically followed.

Elladan let out a deep breath. "You all sure know how to throw a party. That's what I call 'bringing down the house'!"

That broke the tension. Everyone laughed. When the merriment died down, Aksel turned to Brundon. "Where are the mounts?"

The tracker let out a short laugh. "Funny thing about that. For some reason I thought we might want to make a fast getaway. So I brought them down to the woods just before I came looking for you all."

Titan jabbed him in the arm. "Smart thinking."

Brundon grimaced and grabbed his shoulder. "I have my moments."

Another minor tremor rocked the hillside. "I think that's our cue to leave," Seth noted wryly.

The companions gathered their mounts and headed south into

the forest. They wanted to put as much distance as possible between them and the Vogels. A few miles south, they made a brief stop and Aksel finished healing the two warriors. They quickly took off again, riding in silence until they reached the west road. It was nearing sundown when they exited the forest.

Once they were out in the open, Elladan broke the silence. "Who do you think those guys in robes were?"

Aksel shook his head. "I have no idea." He spun around in his saddle and looked at Glo. "Maybe you were right. Maybe they were funding the orc bandits like you thought."

Glo nodded slowly. "It would make sense. Mages with that kind of power might have taught Narthos how to summon demons."

"That still doesn't tell us who they are…or were," Seth chimed in.

The group fell silent for a short while, until Lloyd said, "Could they have been in league with Telvar? He also wore black robes."

Glo raised an eyebrow. Lloyd did raise an interesting point.

Aksel cocked his head to one side. When he spoke, he mirrored Glo's thoughts. "It's an interesting idea, but I don't think we can quite make that connection just yet."

The sunset shown red behind them, briefly bathing the road in scarlet as the companions continued eastward toward Ravenford.

It was very late in the evening when the company arrived back in Ravenford. The town was mostly dark, the streets empty. Very few lights burnt up at Ravenford Keep, mostly along the walls and the main gate. Thus, they decided it best to wait for the morning to report to the captain. The companions headed straight to the Charging Minotaur. It was so late that they had to wake up the stable boy. Lloyd and Brundon stayed behind to help unsaddle and brush down the mounts.

Inside the inn the kitchen was closed; the cook had gone home for the night. The bartender opened it for them and brought out some leftover chicken, potatoes, and pies. Lloyd and Brundon soon joined them, and they feasted together on their late night snack. After getting Elladan a room, the companions all bedded down for the night. Exhausted, everyone slept well past sunrise.

It wasn't until late the next morning that Aksel, Glo, Seth, and Lloyd went up to the castle. They brought Elladan along to tell the story of the caravan. They had asked Titan and Brundon as well, but strangely the duo declined. Captain Gelpas met them in the main hall. After a brief conversation, he decided the baron should hear the rest. He left them there and went to inform Gryswold.

While they waited, Elladan strolled around the hallway admiring the décor. "Nice little keep they have here." He stopped in front of the mural of the dragon battle. "Now that's impressive." Lloyd joined him and explained the history of Gryswold, the Avernos family and their relation to Penwick.

Seth wore an impish grin. "I think I'm experiencing *déjà vu*."

Glo chuckled softly. It was definitely one of Lloyd's favorite topics.

A few minutes later a castle guard entered the hall. "Well, if it isn't the heroes of Stone Hill!" It was Francis. "I hear that you routed those orcs out of the Bendenwoods this time." The guard continued to gaze around as if looking for someone else. Glo had a pretty good idea who that was.

"Yes, we did manage to flush them out," Aksel responded for the group.

A wide grin spread across the guard's face. "Nice. The captain sent me to get you. He is waiting with the baron in his side chambers. Follow me." Francis spun on his heel and motioned for them to follow. He led them down the hall and into the throne room. Once inside, he strode down to the last door on the right, opened it, and then stood aside. They entered a small room, its length and width were almost completely filled by a large wooden table. The baron sat at the head of that table, the Lady Gracelynn to his left, Captain Gelpas at his right. The Lady Andrella stood by her father's side.

Gryswold turned toward the door. "Here they are, Gelpas. Come in. Come in. Please have a seat."

The five of them filed in and found seats around the table. Lloyd sat the farthest away, close to the other end. Once they were all seated, the Lady Andrella walked down to the other end of the table and sat down opposite her father—conveniently next to Lloyd. The pair exchanged a brief glance, the young man smiling at her shyly. A thin smile crossed the young lady's lips, her cheeks turning somewhat rosy, then she quickly looked away.

Gryswold leaned forward in his chair. "Gelpas here was just telling us a bit about your run in with the bandits. Please, fill us in on the whole story."

Aksel stood and cleared his throat. "There is much to tell, your Lordship. To that end we have brought a caravan survivor with us. He was a great asset to us during the course of the mission. May I introduce the bard, Elladan Narmolanya."

Elladan stood up and bowed deeply, his cloak flourishing behind him. "At your service, your Lord and Ladyship."

Gryswold regarded the bard, his blue eyes staring him up and down. "A caravan survivor you say? I thought the last caravan made it through here unharmed?"

"I'm sorry to say your Lordship, but another caravan was waylaid during our hunt for the bandits," Aksel answered his query.

Gryswold's expression grew dark. He slammed his fist on the table. "No! Not another caravan!"

"Another caravan was due in yesterday," Gelpas confirmed.

The Lady Gracelynn reached over and placed a delicate hand on her husband's shoulder, her eyes filled with sadness. Gryswold turned toward her. As he gazed upon her tender expression, his own softened. He let out a heavy sigh, his tensed shoulders relaxing.

After the briefest of pauses, Elladan spoke, his tone tentative, "I was a passenger on that caravan, your Lord and Ladyship. We were attacked by orcs late last night."

The Lady Gracelynn's gaze fell upon him. When she spoke, her voice was low. "Did anyone else survive?"

Elladan bowed his head, his voice filled with regret. "I'm afraid not, my Lady. I'm only alive by sheer luck." He proceeded to tell them the story of the caravan attack. He described it in vivid detail, as bards tended to do, although Glo suspected that he left out the more gory details. When he was done, there were somber faces all around the room.

Gryswold slammed his fist onto the table once more. "The devils!"

Elladan grimaced, his own guilt and anger apparent in his expression. It only lasted for a moment though, the performer in him taking hold once more. "But the story doesn't end there, your Lord and Ladyship. By the grace of the gods, these folks here found me." He spread his hand around the table at Aksel, Seth, Glo and Lloyd. "And let me help rout the fiends."

Gryswold's face was still flushed with anger. He gazed intently around the room. "So they are all gone?"

"To the last bandit, your Lordship," Lloyd declared with clear conviction.

Gryswold stared at the young man for a moment or two, then let out a heavy sigh. "Thank you. I knew I could count on a Stealle."

"Thank you all." The Lady Gracelynn gazed at each of them individually with a gracious smile.

Gryswold's face showed a trace of embarrassment. He immediately followed his wife's lead, his eyes falling on Aksel, Seth, Glo and Elladan. "Yes, thanks to you all."

The briefest of smiles crossed the Lady Gracelynn lips, then she turned back toward Elladan. "Good bard, we are quite sorry for any hardship these bandits may have put you through, and are most grateful for your help in putting an end to these cutthroats and vagabonds. If there is anything else we can do to ease your suffering, please let us know."

From Elladan's expression, he was obviously quite touched. "Thank you, your Ladyship, but I'm just glad to have fallen in with these folks. They are the heroes here. If not for them, I'd still be stuck in the woods, or maybe worse."

The Lady Gracelynn smiled warmly at the young bard. Gryswold seemed impressed as well. He gave Elladan a gruff smile of his own. The baron then began to question the group in earnest, wanting all the details about the various aspects of their mission.

Aksel, Glo, and Elladan took turns filling him in on the specifics. Lloyd and Seth remained silent throughout the ensuing conversation. Glo occasionally glanced over at his quiet companions. He noticed that Lloyd and Andrella would occasionally catch each other's eye, then swiftly turn away. The attraction between the two was almost palpable. He was curious as to which one would eventually make the first move. Elladan, a natural born storyteller, had taken up the tale of their search through the caverns. He had just gotten to the part about the black mages.

Gryswold interrupted him. "Black mages?"

"Yes, three of them," Glo responded.

Gryswold's expression grew thoughtful. He turned to Gelpas. "Didn't you say there was one up at Stone Hill?"

"Yes. According to the accounts I heard, there was a dark mage up at the ruins."

Aksel added to the captain's answer. "Pardon me, your Lordship, but there is no evidence connecting the two."

Gryswold strummed his fingers on the table nervously. "Still, you must admit, that is one heck of a coincidence."

Glo decided to share his theory on how the orcs were being sponsored by some other source. He pointed out the amount of gold coins they had found as well as the ritual they stopped at the summoning circle. When he was done, both Gryswold and Gracelynn appeared extremely concerned. Surprisingly, it was Andrella who spoke next.

"What happened with these three black mages?"

Aksel asked Elladan to finish the story. The bard's uncanny knack for remembering details was a clear asset. Elladan described the entire scene to them including: Lloyd's incredible feat with the fireball, Titan's smashing of the tunnel wall, and the subsequent collapse of the underground caverns. When he was done, Andrella turned to Lloyd.

"That was very brave of you, protecting everyone like that."

Lloyd's face reddened, an uncomfortable smile crossing his lips. His hand went to the back of neck. "It was nothing, really."

"It was stupid, actually," Seth interjected. All eyes fell on the halfling. Seth shrugged. "What? I'm not wrong."

Gryswold broke out in laughter. His gaze shifted from Seth to Lloyd. He regarded the young man warmly. "You remind me so much of your father. During the Eboneye war it was hard to restrain him. He was always wading into battle with little regard for his own safety."

Lloyd was clearly surprised. "My father did that?"

Gryswold sat back in his chair and laughed again. It was a deep, full sound. "Yes, indeed he did. And although he won us many a battle, he nearly got himself killed more times than I can count."

Lloyd shook his head in disbelief. "Really? My father? The man that always yells at me for 'charging in head first'?"

Gryswold threw up his hands. "Well, they say the apple doesn't fall far from the tree." He sat forward in his chair, his expression turning serious. "Don't get me wrong, my boy. Your father is a fine strategist, one of the best Penwick has ever seen."

A wan smile crossed Lloyd's face. "I know, I know. I can't tell you how many times I've heard, 'You must learn to study your opponents first' and 'Never fully engage an enemy until you have properly assessed their skills'."

From Gryswold's expression, it was obvious he had heard those same words more than once. "Indeed, that is sound advice." He leaned further forward and gazed a Lloyd intently. "Trust me, lad, your father had to learn those lessons the hard way. He almost lost your mother because of his own recklessness."

Lloyd's eyes went wide. "I never knew that. Is that how she ended up as Eboneye's prisoner?"

Glo raised an eyebrow. Lloyd's mother was a prisoner of the pirate warlord? He glanced from Lloyd to Gryswold. Both wore grim expressions.

Gryswold nodded slowly. He closed his eyes, an edge to his gruff voice as he continued. "It was the end of the war. We had taken back most of the city. As a last ditch effort, the pirates set a magical trap for us, and your father ran right into it. He was such a charismatic leader that we all followed him blindly. We would have been killed if your mother, quite pregnant with your sister at the time, had not come to save us. And save us she did, but in doing so was captured by Eboneye himself."

Andrella, quite rapt in the story, cried out in dismay, "So how did they save her?"

Gryswold looked at his daughter, a knowing smile on his face. "Kratos saved her. Eboneye had taken her with him aboard his ship.

Kratos, myself and a few others gave chase. He took Eboneye on one on one, while the rest of us freed Lloyd's mother."

Andrella let out a deep breath. "Phew. You had me on the edge of my seat."

Gryswold grinned. "Trust me, daughter, we all were. We were lucky to get her back unharmed. From that day forward, Kratos swore that he would never run headlong into battle again. He almost lost the most precious thing to him in the world, and it taught him a valuable lesson." Gryswold sat back in his chair. The Lady Gracelynn reached over and grasped her husband's arm, squeezing it gently. The baron turned to his wife and gave her a reassuring smile. He reached over with his other hand and patted hers.

At the other end of the table, Lloyd sat with a stunned expression. The Lady Andrella reached over and placed a tentative hand on his arm, mimicking her mother. Lloyd turned to gaze at her, the warmth returning to his face. The two of them sat there staring into each other's eyes. Abruptly, Andrella pulled away, her cheeks turning red. She glanced over at her parents. Her voice was shaky as she addressed them. "Yes, well then…Father, Mother, I think Delara deserves some acknowledgement for her part in foiling those dark mages."

Gryswold and Gracelynn exchanged a brief glance. Gryswold then turned toward Gelpas. The captain, however, had gone rigid. His face was a stony mask. Gracelynn was the one to finally answer, "Yes, you are quite right, my daughter. We will make certain her part in this is duly recognized."

Andrella's response was rather soft, her eyes still fixed on her father and the captain. "Thank you, Mother."

Gryswold turned his attention back toward the companions. "Yes, well…do you think there is any chance those mages survived the cave in?"

All eyes turned to Glo. The elven wizard felt suddenly on the spot. He thought it over briefly before answering. At least one of the mages was a skilled magic user. It really depended on just how proficient he was. "Honestly, it's hard to say. There is a spell which allows instantaneous travel across short distances. If one of them could cast it, then they might well have escaped the caverns."

"Along with my knife and a couple of arrows," Seth said, his dry tone.

Glo let out a short laugh. "That is true. Even if they did escape, they would all still be wounded."

"Still, there is a chance that they survived," Gryswold said.

Glo let out a deep sigh. "Yes."

Gryswold's expression grew pensive. He sat back and tugged on his beard. "Then we can't rest easy just yet. If they did escape, we have potentially three evil wizards who may have been funding those bandits. The real question though is why? Why would someone pay orcs to waylay caravans headed to Ravenford?"

The room fell silent. No one seemed to have an answer to the baron's question. After a few moments, the Lady Gracelynn placed a hand on her husband's shoulder. "Gryswold, don't you think that is enough talk for now? These fine young men have just returned from an arduous journey. They probably have a number of things to attend to."

Gryswold's expression softened. "You are quite right, my dear." He turned to the companions. "Once again, thank you for all your efforts. Master Pheldan has been informed of your success against the bandits. He requested that you meet him at his store for your reward. When you are done with your business and rested, please return here. There are one or two things that we might need your help with. Captain Gelpas can fill you in when you are ready."

"Thank you, your Lordship," Aksel spoke for them.

They all rose as one. Lloyd and the Lady Andrella exchanged glances as they stood. Lloyd smiled warmly at the young lady. Andrella smiled in turn, then excused herself and rushed out of the room. The Lady Gracelynn leaned over and whispered to Gryswold. Glo's keen hearing picked up her words.

"I think we may have found a prospect for Andrella."

Gryswold whispered back, "He comes from a fine and noble Penwick family. He may be a little rough around the edges, but with some polish he would make a fine suitor for Andrella."

"You were rough around the edges once. It didn't stop me," Gracelynn whispered playfully.

Gryswold laughed then leaned in and kissed his wife.

28
CELEBRATION

"Just what are you three up to?"

The companions headed down to Pheldan's store. When they arrived they found a celebration waiting for them. The old half-elf had invited most of the town. Tables had been set up in the clearing behind the store. Pheldan supplied food and wine, the brothers from the distillery brought kegs of ale, and the baker brought cakes and pies. There were even some magical decorations that Xelda had made.

Glo introduced Elladan to Pheldan and Xelda. The old half-elf was delighted to meet yet another elf. Glo was sure Xelda would be enamored with the handsome bard, but to his surprise, neither of them was more than friendly with each other. The foursome had a good time conversing in Elvish. Elladan seemed quite impressed with their command of the language. When he heard Glo was giving them lessons, the bard gave him a sly wink, but Glo was not entirely sure why.

When Elladan found out there was no entertainment, he prompt-ly took out his lute. The bard played a number of lively tunes and invited folks to dance. The clearing quickly filled with folks spinning and cavorting to the spirited music. Glo himself was not much of a dancer, but Xelda grabbed his hand and dragged him out to dance. Luckily he did not step on her toes—at least not too often.

Brundon and Titan showed up, the latter for once not wearing armor. Instead she was garbed in a plain shirt and pants with a red and silver tabard sporting the same crest as her shield—a rearing lion over two crossed swords. The duo sat with Lloyd, Aksel and Seth, sharing in the free food and ale. A short while later, Kailay appeared. Glo saw the young woman approach their table. Xelda noticed it as well.

"Oh, this I have to hear," she told Glo. Before he knew it, he was being dragged back toward their table.

Kailay was speaking to Lloyd for the first time in days. "…sorry I haven't been around much lately. I was…ill."

Xelda whispered to Glo in Elvish, "Ill indeed. More like ill from embarrassment."

Glo stifled a laugh. That was the same thing Delara had said.

Lloyd's expression was sympathetic. "That's okay, Kailay. That can happen to anyone. I'm just glad you're better now."

A bright smile spread across Kailay's face. "Lloyd Stealle, you are so understanding."

"Why don't you join us?" he said. "You know Delara and Brun-don and Aksel and Seth of course. Oh, and here are Xelda and Glo."

They all exchanged greetings. It turned out that Xelda, Delara and Kailay were all old friends. They all sat together and shared more food and ale. It was a fun time, with some interesting stories about growing up in Ravenford. At one point Xelda pulled Kailay aside. The next thing Glo knew, Xelda had dragged Brundon onto the dance floor. Glo thought it strange, but Delara appeared almost resentful. At the same time, Kailay circled around and sat next to Lloyd. She whispered something to the young man, but Delara seemed too pre-occupied to notice. A few moments later, Lloyd rose from his seat and addressed Delara, "Ahem, would you care to dance?"

Delara appeared uncertain at first, but after another glance at Brundon and Xelda, shrugged her shoulders. "Sure. Why not." She rose and followed Lloyd into the crowd. The two clasped hands and began to dance. Titan seemed rather stiff at first, but Lloyd soon had her moving around. His agility on the battlefield translated nicely to the dance floor.

Glo felt a soft touch on his arm. He turned and saw Kailay sit down next to him. "He's rather good, isn't he?"

"Yes, he is."

"I think Brundon noticed as well."

Glo peered over at Brundon and Xelda. The former's eyes were riveted on Lloyd and Delara. Glo nudged Kailay. "Just what are you three up to?"

Kailay smiled sweetly back at him. "You'll see."

The couples passed each other two times. On the third pass, Xelda executed a smooth change of partners. As she danced away with Lloyd, Brundon and Delara were left arm-in-arm in the middle of the crowd.

Glo nearly burst out laughing. He glanced at Kailay. The young woman wore a knowing smile.

"So that's what you were up to."

Her smile widened. "Guilty as charged."

Brundon and Delara stood frozen for a few moments. Slowly, the couple began to dance. They soon fell into a rhythm and moved rather well together.

"It's about time," Seth commented. "They've been dancing around each other ever since we met them."

Kailay grinned. "Try ever since they met."

Seth shook his head. "Humans…" he murmured, his tone exasperated.

Kailay grabbed Glo by the arm. "Come on. We're not quite done yet."

Glo was mystified by her statement, but nonetheless followed her into the crowd. He danced with her for a few minutes, until they passed close to Lloyd and Xelda. The young woman then executed a partner swap and danced away with Lloyd.

Glo watched them curiously. "I thought she had given up on him."

"Oh she has," Xelda corrected him. "The entire town knows he's smitten with Andrella, and that she is smitten back."

Glo raised an eyebrow. "Wow. Is anything private in this town?"

Xelda smiled. "Not really. In a town of two hundred, everyone pretty much knows everyone's business."

Glo shook his head in amazement. His gaze suddenly fell on one disagreeable looking fellow off by himself, nursing an ale. Glo pointed him out to Xelda. "What's his story?"

A thin smile crossed Xelda's lips. "Oh, that's Haltan. He owns the rare items shop."

"Is he always so happy?"

"I don't think I've seen him smile once since he arrived here."

"And just how long has that been?"

Xelda mulled it over. "No more than a couple of years now. Why?"

"Oh nothing," Glo responded. It seemed strange to him that this Haltan was the only merchant who was not happy now that the orcs were gone. Compound that with the fact that he was a relative newcomer in town, and it seemed that much more suspicious.

His thoughts were diverted when the music changed. Elladan suddenly decided to play a slow tune. Glo glanced over at the bard, who returned his stare with a wink. Xelda drew close to Glo and lay her head on his shoulder. Glo felt the warmth of her body press against his. For the first time he noticed the scent of her hair. It smelled like lavender, fresh and sweet. A strange sensation went through the young elf. He felt oddly warm and comfortable.

Glo noted Brundon and Delara leaving the dance floor. Xelda saw it too. She shrugged. "Well, guess you can't have everything."

Glo gathered the couple was not quite ready for that level of closeness. He was further surprised to see Lloyd still dancing with Kailay. The pair stood close together, laughing and talking. Lloyd didn't seem the slightest bit uncomfortable.

He pointed it out to Xelda. "That's new."

"Yeah, like I said before, the whole town knows where his heart lies—even Kailay. She can be very nice when she's not in 'man-hunter' mode."

Glo laughed at her choice of phrase. The young half-elf had a positively delightful wit.

It was late in the day when the party finally wound down. Pheldan made a huge deal of presenting the companions with their reward. Aksel, Glo, Lloyd, Elladan and even Seth made certain to include Brundon and Delara. The two mercenaries were thankful but strangely quiet. The party finally ended and the companions said their goodbyes. Glo promised to meet Xelda the next day for another language lesson. Aksel, Glo, Seth, Lloyd and Elladan then headed back to the Charging Minotaur.

It was late when Aksel asked Lloyd, Glo and Seth to join him in the common room. They sat down in their regular booth next to the hearth. They practically had the place to themselves, most of the town having retired early after a full day of partying.

Aksel glanced around the table. His brow was furrowed as if he had been deep in thought. "I'd like to discuss Elladan. He was quite helpful back in the caves. He was also very skilled at describing all that happened to the baron and baroness. His memory is phenomenal."

"I like him," Lloyd agreed.

"He is rather talented," Glo admitted.

All eyes turned toward Seth. The halfling gazed back at the others, his expression unreadable. After a few moments of silence, he finally spoke, "Well, if you're thinking of asking him to join us, then be my guest. Just be aware he is not like the rest of you."

Glo found Seth's statement rather cryptic. "What do you mean?"

Seth took a deep breath, then sat forward. "Let me put it this way. You are all idealistic. Elladan is a realist."

Aksel stared intently at Seth. "And just how do you know that?"

"Let's just say that I know the type." Seth sat back and folded his arms across his chest.

Lloyd gazed at Aksel and Glo, his expression dumbfounded. He turned to Seth. "And what does that make you?"

"Me?" Seth responded with mock indignation. "Why, I'm neither. The only thing I believe in is myself."

Glo nearly choked. "Dragon dung! If that was true, you wouldn't be with us."

Seth slid out of the booth. "Believe what you want, but if you do induct Elladan into our little group, just be sure to tell him, I'll be watching him." The halfling pointed to his eyes with two fingers then pointed those same fingers toward the others. He then spun on his heel and stalked away.

Lloyd glanced at Glo and Aksel, his expression incredulous. "What was that all about?"

Aksel appeared as mystified as they. "I don't know."

Glo thought about what Seth had said. In what way was Elladan different from the rest of them? He seemed mortified by what happened to the caravans. He also appeared as intent as they were on protecting folks from the orc bandits. The only thing he could think of was what Elladan said about his motto—*trust no one*. That was actually a very Seth-like attitude. "You know, the truth is, Elladan is more like Seth than he cares to admit."

Aksel thought that over. "You might be on to something there. Either way, Seth gave us the go ahead, so I guess I'll go tell Elladan."

"I'll come with you," Lloyd offered.

Glo watched the two walk away. Seth had called them idealists. He supposed they were. Still, he couldn't imagine being any other way. His father had tried to change him, but instead ended up driving him away. Amrod had been a pessimist, though, his complete opposite. If both Seth and Elladan were realists, Glo could deal with that. With that last thought, he got up and headed to his room.

Elladan was surprised when Aksel and Lloyd showed up at his door. When they invited him to join their little group, he was speechless—for a few seconds anyway. He bowed deeply. "It would be an honor."

Elladan liked these folks. First of all, they had probably saved his life. Second, they were very capable, as proven by their exploits beneath the Vogels. Third, they already had a reputation. Eventually, someone would need to chronicle their adventures. That was something he always wanted to do.

A thin smile crossed Aksel's lips. "Excellent. We all have business around town tomorrow, but we will meet first thing in the morning for breakfast."

"Sounds good." Elladan escorted his guests to the door.

Aksel stopped in the doorway and turned to shake his hand. "We will see you later then."

Lloyd extended his hand and smiled broadly. "Welcome to the group!"

Elladan extended his own hand in return. Too late, he remembered the first time he had shaken hands with the warrior. Elladan smiled through it, not wanting to offend him. When Lloyd released him from his vice-like grip, Elladan's hand was throbbing.

"Thanks." He managed a quasi-smile.

Elladan watched the duo disappear down the stairs. As he closed the door, he was still smiling. That was an unexpected development. He had been planning to head to Lukescros for the annual fair, but that wasn't for another month anyway. Lukescros could wait. He had just joined a group of bonafide adventurers. That meant travel, battles, rescues, and rewards. It was a life most bards only dreamed of, and it had just fallen in his lap. With that last thought, the bard sat down and resumed practicing his lute.

Early the next morning, Elladan met the others in the common room. They were seated in a booth along the wall next to the hearth. Flames danced above the stacked logs, radiating warmth around the tavern. The room itself was fairly empty. From Elladan's understanding, the town was comprised mostly of fisherman and farmers. Those folks were either already out on the bay or tending their fields at this hour.

The barmaid, Kailay, served them breakfast. Elladan had met her at the party last night. She was a lovely young woman, with a sweet smile that lit up her heart-shaped face. Kailay seemed to know Aksel,

Glo, Lloyd and Seth quite well. She was talking about the party yesterday. "I almost died when Xelda swapped places with Delara. Did you see the look on Brundon's face?"

Seth let out a short laugh. "Yeah. He turned as white as Aksel's robes, or Elladan's outfit."

Elladan had seen the whole thing. They had gone to great lengths to bring Brundon and Delara together. "So let me get this straight. These two have liked each other for a year or so, but neither one is willing to admit it?"

Kailay turned to face him. As their eyes met, her cheeks reddened slightly. She seemed somewhat distracted as she answered him, "Um…yeah…that pretty much…sums it up."

Elladan gave her a partial smile. "Wow. And I thought elves were slow at courting."

Glo looked at Kailay and Lloyd. "Well I think you two can pat yourself on the back. At the very least, you got them to dance together."

Kailay ripped her eyes away from Elladan. "Oh…thank you, good sir." She flashed him a smile and executed a perfect curtsey. "Well I best be off to the kitchen. Let me know if you need anything else." She cast Elladan a quick glance then hurried off across the room.

The conversation turned toward things to do next. A few items required repairs, supplies needed to be replaced, and the question remained of what to do with that hammer. Furthermore, each of them had studies, or training, to continue.

Glo mentioned he had some new spells to learn. "I stopped off to see Maltar after the party yesterday. He said that after all we went through, I should be ready for them."

"Now that's helpful," Aksel noted said in between mouthfuls.

"He also seemed very interested in our latest adventure, especially when I mentioned those black mages. He agreed that they were most likely behind the caravan attacks but had no idea who they were or what they might want."

Seth's lips curved to one side. "And that wasn't helpful."

Elladan was puzzled. "So who exactly is this Maltar?"

Glo had an apologetic look on his face. "Oh, sorry. Maltar is the town wizard. He's the one who originally hired us to go to Stone Hill."

"Stone Hill?"

Glo put down his fork and explained further. "Our first mission was to the ruined keep atop Stone Hill, a few miles west of here. The place was filled with undead and bugbears, all who worked for a black mage named Telvar."

Elladan cocked his head to one side. "Hmm, I've heard you mention that name a few times. So that's who Telvar is."

Lloyd stabbed another huge forkful of pancakes. "Maltar's also friends with the baron."

Elladan turned toward the young man. "How do they know each other?"

Lloyd put his fork down and sat forward in his seat. "Remember the story I told you yesterday about Gryswold and the black dragon?"

Elladan nodded. "That was a good one. Hard to forget."

"Well, Maltar was the wizard who fought with him. And the town Abbot was with them, too."

Glo took up the story again from there. He told Elladan about the baron's rocky relationship with the wizard, but how Maltar still remained Gryswold's advisor. The whole thing struck a sour note with Elladan. "I wonder what their falling out was over."

Glo shrugged. "Well, Maltar is not the most agreeable of people." It was obvious from his expression that Maltar was more than just disagreeable.

"Did you mention the hammer to him?" Seth interrupted.

Glo shook his head. "No, actually. I thought I would wait until we know what it is first."

Seth's face spoke volumes on how he felt about Maltar. Elladan had to admit, the more he heard about the town wizard, the less he liked him. He turned back to Glo. "Maybe you should be careful just how much you tell this Maltar. Maybe his falling out with the baron was because of his temper. Then again, maybe it was because of something else. Either way, I'd be more careful around him."

Seth slammed his fork and knife on the table. "Yes! Exactly!"

Elladan gave Seth a semi-smile. This was the first time they had agreed on anything. It was not much, but it was a start.

Glo looked embarrassed. "Very well. I'll be more careful about what I tell him from now on."

"Thank you!" Seth raised his hands into the air as if praising the gods.

Aksel talked about going to the temple today. His continued use of healing powers in the name of his goddess should have earned him access to new divine spells. Lloyd said he was going to train heavily. His expertise with the sword had improved after their last few encounters, but there were a number of spiritblade techniques that had previously proven too complex for him. He was hoping to be able to master at least one of them now. Seth didn't say much, only saying he also had some things to look into. The halfling was very closed-mouthed.

Elladan told them about his own research. "A couple of my books contain information on spells and songs. I cracked them open last night and started to look through them. They might come in handy on our next job."

Aksel appeared impressed. "Excellent, Elladan. Now then, back to the hammer, has anyone been able to find out anything about it?"

Glo shook his head. "I couldn't identify it with a spell, and Maltar doesn't let anyone in his library."

Elladan had done his own research but had also come up empty. "And there's nothing about it in bardic lore."

Lloyd wore a puzzled expression. "Bardic lore?"

Elladan raised an eyebrow. "You've never heard of bardic lore?"

Lloyd shook his head.

Elladan laughed softly. "Heh. Well, bards aren't just singers and song writers, we're also historians. We keep track of historical events in song. I know many of those old songs by heart, but they are also recorded in texts. A couple of my books chronicle some of the most important events in history."

Lloyd was clearly impressed. "I had no idea."

Aksel cleared his throat. "So we've established that the hammer could not be identified by spell, nor is it listed anywhere in bardic lore." He turned to Seth. "Well?"

Seth shrugged his shoulders. "Don't look at me. I've never heard of a hammer like that before, and I wasn't going to just go ask around town."

Aksel glanced around the booth. "Okay then. So does anyone have any other ideas on how we identify it?"

They sat in silence for a short while. Finally, Glo offered up an idea. "There is that guy Haltan, the one who runs the rare items shop."

Aksel stroked his chin. "Rare items shop? I guess the hammer could be considered a rare item. It may be worth a shot."

Glo held up a hand. "There's just one thing you should know. Haltan was the only merchant who did not seem happy that the orcs were gone. Also, he's a relative newcomer to town."

Elladan's eyes narrowed. "So you think this Haltan might have some connection to the orcs?"

Glo shook his head. "I don't know."

Aksel reached a decision. "Okay, let's pay this Haltan a visit then after breakfast." He turned to Elladan. "Have you had any experience dealing with merchants?"

"A bit."

"Good. I'd like you to handle this then. The rest of us will hang back and keep silent. Tell this Haltan as little as possible."

Elladan grinned. "I can do that.

29
THE ENCHANTED HAMMER

Martaeu Foudre

The rare items shop was down the street from the Charging Minotaur. It stood around the corner from Maltar's home. There was a
sign over the front door that read *Haltan's Shop of Wonders*. Lloyd
held the door open for them. They filed into the shop one by one,
Elladan leading the way. He stopped inside the door and scanned
the shop carefully. He had seen better. There were a few aisles lined
with a variety of objects, including flasks filled with different colored
liquids, strangely adorned rods and scepters, sparkling trinkets, ornate necklaces, cloaks of just about every shade, boots, belts, gloves,
and even some fancy hats. Along the walls hung numerous weapons,
anything from swords to maces, spears, and axes. At the very back of
the store was a long wooden counter with a number of display cases
showcasing rings, necklaces, headbands and other assorted jewelry
ranging from plain silver and gold to those set with colored gems.

Behind the counter stood the proprietor, Haltan. He still wore the same sour look he had at the merchants' victory party the day before. His eyes narrowed as Elladan strode forward, his tone one of forced friendliness. "What can I do for you gentlemen?"

Elladan gave the merchant a quasi-smile as he navigated the aisle toward the back. "No, friend, the question is, what can we do for you?"

Haltan's face took on an even more pained expression. "Please. I've heard it all. I've been in this business for twenty years. So don't expect to pull anything over on me."

Elladan suppressed a grin. *Ah, a hard case.*

"Wouldn't dream of it, friend. We just have this little hammer we thought you might be able to help us with."

Haltan let out a heavy sigh. "Very well. Let me see it."

Elladan gestured to Lloyd. "Show the man."

Lloyd unslung his backpack and set it on the floor. He pulled out the hammer with both hands, then placed it on the counter. It landed with a resounding *thud*. Elladan watched the shop owner closely. He did his best to feign disinterest, but Elladan had caught a momentary flash of excitement in the merchant's eyes. *So this item is special.*

Haltan shrugged his shoulders, his expression indifferent. "So you have a warhammer. I have at least a dozen of them between here and my warehouse. What use would I have for another one?"

Elladan raised an eyebrow. Even if the merchant had that many warhammers, he doubted any were like this. "Come on now, friend. This hammer is anything but ordinary. Look at the ornate handle, the etched lightning on the sides, and the strange writing on the head; I doubt there is another like it in the world."

Haltan leaned over the weapon and scanned it from top to bottom. He slowly stood back up. "There are some unique qualities to this particular hammer, but that does not necessarily make it worth very much."

Elladan's eyes narrowed. He was certain the hammer was more valuable than the merchant was letting on. "So you have no idea what this hammer is or what it's worth?"

Haltan made a production of looking over the hammer once more. When he straightened up his expression was completely bland. "No, not really."

Elladan heard a snort behind him. He glanced over his shoulder and saw Seth standing at the end of the counter. The halfling's arms were folded across his chest, his eyes rolling to the heavens. Elladan had to stifle a laugh.

If Haltan saw the halfling's expression, he ignored it. He continued on in a condescending tone. "Still, I might be able to do something with this item. I occasionally get customers in here who like to collect unique weapons, even if they are really not worth all that much. I tell you what. I'll trade you something in my shop for this item, something not too expensive, that is."

So he wants the hammer! That confirmed it; it was worth something. Perhaps Haltan even knew what it was. Elladan decided to continue playing along. With any luck the merchant might slip and give them some clue as to its origin. "What do you have in mind?"

Haltan pulled out several items he was willing to trade for the hammer, one at a time. Elladan shot each item down. After the last one, Elladan had enough. This was getting them nowhere. Whether Haltan knew what the item was or not, he was definitely trying to cheat them by trading worthless junk. Elladan shook his head in disgust; he turned to Lloyd.

"Pick up the hammer. We are done here."

"Wait!" Haltan cried. "Perhaps you would be interested in another weapon as a trade for this one."

Elladan halted. He held a hand out to Lloyd, then slowly faced the shady merchant. "I'm listening."

Haltan suddenly seemed very interested in bargaining for the hammer. His tone was practically fawning. "I do have a very fine sword made of star metal. Just wait here one moment."

He hurried from behind the counter to a door that led to the back of the shop. The sounds of frantic rummaging reached their ears. It went on for a while longer, then stopped. A few moments later, Haltan came through the door, his face red from exertion. In his hands he carried an oversized sword. Its hilt and blade were solid black. Elladan had heard of such weapons before. They were made from metal found in rocks that fell from the sky. It was harder than ordinary steel, yet much lighter. Weapons made from that metal were extremely sharp, able to cut through other metals with ease.

Haltan hefted the large sword onto the counter next to the hammer. He took a few deep breaths, then gazed around at the companions. A smug look crossed his face. "I can see your big friend there finds this blade interesting."

Elladan gazed at Lloyd. The young man's eyes gleamed as he stared at the black-bladed sword. Elladan sighed inwardly. He would have to teach Lloyd a thing or two about negotiations. Meanwhile, Haltan prattled on.

"And well he should. It is made of a metal that has fallen from the stars. It will cut through almost anything. Of course, I could not trade something this valuable evenly for this near-worthless hammer. I would need at least 10,000 gold from you to make it an even trade."

Elladan's eyes narrowed. He knew a thing or two about weapons. "That's a fairly steep price my friend, even for a sword of rare star metal."

Haltan ran his hands over the blade. "Ah, but this is more than just a star metal sword. Note the sharpness of its edges. This is a finely crafted blade. You'll find no better this side of Dunwynn."

Elladan knelt down and peered closely at the blade. Haltan was not lying about that; those edges were indeed quite sharp. As he stood back up, Elladan did a quick mental calculation. A star metal weapon with such a keen edge would be fairly expensive—probably a little more than the 10,000 Haltan was asking for. That meant he was giving them next to nothing for the hammer. "Well, this is a fine blade, but you're mistaken about that hammer. I think it's worth far more than you're letting on. I'd wager even with this blade, you'd owe us at least 10,000 gold for it."

Haltan's expression changed to one of outrage. "Are you questioning my ethics? I'll have you know I run a high-class establishment here—one of the finest in this dreadful little town."

Elladan wasn't buying the merchant's act. "I'm sorry you feel that way. I guess our business here is done."

He started to turn away once more when the merchant held up his hand. "No! Wait." Haltan took a couple of deep breaths as if to calm himself. "Perhaps I was too hasty. Let me take another look at that warhammer." The merchant bent over the hammer once more and made a big production of checking it over from end to end. "Hmmm," he murmured. "Hmmm," he murmured once more.

Elladan watched on patiently. This was a game merchants liked to play. Bartering was their way of life. Elladan had frequented shops and bazaars from Kai-Arborous to Lukescros. He had seen it all, but he was not sure about the other companions. A quick glance over his shoulder confirmed his suspicions. Only Aksel seemed calm and collected. Glo and Lloyd appeared impatient. Seth had wandered off altogether. Elladan gave them a quick wink then turned back to the overdramatic merchant.

Finally, Haltan stood back up. "I must admit, my first appraisal was a bit too quick. This warhammer may indeed have more value than I originally thought. I feel bad for my original oversight, so I'll make you a deal—the hammer and 5,000 gold and we'll call it even."

Elladan laughed at the offer. "Ha, that's funny. I think you should have your eyes checked my friend—you're losing your touch. That hammer is worth twice the blade or more."

Haltan's face turned positively scarlet. "That's it. Get out! Take your hammer and get out of my shop!"

Elladan shrugged his shoulders. "If that's how you feel." He waved to Lloyd. "Take the hammer."

Lloyd's eyes strayed to the star metal sword. "But…"

Elladan felt bad for the young man, but this part of the negotiation was crucial. You had to be willing to walk out, even if it truly ended the bargaining. "It's no use, Lloyd. He's just too pig-headed to see a good deal, even when it's right in front of his nose."

He heard Haltan splutter behind him. In front of him, Glo raised an eyebrow. Elladan winked to his elven friend. He was almost certain Haltan was bluffing and would make one final offer before they left the shop.

"Wait!" came Haltan's strangled cry.

Elladan stopped. He spun around and saw Lloyd grasping the hammer. Haltan's hand laid on the young man's arm. Lloyd threw a quick look at Elladan. Elladan nodded to him. Lloyd shrugged and let go of the hammer, stepping back and away.

Haltan glanced up at Elladan, his eyes filled with anger. "You, sir, drive a hard bargain." He huffed for a moment or two then continued. "Very well, an even trade—the sword for the hammer; and that is my final offer!"

Elladan gave the merchant a half smile. "I'll just need to confer with my colleagues first." He walked down an aisle, motioning for the others to follow.

"Well don't take too long," Haltan warned them. "I won't be feeling this generous for very long."

Aksel, Glo, Lloyd and Seth joined him at the front doorway. Glo whispered to him, "This is not getting us any closer to finding out what the hammer is."

Seth wore a twisted smile. "I agree. This is a huge waste of time."

Lloyd wore a forlorn look. "But that sword is so nice…"

He gazed from Glo to Lloyd to Aksel. "Don't worry. If it's okay with you, I can get that sword and find out what he knows about the hammer."

Glo raised an eyebrow. "How?"

Elladan unslung his lute and held it in front of him. "With this."

Aksel eyed him carefully for a moment, then nodded. "Do it."

As Elladan turned back around, Haltan called out across the store, "What's going on over there?"

The bard strolled back down the aisle, strumming a soft tune. Haltan, however, was no novice at this. His eyes went wide. He stepped back and placed his hands over his ears. "Stop that…"

As Elladan continued to play, the shopkeeper fell silent. His hands dropped to his sides and his face went blank.

"Serves him right."

Elladan glanced over and saw Seth standing at the end of the counter. The halfling wore a derisive grin. He flashed him a partial smile, then turned back to Haltan. The shopkeeper stood there, dreamy-eyed, listening to the music. Elladan continued to strum his lute. He spoke to the merchant in a soft voice, "Now what were you saying about an even trade?"

Haltan sounded as if he was in a trance. "Oh, an even trade? Yes, an even trade. The lightning strike hammer of yours for this star sword; that would be a fair trade."

Aksel stepped forward. "Lightning strike hammer?"

Haltan's voice was strangely distant. "Yes, yes, that is what it says on the side here." He stepped forward and pointed to the inscription on the side of the warhammer. "*Marteau Foudre*. Hammer of Lightning Strike."

Glo stepped forward now. "You don't happen to know its origins, do you?"

The shopkeeper replied in that trancelike tone, "No, I don't. It's a mystery."

That appeared to be all Haltan knew. There was no way he could lie under the compulsion of that song. He turned to face the others, still strumming his instrument. "Well, what do you want to do?"

Lloyd gazed admiringly at the black metal blade. "That is a really nice sword."

Glo looked from Lloyd to the star metal blade to the lightning strike hammer. "Well, now that we know what it is, I suppose I could just research its origins."

Seth let out a short laugh. "I think Lloyd is going to burst if he doesn't get that sword."

There was a moment of silence, then Aksel bowed his head slightly. "Go ahead. The hammer is rather unwieldy anyway, and a sword that can cut through almost anything might come in handy."

Still strumming his lute, Elladan turned to face the dreamy-eyed shopkeeper. "Well then, do we have a deal? The hammer for the sword?"

"Done!" Haltan's voice rang out with no real emotion.

Elladan turned to Lloyd. "Go ahead. Pick it up."

Lloyd glanced around at the others and then grasped the black metal sword. A grin broke out across his face as he lifted it from the counter. He hefted it and it almost shot up to the ceiling. The grin on his face grew wider. "This thing is as light as a feather!"

Elladan could not help but smile at the young warrior's joy. Aksel, Glo, and Seth all chuckled in turn. Elladan observed they were still alone, but they really shouldn't dwell here any longer. What he was doing was not exactly illegal, but it was somewhat unethical. Still, it had been the only way to get the truth from the dubious shopkeeper.

"We should leave now," he said quietly. Lloyd looked up from his new blade and nodded his understanding. They all made their way to the door, Elladan following the others. As the others filed outside, Elladan turned back around. He called across the store to Haltan, "Nice doing business with you." He slung his lute over his shoulder, then exited the store, pulling the door shut behind him.

The companions hustled quietly down the street, not slowing until they reached the curve in the road. Haltan's shop was soon out of sight. Seth was the first to break the silence. "You know, he's not going to be very happy when he snaps out of it and realizes what you did."

Elladan shrugged. "Probably not, but short of magic, there was no other way we were getting the truth out of that one. And anyway, his original deal was outrageous. Maybe he'll think twice from now on before he tries to swindle a bard."

30
GIANT

He flew like a mage's missile straight into the monster's back

Early the next morning, the companions returned to Ravenford Keep. When they reached the front gate, Francis was on guard duty. "Ah, if it isn't the Heroes of Stone Hill—or should we be calling you the Heroes of the Bendenwoods now?" The affable guard immediately shook his head. "That doesn't quite have the same ring to it, does it?"

Elladan placed a hand on the guard's shoulder. "Trust me, there's an art to it, my friend. When we're done with this next set of business, stop by the inn. We'll put our heads together and come up with something."

A shy smile spread across the guard's face. "I'll have to take you up on that."

Aksel wore an amused expression as he addressed the likeable fellow. "In the meantime, the baron asked us to return here. He said there were some things he could use our help with."

"Certainly. I'll take you to see Captain Gelpas. He would know what the baron had in mind. Follow me."

Francis left the second guard alone at the gate and led the group into the castle. They followed him through the main hall and down a side hall that led to the officers' quarters. Gelpas had an office there. It was a fairly sparse room, mostly taken up by a desk and some chairs. There were a few cabinets along one wall and a rack where the captain's belt and sword currently hung. The town coat of arms hung on the wall behind him. Gelpas sat at his desk, intently scouring parchments strewn about on the furniture surface.

Francis cleared his throat. "Excuse me, sir. You have some guests."

Gelpas looked up from his desk, his brow furrowed. His expression immediately turned to one of recognition, though his demeanor remained serious. He rose from his desk and stepped around it to greet them. "Ah, gentlemen. Welcome. I trust you have finished all your business around town?"

Aksel spoke for the group, "Yes, captain, as a matter of fact, we have."

"Good, good. You couldn't have returned at a more opportune time. There is something that has come up which could use immediate attention." Gelpas rummaged through the pile of parchments on his desk. After a few moments of searching, he picked one up which had been partially buried. "Here it is."

Lloyd stepped forward anxiously. "What is it?"

A thin smile spread across the captain's lips as he gazed at the young warrior. "It seems that the source of the trouble up north has finally materialized." He read from the parchment aloud. "A hill giant is terrorizing farmsteads up around Bardon's Gap. It started a few weeks ago with broken fences and missing livestock, but the creature has grown bolder over time. Last week, two farmsteads were entirely wiped out."

Elladan stepped forward and gazed over the captain's shoulder. "Bardon's Gap? Isn't that at the eastern end of the Vogels?"

Gelpas glanced up at him. "Yes, as a matter of fact. Why?"

Elladan cocked his head to one side. "I was just wondering if this was somehow related to those black mages we ran into."

Glo's eyes narrowed. "What are you thinking?"

"I was thinking, why would a hill giant suddenly leave its home and raid farms down in the valley?"

Gelpas stared at the bard intently. "You think this creature was driven out? By these black mages?"

Elladan nodded. "Think about it. First the orcs raid caravans, and now a hill giant attacks the farms north of here. It's almost like someone is targeting this area."

Silence fell over the room. It lasted for a few moments until Glo chimed in. "It does make a certain amount of sense."

"Maybe," Aksel said slowly, "but we still have no hard evidence to tie these things together."

Gelpas stood with his arms crossed, his expression grim. "Well, if you do find evidence of such a threat, bring it to me immediately, day or night. For the moment, however, this giant needs to be stopped."

"Consider it done," Aksel responded.

Gelpas gave him a slight nod, then stepped back around his desk. "When can you leave?"

Aksel considered it for a moment. "We should be able to start out within the hour."

"Excellent." Gelpas reached for a quill and noted something on the parchment. "Oh, and there is a 4,000 gold piece reward. Return here for it when you get back."

The companions bid the captain adieu and left the keep. On their way out, Seth rubbed his hands together. "That should do it!"

Aksel smiled at the halfling's exuberance. "That should give us enough gold for those scrolls from Maltar, but how about we finish this job first?"

Seth waved the gnome off. "Details, details. One giant. How hard could it be?"

Glo barely suppressed a smile. When Seth had his mind set on something, there was no talking him out of it. The halfling wasn't the only eager one though; Lloyd was bounding with excitement. His words blurred together as he spoke. "Speaking of details, are we going to work with Titan and Brundon again?"

Seth's lips twisted sideways. "Do we have to?"

Lloyd was taken aback. "I thought you liked Titan?"

Glo placed a hand on the young man's shoulder. "Ignore him, Lloyd. He just likes to complain."

Seth let out a short laugh. "You say that like it's a bad thing."

Aksel decided to weigh in. "We will have more than enough money to afford those scrolls even if we hire them out." He turned toward Elladan. "We've been offering them 50 gold pieces apiece each day."

The bard gave him a slight nod. "Sounds reasonable." He paused a moment, his head tilting slightly. "You know, since you seem to hire them out a lot, I can work that out as a standard fee."

Aksel considered it for a moment. "That would save time."

"Alright. I'll go find them and work out the details."

"Just have them meet us in front of the inn within the hour."

The companions had stopped at the base of the hill below the keep. Elladan flashed them a pearly smile, then took off in the direction of the Charging Minotaur. Glo watched him go with amusement. "I think he likes to haggle almost as much as sing."

"Well, lucky for us he's good at both," Aksel agreed. "In the meantime, Glo and I will pick up rations for the road. Seth, Lloyd, go pick up the mounts."

Seth's tone was rather dry. "Sure."

Aksel chose to ignore him.

Glo went with Aksel to Pheldan's shop. There he ran into Xelda. She greeted him in excellent Elvish. "*Quel amrun. Nae saian luume.*'" It meant *Good morning. It has been too long.*

Glo felt bad. He had come to enjoy these daily lessons, but today he would have to cancel. "*Amin hiraeth, Xelda. Amin aa' il govad yassen lle sina re*" which meant *I'm sorry, Xelda. I cannot meet with you today.*

Her smile faded. "Why not?"

"We are headed up to Bardon's Gap. There's a giant destroying farms up there."

Xelda's expression darkened, her voice thick with emotion. "That is indeed horrible, but why must you always be the one to face these dangers?"

Glo was taken aback. He had not expected such a fervent reaction from her. "It is what I came here for—to help people with my gifts."

Xelda turned away from him, folding her arms across her chest. Her tone was icy. "And what if you die in doing so?"

Glo was at a loss for words. He could not fathom why the young half-elf had suddenly grown so cold. "But…Xelda…if I did not…I wouldn't be who I am."

She whirled around and glared at him, her brown eyes aflame with anger. "Fine!" she spat. "Go ahead and get yourself killed. And for what? Fame? Glory? Those are hollow trophies to put upon one's shelf."

Glo's eyes went wide. He hadn't known she had felt so strongly about this. He took a deep breath and tried to explain once more. "It's…not…like that. I don't care about the fame or the glory. My gifts were given to me for a reason—to make this world a better place. If I do not try, then what good are they?"

The anger in her eyes abated somewhat. She glared at him a moment longer, then turned her back on him. "Well then, you should go. Your destiny awaits you." She took a few steps, then stopped. "I just hope you can live with the lonely path you have chosen." With that she strode away across the store and disappeared into the backroom. Glo suddenly felt numb. His eyes lingered on the doorway where she had disappeared for he knew not how long. A familiar voice finally made him turn away.

"What was that all about?"

Aksel stood next to him. Glo shook his head, still uncertain as to what had just happened. "I do not know. I merely told her I would be away today—that we were hunting down that giant. I am not sure why she got so upset."

Aksel merely shrugged his shoulders.

"Xelda's always been a fiery one, just like her mother," Pheldan said. The old half-elf teetered over to join them. "I never quite knew what would set her off either, but if I had to guess, I would say you got under her skin, young elf."

Glo raised an eyebrow. He had never thought of it that way. As far as he knew, he and Xelda were merely friends. He gazed at Pheldan uncertainly. "Should I go talk to her?"

Pheldan slowly shook his head. "It'll do you no good. Xelda's a stubborn one. Once she's made up her mind, I'm afraid that's that."

Glo felt like an idiot. His stomach churned from the mixed emotions that welled up inside him. If Pheldan was right, he had ended any chance of a relationship with Xelda before it had even begun.

Pheldan drew close, lowering his voice. "It's been rough raising her on my own. My wife, Firla'nes, left us before she was born, and both her mother and father died during the dragon attack." The old half-elf's eyes misted over. "I lost both Firla'nes and my dear daughter, Narila, within the span of two years."

Glo felt his heart wrench. Pheldan had lost so much so swiftly. His voice caught as he spoke, "Was that…the dragon, Ullarak?"

Pheldan wiped the tears from his eyes. He gave them a slight nod. "Yes. It was eighteen years ago, just after Xelda was born. The dragon hit us with no warning. It tore into the keep and slew the old baron before any of us knew what happened. Xelda's father was up there…"

He paused a moment as more tears streamed from his eyes. Glo reached out and placed a hand on his shoulder. Pheldan continued, his voice breaking as he spoke, "We heard…the roars from down here…greenish smoke rose above the keep. Narila went…running up the hillside. She never…made it…"

The old half-elf stopped, his voice choking. Glo felt the blood drain from his face.

"I'm so sorry," Aksel said, his voice barely above a whisper. The little gnome had gone pale as well.

"It's…it's alright," Pheldan managed to say. "Most of us…lost loved ones that day." He wiped his eyes once more and cleared his throat. "When the dragon finished with the keep, it turned on the town. It was a couple of months before Gryswold and his party arrived. They hunted the beast down and in the end slew it, but by that time most folks were either dead or had run away."

Glo was at a loss for words. *So much death. It was horrible.* It also explained why Xelda had gotten so mad at him. She had lost both her mother and father to a monster—she couldn't face the chance of losing someone else. Glo let out a deep sigh. *She is probably better off without me.*

He and Aksel spent a while longer at the shop consoling the old half-elf. The little cleric said a few prayers with him for his lost loved ones. When they were done, they said their goodbyes to Pheldan and left. As they walked down the road, Glo glanced back at the shop one last time. He resolved to himself that he would not return. Xelda was far better off without him.

Less than an hour later, the small company met in front of the Charging Minotaur. Titan and Brundon waited there with Elladan as promised. The company soon headed out, turning north at the end of the block. They continued in that direction, passing to the east of the keep. A short while later, they had left town, headed up the north road toward Bardon's Gap and their inevitable clash with the rampaging giant.

Later that evening, Brundon and Elladan stood at the bar of the Charging Minotaur. They were surrounded by a crowd of patrons, all rapt in the latest tale of the heroes' exploits. The duo took turns describing their clash with the hill giant. Brundon waved his mug around, ale sloshing around in all directions. "The giant was on the run, the ground shaking with its every step. The gap between us began to widen—it was getting away! Suddenly Lloyd launched into the air. He flew like a mage's missile straight into the monster's back. *Boom!*"

Brundon illustrated with his free hand, making a flying motion through the air in front of him. Those gathered around the bar held their breath, waiting for the tracker to continue his story, but Brundon passed the tale over to Elladan. The bard's voice rang out across the entire tavern, rising and falling in a fevered pitch. The crowd was enthralled.

"Lloyd smashed into the giant with all the might he could muster. So great was that blow that it toppled the creature, slamming it hard into the hillside. The ground trembled all around as the earth itself protested from the force of the tremendous impact. When the shaking finally stopped, Lloyd stood over the monster, his great black blade ready. The monster tried to rise, but then the mighty Titan joined the fray. The giant roared, huge arms and legs swinging wildly in all directions, but they were no match for the ferocity of the two warriors. They fought on with swords of vengeance, seeking retribution for the lives of those poor farmers the monster had so callously snuffed out. The battle raged on back and forth until finally, one mighty blow struck true. The sun shone blood red in the west as the foul creature gasped its last breath. The monster fell still, its reign of terror ended once and for all."

At the end of Elladan's narration, the room was so silent you could hear a pin drop. It lasted for a few moments, then the entire inn began to applaud. They rose to their feet as one and cheered, lifting mugs to Elladan and Brundon and the rest of the companions over in their booth. "To Lloyd!" many cried. "To Titan!" others yelled. "To the Heroes of Stone Hill!" even others shouted.

Elladan and Brundon were swarmed at the bar as patrons strode up to shake their hands and buy them more ales. A number of folks came up the booth to thank the rest of them. Lloyd, Titan, and even Glo, Aksel, and Seth received praise and thanks for their part in the slaying of the murderous giant. More rounds of ale were bought, Kailay and Morwen busily hurrying back and forth from the bar with more mugs than the companions could keep up with. Finally, things began to settle down.

Lloyd leaned forward and whispered quietly to the others, "I didn't really look like that, did I?"

Seth leaned back with his feet up, enjoying the aftermath of the show. "Close enough."

Titan raised her mug to him. "I have to say, I was impressed." Her gaze grew wistful. "I wish I could fly through the air like that."

Glo had been curious about that, but in all the mayhem forgot to ask Lloyd about it. "So that was another one of those spiritblade techniques?"

The young man grinned self-consciously. "Yeah, it's called *Soaring Dragon*. I really only mastered it yesterday."

Titan shook her head, a thin smile gracing her lips. "Looks like I'm going to have to step up my game to keep up with you."

More laughter erupted from over at the bar. Brundon and Elladan were still sharing stories with a number of patrons. Titan let out a short laugh. "I think Brundon has met a kindred spirit in Elladan."

"They do seem to be enjoying themselves," Glo admitted.

"It's good for business, too." Seth punctuated his statement with a heavy draft of ale.

Lloyd let out a heavy sigh. "I'm just glad we were able to stop that thing. I wish we could've gotten up there sooner."

Titan reached over and placed a firm hand on the young man's shoulder. "It's alright, Lloyd. We did what we could. That monster won't hurt anyone else ever again."

"Amen to that," Aksel agreed.

They were interrupted by the sound of music. Elladan had taken the stage. The bard sung an impromptu ditty about *Lloyd, Titan and the Giant*.

Afterwards, Seth suddenly grew irritable. "A story is one thing, but now a song? I tell you, I might as well be invisible." He wrapped his cloak around himself and suddenly disappeared. Glo supposed he couldn't blame him. Both Elladan and Brundon had glossed over the fact that Seth had hamstrung the giant. He had crept into its cave and done so while it was still asleep. Had he not, their battle with the monster might have gone quite differently.

Lloyd must have felt the same way. His expression grew troubled. "That's been bothering me, too."

"Unfortunately, that's not what people want to hear," Aksel explained. "The giant wouldn't have seemed nearly as fierce, nor our victory quite as sensational if people knew it had been disabled. Brundon and Elladan's version of the story makes it seem far more dangerous."

Titan shook her head. Her tone was extremely cynical. "Ah, but that is the way of the world. People only see what they want." She took a quick draft from her mug. "Before Brundon came along, no one would take me seriously as a warrior. To everyone else I was just a girl. He was the only one who gave me a chance." Her gaze traveled across the room and fell on her irrepressible partner. Her face lit up, her eyes brimming with emotion.

Glo knew that look. It was the way his mother looked at his father; the way Lloyd and Andrella gazed at each other. She really did care for the man. Glo felt a brief pang as he thought of Xelda but then chided himself. That ship had sailed. Glo's musings were interrupted when Lloyd suddenly rose from his seat.

"Well, I think Seth deserves credit too, and I'm going to fix that right now."

"Sit down, Lloyd!" Seth's disembodied voice hissed.

Lloyd froze in his tracks. He spun around and stared at the empty seat where the halfling had been. Without warning, the halfling reappeared there as if he had never left. Lloyd wore a puzzled expression. "But, I thought…"

Seth interrupted him. "It's alright, Lloyd. I was just griping. Aksel is right. What Elladan and Brundon are doing is really what's best."

Lloyd shook his head but sat back down anyway. "I still don't think it's fair."

Seth stared at the young man, his normally snarky expression visibly softening. He grabbed his mug and raised it high in the air. "Here's to Lloyd, the giant killer!"

They all raised their own mugs and clinked them together. "To Lloyd, the giant killer!"

Lloyd grinned and shook his head, his face turning red. "You guys."

It had gotten late and the tavern emptied out. Titan and Brundon bid them goodnight and headed to their rooms. The companions were left alone in a nearly empty inn. Only Kailay, Morwen, and the bartender, Tapgin, were left bustling around the room cleaning up tables. Kailay strode past their table and stopped, balancing a tray of empty mugs in one hand.

"Well that was exciting! Can't remember the last time we had such a turn out. You all are definitely good for business." She gave them a wink.

Elladan winked back at her. "We aim to please."

Kailay gazed at the bard, her cheeks turning red. Glo found her reaction amusing. This was the second time the young woman had responded so around the bard. He was handsome to be sure, but Kailay was usually the one to make men blush. It was refreshing to see the shoe on the other foot. Her eyes lingered on the bard for a few more moments, then she tore them away. "Anything else I can get you gents before we close down for the night?"

They all shook their heads. "I think we're good," Aksel said.

Elladan abruptly reached forward, his hands full of coins. "These are for you."

Kailay glanced at him, then slowly held out her empty hand. Her face reddened once more. "Thank you, Elladan." The young barmaid pocketed the coins, then turned and scurried away toward the kitchen.

Elladan turned back toward the others. "Well, she's a real sweetheart."

"That she is," Glo agreed. He stifled a yawn. There was one more subject he wanted to discuss before calling it a night. "We'll have the money for the scrolls tomorrow. I can go to Maltar and have him write them up, but we still don't know the magic words that invoke the ring."

Elladan cocked his head to the side. "What was it that Telvar's journal said? Something about his first love?"

Aksel nodded. "Yes, that was the hint he left in his journal."

Elladan turned toward Glo. "And what was it that Maltar told you? That Telvar never loved anyone but himself?"

"That's what he said."

"Then it has to be Telvar himself," Elladan declared. "Or some variation of his name," he quickly added.

"My thoughts exactly," Seth agreed. "It's the only thing that makes sense."

Aksel slowly stroked his chin as he thought it over. "You may be right, but we won't know for sure until we get back to Stone Hill."

They talked a bit more, then everyone decided to adjourn for the night.

31

RETURN TO THE RUINS

The magic exploded from his body, flowing up the shaft
to the golem wedged within

The next morning, the companions headed up to the keep. They were surprised to find the captain already knew all about their adventure. Gelpas's expression was curious. "I just have to ask one question—did Lloyd really knock the giant down?"

Lloyd started to reply, but Elladan beat him to it. "As a matter of fact, captain, he did." Elladan launched into an avid description of the demise of the giant. When he was done, Gelpas had a few more questions. Once he was satisfied, he pointed to a small chest on the floor in the corner of the room. "Flying or not, this is most definitely deserved."

Aksel bowed. "Thank you. We are just glad to be of service."

Gelpas gave him a slight nod. "Very good, but now that the giant is taken care of, I have something else that could use attention." He grabbed a parchment from the top of a pile on his desk. He began to read from it. "It seems that some ships have disappeared off the coast near Cape Marlin over the last month—three to be exact. The Gail Runner, the Sydion, and the Zephyr, all gone without a trace."

"May I see that?" Aksel asked.

"Certainly." Gelpas handed the parchment over to the little cleric.

While Aksel looked it over, Elladan addressed the captain, "That certainly sounds serious, but there was one thing we were hoping to do first, back up at Stone Hill."

Aksel looked up from the parchment. "It should only take a day at most, then we will be ready to head out to the cape."

Gelpas thought it over as he took the paper back from Aksel. "I don't suppose one day would make a difference. And we do need to arrange transportation out to the coast anyway."

"We'll come straight here as soon as we return," Aksel promised.

"Very well," Gelpas agreed.

The companions left the keep. After a quick stop at the inn, Glo headed to Maltar's to get the scrolls. Lloyd carried a couple of sacks filled with gold coins. The mage was rather surprised to see them, but just as obviously pleased to receive his payment. He promised to have the scrolls for them within the hour. In the interim, the companions prepared for the journey back to Stone Hill. They gathered outside the Charging Minotaur just before midday. Glo met them with the freshly finished scrolls in hand. He was surprised to see Elladan sitting in a wagon while the rest of the company were astride their mounts.

Glo halted next to the bard and nudged his head at the wagon. "So what's that for?"

Elladan pointed a thumb behind him. "That? That's for any spoils we find up at the keep."

"And my couch!" Seth added.

Glo chuckled for the first time in a couple of days. He had forgotten about the halfling's obsession with that piece of furniture. He was still smiling as he packed the scrolls into his saddlebags, when a familiar voice called out to them.

"Off for a jaunt, are we?" Brundon stood on the porch of the Charging Minotaur, a lopsided smile on his face.

Elladan called back to him, "Nothing major. Just making a quick trip out to Stone Hill."

Brundon's smirk widened. "Going back to get the golem?"

"And my couch!" Seth added once again.

Brundon's mouth spread into a full-fledged grin. "Of course. Perhaps you would like some company on the journey?"

Elladan glanced at Aksel. The little cleric shrugged. The bard turned back to Brundon. "It's not exactly a paid job."

Brundon stroked his beard. "Be that as it may, I do remember a room full of rather nice antiques out there. Perhaps Titan and I could retrieve some of those and sell them for a small profit?"

Seth stared at the tracker intently. "As long as you don't touch my couch."

Brundon held up both hands in front of him. "I wouldn't dream of it."

Aksel shrugged. "Sure. Why not."

"Done, then," Brundon declared. "I will go and fetch Titan. Give us fifteen minutes, tops."

Brundon and Titan showed up just shy of fifteen minutes later. The seven of them rode off down the street, across the bridge, and down the south road out of Ravenford.

They entered the Dead Forest a couple of hours later. It was just as dreary as Glo remembered it. Elladan rode next to him, peering at the leafless, grey canopy that stretched around and over them. "Well, this is kind of bleak."

"According to Brundon, the entire forest is like this."

Elladan whistled. "An entire forest? What could have done this to an entire forest?"

Glo merely shrugged.

Aksel turned around and gazed up at them. "We said the same thing the last time we were here. Whatever did this, the extent of it boggles the mind."

Elladan continued to gaze around them. "It's giving me the creeps."

The riders soon arrived at the base of the trail up to the ruins. It took awhile, but they entered the courtyard by early afternoon. The front entrance lay wide open, the remains of the inner door strewn to either side of the archway. Large cracks ran through the walls of the structure. Loose rocks lay strewn across the courtyard, most likely fallen from the empty sections of wall. The tall tower stood at the other end of the yard. It appeared exactly as they had left it—the door completely gone. Black stains charred the parapets, a sour reminder to Glo of his explosive mistake during their encounter atop the tower. The main keep rose to their left, its walls a light shade of grey in the afternoon sunlight. It was the only part of the ruins still mostly intact. The companions dismounted.

"I'll stay here and keep watch," Titan offered.

Brundon's face twisted into a half smile. "What, love? No desire to go back inside?"

She gave him a withering stare. "Not really. Anyway, you're the one who wanted 'antiques'. Have fun scrounging around in there."

Brundon let out a short laugh. "Suit yourself."

They left Titan outside and entered the keep. Brundon and Seth made a quick sweep of the first and second floors while the others waited in the foyer. The duo soon returned. The place was empty except for the golem which was still trapped in the chute.

Aksel slowly stroked his chin. "I think we should start upstairs. I don't want to be underneath that thing when it starts dripping down into the basement."

Seth contorted his face in disgust. "Eww."

Glo silently agreed.

Brundon's mind was firmly fixed on looting. "Mind if I take Lloyd and go down to the basement? The day's already half over and we haven't even started scavenging."

Aksel had started up the stairs. He glanced over his shoulder at Lloyd. "It's fine by me."

Lloyd shrugged. "Sure, I'll go with you." He followed Brundon away toward the basement.

Aksel, Seth, Glo, and Elladan went upstairs to the pantry. The four of them gathered around the top of the chute. Glo lit the end of his staff and shone the light down the shaft. Something moved below. They heard a small boom, and the floor shook a bit in response.

Seth lips rose to one side. "See, just like I told you." He reached into his pocket and took out the control ring. Seth slipped it onto his finger. "Well, here goes nothing." He held his hand out over the hole and closed his eyes. His face took on an expression of deep concentration. After a few moments he spoke a single word, "Telvar." Nothing happened. The golem continued to bang weakly against the walls of the shaft. Seth glanced around at the others. "Okay then. Let's try this one more time." Once again, he thrust his hand out over the chute and closed his eyes. He stood in that pose for a half minute, then spoke another word, "Ravlet." The noise from the chute abruptly halted. They all exchanged glances.

Elladan gazed at Glo and Aksel. "Was that it?"

Aksel merely shrugged.

Glo was incredulous. "Really? Telvar backwards? Maltar was right. Telvar really was a hack. That was way too easy."

"Try making it do something," Aksel instructed Seth. "Just to be sure."

The corner of Seth's mouth rose slightly. He held his hand over the chute once again. "Hit the wall," he said in a commanding tone.

Boom! The room shook around them.

Seth looked from Aksel to Elladan and then to Glo, his expression smug. "Hit the wall again," he commanded.

Boom! The room shook once more.

Glo was quite surprised, but there was no denying their success. "I guess that did it."

Elladan gave Seth a pearly half smile. "Nicely done."

Seth responded in an exaggeratedly polite tone, "Thank you." He finished with an accusing glance at Aksel and Glo.

Aksel ignored the halfling's non-verbal taunt. "Well then, now that we know the golem is under our control, let's go down to the basement and use those scrolls."

Seth eyed Aksel suspiciously. "I thought you were worried about the golem dripping on you?"

Aksel gave him a wry look. "I was kidding."

Glo arched an eyebrow. *Aksel? Kidding?* Wonders would never cease.

A short while later, they entered the basement room directly under the pantry. Glo stood beneath the chute and held his staff aloft. The light from it shone up the shaft, just far enough to illuminate something blocking the way.

"I don't think it's gone anywhere."

Glo gazed down and saw Seth standing next to him, the trace of a smirk on his lips.

Glo laughed at himself. "You're right."

The elven wizard took a few steps back and handed his staff to Elladan. He unslung his backpack and drew out a wooden scroll case. Glo popped open the top, turned it over, and let the two scrolls inside slide out into his hand. He gingerly unraveled the first scroll and checked the inscription. This one contained the spell of Stone to Mud. Aksel, Seth, and Elladan stared at him with expectation. With a brief nod, he began to read the spell aloud. It was a very complex spell and thus rather lengthy, but Glo plowed through it, making sure to pronounce each passage properly. When he finished the last sentence, Glo felt a surge of magic stronger than any spell he had cast before. His body practically tingled with power, the arcane mana coursing through his veins. It lasted mere moments, then the magic exploded from his body, flowing up the shaft to the golem wedged within. Glo let out a sharp breath, his body not used to the expulsion of so much power at once. At that same moment, the parchment in his hand began to disintegrate. The paper slowly disappeared from the center outward, until even the handheld sections evaporated. In moments, the entire scroll was gone. Still, that was not unexpected. The magic of a scroll was embedded into the very fiber of the paper. Once invoked, the magic was "used up" and the scroll disappeared along with it.

Elladan took a step toward the shaft, holding Glo's staff aloft. Glo reached out and grasped the bard's arm. "I wouldn't do that if I were you—unless of course you want to be covered in liquid golem."

Elladan gave him a sideways glance, then chuckled. "No, I'm good."

They all stared expectantly at the opening in the ceiling. After a few moments, a thick grayish liquid began to ooze out of the shaft. It slowly dripped onto the floor, pooling up underneath the chute. With only a few exceptions, the ooze did not spread like a normal pool. Instead it slowly piled up, eventually forming into a familiar shape. When it was done, the same grey golem they had faced on their last visit towered over them—with a couple of minor differences. First, the creature's mass shifted around as if it were not completely solid. Second, there were huge gaps in both its arms and sides. Luckily, there was extra "mud" spread on the floor around it.

Elladan let out a short laugh. "He's looking a bit wobbly there."

A thin smile crossed Glo's lips. "He'll be just fine once we change him back, but before that we'll have to re-sculpt him a bit."

The wizard stepped forward and knelt down to scoop up some mud. The others followed suit, gathering the liquid ooze and using it to reshape the golem. They pushed huge handfuls into the empty spots where it had damaged itself, smoothing over the gaps as best they could. When they were done, Aksel cast a spell to produce water which they then used to clean themselves off.

Once Glo was dry, he took out the second scroll, the one with the spell of Mud to Stone. He unraveled it and began to read from the parchment. It was another long, complex spell, but Glo recited it as carefully as before. When he was done, he felt that same potent rush of mana course through his body. The magic exploded out of him and flowed straight into the golem. A bright golden aura encircled the creature as it hardened before their eyes. In a few minutes the golem turned back into stone, looking almost brand new.

Seth walked up to the creature and patted it on the leg. "There you go, big fellow." Seth barely reached up to the golem's knee. "Now we need to give you a name. Hmm, what shall we call you?"

"How about Rocky?" Elladan wore a quasi-smile.

Seth grimaced. "Very funny."

He seemed so annoyed that Glo just couldn't help himself. "How about *Gon-edan*?"

Seth folded his arms and glowered at him.

Glo tried very hard not to laugh. "What? That's Elvish for Rock-man."

Seth's expression turned into a scowl. "How about, no."

"What about…Boulder?" That had been Aksel.

"Boulder," Seth repeated. He cocked his head to the side as he mulled it over. "Boulder," he said once more. A smile slowly spread across his lips. "I like it." He looked up at the impassive stone golem. "That will be your name from now on. You are 'The Boulder'."

Aksel let out a sigh. "Well, now that that's settled, Glo and I are going to go check out Telvar's lab. Maybe we can find some clue as to who those other black mages are. Meanwhile, why don't you two go and scavenge with Brundon and Lloyd."

Elladan glanced up at the golem, his expression speculative. "I bet he can carry a lot."

Seth gave the bard a smug smile, then held out his hand with the golem ring on it. "Come on, Boulder. We're going to go get us a couch!"

Elladan followed Seth through the corridors of the basement to a room filled with large objects, most covered with sheets. Brundon and Lloyd were already there, the former emptying the contents of a curio into a sack the latter held.

Elladan called over to the duo, "I see he's keeping you in shape."

Lloyd gave them a wan smile. "Are you kidding? This is my third trip already."

"Well, we brought along some help." Seth walked in with the golem trudging behind. It was so huge it had to bend over to fit through the doorway.

Brundon eyed the looming creature cautiously. "Are you sure it's under your control?"

Seth halted and glared at the man. He held up his hand with the ring on it and said, "Stop!"

The Boulder immediately halted. Brundon cocked his head, his expression still wary.

Without turning, Seth pointed at a long couch in the middle of the room. "Pick it up."

Elladan and Seth moved out of the way as the large stone golem strode forward. They watched on as it reached the couch, bent over and lifted it easily with one hand.

Seth glanced at Brundon with a satisfied smile. "Well?"

Brundon appeared impressed. "I'd say you could open your own moving company if you wanted."

Elladan let out a short laugh. As Seth directed the golem back out into the hall, he surveyed the rest of the room. It was rather large, but most of its contents were covered with sheets. He did spy an ornate mirror against one wall. Elladan walked toward the mirror. As he approached it, Brundon called out. "I wouldn't do that if I were you."

Elladan halted and gazed at the lean man. "Why's that?"

"Well, you could, if you want a fast trip to the third floor."

Elladan surveyed the mirror from where he stood. It was obviously magic. He had heard of them but had never seen one. "I don't suppose it would work if we took it with us?"

"According to Glolindir, it has a limited range."

Elladan sighed. "Now that's too bad."

Seth and the golem were now gone, Lloyd following close behind. Elladan strode over to Brundon. "Any idea why he's taking that couch?"

Brundon shook his head. "Not a clue. Perhaps it's some kind of elaborate joke."

Elladan thought that over. Seth had a strange sense of humor. He could imagine the halfling going to great lengths to pull off a joke. He was probably taking the couch just to mess with their minds. Elladan flashed Brundon a pearly half smile. "You're probably right."

Brundon's lips twisted upward. "Well then, let's get back to our pillaging, shall we?"

32

A CRY IN THE NIGHT

Without warning the ground rose up around him

It was nearly dusk, the last rays of the setting sun casting long shadows across the courtyard of the ruins. Elladan leaned heavily against the side of the wagon, wiping the sweat from his brow after depositing his last load into the wagon. It had been a long afternoon hauling antiques and valuables from inside the keep. Elladan was nowhere near as strong as Lloyd or Titan, but he had rolled up his sleeves and carted whatever he could up from the basement. Lloyd, Titan and Brundon were still inside, the tracker stuffing as much as he could into the warriors' sacks.

Elladan stood back and peered into the wagon bed looking for some sign of Seth. The halfling had nestled down onto his couch hours ago and was now completely hidden from view amidst the piles of furniture and sacks of smaller valuables around him. Seth had not lifted a finger to help since the Boulder deposited the couch in the cart hours ago. The stone creature stood a few yards away, not having moved an inch since it had fulfilled its master's last command.

Elladan spoke in a loud voice, "Too bad *Rocky* there couldn't have lent us more of a hand."

Seth's response was immediate. "It's the 'Boulder', and I wasn't going to send him back in there and leave my couch unguarded."

Elladan let out a short laugh. It seemed there was no arguing with the halfling.

"Looks like you made out well."

That sounded like Glo. Aksel and the elven wizard strode out of the keep.

"I'm content," Seth's voice came from the wagon bed behind him.

A trace of amusement crossed Aksel's face. "Glad to hear it."

Elladan noted how bleary-eyed the duo looked. They must have spent the entire time going through Telvar's research. "So how about you two? Find anything interesting?"

Aksel's answer was tentative. "We may have come across something."

Glo appeared a bit more excited. "It seems that Telvar had been looking all over the region for traces of the Golem Master's works. In doing so, he had documented a number of old legends. One of them in particular mentioned a cult that existed in the northern branch of the Korlokesel Mountains. There were references to mages in black robes conducting sacrifices to their god."

Elladan found that an interesting coincidence. "The northern end of the Korlokesels are not too far from the Vogels, the same place we had our run in with those black mages."

Aksel still seemed hesitant. "While that may be true, this cult hasn't existed in over a hundred years. It was crushed by the armies of Dunwynn at the end of the Thrall Wars."

Aksel had a valid point. Still, history had shown that evil was never completely stamped out. It always managed to rise again in one form or another. The rest of their conversation was cut short.

"Gods, Brundon, could you have packed these sacks any further? What are we going to do with all this worthless junk?" Titan admonished her partner as they exited the keep. Both she and Lloyd carried huge sacks over their shoulders, each bulging at the seams.

Brundon's expression was smug. "You'll be thanking me later, love, once I convert all this to coin."

Titan glared back at him. "I highly doubt that."

The trio trudged over to the wagon and hoisted the heavy sacks onto the bed. They made a ton of noise as they were loaded aboard.

Seth's head popped up over the piles of loot. "Hey, some of us are trying to rest here!"

Elladan flashed him a pearly smile. "Sorry to disturb your beauty sleep, your highness."

The corner of Seth's mouth lifted upward. "Apology accepted. As you were."

Elladan let out a short laugh. "Would you like us to draw you a bath? Maybe set out some tea and crumpets?"

"I'll never say no to food," Seth said, not missing a beat.

Their verbal sparring was interrupted by Lloyd's voice as it rang across the courtyard, "Guys, you might want to see this."

The warrior stood near the front gate. They all walked over to join him. The sun had just fallen behind the Korlokesels to the west and the night sky was turning dark. Stars began to poke through the inky firmament. Down the hillside in the midst of the Dead Forest there was a faint glow.

"Looks like…a campfire," Brundon observed, "but who in his right mind would camp out in those woods?"

Elladan turned to Glo. "Why don't you send your raven out to see?"

"I just did," the wizard replied, "but she can only get so close. There's not much cover in those dead trees, and a black bird would stand out like a sore thumb."

Aksel gazed around the group, then back at the wagon. Seth had not moved from it, still perched on his couch. The little cleric raised his voice. "Well then would anyone else care to check it out?"

Seth shook his head. "Don't look at me. You're crazy if you think I'm leaving this couch."

Brundon let out a sigh. "Fine. I'll go." He trotted forward through the open gate. "But you better keep an eye on my loot," he called back over his shoulder.

Titan called after him, "Stop worrying so much about money. Watch yourself out there!"

Brundon spun around and jogged backwards. His tone dripped with sarcasm. "Why, Delara, you do care!"

"I just don't want to be the one to have to unload all this stuff," Titan shot back.

"Don't worry, love, I would never do that to you!" With that last jab, Brundon turned around and took off across the hilltop. He swiftly disappeared into the darkening night.

The tall warrior shook her head slowly. "Brundon…" she murmured under her breath.

Brundon made it to the edge of the hilltop and was soon down into the tree line. He traveled swiftly through the woods in the direction of the campfire. As he went, his mind drifted back to Delara. He was not quite sure what was going on with her, but something had changed between them since the day of the party. It was subtle, but it was there. Her digs at him were just a bit more biting, and her jabs were just a shade harder. He had almost brought it up but then decided against it. She would never tell him outright. In fact, she might not even know herself. Delara was one to bury her feelings; it was what he liked most about her. Working with Delara was like working with a guy.

Yet, all that had changed since the party. Xelda and Kailay had cleverly maneuvered them into dancing together. They had even conscripted Lloyd into their little scheme. Brundon found it amusing at first, but once he was arm in arm with Delara something happened. For the first time ever, Brundon had seen her as a woman; a rather pretty woman for that matter. He had not been able to look at her the same since.

A sudden thought made Brundon nearly stumble. *What if Delara feels the same?* He halted in his tracks. *Is it possible? All this time we've been working together she's secretly had feelings for me?*

As soon as he thought it, Brundon realized how foolish it sounded. Delara just didn't think that way. She was all about weapons and fighting. There was no room in her life for love. Brundon let out a deep sigh. His mind felt clearer now. He began to move forward again, then abruptly froze. Something rustled in the dead brambles up ahead. *Brundon, you idiot.* He had been so preoccupied with Delara that he had forgotten one of the most basic rules of survival in the wild—be constantly aware of your surroundings. Now his brooding had put him in a dangerous situation.

The tracker stood completely still. In the darkness, he could see nothing through the leafless grey bushes. He waited and listened, but the rustling had stopped. Without warning the ground rose up around him. Brundon tried to leap out of the way, but something big wrapped around him. He tried to twist free but was held fast. His eyes went wide as the bushes parted and something large and grey stepped out in front of him. Out of options, Brundon yelled at the top of his lungs, "Help!"

With no leaves to stop it, the sound echoed through the lifeless forest all the way up the hillside. A moment later, the pressure around his body increased and everything went black.

Elladan glanced at Glo. "Did you hear that?"

He had heard something—a faint sound rising up from the forest below. "I think it was a cry."

Titan's voice was filled with concern. "Do you think it could have been Brundon?"

"Probably," Seth's voice rang out from the wagon.

"Seth!" Aksel admonished the halfling.

Titan's concern turned into irritation. "Well, I'm not waiting around here to find out." She trotted toward the horses.

Lloyd took off after her. "I'm coming with you."

"Wait!" Aksel cried after them.

Both Titan and Lloyd halted. They turned around and gazed at him impatiently.

"We don't know what we're running into."

Titan sounded angrier by the moment. "I don't care. I'm not leaving him alone out there."

Aksel tried to calm her down. "He won't be." Aksel turned toward Glo. "Anything from Raven?"

Glo closed his eyes and concentrated on his tiny friend. It only took a few seconds for him to feel her apprehension. "Raven is uneasy. There is definitely someone, or something, dangerous out there."

That was all Titan needed to hear. "That's it. I'm going after him." She vaulted up onto her mount. Lloyd was a second behind her.

"Wait!"

The moon had just risen, its silvery light illuminating the small dark form that leapt down from the wagon. Seth stalked over and placed himself in front of Titan and Lloyd's mounts. "I'll go check it out. You two go crashing through the forest like a couple of lumbering oxen and whoever, or whatever, it is will hear you coming from a mile away. Brundon could end up dead before you even get near him."

The two warriors were left speechless. Before either could reply, Seth stomped away toward the front gate. "Leave it to a professional," he called back over his shoulder.

"Um, Seth?" Aksel called after him.

The halfling halted. "What now?"

"You plan on bringing the golem with you?"

Seth's voice was laced with sarcasm. "Sure. That'll make sneaking around easy."

"Well then, maybe one of us should hold onto the ring while you are out there."

Seth stomped back toward Aksel and held out the ring. "You know, sometimes you make too much sense."

As Aksel put his hand out, Seth momentarily drew his away. "You can have it for now…but I want it back." Aksel stared at his friend, his expression impassive in the pale moonlight. When Aksel did not react, Seth placed the ring in his outstretched palm, then stalked out through the front gate.

As soon as he disappeared, Aksel whirled around toward the others. "As for the rest of us, let's start moving out in the direction of that campfire. We'll assume for now that whoever, or whatever, is out there is hostile."

Elladan glanced at Aksel. "I've studied a lot of history, especially the wars. If you want, I could draw us out a battle formation."

Lloyd and Titan both dismounted. Titan's voice was fierce. "Sounds like a good idea."

Lloyd's tone was uncharacteristically hardened. "Let's do this."

Aksel nodded. The five of them gathered around in a circle on the ground of the stone courtyard. Glo lit his staff and they began to formulate their plans.

Brundon woke up and found he still could not move. He was on his side, facing a roaring campfire, with his hands and feet bound. He could kick himself for getting caught in the first place, but now was not the time. He would berate himself later—if there was a later. For now, he needed to keep his wits about him.

"He's finally awake." It was a woman's voice, but it was quite deep for some reason. Suddenly, a face appeared in front of him. It was most definitely female and might have even been attractive considering the curve of the face and those deep brown eyes. What threw him off was the greenish pallor of her skin and the two small tusks that protruded from her lower lip. She was a half-orc!

This just got a whole lot more dangerous. Brundon needed to buy time. If he played it right, he might just make it out of this alive. He put on his best smile. "And what can I do for you now, love?"

"Oh, love is it?" She let out a deep laugh. The half-orc stood up and all he could now see was her lower body. She wore thick brown leather boots and studded leather leggings. The very top of her thighs and midriff were bare, revealing a smooth, muscular physique. Strapped around her waist was a wide leather belt from which hung two long curved blades. This woman was most definitely a warrior. "Looks like we have a charmer here." Abruptly her face appeared in front of him again.

Brundon fixed her with a smoldering gaze. "I just recognize beauty when I see it, and beauty comes in many forms. It's not just in fair hair and pretty eyes. There is beauty in strength and muscle as well. From here, I see all that and more."

Her eyes narrowed as she studied him, but then her face notice-ably softened.

"Don't let this one sweet-talk you," came a cold voice from be-hind her.

Rough hands grabbed him and pulled him up into a sitting posi-tion. Brundon swiftly surveyed his surroundings. He sat in the mid-dle of a camp. Two covered wagons were parked on either side of a campfire. Two men strode away from him, each wearing bronze-colored half plate across the torso, their lower halves garbed in leath-ers with a longsword sheathed at the waist. A third man dressed all in leathers sat by the fire—perhaps a woodsman like himself. In front of him stood a figure in dark robes. Brundon could make out noth-ing of its features, its face hidden by a low hanging hood. The half-orc female now stood to one side. She wore leather from her midriff up to her neck, with a necklace of large tusks hanging down across her chest. Her arms were wrapped in the same thick studded leather that covered her legs.

"Like what you see?" she said with a smug smile.

She was impressive, he had to admit, but then Brundon admired strong women. He cocked his head to one side and gave her a wink. "So far, love. So far."

The half-orc's eyes widened. It was hard to tell from her skin col-oration, but he thought she was actually blushing. Their flirtation was interrupted by the figure in dark robes. Its tone was contemptuous.

"Enough of this frivolity."

Brundon slowly turned his gaze toward the figure. The voice was most definitely male, human-sounding, in fact. "Wondering how you got into this mess?" the man asked. His tone was condescending.

Brundon berated himself. *Oh I know how—I got careless.*

The man mimicked his thoughts. "Quite careless of you, wasn't it?"

Brundon stared back at him. That was probably just a lucky guess, unless this 'man' was some kind of mage. If that was the case, then mind-reading was quite possible.

The man laughed. It was a cruel sound. "You're wondering if I can read your mind, no doubt. Not exactly. Let's just say I have a talent for studying people. You are in a particular predicament and are reacting in a typical manner."

Brundon also made a quick study of people. This man was arrogant. He could have let Brundon believe he read minds, but instead chose to brag about his ability to read reactions. Well two could play at this game. He would feed the man's ego and see where it led. "Fair enough. You're obviously the man in charge. What can I do for you?"

The man in black robes snorted. "Ah, you are a smooth one. Very well, all you have to do is answer a few of my questions, and you'll be set free."

Right. More likely you'll slit my throat. Brundon kept his tone even. "I tell you what—I tell you what you want, and then you let me join your merry little band."

The man scoffed. "Join us?" He turned toward the half-orc warrior, his tone biting. "You hear that Tazira? He wants to join us."

Tazira looked him carefully up and down. Brundon met her gaze with a wry smile. "Perhaps he does like what he sees," she answered with an appreciative nod.

"No doubt about that, love." He turned back toward the man in black. "Look, I'm just a mercenary for hire. You caught me off-guard, but I'm not bad in the woods or a fight. I also don't care exactly what I do, as long as I'm well paid for it."

The robed figure did not move. "Go on."

Brundon shifted his weight around and got more comfortable. "You're obviously a smart man—not one to run into battle without knowing his enemy. So, I'd wager you want to know about the group up at the keep."

"Yes," came the cautious reply. "Who are they? Where are they from?"

"They don't have a name as a group. Some folks call them the *Heroes of Stone Hill.*"

The man scoffed. "Heroes of Stone Hill?"

A small smile crossed Brundon's lips. "I know, it's a stupid name. Anyway, I was with them last week when they raided the ruins and killed a dark wizard."

There was the slightest hint of concern in the man's voice. "A dark wizard? You wouldn't happen to know this wizard's name?"

It wouldn't hurt to tell him. The wizard was dead, after all. "Telvar. His name was Telvar."

The note of concern disappeared from the man's voice, once again replaced with that arrogant tone. "Telvar. Yes, I believe I've heard of him. A third-rate wizard at best. Do you know what he was doing at Stone Hill?"

Brundon had to be careful here. The information he gave the man had to sound valuable, but he didn't want to tell him too much either. It was a fine line, but Brundon knew the best lies were hidden in half truths. "He was searching for the secret to golem creation."

"Telvar? That fool couldn't create a golem if his life depended on it."

So he did know of Telvar. According to Glo, Maltar had much the same opinion of the now-dead mage. Brundon's face twisted into a half smile. "Oh trust me, he didn't, but somehow he managed to get his hands on one."

The man's voice took on a dangerous edge. "What kind of golem?"

"A stone golem." Brundon proceeded to describe the Boulder.

When he finished, the dark-robed man remained silent as if weighing the truth of his words. "And what happened to this golem?"

They had reached a delicate point in the questioning. From his tone, it was obvious the man did not trust him. Still, he was rapt in Brundon's story. If he could twist it around just right, he could gloss over the fact that the companions had a golem. That might give them an advantage in the battle that was sure to come. "They destroyed it."

"They destroyed a stone golem?" His tone was incredulous.

Brundon snorted. "It was more luck than anything else. They found its control ring and smashed it."

"Really?" the man drawled. He paused as if mulling over the possibility. "That's actually rather clever."

Brundon let out a short laugh. "You're giving them far too much credit, my friend. They nearly got themselves killed doing it. If the little thief they had with them hadn't stolen the ring, they'd all be dead."

A cold, soft laugh came from underneath the dark cowl. "And then they killed Telvar?"

"Yes. They buried him just outside the keep."

"Good. Good."

The robed figure's voice rose just a bit as he asked the next question, "So then, what are they doing back here now?"

Here it is. This was crucial. "Not much of a surprise there. They went back to town and celebrated for a few days. Once everyone sobered up, they grabbed a wagon and headed back up here. There's a lot of fine items stored in that basement."

The figure was quiet for a few moments. Brundon kept a wry smile on his face, acting far more confident than he felt inside. Abruptly, another chilling laugh came from underneath the hood. "Excellent. Now, tell me more about this group."

"Well, they have a wizard, a cleric, and a large warrior. They also have this bard—a real showoff. Then there's that little snot halfling. He brags about being an assassin, but he's a second-rate thief at best." Brundon allowed a trace of annoyance to seep into his voice. That was not hard. It was easy to be annoyed with Seth.

"Are there anymore?"

Brundon shrugged. "Just one. Another mercenary—a warrior in full plate." He did his best to sound indifferent, but it proved harder than he thought as a vision of Delara popped into his head. If he didn't die from this, she would kill him for getting himself caught.

Tazira snorted contemptuously. "Humph, a friend of yours?

Brundon's heart skipped a beat, but somehow he managed to maintain his outward composure. "Oh, we've been on a job or two together, but we're not close; no good mercenary is."

She eyed him carefully, then a thin smile spread across her face. Her tone was suggestive when she spoke, "You obviously haven't been hanging around with the right mercenaries."

If Delara were here, she would have taken Tazira's head off. Brundon kept his emotions in check, giving her a sly wink. "That remains to be seen, love."

The man stepped in closer, his tone menacing. "That's enough of that, you two." The hood turned toward Brundon. "Tell me about the wizard."

"His name is Glolindir. He's an elf, from the west. He's an apprentice of the wizard, Maltar."

The man's voice took on a slight edge. "Maltar? He's involved in all this?"

Brundon immediately realized his mistake. He should never have mentioned Maltar. He covered it with a derisive snort. "Are you kidding? Maltar wouldn't waste his time with something as small as this."

There was a short pause. When the man spoke again, his tone was smug, "Okay then, an apprentice of Maltar's. That I can deal with easily. And this warrior. What of him?"

Brundon gave them a knowing look. "Now he's a big one. Really strong, but slow as an ox. Just don't let him hit you, and you'll be fine."

"No worries there," Tazira boasted. "I'll take care of that one."

Now that will be a battle to see. Half-orcs were notoriously strong and from the looks of it, this Tazira could handle herself. Hopefully the little bit of misinformation he had just fed her would make the difference. At that moment, something flashed over by one of the wagons. The cloaked figure strode over to it. It was a crystal ball. He gazed into it a moment then stood back up. "Well, they're coming this way."

"Good," Tazira responded. "That's better than having to hunt them down."

The man whirled around toward Brundon. "Now you stay there until we get back."

Brundon feigned disappointment. "Wait. I thought we had a deal."

The man's tone was arrogant. "We still do. If your information proves to be good, then we will discuss you joining us."

Sure. And I'm the Queen of Lanfor, Brundon thought wryly.

With that, his captors walked off. Hopefully those little twists of truth would buy his friends the edge they needed in this upcoming battle.

33
BATTLE IN THE DEAD FOREST

The raw power in these two behemoths was frightening to behold

Seth sat high in the branches just above the outskirts of the camp. He had taken to the trees after sensing something large in the forest below. It was a good thing, too. When he finally spied the thing from above, he saw that it was an earth elemental. Those creatures were deadly opponents on the ground. They moved through the earth as easily as people did through air. They could sneak up on you underground and grab you before you knew it. More than that, they were incredibly strong; once they got a hold on you, escape was near impossible.

Seth was certain that was what had happened to Brundon. He stuck to the treetops after that, leaping his way toward the glow of the campfire. The trees ended, and below him lay a long clearing, sparsely filled with leafless brambles and the occasional rocky outcropping. The camp was set up at the southern end. Seth immediately spotted Brundon tied up at the other end of the campsite. A figure in black robes and a female half-orc in warrior's garb stood over him. There were three other men moving around the camp. Two were dressed in half plate with swords strapped to their sides. The third sat by the fire—a bowman loading his quiver with arrows.

Seth also caught sight of a dark bird perched a few branches over. It was Raven. He reached into his backpack, pulling out a small piece of parchment, a thin quill and a small vial of ink. He scrawled a quick message and tied it to the bird's leg. He then waved the bird off, mouthing the word, "Go."

Raven took off into the darkness.

Seth turned back to the camp. He was too far away to hear the conversation with Brundon. He could sneak down there, but there was always the chance that the figure in black could see the invisible. Thus, Seth thought it best to remain hidden until the opportunity arose. He would then enter the camp and free the tracker. Of course he would rub it in that Brundon had been caught in the first place. A while passed before an object flashed in the middle of the camp. The robed figure went over to it, then called out to the others, "Well, they're coming this way."

That flash must have been from a crystal ball. It had to be focused on his friends. Hopefully his message had reached them in time.

The companions entered the north side of a long clearing. The moon had risen above the tree line, throwing its pale silver light across the area. The glade was mostly empty, with just a few dead brambles and a couple of rocky outcroppings; the glow of a campfire outlined a pair of wagons behind a slight hillock at the other end. The companions rode in a wedge formation with Lloyd in the lead. Titan and Glo were fanned out a couple of horse lengths behind him. Aksel and Elladan brought up the rear, driving the wagon, its bed covered with a canvas sheet.

A sudden whizzing sound caught Aksel's attention. His gnomish eyes barely caught sight of an arrow as it crossed the clearing. It was headed straight for Glo. He had no time to even shout out a warning as the projectile found its mark. Yet, instead of embedding itself into solid flesh, the arrow passed right through the elven wizard. Glo's body appeared to waver back and forth, then popped out of existence as if it were never there. His horse continued on rider-less.

At that same moment, the ground in front of the wagon began to shake. It broke apart, two large, rocky hands reaching up out of the dirt. They grabbed the horses, stopping them in their tracks. The spooked animals whinnied in fear but could not break free of that powerful grip. A huge form rose out of the ground. It grew in height until it towered over the frightened horses. Aksel immediately recognized it as the earth elemental. Seth's message had warned them about the creature. Still, his knowledge of the situation did nothing to assuage his fear.

Elladan suddenly spun around and yanked the tarp off the back of the wagon. "Now!"

Aksel forced down his fear. He held out his hand, the pale ring on his finger gleaming in the moonlight. "Attack the elemental!"

A large figure rose out of the back, a huge leg swinging over the side. The wagon tipped, almost knocking Elladan and Aksel out of their seats. The figure swung its other leg over the side and landed on the ground with a huge thud. The cart rocked wildly in the opposite direction; it was all they could do to hold on to their seats. The wagon righted itself with a thud. When Aksel's eyes focused he spied the earth elemental lumbering forward to meet its new foe, the Boulder.

A head popped out of the wagon behind them. "Wild ride there!" Glo cried. "So did it work?"

Aksel pointed toward the impending battle. "We're about to find out."

The stone golem and earth elemental came together, the sound of rock grinding on rock as they locked their hands. The strain was visible as both creatures threw their weight into the struggle. Two pairs of stone feet dug deep into the soft earth as the titanic battle ensued.

Up ahead, a dark figure rushed out of the bushes. Two blades gleamed in the moonlight as it leapt off the ground directly at Lloyd.

It appeared as if the warrior would be cleaved in two. At the very last moment, Lloyd flipped backwards out of his saddle. The dark figure went flying over the empty saddle, barely missing the young warrior.

Lloyd landed in a crouch. He stood and drew his blades, falling into a defensive stance. A few yards away the figure whirled to face him. It was the half-orc warrior he had been warned about. The figure was smaller than he expected, but the moonlight revealed it to be female. It made no difference though; half-orcs were strong, and this female had already proven to be quite agile. He was definitely in for a tough fight.

His opponent slowly walked toward him. "And here I thought you were slow!"

Lloyd shifted his footing in preparation for the coming attack. "You're fairly quick yourself."

The half-orc halted a short distance away and fell into a defensive stance. A wicked grin crossed her face. "This is going to be fun."

As one, the warriors launched themselves across the intervening space, weapons raised and battle cries on their lips.

The sound of steel against steel rang all around them. Blades flashed swiftly in the moonlight as the two warriors traded blows. They appeared evenly matched, Lloyd's foe just as fast as the spiritblade.

Off to their right, Titan faced off against two more warriors. The pair launched staggered attacks against the silver-clad warrior, but Titan ably fended them off with her own sword and shield.

Bam! Bam! The noise was so loud that Glo nearly jumped. The Boulder had just shrugged off a pair of blows from the earth elemental. The force of those strikes was so great that it traveled through the golem's body and into the ground, causing the very earth to shake around them. The Boulder's response was immediate. It wound up its huge grey arms and struck back with frightening speed.

Bam! Bam! The earth elemental shook visibly from the two-fisted blows, as did the ground surrounding them. The raw power in these two behemoths was frightening to behold. In between those huge booms and the ringing of steel, the sound of falling pebbles could be heard—tiny pieces chipping off the two earthen creatures.

Elladan wrestled with the reins, doing all he could to keep the horses from bolting. The poor creatures whinnied nervously, shying away from the nearby battle. As awesome as that battle was, Glo wrenched his eyes away and swept the clearing with his keen elven eyes. There had been no sign of the archer since the one arrow cleaved his false image. That image had been Elladan's idea. He had said it was a standard battle tactic to take out the opposition's casters. Glo was thankful he had listened to the bard. Still, he was more worried about that black mage. The last time they had faced one, they were all nearly burnt to death.

Aksel also scanned the area, mirroring Glo's thoughts. "Do you see the mage?"

"A little busy here," came Elladan's answer as he continued to grapple with the horses.

"No," Glo responded, still gazing all around. *Where is he? What am I missing?* As if in answer to his silent question, a memory flooded to the forefront of his mind.

"You are thinking too small, Glolindir," Amrod chastised him. *"A powerful enough wizard can attack from any direction—above or below."* Glo's eyes went wide. How could he be so stupid? He immediately shifted his gaze upwards, scanning the heavens. It was not a moment too soon. A sudden red flash in the dark sky above sent a cold chill up his spine.

"Out of the wagon!" he screamed, thinking it already too late. Glo only vaguely remembered what happened next. One moment they were in the wagon, the next they were in a heap a couple of yards away.

Baroom! There was a sudden flash of light, and a rush of heat passed over their bodies. Glo lifted himself up and saw the wagon was in flames. The horses were yards away, bolting for the forest. Miraculously, he and his friends were unscathed. Somehow they had been spared.

"What was that?" Elladan exclaimed.

"Fireball." Glo scanned the sky once more.

Elladan let out a low whistle. "How in the heck are we still alive?"

It was Aksel that answered, "I think it hit in the wagon bed. The wagon took the brunt of the explosion."

Elladan followed Glo's gaze. "It came from up there?"

"Yes." Glo nudged his head in the direction he was looking. He focused on the portion of the sky where he had seen the first flash. He could just barely make out a darker area hovering against the star studded backdrop. Glo began an incantation; he lifted his fingers into the air and pointed at the dark spot. *"Radius Ardens."*

A red hot ray of light leapt from his fingertips and raced upward, streaking across the star strewn sky. Just as it was about to hit, the ray flickered and faded out of existence.

"Dragon dung," Glo swore. "He's out of range."

Elladan reached inside his vest and pulled out a short wooden wand. "Maybe this will work." The bard pointed the tip of the wand up toward that same dark patch in the sky. *"Nullam Telum."*

A purple projectile leapt from the tip and rocketed upward. It lanced through the night, swiftly closing on its target. About a yard away from the dark form, the missile abruptly exploded. An evil laugh floated down from the sky above.

"Son of a hellhound," Elladan swore. "He must be shielded."

Elladan was right. A shield spell would have the effect they saw. It put an invisible barrier around the caster that would block projectiles such as missiles or arrows. This mage was experienced and clever. They were in a lot of trouble.

Aksel must have had the same thought. "Um, guys, maybe we should look for cover." He nudged his head toward a rocky outcropping not five feet behind them. The little cleric had not spoken a moment too soon. There was another red flash in the sky where the dark mage hovered.

"Look out!" Glo cried.

The three of them scrambled for the rocks, Glo and Elladan grabbing onto Aksel from either side. The trio vaulted over the top of the outcropping, barely hitting the ground before the night lit up behind them.

Baroom! Another rush of heat passed over them, but this time the rocky wall spared them from being burned. Glo, Aksel and Elladan slowly rose and dusted themselves off.

Elladan's tone was filled with irony. "So what do we do now? We can't reach him, but he sure can reach us."

Glo exchanged glances with Aksel, but the little cleric just shook his head.

The elven wizard was just as stumped as his friends. He slowly shook his head. "I don't know. I just don't know."

Seth had watched silently from the trees as the warriors and the archer moved out. The black-robed figure was left alone. It disappeared into one of the wagons, emerging a few moments later with a red garment. The figure flung the cloth over its shoulders, then waved its arms around as if casting spells on itself. When it was done, the figure grasped the edge of its cloak and launched into the air, disappearing into the blackness of the sky.

Interesting, a flying cloak. That must come in handy.

The halfling carefully scanned the camp below. Once certain that everyone was gone, he wrapped his cloak around himself and became invisible. Seth cautiously climbed down and circled around through the woods until he was behind Brundon. He silently crept up to the tracker and whispered, "Don't move."

Without turning, Brundon whispered, "Took you long enough."

Seth snorted as he pulled out a knife. "Well, at least I didn't get caught by an earth element."

"Touché," Brundon said.

Seth cut through the ropes binding his wrists.

"That was rather stupid of me." Brundon rubbed his wrists where they had been bound. "Hopefully I was able to buy our friends an advantage."

While Seth went to cut the ropes around his legs, Brundon explained how he had slipped misinformation to his captors. Seth had to stifle a laugh to avoid slicing the tracker. He stepped back, his mouth twisting sideways.

"Well played, Brundon. Well played."

Brundon leaned forward and rubbed his ankles where they had been bound. "Easy, Seth—that could be mistaken for a compliment."

The retort on Seth's lips died as the sounds of battle reached his ears. He peered in that direction, but the hillock blocked his view of the clearing beyond. Brundon rose to his feet next to him.

"Sounds like it's begun."

A trail of flame crossed the night, lancing downward in the direction of the battle. Seth followed the trail backward, his keen eyes fixing on a small area devoid of stars just above the trees. He spoke to Brundon without taking his eyes off that spot. "I've got to go. You going to be okay here?"

"Fine now," Brundon replied. Out of the corner of his eye, Seth saw the tracker holding up his bow and quiver in one hand and short sword in the other.

"Good," Seth said with a quick nod. "I have a wizard to kill." Without another word, he took off in the direction of that dark spot. Seth swiftly reached the trees and launched himself upward. As he climbed, another red streak crossed the sky, but this one shot up from the ground.

That must be Glo's fire beam spell. Unfortunately, the ray faded just before it reached its target. Still, it had lit up the section of sky Seth was focused on. It was only for a moment, but it was just enough for him to see a clear outline of the black mage. A grim smile crossed Seth's face as he continued to climb. He had nearly reached the top of the tree, when a purple projectile came whizzing through the air. It homed in on the mage and appeared as if it were going to hit, but exploded about a yard too short. The detonation was followed by an evil laugh. Seth kept his eyes locked on the dark form as he pulled out his venom knife. It was hard to focus in the inky blackness, but he didn't have much choice. Seth was just about to let loose his dagger when a red glow appeared next to the figure.

He's casting another spell. A wicked smile spread across the halfling's face. As the red light coalesced into a ball of fire, the mage's silhouette was perfectly outlined.

Gotcha! Seth adjusted his aim as the small red ball sped away. In one swift motion, he let loose his dagger, sending the knife straight toward its unsuspecting target. A high-pitched scream erupted from the direction of the dark spot—the dagger had found its target.

"*Venenum*, scumbag," Seth said with satisfaction.

Lloyd and the half-orc warrior were locked in combat. Blades flashed swiftly in the moonlight as the fierce battle weaved back and forth. Each strove to gain an advantage, but neither was able to land a blow. Every advance he made, she countered, and every attack she made, he blocked. The half-orc abruptly halted, her chest heaving as she paused to catch her breath.

"It's been awhile since…I've had such…a skilled opponent."

Lloyd's own breath was ragged. He managed a smile. "I could say…the same."

She grinned in turn. "Too bad…only one of us…will walk away from this."

The two warriors slowly circled each other, their long shadows crossing in the pale light of the moon. They kept their eyes firmly fixed on one another as the sounds of battle raged around them. Half-orcs were known for their stamina. Lloyd had kept up with this warrior till now, but he was tiring. One slip could bring his downfall. He had to do something soon or the outcome of this battle was inevitable.

His best bet was to use a spiritblade technique, but he was facing a seasoned warrior. With her quick reflexes and battle expertise, there was no guarantee a technique would work. Perhaps if he drew her off-guard first…

A desperate plan flashed through his mind. Lloyd steeled himself, then abruptly launched into his opponent. He struck with a typical two-weapon combo to lull her into a false sense of security. The half-orc wore a smug smile as she parried each of his swings. At the last clash of steel, Lloyd began his technique. Time slowed for him as it always did, dragging out those few moments when he would be most vulnerable.

The half-orc mistook his hesitation for fatigue. She let loose a triumphant battle cry as her blade rushed toward Lloyd's unprotected neck. The keen edge of her sword glimmered in the moonlight as it closed in on him, but Lloyd's mind was elsewhere. It dug deep into his innermost being, searching for that spark of spirit.

The blade was mere inches from his neck when he finally made that connection. The world suddenly blurred around him, then came back into focus. The half-orc warrior was now behind him. Lloyd reacted swiftly—he whirled around, bringing his right blade with him in a tight arc.

His opponent stood flat-footed. She had put too much weight into that killer blow, and his sudden disappearance had pulled her off-balance. His blade caught her in the side, slicing through the thick leather armor and sinking deep into the flesh underneath.

The warrior screamed in agony, trying desperately to whirl out of the way. She was not quite fast enough; the tip of Lloyd's other blade slashed across her exposed torso. With his opponent injured, Lloyd pressed his deadly assault. She managed to parry his next two blows, but she was definitely moving slower.

The warrior cried out in rage and frustration, "How did you get behind me?"

Lloyd did not answer but instead pressed his advantage. He launched another deadly assault, his blades flicking and arcing in a dance of whirling steel. He ripped through her defenses, inflicting new wounds on top of the old. The half-orc was now bleeding profusely, dazed and sweaty from exertion and the loss of blood.

Lloyd sprang forward once more, slicing away at his opponent, but on the last swing, feinted and thrust instead. His blade went past her guard and slid into her chest. Her eyes locked on his, a stunned expression on her face. Lloyd paused for only a moment, then drew back and fell into a defensive position. His opponent did not move. She stood frozen in place, glaring at him as ragged breathes escaped her throat. Her voice was barely a whisper.

"I still don't know…how you got…behind me…"

The grip on her weapons loosened as they tumbled out of her hands. The warrior's body teetered a moment, then collapsed onto the ground. Lloyd stood there silently, his chest heaving as he watched his valiant opponent draw her last breath.

Titan was angry—mad at Brundon for getting himself caught,

but even angrier at herself for letting him go off on his own. She had
a bad feeling about it from the start and should have said something.
Brundon was so infuriating though, with his devil-may-care attitude
and insinuations about her feelings for him that she merely sniped at
him in return.

Now the idiot was in peril and she could do little about it. She was
in the midst of battle with a pair of warriors, and despite her best
efforts, the duo had flanked her. These two were quite skilled, coor-
dinating their attacks so as to keep her constantly on the defensive.
It was a tactic she knew well—wear your opponent down until they
made a mistake. Luckily, she also knew how to defend against it.

Titan's father was an excellent swordsman—one of the best in
Ravenford. He had run Titan and her brothers through hours of
drills, preparing them to be the town guards. Although Titan had
chosen not to join the guards, she had always bested her brothers—
even with both of them pitted against her. Her superior size and
strength helped, but it was her keen mind that allowed her to prevail.
She soaked up her father's lessons on tactics like a sponge.

Titan now put that knowledge to use. She subtly shifted her stance
between attacks, inexorably drawing her opponents into a rhythm. It
took careful timing and patience, but once she had them in a predict-
able pattern, the tall warrior struck.

She caught the first warrior in mid-attack, lashing out hard with
her shield. Her preemptive strike was met with the sound of snapping bone. The man cried out in pain and staggered backward, his
sword dropping from his hand.

Titan was tempted to finish him off right, but was too experienced to make that mistake. She immediately spun around and parried the blade bearing down on her back. She followed with a full out
assault on the second warrior. She bore down on him, using her superior strength and height to her advantage. She hammered away at
him, driving him back until he lost his footing and fell to the ground.
The man went sprawling, stunned and completely at her mercy as he
lay there.

She could have slew him right then, but her eyes had been off
the second warrior too long. A furtive glance over her shoulder

confirmed her peril; the warrior bore down on her, sword poised for a strike in his left hand.

Titan dropped her shield and grasped the hilt of her sword in both hands. Turning slightly, she stabbed backwards swiftly and viciously, the blade catching her attacker in the abdomen. The warrior's eyes rolled back in his head. A gasp left his body and the sword fell away. He shuddered once, then went limp.

Titan immediately withdrew her sword and faced her second attacker. He was just scrambling to his feet. Not waiting to retrieve her shield, she launched into him once more. He moved slower now, perhaps still slightly dazed from his fall. Titan drove on mercilessly, her blade flicking around more like a fencer now.

Her opponent slowly retreated until he faltered once again. Titan lunged forward, the tip of her blade sliding past his guard and skewering him neatly through the upper torso. The warrior let out a short cry, then collapsed to the ground in a heap.

Titan swiftly surveyed the battlefield. Loud booms resounded from the stone golem and the earth elemental as they continued to beat on each other with those huge fists. A fiery ray shot across the sky above her, ending somewhere above the trees ahead. A reddish ball flew back in the other direction in response.

Wizard's battle, she thought wryly. *Nothing I can do about that.*

Her eyes then fell on Lloyd and his opponent. The duo circled each other cautiously. Titan went to pick up her shield. Now there was somewhere she could lend a hand. She sprang forward at the same moment Lloyd launched into his adversary. She swiftly closed the gap but was still too far away when Lloyd faltered.

Titan's heart leapt into her throat as that blade bore down on his exposed neck. Suddenly, Lloyd was gone. His body shimmered out of existence and reappeared a moment later behind his opponent. Titan stopped in her tracks and watched in awe as he assailed his adversary from behind. The other warrior had no chance now. Lloyd had connected with a vicious swipe followed by a furious onslaught of flashing blades. It was over in less than a minute.

Titan slowly shook her head. Those spiritblade techniques were extraordinary. There was no way she could compete with something like that. Something clicked in her mind at that moment—a decision she had been putting off for a couple of years now. It was time to step up her game.

A sudden cry in the night interrupted her musings. It came from above the trees.

34
THE SERPENT CULT

They practice a dark magic

Glolindir, Aksel and Elladan huddled together behind the rocky outcropping. The trio wracked their brains as the sounds of battle raged around them. Elladan urged them to hurry. "If we don't do something quick, that black mage is going to start taking pot shots at the others."

Before either Glo or Aksel could respond a cry pierced the night. "Ahhhhhhhh!"

A chill went up Glo's spine. He scrambled up the rocks and peered across the clearing. Thankfully, Lloyd and Titan appeared okay. Their opponents lay on the ground around them.

"Look!" Aksel cried. He pointed in the direction of the camp. A dark figure floated below the tree line, clearly silhouetted by the campfire's glow. Yet there was something strange about it—it wobbled around erratically.

"He don't look so good," Elladan observed.

Glo wasn't sure what had happened, but he wasn't going to look a gift horse in the mouth. "Well he's in my range now. Let's see if we can add to his discomfort."

Glo pointed at the flailing figure and repeated the words, "*Radius Ardens.*" A red beam of light leapt from his fingertips and raced across the clearing. This time it did not fade. It hit its mark with a satisfying flare, causing small trails of flame to sprout around the bobbing mage.

"Arrrrrrrrrgh!" the figure shrieked.

"My turn," Elladan announced. He drew out his wand once more and pointed it at the struggling mage. "*Nullam Telum.*" A purple projectile leapt from the tip and sped across the clearing. It swiftly closed on its target, yet again exploding just short of the mark.

Elladan shrugged. "Can't blame a guy for trying."

The dark figure managed to right itself, though it still appeared wobbly. A shrill voice pierced the night. "You cannot win. No one can…stop the…Scrp…"

The voice faded as the dark form tilted backwards, then abruptly plummeted toward the ground below.

Elladan clapped Glo on the back. "I think you got him."

"Let's go make sure," Aksel responded.

As the trio vaulted back over the rocky outcropping, loud booms resounded across the clearing. A quick glance confirmed that the Boulder was still trading blows with the earth elemental. Whole chunks of rock and dirt were missing from the earthen creature.

The trio paused for a moment as the golem wound up and struck the elemental twice more. This time the creature did not strike back. Instead, its huge body shook violently. Without warning, the elemental broke into pieces. They fell to the ground and lay there inert—a pile of boulders in the pale moonlight marking all that was left of the powerful opponent.

The trio let out a brief cheer then took off at a run toward where the wizard had landed. They swiftly caught up to Lloyd and Titan.

"Did you see where he landed?" Elladan asked the duo.

Titan nodded a short distance ahead. "Over there."

Glo lit his staff as they ran and held it aloft. They swiftly came on the body of the fallen mage. A small figure kneeled next to it. It was Seth. The halfling glanced up as they drew up in front of him.

Seth wore a half-twisted grin. "He's dead."

He seemed to be searching underneath the body for something. A moment later he pulled a knife out from under the lifeless corpse. Glo caught a glimpse of shining steel as Seth wiped the blade off on the grass. It was that venom knife they had found in the ruins. Seth snorted as he cleaned the blade. "That'll teach you to turn your back on a ninja."

Glo, Elladan, Aksel, Lloyd and Titan all exchanged glances then burst out laughing.

"Nicely done, Seth," Elladan said in between chuckles.

"Yeah. You saved the day yet again," Glo agreed.

"What does that make? Two wizards you've killed in the last couple of weeks?" Lloyd added.

Seth winked. "Three if you count that jackass Flibin."

Titan weighed in to the conversation with a slight edge to her voice. "Well then, Mr. Mage Killer, you didn't happen to find Brundon by any chance?"

Seth looked up at the tall warrior and nodded. "He's fine. Found him back at the camp all trussed up like a goose. I set him free before I went after this loser." Seth gave a slight nod toward the corpse on the ground in front of him.

"So then where is he now?" Titan asked.

As the question left her lips, two figures appeared in the glow of the fire over the rise that hid the camp. Seth stood up, casually holding his blade. Lloyd and Titan fell into defensive stances. As the two figures came closer, the light of Glo's staff revealed their features.

The man on the left was none other than Brundon. The tracker strode along casually next to the second figure, a man with long brown hair and a close-cropped beard and mustache. The man was unarmed, Brundon holding an extra sword and bow in his hands.

Titan let out a sigh. "Brundon…"

"Did you miss me, love?" came the nonchalant response.

She strode up to him and jabbed him hard in the arm. "You idiot. You could have been killed."

Brundon flinched. "Easy there, love. I missed you too."

Titan shook her head. "Idiot!" she spat at him, then stormed off.

The others watched her stride away until Elladan broke the silence. "So Brundon, who's your friend?"

"Oh, yes. This is Martan—and no worries, folks, he's already surrendered."

Aksel surveyed the second man with curiosity. "So then, that's all of them?"

Brundon ticked off on his hand. "Two warriors, a half-orc, Martan here, and the black mage in the camp. Did I miss anyone, Seth?"

"Just the elemental that caught you," the halfling said with a smug smile.

Brundon smiled wanly at him, his reply laced with irony. "Yes, of course. How could I forget that?"

Martan nodded. "You are correct. There were five of us not counting the earth elemental."

"Well, I took care of the half-orc," Lloyd said with just a trace of regret.

"And Titan took out the other two warriors," Glo confirmed.

There was just a trace of nervousness in Brundon's voice. "What about the elemental?"

Elladan pointed a thumb behind them. "Nothing left but a pile of rocks after the Boulder got through with it."

"Guess it was a good thing we had a stone golem after all," Seth added, his tone quite smug.

Aksel sighed. "Yes, Seth, it would have been quite difficult without it."

Glo had to agree. It was a sound victory, but something still nagged at him. This was yet another black mage they had encountered—the fifth in a week. There had to be some connection between them all. This last one had tried to say something before he died, "*You cannot stop the Serp…*"

Glo fervently wished the mage had finished that sentence, but perhaps all was not lost. This newest member of their group might be able to shed some light on the subject. "Martan, who were these people?"

Martan turned toward Glo. A strange expression crossed his face, but immediately disappeared. "First, let me say I am sorry for taking that shot at you."

A thin smile crossed Glo's lips. He had never received an apology from an attacker before. "It was only an image of me. Answer my question and we'll call it even."

Martan's eyes widened slightly. He appeared surprised at Glo's cavalier dismissal of the incident. He briefly nodded then said, "They called themselves the Black Adders. They are a sect of the Serpent Cult."

Glo raised an eyebrow. *The Serpent Cult.* That must have been what the mage was going to say before he died.

"And just what is the Serpent Cult?" Elladan asked.

Martan turned to the bard and displayed that same reaction that he had to Glo. It disappeared almost immediately. "It's a group of mages who worship serpents. They are based out of Serpent's Hollow."

Elladan's eyes narrowed. "Serpent's Hollow. Is that in the northern end of the Korlokesels?"

"Yes," Martan confirmed.

Glo and Aksel exchanged a glance. A cult of black mages based in the northern Korlokesels. That matched the legend they had found in Telvar's notes—the cult that conducted sacrifices to their 'god.'

Elladan continued questioning Martan. "Tell us more about this Serpent Cult."

Martan appeared eager to answer. "They practice a dark magic that lets them control serpents. In fact, some of them can even change into snake form."

Glo raised an eyebrow—that was dark magic indeed. Serpents and snakes had long been associated with the darker side of the arcane. If these folks were shape shifters, and controlled serpents, they were extremely dangerous. "So who was this particular mage?"

Martan gazed down at the still, black figure lying at their feet. "He was called Voltark. He and his crew were traveling to Ravenford."

A cold chill raced up Glo's spine. "Do you have any idea why they were headed there?"

Martan shook his head slowly. "Not really. I was just hired to guide them. They didn't really confide in me much."

"So you're not part of the Serpent Cult?" Elladan asked.

Martan shook his head vigorously. "Me? No! No way. I hate snakes."

"Then how did you get mixed up with these folks?" Elladan pressed.

Martan let out a heavy sigh. "Well, that's a long story. Let's just say I upset the wrong people and ended up in a jail cell in Kai-Arborus."

Elladan appeared visibly startled. "Kai-Arborus?" His expression changed to one of understanding. "Let me guess. You were hunting game in the Ruanaiaith and without any warning were grabbed, hauled off and thrown straight into a cell. I'll bet you never even had a trial."

Martan stared at Elladan dumbfounded. "Yes. That is exactly what happened. How did you know?"

Elladan let out a deep sigh. "I've heard stories. The elves of Kai-Arborus have grown suspicious of the other races. They're even less tolerant of anyone trespassing on their lands. You were probably just hungry."

Martan stared at Elladan with appreciation. "That's true. I was just trying to feed myself." He paused a moment and gulped with obvious emotion. "The Black Adders offered to pay my bail if I guided them to Ravenford. I didn't have a lot of options, so I accepted their offer. I really didn't care much for them and was hoping to go my own way once we reached Ravenford."

"More than likely they would have cut your throat when they were done with you," Seth interjected.

Martan glanced at the halfling. "You are probably right. They never trusted me all that much."

Glo had one last thought. "Martan? Did you meet with any other black mages on your trip, or perhaps see Voltark communicate with any?"

Martan appeared to think it over for a moment. "Now that you mention it, I do remember overhearing him talking to someone when no one else was there."

"Do you remember what he said?" Glo asked.

Martan's face screwed up and his eyes closed as if deep in concentration. "Something like, *Things are going as planned. We have them cut off on all sides.*" Martan opened his eyes again. "He saw me listening after that and warned me off."

The companions all exchanged glances. That sounded far too much like what was happening around Ravenford. Aksel addressed the archer, "Thank you, Martan. This information you've given us may be vital to the safety of Ravenford. I think it best if you come back there with us and tell your story to the baron."

Martan's expression grew suddenly nervous. Elladan reached out and placed a hand on the man's shoulder. "The baron's a fair man. Once he hears your side of the story, he's more than likely to let you go."

Martan glanced at Elladan and then back to Aksel. "Okay. I'll come with you if you think it's important."

Brundon, quiet up till now, spoke up. "Now that we've settled all that, there's food back at the camp. Maybe we should eat something and rest up before starting the journey back?"

Aksel grinned up at the tracker. "That's an excellent idea."

When the companions reached the Black Adder's camp, Titan was already there. "The camp's secure."

"Yes, love. We already established that fact thanks to Martan here." He pointed to the cooperative archer.

Titan gave him a withering look. She continued to stare at him as she replied, "No offense to Master Martan, but I'd rather confirm that for myself."

Brundon threw up his hands. "Whatever, love. Whatever." He peered at Aksel. "Perhaps Delara is right. I think I will go scout out the surrounding woods."

"Good idea," Aksel agreed.

Brundon cast a quick glance at Titan. She continued to stare at him, her eyes still smoldering. The tracker then took off, swiftly disappearing into the surrounding trees.

"And be careful this time!" Titan called after him.

Her words were followed by the sound of loud snickering. Titan turned her gaze on Seth, her countenance fierce. Abruptly, a wide grin broke out across her face and she winked at the halfling. Seth responded with a wicked grin of his own.

While Brundon went to scout the area, Aksel sent the Boulder to retrieve the bodies of their fallen enemies. At the same time, Elladan prepared dinner and Seth searched the wagons. When the halfling was done, he approached Glo. He held a silver helmet with large wings on either side of it in his hands.

"I found this in a locked chest inside the wagon."

Glo had never seen anything like it. He cast a spell of identification, took the helmet and concentrated. He tried for quite a while, but nothing came to him—no images or feelings of any kind. His eyes snapped open again.

"Well?" Seth asked.

Glo shook his head in response. "I couldn't get anything."

Seth peered at him quizzically. "Does that mean…"

"…it's probably an artifact," Aksel finished for him.

Artifacts contained so much concentrated magic that they actually defied detection, their own magic scrambling those trying to identify it.

"It is rather beautiful," Titan said. She turned to Elladan. "Ever hear of anything like this before?'

The bard peered over from the campfire. Glo held the helmet aloft so he could get a better look. After a few moments, Elladan shook his head. "Can't say that I have." He turned toward Martan. "Do you know what that is?"

The archer shook his head. "Never seen it before."

Elladan shrugged. "Guess I'll check the history books after dinner."

Glo turned to Aksel. "Do you mind if I hold onto this for a while?"

Aksel shrugged. "Might as well."

"There's also this." Seth reached into his pack and pulled out a crystal ball. He held it up for Glo to see.

Glo peered closely at the round crystal. It was clear with no markings.

"Voltark used that to spy on you folks," Martan explained.

Glo raised an eyebrow. "A scrying crystal?"

Martan nodded. "That's what he called it."

Glo was impressed. A scrying crystal did exactly what Martan had described, allow the user to spy on others, no matter how far away. Of course, there were limitations, but one of these was quite a find. Dinner was soon served. Afterwards, Seth examined the bodies of the Black Adders. He pulled a book from one of Voltark's pockets and held it out to Glo. "Voltark's spell book. I figured you would want it."

Glo raised an eyebrow. This was the second wizard's spellbook he had received in the last week. If this kept up, he would know every spell there was within a year. "Thanks."

Seth then rolled Voltark's body over and removed his cloak. He bundled it up and then turned around and strode over to Lloyd. Seth motioned the tall warrior to bend down and then whispered in his ear. Lloyd's eyes went wide. He took the cloak from Seth, unfolded it and wrapped it around his shoulders. Lloyd then spoke a single soft word, "Fugere."

All eyes were riveted to the tall warrior as he launched himself up into the sky. He swiftly rose, disappearing into the darkness above the trees. A cry wafted down from the inky night above, "Wahoo!"

Glo glanced at Seth. "How did you know it was a flying cloak?"

Seth folded his arms across his chest, his expression smug. "I have my ways."

Titan lips curved up to one side. "Well, however you did it, you made his day."

Seth smirked back at her. "Apparently."

A few moments later a red blur buzzed over their heads. Glo caught a glimpse of the wide grin across Lloyd's face.

A short laugh escaped Elladan's lips. "Looks like he's a natural."

Amazing as Lloyd's airborne prowess was, Glo was even more amazed at Seth. He had given Aksel that ring, two spell books and the crystal to Glo, and now gifted Lloyd with the cloak. It was apparently

Seth's way of showing friendship—that and twice now that he saved all their lives. Underneath that cynical exterior lay a fiercely loyal friend.

On Lloyd's third pass, Aksel called out to the warrior, "I know that's fun and all, but I think we've had enough for one evening."

"Alright," came the reluctant reply from above.

Lloyd reappeared a few moments later, flying slowly over the camp this time. He stopped completely, hanging in midair over the fire. Lloyd then slowly floated down, touching the ground softly with his feet.

Elladan and Titan firmly clasped him on the shoulders.

The bard gave the young man a pearly semi-smile. "Definitely a natural."

Titan's tone was wistful. "That did look like fun."

"You can try it yourself if you want," Lloyd told her. He started to unfasten his cloak.

Titan reached out and stayed his hand. "Thank you, but not right now." She pointed to her armor-clad figure. "Not in this, anyway."

"When we get back, then," Lloyd declared firmly.

A wide grin broke out across Titan's face. "When we get back."

Brundon returned a short while later with the horses from the torched wagon. He reported the surrounding woods were all clear. The companions buried the bodies of their stalwart foes, all except for the mage, Voltark. Aksel insisted on bringing the body back with them. There was a spell he could use to speak with the mage's spirit, but he did not want to try it out here in the open.

The companions camped out until daybreak, resting and regaining their strength. After a quick breakfast, they took Voltark's wagon back up to the ruins. There they loaded it with the spoils so abruptly left behind the prior evening. Elladan and Martan took turns driving the wagon when they finally set out back to Ravenford.

It was midday when the small company arrived at the little seaport town. Glo, Aksel, Brundon, and Titan rode ahead, the Boulder trailing behind. Elladan and Martan brought up the rear while Seth relaxed inside the wagon on his couch. Lloyd's horse was hitched to the back of the wagon, the young warrior, unable to resist the urge to fly, flew over the open seaport and bay beyond.

The people of Ravenford came out in droves to see them. It turned into an impromptu parade of sorts. The townsfolk cheered as Lloyd flew overhead and appeared in awe of the Boulder. The word *Heroes'* kept springing up amongst the crowd. The throng grew as they marched along, following the small company up the hill to Ravenford keep. The entire entourage finally drew to a halt at the front gate. They were greeted by the guard Francis and Lieutenant Relkin.

Francis wore a wide grin. "Well, well, look who it is."

Relkin eyed the golem with curiosity. "Back victorious, I see?"

Aksel leaned forward in his saddle and spoke softly to the duo, his tone grim, "We need to see the baron at once. It's urgent."

Both men turned immediately serious. Francis nodded. "Right then. I'll notify the captain at once." He spun around and disappeared through the open gate. At the same time, Relkin motioned to a group of guards just inside the courtyard, then spoke to the companions, "You can leave your mounts and wagon here if you like. We'll bring them inside for you."

Aksel gave Relkin a quick nod. "Thanks."

The small company dismounted, even Seth finally appearing from inside the wagon. The halfling jumped down, patted the Boulder affectionately on the leg, and strode forward to join the others. The group all gathered together in front of the lieutenant.

Relkin addressed Martan, "And just where did they find you, friend?"

An ironic smile crossed the archer's face. "In the Dead Forest. These heroes of your town more or less saved my life."

The townsfolk nearest to them picked up on the archer's statement. A low chant ensued. *"Heroes. Heroes. Heroes of Ravenford."*

The companions gazed around at the throng in amazement.

"Well, that just happened," Seth said in a wry tone.

They waved briefly to the townsfolk, then Aksel addressed Lieutenant Relkin once more, "Gratifying as this may be, we still have that urgent business."

Relkin nodded. "Right. This way."

He led the *Heroes of Ravenford* through the gate and into the courtyard beyond.

Here ends Book One of
the Heroes of Ravenford
the story continues in Book Two
Serpent Cult

ABOUT THE AUTHOR

F.P. Spirit writes high fantasy fiction inspired by the likes of Tolkien, Eddings, Brooks, and Piers Anthony. An avid science fiction fan, he became hooked on fantasy the moment he cracked open the Lord of the Rings in high school. When he is not writing, F.P. is either spending time with his wife and sons, gaming, doing yoga, Tai Chi, or walking their dog.

A long-time lover of fantasy and the surreal, he hopes you enjoy his fun contributions to the world of fantasy and magic.

You can learn more about F.P. Spirit by visiting his website at:
Fpspirit.com

www.ingramcontent.com/pod-product-compliance
Lightning Source LLC
Chambersburg PA
CBHW031932110726
47902CB00001B/137